# FLIPPING LOVE YOU

## BOYS OF THE BAYOU GONE WILD

### ERIN NICHOLAS

ISBN: 978-1-952280-16-0

Editor: Lindsey Faber

Cover photo: Wander Aguiar

Cover design: Najla Qamber, Qamber Designs

# ABOUT THE BOOK

*He's the tattooed bad boy her mama warned her about.*
*She's his hot mess--but mostly hot--next door neighbor.*
*Until a two-night-stand gives them the surprise of a lifetime...*

Jillian Morris is a workaholic who forgets to watch the time. And to eat. And to change her shoes. And to keep even a house-plant alive. And to have any kind of a personal life.

Now an eccentric millionaire has left her sixteen million dollars. And eight penguins. Yes, real live penguins. She's a wildlife vet who specializes in penguins, so that makes sense. Kind of. She can, and does, keep penguins alive and well. She now just has to move them cross-country to her friend's new animal park.

So if anyone deserves a one-night (or two) stand with a hot, younger, tattooed bad boy on a motorcycle, it's her. Or so Jill tells herself when Zeke Landry flips his bike in front of her motel.

If only she'd known who he really was.
And that he was the fall-hard-and-fast type.
And the protective type.
And that one night would turn into more like nine-months of
being ...sigh...very personal.

*To A.J.*
*Here you go.*
*(Told you I was going to kill you).*

# AUTHOR'S NOTE

Thank you for picking up this book! Just a quick note before
you dive in!
This is a work of fiction. I absolutely do not condone the
owning of endangered species by unqualified people for any
reason.

I also don't go into detail in these books about the paperwork
and licensing that is required for zoos and animal parks.
However, there is a lot of it, I'm aware of it, and it would be a
very boring addition to an otherwise (in my opinion anyway)
light and fun story. So, I left that in the background. Rest
assured, Fiona, Griffin, Tori, Donovan and the rest are taking
care of it all and Knox is making sure they're crossing all the T's
and dotting all the I's!

Specifically regarding the Galapagos penguins in this story...

There are no such programs like the one I've described, at least
as far as I know. I made it all up. But then, I made up the entire
town and all of these people too. It's what I do. Galapagos

penguins are real though, and they are critically endangered. We should all be concerned about that and do what we can to protect them. It is not my intention to make light of their plight or to minimize the real, actual efforts to protect them. The opposite is true, in fact. I hope this story will shine a light on their situation and will make people want to get involved.

Galapagos penguins are not, as far as I can find in my research, kept in captivity anywhere in the world because of their endangered status and protections around them. So, yes, I took some artistic licenses with this story to spotlight an important issue. I hope that you'll take that in the spirit it was intended.

# PROLOGUE

Jillian Morris would never admit it, but the fact that her mother believed she needed help dressing herself, even at age thirty-four, came in handy sometimes.

Because she did need help dressing herself.

Sometimes.

Certainly not on a regular basis. Her basic v-neck t-shirts in various solid colors and her jeans or khakis worked perfectly three hundred and sixty-two days a year. And it was awesome to be able to reach into her closet and, literally, pull on the first thing her hand touched.

But every once in a while, the clothes her mother sent her were actually appropriate. Never for Jill to wear to work, of course. But for...other things.

Like funerals.

And meetings with lawyers for reading the will a couple days after a funeral.

She'd worn this same dress to the funeral, but she'd grabbed it again this morning when she'd remembered the meeting and realized she'd need to change after work and had run back up the stairs to her apartment.

She hoped a basic black dress was appropriate for a meeting with a high-powered attorney at an enormous, intimidating mansion on the outskirts of town regarding the last will and testament of a man she'd loved and who she'd had no idea was a multi-millionaire.

Was there a handbook or blog or something that she could have referenced for this meeting? Maybe she should have Googled.

She studied the toe of her shoe.

Okay, it was a boot. One of her work boots. Because, while she'd been so proud of herself for remembering to grab the dress, of course she hadn't thought about *shoes*.

Her mother would be appalled.

The boot probably had penguin poop on it.

No, the boot *definitely* had penguin poop on it.

Which was why she had also arrived to this big-time fancy meeting in her truck. She drove her truck to and from work because then she didn't have to worry about things like penguin poop on the floor mats or if she'd remembered her work bag. She just kept it in her truck at all times. And wore the same thing to and from work every day.

Having a big meeting that required a dress and nice shoes right after work was really not a good idea for Jill.

Had she gotten penguin poop on the carpet in A.J.'s stuffed-with-books-covered-in-maps-and-filled-with-probably-expensive-stuff office?

Very likely.

But she smiled slightly. A.J. would not care about penguin poop on his carpet.

Though she couldn't help but wonder how much the carpet in here cost.

A.J. had been a *millionaire*. More precisely, Allan J. Reynolds III had been a millionaire.

*What?*

She'd known the man for almost four years. He'd come to the zoo every Thursday afternoon to watch her feed the penguins. After a couple of weeks, they'd started chatting politely. Then they'd started actually *talking*. And laughing. And sharing their stories and passions. And caring.

The older man had been fascinating. He'd had a dry sense of humor and had led an incredible life, traveling the globe, studying and photographing wildlife. He'd been especially fond of penguins. They'd shared that passion. Which was how they'd become friends.

When he hadn't showed up last Thursday, she'd been so worried.

Turned out, for good reason.

He'd passed away Wednesday night.

From cancer that she hadn't even known he had.

Jill felt her throat tighten and her eyes sting. She was going to miss him so much. It still didn't feel real that he was gone.

"Jillian?"

She lifted her head and focused on the man sitting behind the enormous, polished cherry-wood desk. "Yes?"

"I asked if you're ready?"

Oh, he'd been speaking to her. She glanced at the other two people in the room.

Christine Jones had been A.J.'s long-time personal assistant, housekeeper, and friend. She was inheriting this gigantic house and all of the furnishings and artwork. Apparently, A.J. felt that the woman who had vacuumed, dusted, polished, and shined the place should get to keep it in the end.

Christine was a little overwhelmed by the whole thing.

But Mathias Alcazar, the twenty-one-year-old man sitting between Jill and Christine, was more than overwhelmed.

Mathias had been picking A.J. up and driving him to church then taking him out for breakfast every week for two years.

A.J. had left Mathias his cars. Yes, plural. Six of them. There was a silver Bentley, a maroon Rolls Royce, a black 1936 Mercedes Benz Roadster, a beat-up blue pickup, the basic tan Buick they'd driven to church, and, Mathias's favorite, a fire-engine red Ferrari.

A.J.'s taste in cars had been eclectic. As had his taste in artwork, hobbies, and, clearly, personal relationships.

Jill was still smiling over how amazed and touched both Christine and Mathias had been, not only with what A.J. had left them in his will, but the kind words about what their friendships had meant to him that William, his attorney, had read.

A.J.'s children—two sons—were grown and wildly successful themselves. One lived in New York and one in London. They had inherited shares of A.J.'s company—Jill wasn't clear on what exactly A.J. had done to become a million-aire—and money, but they didn't want or need his house, furni-ture, artwork, or cars.

Now it was her turn to find out what A.J. had left to her.

She swallowed and sat up straighter, tucking her boots under the chair. "Yes, I'm ready."

She wasn't ready at all.

She was here with two people who knew A.J. really well. They'd known he lived in a gigantic house and had millions of dollars to his name. They'd done things for him.

All A.J. and Jillian had done was chat about animals and travel and her work. Some days they talked about recent research in wildlife veterinary care. Sometimes they talked about conservation efforts around the world. They talked about everything from deforestation of the rainforests to the news story about a mother tiger that had adopted a stray litter of puppies as her own.

They'd shared their love of animals, but she hadn't taken him anywhere, or helped him in any particular way. She'd been touched to find out that he'd remembered her in his will at all.

If he was going to leave her some of his wildlife photography or even one of his journals from his travels to the Galápagos Islands where he first fell in love with the penguins, she would be ecstatic and treasure it forever.

"To my dearest Jillian."

Jill's throat constricted with even those first four words.

"Everything I needed to know about you, I learned on the very first day I saw you. I was watching you caring for the penguins in the exhibit. You didn't know I was there at first, and I overheard you talking to them. You were loving and sweet and patient. You were not just feeding them, but truly interacting, and taking the time to give each of them individual attention and care. It was clear they loved and trusted you implicitly. After that, we became fast friends and you always treated me similarly."

Jill had to blink rapidly. A.J. had been surprisingly verbally affectionate toward her. He praised her care of the penguins and had told her many times what her friendship meant to him. But hearing it like this in a letter, that he'd clearly taken time to write, knowing it would be his final chance to say it, made her heart ache. She dashed the tear off her cheek that had slipped from her lower lashes.

"There is no one else I could possibly entrust my beloved animals to. I know that you will give them the love and attention and care they need and will make the choices for them no one else can."

Jill lifted her head and met William's eyes.

Animals?

Oh...shit.

Clearly, A.J. had had pets. That didn't surprise her.

But he thought *she* would be good at taking care of them?

Of course he had. She was a veterinarian. Sure, she specialized in wildlife, but yeah, they'd covered cats and dogs in vet school. She remembered the basics. Plus, tons of non-veterinarians had cats and dogs. Obviously. *Most* cat and dog owners weren't vets.

But Jill was...not good at taking care of other things. Laundry. Home repairs. Feeding herself. Other things with a pulse.

Unless the other thing was black and white and had flippers.

Nope, that wasn't even true. She would have no idea what to do with an orca whale.

She was good at taking care of *penguins*.

And that was pretty much it.

Penguins were all she cared about. Caring for penguins, helping save them from extinction, was her life's work and well, she didn't *want* to do anything else.

She'd fallen in love with penguins at age eight. When she was thirteen she'd found out that she could work with them—like actually touch them and feed them and pet them *every day* —if she became a wildlife vet and that had been that. It was all she'd ever cared about.

Okay, so A.J. hadn't known her as well as he might have thought.

William was watching her, seemingly finished reading aloud.

Jillian sighed. "How big is it?"

William lifted a brow. "How big is what?"

"The dog."

She supposed it could be a cat. Or, God forbid, multiple cats, but A.J. seemed more like a dog person.

Her heart thumped. That wasn't true. A.J. was more of a cat *and* dog person. With maybe a ferret and something odd like a snake—she shuddered—and, now that she'd seen his house, maybe a pony. And the type to have multiples of each.

Crap. He was giving her *living beings*.

He couldn't have given her...a vacation home? He'd often said that she worked too much. That would have fit. She could have used a vacation house. Or a car. He had *six*. Did Mathias need all of them? She couldn't have had one? She'd even take the pick-up.

But no, A.J.—the sweet man who'd thought she was amazing and she'd let talk her into thinking so too...at least on Thursdays—wanted her to take care of a living creature. Probably more than one.

That was just great.

She was going to freaking forget to feed and walk it, and probably kill—though accidentally of course—one of her sweetest friends' beloved pets.

Awesome.

William shook his head. "There's no dog."

Jillian stared at him. Then felt her breath whoosh out. She covered her chest with her hand. "Oh, good. Sorry. I just..."

*You can't tell them that you, a freaking veterinarian, don't want to be responsible for keeping a bunch of non-penguin animals alive.*

"...have a very small apartment. And I don't think my lease allows pets. And I work a lot, so I'm gone a lot."

There were probably other good reasons she shouldn't have pets. Other than the 98% chance that she'd forget about the poor things entirely.

William smiled. "We won't have to worry about keeping them at your apartment. You'll have plenty of funds to be sure they are housed appropriately."

So it was a "them". As in more than one. But she was going to have funds to house them. What did that mean?

Dammit. They were horses or something.

She *liked* animals. She really did. She just shouldn't be in charge of taking care of them. And she honestly didn't know much about horses.

"Where are they housed now?" She assumed a barn. But was it here on this property that was now Christine's or—

"It would be better to show you," William said. He pushed back from the desk and stood.

It probably would. They'd taken Mathias down to see the cars. That was when it had really sunk in for him, and William had been able to answer his questions. Maybe it would be good for Jill to meet the horses.

She rose and followed William out of the study. Christine and Mathias were right behind her. She and Christine had gone down to see the cars too. And on the way, she'd gotten a brief tour of at least a portion of A.J.'s—now Christine's—house.

Holy shit. The man had lived in *this*? It was three stories and had to be thousands of square feet. Jill wasn't that good at estimating things like that, but the place was *huge*.

A.J. had worn blue jeans with red suspenders and white t-shirts and tennis shoes every day she'd seen him. When it was cool, he'd wear a tan jacket. And a red cap. When it was cold, he'd wear a navy-blue coat and a red stocking cap. It was all basic, non-descript, totally average stuff. He'd looked like every other seventy-something man in any other setting.

"Down this way." William turned into a hallway that led to the east part of the house.

Jillian's heart started beating faster for some reason.

Anything that had been important to A.J. was important to her. If he wanted her to take care of something, she would. Or she would try. Or she'd hire someone to do it. And hope A.J. wasn't the type of guy to haunt someone for half-assing what he'd asked her to do.

Or for finding the animals a new home. Someone who would actually want a horse. Or four. But damn, that made her feel instantly guilty. William wanted *her* to take care of them.

*Please don't let there be more than three or four. Please don't let there be more than three or four.*

Lord, even four horses was a lot. Who did she know that would take four horses?

William led them down one hallway. Then another. They took another left turn, then a right, then descended six stairs and then went through a large door. As Jill stepped into the room behind William, she was still thinking through all the people she knew who loved horses. It wasn't that many.

If A.J. was giving her dogs, she could find them homes. If they were cats, she could definitely find them a place to go. Maybe even all together. Margie Perkins might even...

"Ms. Morris?"

It took her a moment to realize they'd stopped. She blinked.

The room they stood in looked like what she would assume an indoor in-home swimming pool would look like. It was a large open area with two glass walls that overlooked the property. A property that was just as gorgeous as the rest of the house.

There was emerald grass, tons of trees that were starting to change color now that it was early September, and numerous bushes and a gorgeous flower garden. But that wasn't the most stunning thing.

What she couldn't believe was the dirt, sand, rocks, and greenery *inside* the enclosure. Along with the man-made swimming pool, with its very own waterfall. And then of course the inhabitants of the area.

Penguins.

There were penguins in this room.

Five of them that she could see.

Real, live penguins.

Jill was barely aware of Christine and Mathias coming into the room and joining William at the small, waist-high gate that separated the doorway from the rest of the enclosure. The penguins were nowhere near the gate. And why would they be?

They wouldn't want to escape this room. It had everything they needed. It was a penguin paradise.

"I didn't know that penguins didn't need ice and snow until I met A.J.," Mathias said.

So Mathias had known about the penguins. She assumed Christine had as well. She took care of the house, after all. Not that Christine looked to be the type of woman who probably routinely got into the penguin enclosure. Plus knowing A.J., he'd done all the hands-on work. This wasn't just a penguin paradise, this was an A.J. paradise.

Then what Mathias said truly sunk in. Of course, *Jill* knew not all penguins need ice and snow. In fact, there were more species of penguins that lived in warmer climates than cold. But *these* penguins were specifically Galápagos penguins. Not only were they tropical penguins, but they were one of the most endangered species on the planet.

She knew they were A.J.'s favorites. These penguins were the reason he'd traveled to the Galápagos Islands the first time. He and Jill had talked at length about his trips.

But he'd never brought up the fact that he actually *owned* Galápagos penguins.

How did that even work? How did a guy come to own an endangered species and keep them in his house?

She looked at William. "A.J. is leaving me his *penguins*?"

"All eight of them."

Her eyes widened and she looked back out over the penguin enclosure. She only saw three now. "There are *eight*?"

"Six adults and two juveniles."

"Are any of them breeding pairs?" Jill asked, perking up. Penguins mated for life. If the penguins had laid viable eggs and hatched new penguins in captivity with A.J., that was huge.

"Yes, three pairs."

"And the babies are theirs?"

"No."

Jill deflated slightly.

"But A.J., and all of this, is part of a program where some wealthy investors with interest in wildlife conservation have each taken in a group of penguins. They are experimenting to see what private sanctuaries can do for preservation and propagation."

Jill blew out a breath. "But what am *I* going to do with them? Am I leaving them here?" She looked at Christine. "This is your house now. Are we working together to keep the penguins here in this sanctuary?"

That was her immediate reaction and her first concern. These were not just eight horses. They really weren't even just eight penguins. They were a penguin species that was vulnerable and threatened. All penguins needed protection, but the Galápagos penguin population in particular had dwindled.

In the back of her mind, Jill understood why A.J. had left the penguins to her. It was rare to come across someone who shared such a passion for penguins. She knew that well.

She'd been in love with the bird since she'd been eight years old and A.J. was the first person she'd found, including other veterinarians, who truly felt the same love and dedication to the birds she did. She understood now why he had been so excited to meet her and why he had continued their relationship over the past four years. But why hadn't he told her about these penguins? Why hadn't he told her he had a whole sanctuary here? Why hadn't he warned her that he would need someone to care for them when the time came?

Okay, the last part wasn't such a big deal. He had to know that there was no reason for her to turn down the request. Now that she knew about the penguins, even if she didn't know exactly how this was going to work, there was no way she would let anyone else take care of them. Even the other veterinarians at the zoo wouldn't do as well as she would.

Jill knew that she was kind of a mess. She never showed up

on time for social events. She needed her mother to dress her for important professional engagements—or any engagement other than work, really. She ate cold cereal three nights a week —okay sometimes four, and she ate peanut butter and jelly sandwiches the other nights. She *liked* other animals and would certainly care for them if needed, but she *always* preferred penguins over other animals. Always.

She knew who she was and she owned it.

She was a damned penguin *expert*.

It was the one thing she was good at. It was the one thing she'd focused on and concentrated all of her time and energy on.

And it had paid off.

Veterinarians and zookeepers from around the world called for her input. She wrote papers and taught on the subject. She'd led scientific expeditions to the Galápagos , Antarctica, and Argentina. She was part of two different world-wide teams working on the problems causing declines in penguin populations globally. And none were more threatened than the Galápagos.

And now she *owned* eight of them personally.

But Christine was shaking her head. "I'm really hoping to turn the house into a bed and breakfast. I intend to live in the west wing of the house and use the main section in this east wing as the bed and breakfast. As much as I love the penguins and have always found them fascinating, I have no desire to help take care of them. And I'd really rather not have them here."

Jillian understood that. They were wild animals after all. They were adorable, of course, but they were not something that a typical person would want in their house. They weren't pets.

In fact, the more she thought about it, if Christine didn't have the passion and knowledge that A.J. had had, then she wasn't the best one to care for these birds. And if she was going to have a lot of people in and out of the house, that wasn't good either. Who knew what people might do to the penguins?

They'd had an incident a year ago at the zoo where a little boy had somehow slipped into the penguin enclosure. They'd found him wet, sitting by the side of the pool when his class had discovered him missing. His mother had come to pick him up and when she got him home and into the bathtub to clean up, she'd unzipped his backpack and found a baby penguin inside.

Jillian had almost had a heart attack. She'd also almost lost her job for yelling at the child's teacher and the parent chaperones for the trip.

She'd been called into the director's office and had had flashbacks to when her friend Griffin had been fired from the zoo for a similar incident. That had been the start of her issues with the zoo director. But it hadn't been the end of her issues.

"And A.J. didn't want to just donate the animals to the zoo?" Jill asked William.

That seemed the obvious choice for someone who had a group of wild animals that needed care, but she was so glad A.J. hadn't chosen that option.

William was watching her closely. "He actually considered that, but apparently as he got to know you better, you shared with him that you had some...issues with the zoo director. A.J. realized that you may not be employed at the zoo for the rest of your career and it occurred to him that if he wanted *you* caring for the penguins, the only way to ensure that was to actually give the penguins to you and let you decide where they would live."

Jill was touched by that. She really was the best choice. She, by far, would take the best care of these animals.

But she certainly didn't have a huge enclosure that included everything from sand to waterfalls for them to live in.

"If I don't give them to the zoo, what will *I* do with them?"

"Each penguin comes with two million dollars," William told her. "So you have a total of sixteen million dollars to work with. Of course, that money has to be used directly or at least indirectly for the penguins' care. But that can be used to relocate them, of course, as well as to care for them long-term, including food, shelter, medical care. It can also be used to house *you*, since you are essential for their well-being. If you need to build a new house or move to a new place, that money can certainly be used for that."

Jill knew she was staring at him. He had just said the words *sixteen million dollars* to her. That definitely deserved a stare.

She turned back to the enclosure. She could now see six of the penguins. Correction, six of *her* penguins.

Suddenly her chest felt warm and she felt her eyes stinging again.

She now had eight penguins. Galápagos penguins.

Thanks to a sweet little old man who had come to the zoo one Thursday and had started up a simple conversation with the words, "Some scientists think that penguins sometimes jump for sheer joy."

She'd instantly known that this man knew more about penguins than the average person. Penguins leapt from the water like dolphins, an act called porpoising, and it was true that some scientists thought it truly was out of happiness more than for any other reason.

Watching the penguins, she felt a little like jumping for joy herself. This was an amazing opportunity. And she suddenly understood why A.J. hadn't told her about them.

He'd wanted this to be a surprise. He wanted to make her dream come true and he'd wanted to do it in a way that would give her joy even as she was sad and grieving losing him. It was his way of showing her that their bond would go on.

"How long has he had the penguins?" she asked.

"They started the program just over a year ago."

She frowned. "And...when did he get his cancer diagnosis?"

"About fifteen months ago."

Her breath caught in her chest. A.J. hadn't gotten these penguins for himself. She was certain he'd been optimistic about beating the cancer at first. That was just A.J. But she also knew that he'd agreed to be a part of the program, even with cancer, because he knew he had *her*.

"He has all of the permissions, licensing, and paperwork in place. You can relocate the penguins as needed with a little help from me," William said with a smile. "But you are officially the owner and caretaker of these penguins as far as the program and all the pertinent government entities are concerned."

Jillian sucked in a huge long breath. "So I have eight penguins and sixteen million dollars. And I need to move them out of here in time for Christine to turn the house into a bed and breakfast."

"You can keep them here, of course, until you have a plan," Christine assured her.

She appreciated that, but knew that Christine didn't mean that she could take a year or more to figure this out.

"So, I guess I need to try to make some plans," Jill said.

"I'm happy to help with anything you need," William said. "I have all the contacts that you might need. A.J.'s partners in the private sanctuary program are eager to talk with you." William smiled again. "A.J. told them all about you. They're excited to have your expertise."

"They don't have expertise?" she asked.

"They are mostly just people with money who want to help with wildlife conservation and really like penguins."

Oh. So she really would be the expert of the group. Well... great. She was used to that, actually. Truly, in any group of humans, 99.8% of the time she would know more than anyone else about penguins.

Nothing else, of course, but penguins? Absolutely.

"Are there rules about where I take the penguins?"

She supposed she could stay here, but she wasn't from Omaha. She'd come here specifically for the job with the zoo. But she didn't really have a desire to go home to Kansas either.

"No, the location has nothing to do with the program. They just require the penguins' environment be protected and controlled. They want it as natural as possible, with no other penguin types. They want to strictly limit the number of care-givers as well, in a quiet, non-disruptive environment, with plenty of food, of course, so that they feel secure to breed regu-larly and produce viable eggs."

That made sense. Food availability was the primary factor that impacted the penguins' breeding habits in the wild.

So where did she *want* to take the penguins? What made the most sense? With sixteen million dollars she could prob-ably relocate the penguins anywhere she wanted.

But she was suddenly feeling a little alone.

She often felt alone. She liked being alone. She liked doing her own thing.

But she'd never been responsible for eight other living beings before.

On purpose.

And even if they were penguins, she was feeling intimi-dated and overwhelmed.

Killing a houseplant was one thing. Something she still felt bad about and why she'd stopped getting them.

Killing a goldfish was also pretty terrible and it had only taken her a weekend to give away the one she'd gotten impul-sively two years ago.

She'd never even entertained the idea of getting so much as

a gerbil or a bearded dragon or anything. And definitely not a cat or dog.

Now she had penguins. And while, yes, she knew *everything* about them, these were an *endangered species*. If she couldn't keep them alive, it would be devastating. Not just to the general welfare of the penguins, but to *her* mentally and emotionally.

This was her passion in life.

This was what she'd dedicated her entire career to.

This was what she did instead of having friends, or dating, or going to concerts, or book clubs. Hell, she read research articles—or wrote them—instead of reading books.

Jill felt her heart hammering and her breathing coming in near pants now.

She was freaking out.

Yes, she worked with penguins all day, every day. Yes, including Christmas. Just ask her mother.

But that was in controlled environments. With other people around to help feed them and watch for problems.

No, she'd never forgotten to feed them and yes, she was always the one who caught problems first but she didn't *have to be*.

Now, with these eight, she did.

She was on her own.

They were her responsibility. Just hers.

The woman who couldn't even remember to change her *shoes* before an after-work meeting.

"Ms. Morris? Are you all right?"

Jill was staring at her penguins. All eight of them were now out in view and she watched them waddle and talk to one another and splash at the edge of the water and in spite of the adrenaline rushing through her veins, her heart swelled.

They were so beautiful.

And they needed her.

*Her.*

*She* was their best chance for survival.

She nodded. "I think so."

"Will that all be possible?" William asked.

Without looking at him, Jill asked, "Are you asking if I'm willing to dedicate all of my time and energy to these penguins and making sure they are safe and stay healthy and continue to breed and multiply?"

"Yes, that is what I'm asking."

She nodded. "It's an absolute dream come true."

# 1

*One month later...*

Zeke Landry pulled into Autre, barely pausing his motorcycle at the stop sign before he turned onto Bayou Road, the street that would lead past Boys of the Bayou Swamp Boat Tours and his grandmother's bar, and would eventually dead-end at his house about a mile from the bayou.

The first stretch of the road in the main part of town was paved, however, and even had a couple stop signs. It ran past the grocery store, the fish market, the city park, and the convenience store and gas station that marked the beginning of the dirt portion of the road.

That was the segment they should've called Landry Road. Not only was the family's swamp boat tour company there, and of course Ellie's bar, but Zeke's own construction company office also sat along that road beside his uncle's auto shop. On past those businesses were several Landry family homes.

The Landry family had been in Autre for generations, and if

you lived in Autre and weren't related to one of them, the chances were you owed a Landry money, an apology, or a black eye.

Hell, even if you *were* related to them, you probably owed a Landry one of those three things.

Zeke waved as he passed his cousin Mitch in his truck, but he didn't slow his bike. He was not in the mood for conversation. Which was, in itself, rare. Like most Landrys, Zeke loved to talk. But tonight, he was distracted. And, even more unusual, frustrated.

Zeke was not, by any stretch, the most patient or level-headed of the Landrys, but he was pretty fun-loving and easy-going most of the time. Unless it came to one of his projects not going according to plan.

His work was straightforward. He built stuff. He tore stuff down. He rebuilt stuff.

Simple.

Or it should have been.

Someone wanted a building put up? Zeke put up a building. Four walls, a floor, and a roof.

None of this needed to be *difficult*. That was what he liked about it.

But every once in a while, something went off the rails. Weather blew in and screwed up a timeline. Supplies got back-ordered. There was a bigger problem with an old foundation than expected when they got down to it. One of his guys showed up drunk.

But he dealt with it. He got things back on track.

Like he needed to do with this new job he'd just gotten.

His cousins were expanding their petting zoo into an animal park. Which was super fucking cool.

And good for business. Zeke and Mitch had been the ones in charge of designing and building all of the animal enclosures. It had been a hell of a lot of fun. Mitch was super easy to work with and they had plenty of extra hands whenever they needed them. They'd been putting up the new animal enclosures in crazy short time frames.

And now they had penguins coming to town.

Fucking penguins. It wasn't every day a guy got to build a habitat for penguins. These weren't cold-weather penguins, so he hadn't had to figure out a way to install any kind of refrigeration system—much to his disappointment—but still, there were going to be *penguins* in Autre, Louisiana.

The thing was, the penguins came with their very own veterinarian. Technically, she was their owner too. But Dr. J. Morris—he didn't know her first name, he'd just been referring to her as Dr. Morris in his emails—was totally in charge. All the money being spent, all the decisions being made, were hers. And that had been great. She was detail oriented and completely on top of everything when it came to the birds. Every time he had a question, she got right back to him.

But, in addition to building the penguin enclosure, he was also remodeling a house for her.

And she wouldn't answer one damned question about *that*.

He was convinced at this point that she didn't know he was the same guy building her penguin habitat. He'd used the petting zoo email to communicate with her on that project and they'd quickly moved to texting. It was the Landry Construction emails she was ignoring.

And she was supposed to be here in three days.

Zeke consciously unclenched his jaw as he drove past the grocery store. It was not his problem if she got to town and had no place to live.

Except that he really hated not being able to get a job done and get it done well.

Suddenly a dark shape darted out in front of him.

Swearing, Zeke jerked the wheel to the right. The front tire of his bike hit gravel and he felt the bike shift and start to slide underneath him.

*Fuck.* This was just what he needed.

That was his last thought before the bike tipped, hit the ground, and slid along the pavement and into the roadside ditch.

*Fucking son of a bitch.* That hurt.

Plus, now his bike was going to be dinged up.

Zeke lay just breathing for a few seconds, mentally cataloging what he was feeling. He'd been going slow so there weren't going to be any serious injuries. His right leg hurt, but he was fairly certain it was just bruised and scraped. He'd broken enough bones to know the difference. His right arm throbbed, but he was sure his jacket had kept him from getting any skin-to-pavement injuries. His helmet was sitting askew, and he knew that it had kept him from smacking his head too hard, but his ears were still ringing a bit.

He lifted a hand to his temple. His fingertips came away sticky and red.

Dammit, and he was bleeding. How the fuck had that happened?

He'd better not need stitches. He hated getting stitches and they bothered his mom more than bruises.

He sat partially up and shoved at the bike. It only moved a little. Suddenly annoyed at *everything*, he gave a loud roar and lifted the bike as he jerked his leg out from under it.

There. At least he was free.

He flopped back into the weeds and grass.

With his luck he was going to run into a snake or a gator down here in the ditch. But honestly, at the moment, he didn't give a shit.

He reached into his pocket for his phone. He could walk to his grandma's bar, or to his shop, or to one of many houses, but he needed someone with a pickup to help him haul his bike. And he was feeling a little dizzy.

"Fuck. This is inconvenient," he muttered to himself.

Zeke stared at his phone trying to decide who to call. The gamble was trying to get someone who was alone. One phone call could turn up anywhere from four to twelve Landrys.

No one needed twelve Landrys all at once for anything.

Unless it was a crawfish boil, of course.

But even two or three would just make the headache that was starting to brew behind his eyes worse.

"Leo'd be best," he said out loud.

His grandfather wasn't judgmental and had helped all of his grandsons out of worse than this at one time or another.

"But Leo's *never* alone," Zeke realized. Also out loud.

Leo would tell you it was because of the good-old-boy charm that was his curse, but the truth was, Leo never wanted to miss a thing, whether it be a tall tale, a bit of gossip, a dramatic moment, or a funny story. Or a chance at the last piece of pie—no matter the flavor.

"Could call Mitch." Mitch had just driven by. And he was by far the *nicest* of the Landrys. Old or young. Not that the bar was very high.

Zeke started to dial Mitch's number.

"Oh, baby, are you okay?"

His finger froze and he rolled his head at the sound of the feminine voice.

Or he could just let the owner of that voice take care of him.

"I'm a little sore, actually."

The woman plopped onto her knees in the dirt beside him.

It was dark, so he couldn't see her well.

That was also why he hadn't clearly seen whatever it was that ran out in front of him until it was too late. He also hadn't really been paying attention. He'd been too caught up in his thoughts about the penguin veterinarian and her new old house.

He was suddenly *much* less annoyed though.

The woman kneeling next to him leaned in and he caught the scent of coffee and soap.

He wasn't sure why that struck him. Maybe because it was simple. She didn't smell like perfume or flowery shampoo. She just smelled clean and comforting. Like that first cup of coffee in the morning after a shower.

That was a really weird thing to notice. And who drank coffee at eleven o'clock at night?

He probably had a concussion.

Great. *That* was just what he needed.

"Oh, sweetie," she cooed.

And yep, he definitely felt a little better.

"I'll be okay, but I could use a hand," he said. Specifically, a woman's soft hand rubbing his head and maybe her lips kissing his bump better.

Did he know her? She had long, dark hair and that was about all he could tell.

"Are you hurt or just scared?"

Zeke pushed himself up to sitting, wincing as his head swam and his leg ached as he shifted it. "A little hurt. Not scared at all."

The woman looked up at him. "What?"

It was then that he realized she wasn't talking to him.

And that she was holding a goat.

The little thing was cradled in her lap. It was also black.

He was ninety percent sure this was the reason that his bike was lying on its side in the ditch and he was bleeding from the head.

The woman was calling *the goat* "baby".

"Wait, you're worried about the *goat*?"

"You almost ran him over," she said. "The poor thing's probably terrified."

"Do you see me lying here? Under a motorcycle? Bleeding?"

"Your own motorcycle. That you almost hit this goat with."

Unbelievable.

Besides her long, dark hair which fell in waves to nearly the middle of her back, he could see she was small and slender. Her skin was pale, glowing just slightly in the moonlight and the dim light offered by the streetlamps across the road.

"Did you come over here to check on the goat?"

"Yes."

"No concern for the human being at all?"

"I came over to make sure you were alive. But I immediately realized you were conscious and breathing."

"How's that?"

"You were moving around. And swearing. I saw you move the motorcycle off your leg. And I heard you talking to yourself. About Leo."

Okay, so he was *alive*. There was a lot of space between that and totally fine though. "What if that's the sign of a brain injury?"

"I certainly hope it's not," she said. "I talk to myself all the time."

He noticed she was stroking her hand over the goat's back as she held him and he seemed quite content in her lap.

Yeah, it was his experience with these goats—yes, he had experience with these goats because they belonged to his cousins' petting zoo—that they loved attention in general and were smart enough to prefer female attention.

He frowned at the little animal. This one was Sneezy. Not because he actually sneezed a lot—or ever, as far as Zeke knew —but because some of the goats were named after the seven dwarves and, well, someone had to be Sneezy.

What the hell was Sneezy doing down here?

"Baaaa!"

He glanced over to the front of the motel across the street.

Ah. Well, that explained it. The other ten goats were clustered in front of the motel's front office.

"Arf! Arf!"

Along with Benny—short for Beignet—Fletcher's border collie.

Benny was just a pup and was learning about herding. Her instincts were spot on to...herd things. The *details* were a little bit much for her though. Like that she should herd them back to their *barn*.

Instead, she just herded them to whatever structure was closest when she found them.

It had turned into a game around town. Spearheaded by his grandmother, of course. She called it Goat Bingo and handed out cards at her bar.

It had started when Benny had herded the goats into the bar. Twice. The squares had various locations around town— the gas station, the church, the bridal shop, the gazebo, etc.— and when the goats ended up in one and you saw it, you could mark that square. If you got bingo and were the first to bring your card in to Ellie, you got a free drink and an order of fried pickles.

Charlie, his cousin and head of marketing for the petting zoo, had tried to get Ellie to do fried goat cheese balls, insisting that was funny and tied into a theme. Ellie had told her she wasn't going for a theme and she didn't have any goat cheese.

The conversation had gone on for ten minutes. Which was about eight longer than it took most people to realize they couldn't win a debate with Ellie.

Zeke focused on the woman again. "So no petting for me then?"

"I called 9-1-1," she said. "And like I said, you're breathing and moving and I don't see blood gushing from anywhere so you don't need compression or a tourniquet or anything."

He wasn't so sure about fine, but he groaned. "You called 9-1-1?"

"That is the typical course of action when someone witnesses a motor vehicle accident."

"Shouldn't you have attempted some mouth-to-mouth or something first?"

He saw her dark brows rise. "Like I said, I heard you talking to yourself this entire time. Obviously your airway is working. And I don't know that you don't have any communicable diseases and that you're not an ax murderer. So I thought keeping a little distance and being prepared to run might be a good idea."

Fair enough.

But, shit. 9-1-1 meant his brother might be showing up. Then again....

"What did you tell them?"

"That I had witnessed a single motorcycle accident. And told them it was in front of the motel."

He might get lucky. It might not be Zander, the cop, who responded to the call if they believed it was more of a medical call.

And yeah, okay, he wasn't very hurt. A little banged up was all.

Zeke shoved to his feet. The goat startled slightly, but the woman tightened her arms around it and cooed to him softly that everything was going to be okay.

"He's not hurt a bit, right?" Zeke knew he hadn't hit the thing. He definitely would've felt that. Plus, he had great reflexes.

The woman shook her head. "He doesn't seem to be. I should take him over where there's more light and make sure." She glanced over her shoulder as she got to her feet, still holding the baby animal. "He really just wants to be with his friends."

Zeke nodded, then regretted it. His head was aching a bit.

"Griffin must be around here somewhere. If Sugar saw his truck, she would want out."

"Sugar?"

He pointed across the street. "The white goat. She's in love with our local veterinarian. Whenever she sees him, she wants out of the pen. Stan"—he pointed at the large goat who was off by himself, munching on some grass—"opens the gate for her. She'll stand at the gate and cry until Stan gets sick of listening to her."

The woman looked from him to the goat and back. "You're serious?"

"Yeah. Anyway, whoever shows up to the 9-1-1 call will have to get them back to the barn. Good thing I'm fine," he said dryly.

Just then a red pickup with a white cross and Autre Emergency Services in block letters on the side pulled around the corner.

Zeke let out a relieved breath. It was Michael, one of the firefighters and paramedics, not Zander.

Michael got out of his truck and approached. He was already grinning by the time he reached them. "Zeke."

"Hey, Michael."

"I got a call about a motorcycle accident."

Zeke pointed at his bike, then pointed to Sneezy, still in the woman's arms. "No worries. The goat is fine."

Michael chuckled. "Knox will love this."

Knox was the city manager who generally thought the petting zoo was a damned nuisance. Especially with the escaping goats and now the herding dog. And the Goat Bingo. And…okay, all of it.

There was also increased traffic from the uptick in visitors to the town and all of the issues that went along with that including more accidents, traffic flow problems, complaints from the locals about the noise and crowds, overflowing trash and recycling bins. His list of complaints went on and on.

In fairness, a lot of the complaints were things he heard about from citizens. But Knox also liked to think ahead to all the things that *might* happen as well. Goats escaping and crossing one of the main roads and causing accidents was definitely on his list. Having it come true was not going to make his day.

"Maybe we don't tell him. No harm, no foul."

Michael squinted at Zeke in the dark. "No harm? Your bike looks beat up and I think you're bleeding."

Zeke touched his temple again. "I'm a Landry. It'll take a lot more than a shot of pavement to the head to do any damage."

"I'm going to take a look at it," Michael said firmly.

"You want to shine a light in my eye and ask me to say the alphabet backwards?"

"Yeah, I kinda do. And I wouldn't mind putting a butterfly suture on that thing."

Zeke glanced at the woman who had caused all this trouble. Well, okay. The goat in her arms had caused trouble...okay, the goat across the street that was in love with Griffin that *this* goat had been following had caused the trouble...but she'd been the one to call 9-1-1, for fuck's sake.

Zeke sighed. But now that Michael was here, he knew the paramedic wasn't leaving without checking him out. "Fine."

He followed Michael to the truck and let his friend shine a flashlight over his face and ask his questions. Finally, Michael cleaned him up and taped a couple of white strips across the gash on his forehead and told Zeke he was probably concussion-free but what signs to watch for over the next day or so. Then he determined that Zeke didn't use his common sense much anyway so it didn't really matter if he'd lost a few IQ points.

Michael was hilarious.

Zeke was surprised to find the woman still standing there holding the goat when they were finished.

"You want Michael to take a look at the goat, cher?"

She shook her head. "He's fine. I'm just hanging onto him so he doesn't go wandering out into the street again. You said whoever responded to the call would take him and his friends back to the barn."

Zeke looked at Michael, who was watching at him with both eyebrows up.

"I did say that."

"And why would you say that?"

"Animal control isn't in your job description?" Zeke asked with a grin.

"You know damned well that when I'm on call almost everything falls into my job description," Michael said.

It was true that small town job descriptions definitely overlapped and there were a lot of blurred lines, especially when it came to emergency services.

Michael was a firefighter and paramedic, but he showed up to help break up bar brawls and had definitely herded a few goats in his time. A couple of months ago, he'd helped search for two fishermen that had gone missing on the bayou. Last year he'd helped run some illegal arms dealers out of town with Zander. And he'd definitely wrangled a few gators. He'd even been in on trapping a couple black bears and relocating them when they decided they'd rather hang out in the city limits for an extended period.

"Would you like some help?" the woman asked.

Obviously she was comfortable handling the goat.

"Any time a beautiful woman wants to do something for

me, I'm inclined to say yes," Michael told her. He even tipped his hat to her. Like literally tipped his hat.

Zeke rolled his eyes.

He knew that the women of Autre found Michael LeClaire handsome and charming. Zeke had been hearing about it since they'd all hit puberty.

Michael was an Autre boy born and raised, and though he was a couple years older than Zeke and Zander, Zeke had spent plenty of time around Michael and his family. Their grandfathers were best friends, and their families knew each other well.

The black man stood six-two, had a quick, easy smile, and an even easier Louisiana drawl. He also peppered his speech with French, learned from his grandparents, that made women swoon. It was quite a sight to behold actually.

Zeke usually found it hilarious. Michael was no saint, that was for sure. None of the bayou boys were. But being a firefighter and paramedic added to the swoony heroic good-guy image that Michael had going and that women fell for. Every time. Even women who had known him his whole life. It was amazing and Zeke had to admit he was envious.

But right now, he wasn't feeling exactly envious or entertained.

Michael flirting with this woman was annoying for some reason.

"It's a little ways back to the barn," Zeke said. "Can't believe one of them tried to kill me and you want me to escort him back home and tuck him into bed."

"He didn't try to kill you," the woman said. "He's just a baby. He was going to meet his friends across the street, and suddenly you came barreling through and nearly ran him over. You didn't even come to a full stop at the stop sign."

Zeke stared at her. "You saw me come through the stop sign?"

"Maybe," the woman said, tipping her head.

She hadn't. She was messing with him. Right? Then again, she could have. She must've been right there to have come over to check on him—okay, the goat—so quickly. Had he stopped at the stop sign? He knew he'd rolled through the one coming off of Main Street. But he was pretty sure he'd stopped at this one. Then again, it was possible he hadn't.

"So you're saying the goat had the right-of-way?"

She lifted a slender shoulder. "He was crossing the street and you should have stopped."

"Was he in the crosswalk?" Michael asked.

The woman looked at him, then looked at the street where there was actually the faint outline of crosswalk. She lifted her chin. "He was. Clearly the motorcycle driver was at fault here. How much would a ticket like that cost you?"

Zeke narrowed his eyes. "Are you saying that if I don't help get these goats back safe and sound in their barn you're going to turn me in and I might end up with a ticket?"

The woman shrugged. "I don't make the rules."

He actually huffed out a laugh. "Would it make a difference to you if I told you my brother is the cop in town?"

"Surely a lovely town like Autre, Louisiana, doesn't believe in the cop doing favors for his family when they clearly break the law."

Zeke liked her. That was ridiculous, of course. She was siding with the goat over the human being. He was actually hurt. Not enough that he actually needed Michael's services. But he was going to be sore in the morning.

Still, there was something about her that he found intriguing. There was no question in his mind that it had to do in part with the fact that she was gorgeous.

Now that they'd moved closer to Michael's truck and the street lights he could see her more clearly. He couldn't tell what color her eyes were exactly or if she had freckles or if her teeth were perfectly straight or anything. But she had a cute turned up nose, that long, tightly wavy hair, and a great body. She was very petite. She only came to chest level on him and he was sure he could span her waist with both hands. She had small perky breasts, slim hips, and a tight ass. He'd bet she was a runner or something.

Most of all though, he wanted to make her smile.

That was very strange. But she seemed so serious.

She had a bit of a sense of humor that had peeked out. At least he assumed she was joking when talking about turning him into the authorities and getting him written up if he didn't help her goats. But she also seemed...detached. She truly seemed unconcerned about his medical condition and she was willing to manipulate him into helping the animals.

Detached was not something that Zeke understood. He had never been detached about anything in his life that he could think of. He wasn't sure anyone in his family could actually define that word.

Landrys attached. Period. To recipes. To favorite fishing spots. To favorite embarrass-your-relatives stories. To people. Most definitely to people.

Like leeches.

"Okay, fine," he said. "We'll get the goats back home. Then you have to let me buy you a drink."

She shook her head. "No, I don't."

Zeke heard Michael snort. He cast his friend a glance.

"How about coffee?"

"I'm okay."

"How about the best pecan pie you'll ever have in your life?"

"No, thanks."

"Goat cheese balls?"

Michael laughed out loud at that.

If she said yes to those, Zeke was going to be in trouble, but he knew this woman wasn't going to let him buy her anything so he was just being sarcastic.

"Or goat steaks maybe?" he asked. He eyed Sneezy as he said it.

"No," she said, clearly a bit exasperated.

Which was fine. Zeke was *very* familiar with people being exasperated with him.

"Look, it's not like either of us is doing the other a favor by getting the goats to the barn," the woman said. "They just need to get back. If you'd rather call someone else, I suppose we could do that. But the three of us are here and I think that's more than enough to handle the goats, especially since there's also a dog."

Zeke snorted. "That dog is part of the problem."

"She's clearly still learning."

"Clearly."

"It just seems like a waste of time to wait for someone else to get here." She paused. "Also seems like a waste of time to stand here talking about all of this instead of just getting it over with."

Zeke wasn't sure what to say. He was actually…offended.

He was very well-liked. That wasn't his ego talking. That was just a fact. Yes, he was very well-liked by women in particular. It was unusual for women to not want to…consume things with him. But it was very uncommon for people in general not to want to spend time with him.

Then again, it also seemed unusual for someone to come upon another person who had just had a motorcycle accident and not be at least slightly concerned about them.

So the woman was weird.

It was her, not Zeke.

Okay, good. He could accept that.

It was better they not have a drink, or any goat products, together.

## 2

Zeke would've really preferred, however, to not have had a friend witness all of this. Especially a friend who would repeat it to the rest of his friends, most of whom were his relatives.

"Okay, let's go."

The woman went to the dog and told her she was a good girl and to come. Then they each picked up a goat and started in the direction of the petting zoo barn that was down the road.

The rest of the goats followed along behind them with Benny running from one side of the group to the other, barking and woofing. Zeke rolled his eyes. She had the general idea, but the goats were definitely following the humans, not listening to Benny.

The petting zoo was located directly next to the Boys of the Bayou Swamp Boat Tour Company office and docks and across the street from Ellie's bar. Zeke was tempted to walk straight in there after they got the goats settled and the gate secured. But his bike was still up by the motel and for some reason, he wanted to make sure the woman got back to where she'd come from.

"Were you just passing through?" he asked her.

"I'm staying at the motel," she said. "I was over at the convenience store getting food and was walking back when I saw you barreling toward the goat."

Zeke looked at her as they walked. He could not read her. Was she joking? Surely, she had to be joking. "I wasn't *barreling*," he felt inclined to say.

"You would have been if it hadn't been for the stop sign."

He stopped walking. "I knew it! I knew I stopped. You manipulated me to get me to take those goats back to the barn."

She gave him a look that said, "obviously". "I wouldn't have had to if you were a good guy and had just agreed to do it in the beginning."

"I'm a very good guy. I was going to do it."

"You sure were whining about it."

Again, Michael snorted, but said nothing.

"I wasn't whining. I've had a long day. And I just wrecked my motorcycle," Zeke pointed out.

"You stopped at that stop sign. The goat was crossing the street. You started forward and then saw him and swerved. You were clearly not paying attention."

"So?"

"So it's your own fault." She turned and started walking again.

Michael walked along beside her.

Zeke watched them for several steps.

He realized he was having a hard time processing this whole situation.

And yes, he was self-aware enough to realize what it was.

This woman wasn't a bit charmed by him.

And she wasn't letting him off the hook.

That sounded a little pathetic. He was twenty-five years old. It wasn't like consequences were an entirely foreign concept.

But he was the baby of the family. He didn't have *a lot* of consequences. Yeah, he knew how that sounded, but it was true. He was the youngest grandchild, except for a couple of girl cousins who didn't live in Autre. He was the youngest boy in his family, even if it was only by two minutes behind his twin Zander. And he loved being the youngest.

Youngest children got away with all kinds of shit. He'd been aware of that from a very young age. Also everyone worried about him more. Everyone loved to take care of him. And he loved to let them. Could he have survived on his own if he had to?

He really wasn't sure.

He'd never had to try and he couldn't think of a time, at any point in the near future, when that would change, so he didn't really think about it too hard.

He finally jogged a few steps to catch up with Michael and the woman.

"So you're judging me to be a bad guy just based on this goat situation?" he asked.

Why did it bother him? He didn't know her. She was clearly just traveling, spending the night in Autre. He'd probably never see her again. Why did he care what she thought?

But everyone thought he was a good guy. Okay, sure he was the baby and his brothers and even a couple older cousins, at times, rolled their eyes about how spoiled he was. But he knew it was mostly because they were jealous. No one thought he was actually a *bad* guy. No one believed he was lazy.

"How am I supposed to base who you are on anything else?" the woman asked. "I don't have any more data to use."

Well, she had a point. Zeke was so used to spending time around people who'd known him, literally, his entire life, that he didn't have to worry too much about making good first impressions.

"I'm a great guy," he said.

She glanced at him with one brow up.

Okay, so maybe even bad guys said that they were good guys.

He elbowed Michael. "Tell her I'm a good guy."

"He's a good guy," Michael said.

The woman didn't reply. She also didn't seem that impressed.

But even more, she didn't seem concerned, or unimpressed, or really like she had any feelings about it whatsoever.

That almost bugged him more.

Why did he want her to have feelings? He wasn't even specifying that they needed to be *good* feelings. He just wanted her to have feelings about this, or him, or something.

They were back at the motel.

Michael started for his truck and Zeke thought fast.

He focused on the woman. "Do you have any ibuprofen in your room?"

Now she at least seemed surprised. She thought about the question for a few seconds. Finally she nodded, "I do."

"Can I have some?"

"I'm sure your paramedic friend has some."

Michael opened his mouth, but Zeke shot him a frown. "He's out."

The woman looked from Zeke to Michael and back. "I'd guess the convenience store has some." She pointed in that direction. About twenty yards behind Zeke.

"It's way over there and my head is pounding."

She put a hand on her hip. "You can't wait till you get home?"

"My motorcycle is trash."

So it wasn't exactly trash. He wasn't even sure that it wasn't drivable. But he wanted something more from this woman than detached and dismissive. He wanted her to either tell him to fuck off or come on in.

Yes, he was generally well-liked. He was definitely spoiled.

But he was something else that younger brothers tended to be experts at—he could be annoying to the point of making anyone snap.

"And your paramedic friend won't give you a ride?"

"Michael is very busy. He can't be using his work truck, and his work hours, to chauffeur a friend around."

"There's no one else you can call? I assume this town doesn't have Uber or Lyft?"

"Nope, no taxis. Nothing like that."

"And you have no friends."

"Well as you've seen tonight, I'm kind of an asshole."

She studied him for a long moment. Zeke just let her. He met her eyes directly. His head really was hurting, so if she did have ibuprofen in her motel room, he would absolutely take her up on it. But he was a thousand percent certain that she knew that wasn't what he was looking for.

Thing was, he wasn't exactly sure what he *was* looking for. A reaction more than anything. A smile, an outraged gasp, an exclamation of some kind. A moan.

That last one hit him out of the blue.

But then he thought about it. Yeah, a moan. He would absolutely take one of those.

Zeke was aware that Michael was still standing by his truck. He was off far enough that the conversation was mostly happening between the woman and Zeke, but Michael was there in case she felt uncomfortable. Or, honestly, if Zeke ended up needing a ride.

Which Michael was probably pretty sure he would.

Finally, after what felt like two hours of thought, the woman shocked Zeke when she said, "Okay. I'll give you ibuprofen."

"Awesome," Zeke said sincerely. Regardless of what *ibuprofen* really meant.

"So I'm okay leaving you?" Michael asked.

Zeke waited for the woman to answer.

"I assume that as a first responder you wouldn't leave me alone with an ax murderer."

Michael chuckled. "No, ma'am. Even if I wasn't a first responder, I think I'd try to keep people away from ax murderers."

"Or really a murderer of any kind? I guess ax murderer is pretty specific," she said, showing that hint of humor again.

"I would not leave you with a murderer of any kind," Michael said. "He's a good guy. And I mean, after all, you're not a goat so you don't have to worry about him trying to run you over, or being neglectful, or uncaring."

"Fuck off," Zeke muttered.

But the woman nodded. "I guess that's a good point. He seems to think that I should be very concerned about him just because we're both human beings. I assume that he would extend that same level of care and concern to whatever I might need from him."

Zeke's gaze snapped to hers.

That sounded dirty. He didn't care what anyone said. That sounded dirty. And not just because he'd whacked his head earlier.

The woman's face was completely impassive however.

He looked over at Michael. Surely his friend thought that sounded like innuendo.

But Michael was already climbing behind the wheel, giving them a quick wave over the top of the truck. "Goodnight."

Zeke turned back to the woman, planning to ask her just what kind of needs she was talking about, but she, too, had already turned away and was walking toward the motel.

Well, that was where the ibuprofen was and he was starting to think some painkillers were a good idea. He followed her.

The woman unlocked the door to number one eleven.

One eleven was funny, considering the motel had thirty rooms.

The door swung in, the woman stepped inside, and he followed.

She shut the door and turned to face him with her back pressed against it.

"I'm not sure if I have ibuprofen, actually," she said.

He lifted a brow. That was...interesting.

It occurred to him briefly that she had asked Michael if she was safe with Zeke.

But no one had asked if Zeke was safe with her.

She was tiny, but she might have a weapon. She might be a black belt in karate. She might be about to release toxic fumes into the room. All of those things would really suck because they would certainly even up the physical playing field here.

But if it was just one on one, he could totally take her.

His body should *not* have responded to that thought the way it did.

But there was no denying the heating and hardening he experienced.

Now that they were inside in full light, he realized that her eyes were a deep moss green. Her skin was fair, as if she rarely spent time outdoors. She was slim but her arms, in the sleeveless shirt, showed muscle definition. Either she worked out or she had a physical job.

He was willing to take a chance here that *she* wasn't an ax murderer.

"If there is any, it's in the little travel bag in the bathroom next to the sink."

"I'll look. I need to wash up a little anyway."

He didn't find ibuprofen but he did find some tablets for menstrual cramps when he went through her bag. He read the back. Headache and body aches were two symptoms the tablets helped with—and wow, it sucked a woman could depend on getting those *plus* bloating, fatigue, and cramps once a month— so he figured what the hell? But he decided to take just one since he wasn't bloated or cramping. He washed his hands and face and stepped back into the main room.

He decided to just cut to the chase. "So you think I'm kind of an asshole to goats," he said. "What am I doing here?"

She tipped her head and let her gaze roam over him.

Zeke felt his eyebrows climb.

"I've had a really crazy week." She took a deep breath and let it out. "Actually, a couple of weeks. A really good friend of mine died recently."

"I'm sorry to hear that."

"Thanks." She lifted her eyes to him again. "How do you feel about sex as a stress reliever?"

Awesome. He was now on the same page. A non-poisonous-gas-or-other-weapons page.

"In general, I am of big fan of sex, for almost any reason."

The corner of her mouth curled up. And nothing could've removed Zeke Landry from that room now.

A reaction. An emotional reaction. Toward *him*, not a goat.

"How do *you* feel about sex as a stress reliever?"

"Big fan. It works really well for me."

His body liked the sound of that. Not that he liked the idea she was stressed. He wasn't an asshole, in spite of his previous goat interaction. But this conversation seemed to be going in a very nice direction.

"I'm happy to help," Zeke told her. "I can be your personal therapist tonight."

She waved her hand like she was flicking a fly away. "Sex is faster and easier than therapy. It's also easier to get up the next morning than if I drink too much wine. And it costs less than going for a massage." She tipped her head. "Can be faster than that too. But not always."

"So your stress-relieving list is sex, therapy, wine, and massages. And sex is your preference because it's faster, easier, and cheaper than all the others."

"Yep."

Wow. She was...something.

"Except, like I said, it's not *always* faster than a massage."

Right.

"How long are your massages?"

"An hour. Hour and a half if I'm *really* tense."

"Yeah, this is going to take longer than that." He didn't know *why* he felt so compelled to make an impression on this woman, but now that he'd made her smile, and had her full attention, and had seen her green eyes up close, he *was* going to send her on her way with a *huge* grin and very fond memories of Autre.

"Do you have more tattoos?" Her eyes were back on his arm where his full sleeve showed beneath the edge of his t-shirt. Oh, she liked tattoos.

"I do."

"Are you any good at dirty talk?"

The woman knew what she liked.

His entire body felt like he'd just taken a big shot of his grandpa's moonshine. He was hot, on edge, and ready for the unexpected. Because when Leo Landry's moonshine came out, you never knew what could happen.

"As a matter fact, I can't really help it."

She let out a breath. Then she gave him a full smile.

Yeah, he wasn't going anywhere for a nice, *long* time. And suddenly his head felt fine.

"Do you have a wife, fiancée, girlfriend, woman who thinks she's your girlfriend even if you don't think so?"

"No. No. No. And I did but we cleared that up."

She gave him another of those little half smiles. Like she didn't *want* to be amused by him, but she couldn't resist.

"How do you feel about one-night stands? Because I'm not looking for anything serious."

"They are my favorite kind of night stand."

Her smile grew and Zeke felt a strange warmth along with the heat.

"And you won't brag about this to your friends tomorrow?"

"Oh, I'm absolutely going to brag to my friends about this tomorrow," he said. He took a step closer to her. "Especially Michael. Since he was out there saving goats and being all charming and sweet and you didn't invite him to your room."

"He was on duty."

Zeke lifted a brow. "That's the only reason."

"Probably. He's hot. And has the heroic, sweet thing going for him."

"He fakes most of the sweet stuff."

"How about the heroic stuff?"

Zeke gave a dramatic sigh. "Unfortunately for the rest of us assholes, that's all real."

She gave a soft snort. "Maybe I actually *am* concerned about your head and thought I should keep an eye on you to be sure you don't slip into unconsciousness and never wake up."

"I'm going to accept that only because I like it better than the realization that Michael could be in here with you right now." He leaned in. "But I don't believe you. I think you took a look at my boots and Michael's and realized that mine were bigger."

Her eyes widened. "How did you know I did that?"

He paused, then shook his head. "You *did* do that?"

"Of course."

"You are..."

"I know," she said, when he trailed off.

He wasn't even sure what he'd been intending to fill in there. Odd? Quirky? Fascinating?

Yep. To all of that.

"So, can I brag to *my* friends about it tomorrow?" she asked, her voice huskier now.

"You better," he said, dropping his voice to a gruffer note.

The next smile she gave him was one that said he'd given all the right answers, but even more, it was filled with heat as well.

"There it is." He reached up and cupped her face.

Her breathing got more ragged as she looked up at him. And she had to look up a ways. She was small. She probably stood about five-three to his six-four.

"What?" she asked softly.

"The reaction I've been going for."

"Reaction?"

"Yes, until now. You've seemed very...dispassionate towards me."

Her eyes narrowed slightly as if she was thinking about that. "Have I?"

"You have." He leaned in, bracing a hand on the door just above her ear. "Quite insulting."

This smile was a little more sly and definitely had a touch of mischief. "Maybe you should see how passionate you can make me."

"Oh, challenge accepted," Zeke told her.

---

His posture with his one hand braced on the door and him leaning over her could have felt intimidating, like he was caging her in.

But Jill only felt excitement.

Her mother would have heart palpitations if she knew. She was in a hotel room in a strange town with a man she had literally just met.

And had just agreed to have sex with.

No, she hadn't agreed. She'd been the one to initiate that entire conversation.

Well, hey, she didn't have a masseuse or a therapist here. And yes, the convenience store did have wine but she'd have to walk *way* over there while this big, hot Louisiana man with long hair and a beard and tattoos and a motorcycle was right here.

And clearly willing.

And she wasn't worried at all. She didn't know if it was because of the paramedic reassuring her that this man was a good guy, or the fact that this was actually a town much like the town where she'd grown up, or what.

Autre was tiny and everyone knew one another. Her friend Griffin was here. Granted, he'd accidentally settled here, but he seemed grudgingly happy. In fact, he seemed more than grudgingly happy. His girlfriend, Charlie, had family here and had, evidently, spent a lot of time here growing up. If she and Griffin both liked this town, Jillian felt safe here.

Yes, that all seemed probably a little convoluted as far as rationale went, but it was working. Her conscience was very cool with this.

She studied him up close.

His dark brown hair was gathered back in a ponytail, but she would guess it would hang past his shoulders when loose. In the dark brown were lighter streaks that gave him the look of someone who worked outside, or a model. His beard was short, but dark and full, and even his eyes were a deep brown.

He also had piercings in both ears, a gold stud and a hoop on the left and one gold stud on the right.

Dammit, everything about him was her type.

She knew that good guys with steady jobs and day planners were who she *should* be attracted to and they were who she'd dated almost exclusively. Jillian knew that in the big picture, she was looking for an opposites attract romance. But not like this.

She didn't have any tattoos and she'd only ridden on a motorcycle once. She'd had her ears pierced when she was twelve, but she'd let the holes close up and didn't own any earrings anymore.

But no, the opposite type of guy she was looking for was the 9-to-5-Monday-through-Friday-had-a-401k-put-appointments-in-his-phone-and-never-forget-a-birthday type. Not the clearly-wasn't-afraid-of-needles type.

She wasn't even concerned about her own birthday so much as she was hoping for someone who would help her remember *other people's* birthdays.

Because she sucked at that kind of stuff.

She needed someone in her life to keep everything else straight so she could focus on work.

She needed someone who had a normal, sane life because they could then add some sane and normal to *her* life.

That's how it had been with Stephen anyway. No, they hadn't worked out, but he'd showed her what was possible. She was definitely looking for another Stephen.

She was *not* looking for a smooth-talking, tattooed, motor-cycle guy who didn't even care when he almost killed a baby goat.

But her body and her brain did not agree on what she was looking for in a man. And every once in a while, her body won the battle.

She'd had a very nice friends-with-benefits thing going with Dan back in Omaha. It had been very low-key. About once a month one of them would call the other, they'd compare their calendars, pick a night, and scratch their itches.

Then they'd go on their merry ways for another month or so.

It had been perfect. No letting him down when she had to work late—or worked late because she forgot she'd promised to go to the theater with him.

Stephen had really liked the theater. The third show he'd

ended up attending alone at the last minute had been the final straw.

Dan had never asked her to the theater. Or to a movie. Or to dinner. They literally got together, said hi, and took their clothes off.

It had been amazing.

But it had been a while.

She looked up into the brown eyes of the goat terrorist.

She was really going to enjoy having sex with this guy. She could just tell. There was something about him, goat terrorist or not, that said he could deliver on orgasms.

And hey, even if there was a little false advertising going on, he had all the parts she needed and she knew how to help herself. He was big, claimed to be able to talk dirty, and he had tattoos.

She could do the rest of the work if needed.

"Maybe I should get your name," Zeke said.

Jill felt a little shiver dance down her spine. She loved his voice. Deep, rumbly, and that drawl. Yum. She was from the Midwest. Everybody talked the same there. There were no drawls or accents. She already liked a few things about the south a lot. The beignets she'd had earlier that day had also been amazing.

"Jillian."

Sure, it was really a small town and she was going to be living here, and there was a chance they might run into each other again. But she fully intended to be an eccentric, anti-social millionaire who owned penguins. She didn't think they'd be seeing each other at the local bar or anything.

And hey, if tonight turned out well, she might *want* to run into this guy again. Every once in a while. With very long stretches in between. And only for a night at a time.

Still, he really did put off playboy vibes that said he could easily be trained to be her new Dan.

"Hi, Jillian. I'm Zeke."

She opened her mouth to respond, but he covered her lips with his before she could.

Fine. Talking, especially at moments like this, was overrated.

## 3

She gripped his biceps and leaned into the kiss.

He was good at this. Thank God.

He took his time easing into it. He kissed her softly at first, tasting her, pressing and then lifting, tilting his head, coming at her from another angle. She ran her hands up his arms and under the edge of his sleeves, exploring the contours of his muscles. He was definitely in good shape. Biceps, triceps, deltoids, pecs. All had sculpted definition. And he seemed to love her touch. He gave a low groan as she smoothed her hands down over his abs and then up under the t-shirt onto hot, bare skin. She ran her palms up and down his ribs, loving the way his abdominal muscles jumped.

His groan sent a shaft of heat through Jillian's stomach that arrowed down between her legs.

He teased her lips with his tongue and she gladly opened, but as she tried to press closer she realized their height difference was going to be an issue.

She nudged him back, wanting to walk him to the bed, but he mistook it for her wanting him to stop. He lifted his head and looked down at her, breathing a little raggedly.

"You okay?"

"Need you on the bed."

He looked surprised for a second. "Well, damn. Yes, ma'am." He started to take a step back, but grabbed the loops on her pants, and tugged her with him. "Feel like that would be a good place for you too."

"I'm right there with you."

In two strides he was at the mattress, sitting and pulling her into his lap. She climbed up, straddling his thighs, and pressing into him.

*Yes.* That was much better.

His hands settled on her hips and she became aware of just how big and hot they were. The heat from his touch soaked through her pants and she wiggled, pressing their flies together.

He was hard. And huge.

That shaft of heat warmed her belly again and seemed to spiral out from her bellybutton to set all of her nerve endings on fire.

She couldn't remember being this turned on in a long time.

"Damn, girl, you feel good," he told her roughly.

She leaned in and pressed her lips to his, picking up right where they'd left off. She opened her mouth, stroking her tongue along his lower lip.

He groaned and one hand lifted, his fingers slipping into her hair while the other gripped her hip.

So far this was very promising.

She tasted him for a long time, before sitting back and reaching for the bottom of her shirt. She pulled it up and over her head, tossing it toward the pillows.

Zeke's gaze dropped to her breasts and the plain white bra she wore.

She didn't have time, or the inclination, to worry about

what he thought about her underwear. All of her bras and panties were basic. Everything in her wardrobe was basic.

But he wasn't here for her bra.

She reached back and unclasped the tiny hooks, releasing the bra and tossing it over her shoulder. In her experience, once the bra was gone, he'd be easily drawn back to the task.

Predictably, he made no comments about the white cotton lying on the floor by the bed. Instead, he lifted a hand to cup a breast.

Jill was not well endowed, and his hands were huge, so her A-cup easily fit in the center of his palm.

He didn't seem to mind. He kneaded and willingly took her direction as she covered his hand with hers and moved it so her nipple was between his thumb and finger. He rolled the hard tip, squeezing and plucking, then moving his other hand to her unattended breast.

"Harder," she coached.

He complied, squeezing tighter, and tugging harder. She tipped her head back. "Yes, like that."

He kept going, giving her even more pressure, sending jolts of heat and desire coursing through her.

Jill rubbed against his hard cock, not wanting to interrupt what he was doing, but wanting so much more.

"I—"

Without any input, he slid one hand to the middle of her back between her shoulder blades and tipped her back, lifting her and fastening his mouth over one nipple.

She gasped with pleasure that was both physical and emotional. The sensations were delicious, but she loved that he'd realized what she needed. She had no trouble with open communication about what it took to get her to orgasm, but she certainly didn't mind if the man could figure some of it out on his own.

Zeke sucked hard, then swirled his tongue around the tip, sucked again, then grazed his teeth along the tender point.

Jillian gasped and tightened her thighs, squeezing her knees into the outside of his legs. The ache in her core was suddenly intense and she was wet and hot to a point she hadn't been in forever.

"Zeke—" she started again.

But he switched sides just as she was about to ask him to.

He sucked, licked, sucked, and then bit again, scraping his teeth with the perfect amount of pressure to give her that little burst of pleasurable pain.

Oh, yes, this was going very well.

She clutched the back of his head, holding him close, encouraging him. She gripped his ponytail.

"Can I take your hair down?" she asked.

He barely lifted his head. "If I get to keep my mouth against these tits, you can do anything you want."

She didn't really want his mouth anywhere else. Okay, that wasn't entirely true. She had some other ideas about where she'd like his tongue. She didn't think he'd object either.

She pulled the tie from his hair, the long strands falling to his shoulders. She ran her fingers through it, combing it out. It was silky and soft, falling just past his shoulders, and had a slight wave.

She wanted to feel it brushing against her skin. All of her skin.

"God, that feels good, cher," he muttered, before he sucked hard on her nipple again.

"I love your hair," she told him.

"Yeah? Well, I'm a big fan of everything of yours so far."

She laughed softly. "I'm not saying it's going to be my favorite part."

He lifted his hands and ran them both through her hair, then gathered it in one fist. Her hair was thick and naturally curly, but he seemed to have no problem holding the coiled dark strands in one big hand. He tugged slightly, tipping her head back and peering into her eyes.

"Just how much of this sweet body are you going to let me see?"

"As much as you want."

His eyes flared with heat. "I want it all."

"Very good answer," she told him. "Because I want the same from you."

He shook his head slightly. "I wasn't expecting you..."

"You weren't expecting me to what?"

"No, I think that's it. I think I just wasn't expecting you."

That was actually kind of sweet. "You didn't expect a one-night stand tonight?"

"Honestly? No. Not even after I met you. And I'm still not sure."

"And why is that? Do I seem like a good girl?"

"Maybe. But I think it's more that you seem to not like me very much."

Huh. She wasn't sure that was entirely true. But then again, she didn't really *know* him. She hadn't slept with a stranger before. She and Dan didn't even know each other's birthdays, but she liked his taste in wine, loved his taste in bed sheets, and preferred sex at his place because he had great after-sex snacks.

Okay, that all sounded pretty shallow.

"Would you have taken the goats back to their barn if I hadn't made you?"

He was obviously surprised by her question for a moment. Then he seemed to be considering it. Finally he said, "No, probably not."

"Because you really didn't care what happened to them?"

It was possible that she *didn't* like him.

"Because someone else would have taken care of it." He lifted a shoulder. "That's how things work here. For me. No matter what I might *intend* to do as far as good deeds are concerned, someone else nearly always gets there first. I guess I just...assume things will get taken care of."

She narrowed her eyes. He seemed completely sincere. "And are your assumptions correct? All the time?"

He looked up at the ceiling, thinking. Then he nodded. "Yeah. There are *a lot* of people here who love to take care of things and are pretty kickass at it. So, yeah, my assumptions about that are always right."

She supposed that didn't make him a *bad* guy then. Just a little...irresponsible, maybe.

And hell, she didn't need him taking care of her. She just needed an orgasm.

"Okay, I like you," she decided.

"Yeah?"

He seemed to really want that to be true.

"Yep. And I *really* like what you do to me." She wiggled her hips against his, which caused her breasts and the hard nipples he'd been so good to just a few minutes ago to brush against his chest.

He looked at her for a second as if thinking things over. "Then I say we keep going."

"I say hell yes."

With his hand still in her hair, he brought her head forward, covering her lips with his and immediately kissing her deep and dirty.

His tongue tasted and taunted, and all Jill could think was how much she wanted his tongue between her legs.

She was *not* a good girl but...

Yes, she was. But mostly because she didn't have a lot of time or attention to give to things like flings and partying and being wild and free. And that was fine. She had chosen to dedicate her life to her work.

But when a hot guy with long hair and tattoos was kissing

her and playing with her nipples and making her think about body parts that got attention mostly from her vibrator, she did realize that there were good reasons to leave the penguins. Once in a while.

Sex and cheesecake.

And not the no-bake kind made with whipped topping.

*Real* cheesecake that had to be baked.

Those were two things she was willing to leave the penguins for periodically.

But other than that, she had a hard time coming up with things that were more important than what she did for a living. She was not good at relationships because she rarely put anything or anyone above her work. Men—and to be fair, most people—got tired of coming in second. So, to avoid arguments and break ups and generally hurting people's feelings, she made sure her relationships were very clear from the beginning.

But this guy? And his tongue? She might be willing to make a few exceptions for him.

Zeke pulled back, staring at her eyes, and ran his hands from the back of her head down her shoulders to her wrists where they were linked behind his head. He pulled them apart and nudged her off his lap.

"Want the rest of those off," he said, nodding to her clothes.

She started on the button of her pants, but he stretched to his feet just then and stripped his t-shirt up his torso and over his head.

Holy crap.

The guy was ripped. He had muscles. She'd already known that he had great muscles in his arms, shoulders, and chest, but seeing them without the black cotton covering them was hot-fantasy-at-night-in-bed-with-her-vibrator-alone level. The guy had suntanned skin and just the right amount of chest hair that narrowed into a line that bisected his sixpack abs, and muscles that were not only incredibly defined, but were covered in gorgeous dark ink.

His right shoulder was covered from the top curve to his elbow with a huge grizzly bear head that spanned onto his chest and wrapped around to the back of his shoulder. Across his chest were words that appeared to be French and were wrapped with magnolias and met up with a dove on the front of his left shoulder and an eagle on the back. Then down his arm all the way to the wrist was a combination designs, feathers, and vines.

She wanted to explore every single line. She wanted to know what they were all about, what they meant to him, why he'd gotten each one.

But mostly, and first, she wanted to run her hands over them, followed by her lips and tongue.

With his hair down and wild around his shoulders, the glint of an earring from his left ear, the ink covered muscles and the low-slung blue jeans along with the black leather riding boots, he was the epitome of an indulgent fantasy in a roadside motel and Jill was suddenly filled with swirling hot, oh-my-God-yes excitement.

The last few weeks since A.J. had passed and she'd inherited the penguins, her life had been crazy.

She'd quit her job, found a new place to live, prepared to move several states away, broken the news to her family and friends, and learned all about the penguin conservation and propagation program she was now automatically a part of.

She'd spent her time trying to get the penguins used to having her around, figuring out how to actually be in charge of endangered wildlife, getting licenses and paperwork transferred, and figuring out how to be in possession of millions of dollars.

Everything in her life had been turned upside down, it seemed, and if anyone deserved a hot night fulfilling a whole bunch of I-probably-shouldn't-but-I-really-want-to urges that no one would ever know about, it was her. This was actually the perfect situation and she was all in.

"You okay?" Zeke asked, his hands pausing on the button in front of his jeans.

Jill lifted her eyes to his. She realized that she had been frozen, just staring. She swallowed and nodded. "It just hit me what an amazingly wonderful idea this is."

The corner of his mouth curled up and he took a step closer. "Which idea exactly?"

"Getting you naked and riding you 'til dawn."

For just a second Jill was shocked those words had come from her mouth.

But the way his pupils dilated and his mouth fell open, made every bit of shock and embarrassment fade quickly. She loved having an effect on this guy, and there was something about not knowing him, not expecting any of this, and him looking at her the way he was right now that made her feel very brazen.

"Well, since we have until dawn, there's a whole lot of stuff I'd like to do before we get to the riding," he told her. "But while we're both gonna enjoy me bending you over and fucking you from behind, taking you up against the wall, and some good old missionary before we get to that, I'm going to think about you straddling me the whole time."

Heat blossomed in Jill's lower belly and spread quickly through her body. God, she loved a guy who talked dirty. And she very much loved the fact that he was meeting her brazen talk with his own.

He reached for the front of her jeans and dragged the zipper down slowly as he said, "And please tell me that you like cowgirl more than reverse cowgirl, because I'd really love to watch your tits bouncing and see your face when you come."

Her breath caught in her chest and Jill didn't speak for a

moment as he pushed her jeans over her hips and down her legs.

She braced a hand on his huge biceps as she lifted a foot to kick free of the jeans absentmindedly. Her brain was fully focused on what he had said.

"I actually like both lots. Reverse is a fantastic angle and there can be something sexy about getting off without seeing your partner's face."

That actually made Zeke stop in the midst of helping her get her jeans off.

"Is that right?"

She looked at him, realizing he was surprised that she'd answered completely honestly. She hadn't been teasing, flirting, or just talking dirty. All of what she just said was true. "But I'm willing to do cowgirl for you."

He laughed. "Thanks. I do really appreciate it."

She let her gaze wander over his body.

He was hard and ripped but he didn't have a weightlifter's physique. He had very natural muscle definition, clearly built from hard work.

"What do you do for a living?"

"Construction. Mostly."

"Shows."

"Thank you." He seemed surprised.

She looked up at him. "Are you telling me that I'm the first woman to think you're good looking?"

"You're the only woman who matters right now."

She gave a soft snort. "Good answer."

He reached out, snagged her wrist, and tugged her forward. He put her hands on his chest and covered them with his. "I hope it goes without saying, but this isn't show and tell. Feel free to handle anything you see that you like."

"There's going to be a lot of handling then."

"*That* is a good answer."

He ran his hands up her arms and down her sides. Goosebumps broke out over her body and she couldn't help but move her hands over his skin as well. He was hot to the touch and she loved every sensation from the soft hair on his chest to the firmness of his nipples to the hard contour of his chest to the way he shuddered as she ran her hand down his ribs.

His hands went to her panties and he quickly pushed them down her thighs. They dropped to her ankles.

Naked now, Jill wasn't sure she'd ever felt this turned on. It was strange. Sex was very purposeful for her. She enjoyed it, immensely. She'd been lucky to hook up with Dan. But they could go two months without seeing one another. She was generally fine in the time between their visits with her vibrator.

But she did like the real thing and Dan was very good. Over the couple of years they'd been seeing one another they'd learned each other's buttons and turn-ons. He could deliver every time. She very much appreciated him and knew she was going to miss him.

But right now, with this complete stranger, she was feeling jumpy and tingly and hot from head to toe in a way that she couldn't remember ever feeling.

Maybe it was the newness of it. Maybe it was the impulsive, unexpected act of picking someone up. Maybe it had just been a while. She couldn't remember exactly when she and Dan had last been together. They hadn't been able to make their schedules jive for one last hurrah before she'd left Omaha.

But then Zeke's hands skimmed down her back to cup her butt and pulled her forward and she completely forgot about anything except the hard, hot body in front of her.

"God, you're gorgeous," he told her huskily. "And little."

She huffed out a short laugh.

He gave her a crooked grin. "Sorry. That came out wrong. You're just very...petite."

"I'm short."

And he was *big.*

"Sure. But you're just littler than me."

He brought his hands around her sides, running them up to cup her breasts. As he ran them over her hard nipples, she took a shaky breath.

"Not that I'm complainin'," he said. "Puttin' you up against the wall is going to be a lot easier."

"Awesome. It will use less energy and you'll be able to go longer," she told him.

He nodded, that same grin still in place. "I like the way you think."

"Then you might like to know that I'm thinking about how I'd like to suck your cock."

He sucked in a sharp breath. "How about you lie back on the bed and let me eat your pussy?"

Her eyes widened, partially in surprise, but also with excitement. She'd intended to ask him for exactly that. Again, he was just a second ahead of her and she very much appreciated that.

"How about we do both those things?"

He chuckled softly and shook his head as if he wasn't sure what to think of her. "I'm keeping my pants on until you come in my mouth at least once."

"Why is that?"

"Honestly?"

"Has anything about this conversation made you think that I don't want to be totally open and honest?"

"Fair enough. Okay, I want to come inside you the first time."

God, she loved this. She loved the frank talk, the words, the sentiments, and most definitely the plans he was laying out. "Such little self-control?"

"I'm not well known for suppressing my urges."

There was something so refreshing about his unabashed, self-deprecating honesty.

"You just have to do whatever feels good?"

"Pretty much. My whole world is about your nipples right now."

She laughed. "Wow, not even the kissing? Or the depths of my blue eyes?" She batted those eyes at him as she teased.

Laughing as well, he reached up and slid his fingers into her hair again, tipping her head back and leaning in to touch his lips to hers.

Against her mouth, he said, "Your eyes are green, cher. And I really need you to lie back on that bed and spread your legs for me."

Hey, he'd noticed the color of her eyes. That was definitely a good enough reason to do exactly what he'd suggested.

Plus she just really wanted to.

He crawled up the bed after her, his eyes on the area between her legs. Her clit tingled and she ached deep in her pelvis. It was lust and anticipation.

*Please let him be good at this.*

She wanted to have bed-rocking sex tonight. She hadn't realized it until she met Zeke, but this was exactly what she needed.

He looked so hot climbing up the bed, shirtless, his jeans low on his hips, unbuttoned, with just the hint of black underwear peeking at her as he moved. His tattoos shifted over his chest, shoulders, and arms as his muscles bunched, his hair swung forward, and she swore she could already feel his beard against her inner thigh.

When she got to the pillows, she laid back. He was already there, between her legs. He wasted no time. He ran his big hands up the outsides of her thighs and then under her ass. He cupped her butt and lifted, then settled his broad shoulders between them, his hot breath on her mound.

"Damn, girl, you are pretty," he told her, his drawl seeming lower and slower, more pronounced now.

"Thank you," she said breathlessly. What was a girl supposed to say when a guy complimented her most private parts?

He lifted his eyes. "You comfortable? I want you to be okay to settle in here for a while, 'cause I have no place I'd rather be."

Her breath caught in her chest. There was so much hot intent in both his tone and his expression that she felt as if he had already put his mouth on her. She pulled her lip between her teeth and nodded.

He gave her a hot, cocky grin, then licked his lips, then lowered his head.

---

D amn, he was glad he'd flipped his bike in front of this girl's motel. She was smooth, tight, sweet, and hot from head to toe. He wasn't sure he'd ever been with a woman this petite. Which sounded so stupid. But she had small hands, tiny breasts, even her nose was tiny.

He'd also never been this turned on. It was weird. He'd always considered himself a boob guy.

Some of the hottest sex of his life had been with a hot blonde with gorgeous big tits and long legs, a fiery redhead who had freckles *all* over, and a brunette who had spiked-up pink hair and tattoos up and down her arms and legs. Not all three at once, of course. Though the brunette *had* offered to bring a friend.

This girl wasn't...any of that.

Jillian had pale, creamy skin without a freckle or a birthmark. Her long, dark hair was stark against her pale skin, and she was just...tiny. He couldn't get over it. In fact, as much as it was a turn on to think about putting her up against the wall, he was actually slightly concerned about hurting her.

He wasn't freakishly big or anything. But he was tall and broad and had been well gifted when it came to certain parts of his anatomy. But damn, it was hot that his hands were so big on her body, and, frankly, how far she had to spread her legs for him to fit between them right now.

Yeah, he was *really* glad he'd flipped his bike in front of the motel tonight when this woman had been here. He knew he lived a charmed life, but he wasn't sure he'd ever been as aware of that and as thankful for it as he was at this very moment.

He lowered his head and kissed her inner thigh. She shivered and he stroked the back of her opposite thigh and kissed his way to her mound, then down to her clit where he gave a little lick.

She gasped and arched closer.

He gave her another lick, firmer and with more tongue this time.

Her hand went to his hair and she grabbed a fistful.

Oh yeah, that's what he wanted.

He moved his thumbs to part her slippery sweet lips. She really was pretty. He was a fan of all the pussies he'd been this close to, but this one had *lick me* written all over it.

He tasted her again, sucking gently on her clit before moving lower and swirling his tongue around her entrance.

She moaned and pressed against him.

He tasted her gently for a few seconds, but then she tightened her fingers in his hair and said, "Harder. Suck harder."

Two of his favorite words when put together.

He took her clit between his lips and sucked and licked, then sucked again, harder as requested. She lifted against his mouth with a, "*yes!*"

He licked and swirled and sucked for nearly a minute, her fingers continuing to grip his hair. Her other hand grabbed the bed comforter as if she were holding on for dear life. She lifted her hips closer to his mouth and made the most amazing sounds.

"Zeke! Zeke, yes!"

He dipped his tongue into the sweetness below, teasing her and making her tug his hair harder.

"Your fingers," she said breathlessly. "Please use your fingers."

He lifted his head, looking up her sweet body into her face. Her eyes were closed, her head tipped back. She looked completely rapturous, and he felt a surge of satisfaction and freaking pride at that. Damn, this was such a turn on. He wanted to give her exactly what she wanted and needed and it was definitely a lot easier to do that when she told him exactly what that was.

She wasn't indifferent now, was she?

"Anything you want, cher."

He slid a thick middle finger into her and she gave a happy sigh.

"More."

He added a second finger, thrusting in and out slowly.

She was tight and his cock ached with the knowledge that he was going to be next.

*In a bit, buddy*, Zeke thought. He was staying right here for a while. He was going to drag this out.

"Your mouth," she said. "Suck me."

The lady didn't have to ask him twice. He was a gentleman after all.

He lowered his head and gave her a lick, then sucked, at first gently, but quickly working up to harder pressure. The way her pussy clenched around his fingers told him everything he needed to know about the amount of suction even without her sweet, breathless, "Oh, God!"

But damn, he fucking loved that breathless open praise she was giving him. Zeke liked to be praised. He very much liked people appreciating him, and he was very into this woman in particular appreciating him at this moment.

"Faster. Deeper."

Yeah, he liked her coaching. He pumped his fingers faster and deeper just as she asked as he sucked and licked and felt the response around his fingers clearly. Her inner muscles were clenching, her grip on his hand tightened, and she was lifting and lowering her hips as if he was fucking her. He curled his fingers, dragging them over her G-spot and gave her a hard suck, sending her over the edge with a loud cry.

He continued to stroke her as she came down from her climax, but pressed kisses to her inner thighs and then up over her stomach. When she had quieted, he eased his fingers from her body and lifted them to his mouth. Her eyes fluttered open as he licked her from his fingers.

She was still breathing hard. But she gave him a smile. "Thank you."

He chuckled. "Anytime."

It struck him how unfortunate it was that she wasn't going to be here for long. He wouldn't mind going over a few more things she liked with her clear and graphic coaching.

But he didn't have to tell her that. Or wait long. She sat up, pushed him over to his back, and straddled his stomach. She leaned down and pressed her mouth to his, giving him a deep, hot kiss. She lifted her head after a moment, braced her hands on his chest, and smiled down at him.

"Now can we take your pants off?"

"I'm completely on board with that."

# 4

He was aching and hard, and his cock was pressed almost painfully against his fly now. She scooted down his body until she sat just above his knees. He was already unbuttoned and unzipped, so she started working the denim and cotton down his hips. His cock was free within seconds and she took a moment to stop and run her hands over his thick shaft.

"Ooh, this is going to be fun."

Again she surprised him and his heated reaction seemed to stab him in the gut.

She was more enthusiastic about sex than any woman he'd been with in a while. As a teenager, the girls he messed around with had been either enthusiastically interested in everything new or shy and stiff. As he'd gotten older, he'd found a variety of women to date, flirt, and hook up with. Most women he knew enjoyed sex and they had a good time. But he definitely led the way.

He'd learned a lot being the youngest in a large clan that had more than its share of testosterone. His brothers and male cousins were all older than Zeke, and the Landry males were well known for loving women and loving to love women. They also had no filters and there were no topics off limits. So he'd heard plenty of talk about sex and other things that happened in bedrooms, truck beds, and the backseats of cars.

Of course, practice made perfect, and the bayou girls ran a little hot too. It also didn't hurt that the steamy summer nights in Louisiana made it easy to talk people out of their clothes.

In general, Zeke knew that he delivered in this area and enjoyed doing it, but he didn't mind at all having someone tell him exactly what she wanted and having her enthusiastic input as he followed her directions.

He lifted his hips and shoved his jeans and underwear down. She had to lift her butt off of him to get everything to his ankles and then off. She had to slide down his body to undo his boots and throw everything on the floor. Having her kneeling over him, undressing him and taking plenty of time to run her hands over all of the skin and body parts she was exposing, was a fun and unexpected torture.

By the time she had him naked and crawled back up his body, he was raring to go. She straddled his thighs again, wrapping her hand around his cock and stroking. With that he was going to last about thirty seconds. He grasped her wrists and gave her a little tug, pulling her up off his body. She tumbled over his chest, their noses almost knocking together.

He cupped her head in one big hand and kissed her deep, stroking her mouth with his tongue the way he had her pussy. She ran her hands over his shoulders, chest, and down his sides. Her hot naked skin pressed against his cock and he knew that his first time inside her wasn't going to last long.

He reached down and grasped her by the waist, shifting her to the side and onto her hands and knees, loving the way he could move her so easily. That was hot.

"Oh, yes," she said enthusiastically.

He loved her enthusiasm. He loved that she knew exactly what he was doing and thinking and wanted it all.

He ran a hand up and down her spine. "You're sexy as fuck this way," he told her, his voice rough. "You okay?"

She lowered her upper body, resting her head on her crossed forearms, her ass up in the air. She wiggled it, and said, "So okay."

Damn, he hadn't even been inside her yet and he already knew that he would want this again and again.

His hands cupped her ass and he squeezed, kneading for a few seconds. Then he leaned over and snagged his jeans, pulling his wallet out of his pocket, flipping it open, and withdrawing three condoms.

Three. They had three times at this.

And again, having not even done it once, he knew three would not be enough.

He tossed the other two onto the bedspread next to them, and ripped the one open, rolling it down his shaft.

He stroked himself a few times trying to tamp down some of the pent-up need. But looking at this woman prone on the bed with her gorgeous ass in the air, there was no hope for tamping down this burning desire.

"You ready, cher? Here I come."

"Well, I hope not right away," she teased.

On impulse, he gave her ass a little slap.

She gasped and moaned.

Perfect. She just might be perfect.

"I love this position," she said. "And I love it hard and fast. Just so you know."

Yep, perfect.

Zeke took his cock in hand and lined it up with her opening, pressing forward slowly. Damn, she really was a tight fit. But it felt like fucking heaven. He eased in, her pussy squeezing him.

She clenched around him with a gasp as he got about halfway.

"You good?" He realized he was gritting his teeth.

This was exquisite. And hell. He wanted to slam forward. But he also wanted to take his time. Not just because it felt so amazing and he wanted to draw it out, but because he truly did think he might hurt her.

"You're so big," she said, her voice tight. "Amazing."

He was so glad she'd added that last word.

"You can take me," he told her.

He'd meant to phrase it as a question, but it hadn't come out that way. But he knew she could. Not just because her body was hot and wet and ready, but because of her confidence and attitude so far. She would've told him to stop. She would've changed things up. She would've pushed him away. That gave him the confidence to press forward two more inches.

She gave a long groan and leaned back into him. That made him sink in another inch.

"I bet you get your way with women all the time, don't you?"

He huffed out a breath. He didn't know why she kept surprising him. He supposed because she looked like a sweet little thing. Then she'd made him so easily feel like an ass about the goat and clearly not giving a shit he was bleeding to death by the side of the road. Now she was letting him fuck her and talking dirty to him in a way he hadn't experienced before. She had been a surprise from the beginning. And he loved it.

His life was very routine, very predictable. And he liked that. He was living and working in the town he'd grown up in, surrounded by people he'd known since birth. Nothing happened to shake him up or to knock him off-kilter. Ever.

There were the typical storms and ups and downs of life, but he was enveloped by family and friends who helped him through all of it, and vice versa.

But this woman hadn't been predictable for one minute and the only person getting rocked by it was him.

"I get my way a lot with pretty much everyone." He decided to be honest, even though it was in-bed teasing.

She nodded her head against her arms on the bed. "Yep, I can see why."

He eased in a little further, suddenly loving that this was taking a little time.

He reached around for her clit, but found her hand already there, her finger circling. Well, okay. That meant he could settle both his hands on her hips and hold on while he thrust the rest of the way into her.

They groaned together, and he hesitated for just a second, enjoying...everything about the moment.

Then he pulled back and thrust again. The third time she met his thrust, pushing back into him. She had one hand between her legs, but the other was now braced on the mattress, helping give her leverage.

Zeke had the dominant position here, but it definitely seemed that she was fucking him right back. They moved together like that for several minutes, their bodies slapping, the heat building, their moans and gasps filling the room. He felt her clenching around him and for some reason it hit him that he wanted to see her face when she came with him buried deep.

He pulled out and, even before she got her entire protest past her lips, he had flipped her to her back, pulled her off the bed, and pivoted to put her up against the wall. He leaned into her as she wrapped her arms and legs around him with a smile.

"Well, hi."

"Hey, girl."

He thrust into her and absorbed her gasp with his mouth as he kissed her deeply.

Her legs and arms tightened around him as he held her ass and thrust repeatedly. When he felt her tightening again, he lifted his head so he could watch. She let her head fall back against the wall and within a few strokes was clenching around him and crying his name. That fired his blood and he pumped deep three more times before coming with a growl.

He held her up against the wall as they both fought to bring their breathing back to normal. She stayed wrapped around him, seemingly content to be held against the wall this way.

When his skin felt a little cooler and he could draw a complete lungful of oxygen, he leaned back, taking her with him, and turned back to the bed. He lowered her to the mattress and headed to the bathroom to deal with the condom. When he stepped back into the bedroom, she was still lying on her back on the bed, one arm slung over her face. Her gorgeous body was spread out on full display. The two condoms still lay next to her and he was incredibly grateful he had more than one.

He climbed up on the bed next to her and stretched out along her side. She moved her arm and rolled her head to look at him. She gave him a smile. "I forgive you for almost killing that goat."

He ran a fingertip down her body, from between her breasts to her belly button. Goosebumps broke out and she gave a little shiver.

"If you're still able to remember anything about that goat, I haven't quite done my job here."

"You're thinking you're going to make me forget about the whole incident entirely?"

"I really think that might be in my best interest."

She laughed and turned onto her side to face him. She ran a hand over his shoulder and bear tattoo, tracing some of the ink with her fingertip. "I think you should definitely give it your best shot."

Then she surprised him yet again, by pushing him onto his back, climbing on top, and getting him all worked up again within minutes of one of the hardest orgasms he'd had in a very long time. This time she got to ride him cowgirl *and* reverse cowgirl, both of them getting their way.

Which was really the very best way to have mind blowing sex.

And as he fell asleep next to her, nearly two hours later, Zeke decided that maybe having his world rocked had been underrated all this time.

---

Jill left her hot, hunky one-night stand in bed. He didn't even stir when she slipped out of bed, showered, and got dressed. He slept like the dead. Which was fine. But she did want to have a conversation with him about a possible new friends-with-benefits arrangement here in Autre.

She gave a little shiver of pleasure remembering the night before. It had been a long night but so, so worth it.

Zeke would be perfect for a once-a-month-or-so-scratch-each-other's-itches setup. Clearly the guy scratched other people's itches on a pretty regular basis. No one got that good without a lot of practice. But if he'd come over when she needed scratched, she was okay with that. Great even.

Other girls could watch movies with him and have dinner with him and...whatever else he wanted them to do. If he was into those other things. In fact, it would be awesome if he did that stuff with other girls. As long as he'd give her some more of what he'd given her last night.

She even left him a note that read *Goats? What goats?*

She wasn't typically super flirty. Or flirty at all really. That just wasn't her personality. But something about this guy with the Louisiana drawl and hot tattoos, not to mention the little I'm-pretty-adorable-aren't-I grin and the dirty talk and the way he'd made her body sing, made her feel a little flirty.

Feeling better than she had in weeks, she headed for the penguin habitat that was being built just up the road.

The penguins were due to arrive in three days and it was making her very anxious. She'd hired a couple of the Omaha zookeepers to drive the penguins to her. She was in Autre to make sure the habitat was finished to her standards. The birds needed a place to live when they got here after all. In the ideal world she would be the one driving them down, but it was too long a trip for one person to make by themselves and there was no way to park a trailer full of penguins at a roadside motel halfway between Omaha, Nebraska, and Autre, Louisiana.

So she'd used some of her sixteen million dollars to hire a couple guys she'd worked with for the past two years and knew penguins well to make the trip. She was going to fly the men home so they were only driving one direction. They were leaving the new truck and trailer with her. You never knew when you might need to haul a few penguins somewhere.

She couldn't believe this was her life and the kinds of things she was thinking about now.

She found the arched sign that read Boys of the Bayou Gone Wild and the road that turned into what Charlie had referred to as the animal park, though Griffin had rolled his eyes when she'd said it. Jill parked her car in the little gravel parking lot just inside the fence line.

Her phone dinged with a text just as she shut off the engine.

She looked down and smiled. It was from her best friend, Evan, back home in Kansas.

Evan: *WTH? Have you been eaten by alligators already? Text me.*

Jill knew her mother was trying to "be good" and not text Jill but was, instead, driving Evan crazy asking how Jill was.

Instead of texting, she put in her earbuds, dialed his number, and got out of the car.

"So that's a no to getting eaten by alligators then?" he asked when he picked up.

"Well... it wasn't an alligator."

Evan frowned. "What are you..." He paused. "Wait. Seriously? You hooked up with someone? Already?"

She felt how big her grin was. "The welcoming committee here is *really* nice."

"And I was worried you wouldn't make new friends."

"I was *very* friendly."

"Did you make him lasagna?" Evan teased.

The one and only time she and Evan had crossed over the just-friends line had been years ago after the funeral of a very good friend and Jill had taken Evan lasagna to cheer him up.

"That was my mother's lasagna," Jill said. It wasn't that Jill *couldn't* make lasagna. She just didn't want to. Lasagna was a lot of work. "And I don't need lasagna to get other guys naked, thank you very much." Hell, she hadn't intended to get Evan naked that night. That had just happened.

Evan just laughed. "I guess what they say about southern hospitality is real, huh?"

Evan was pretty laid back and had definitely had his share of what's-your-name-again-baby hook-ups back in the day, but she knew her friend would not approve of picking up a stranger in a roadside motel in small town Louisiana where she knew exactly two people, so she decided to change the subject.

Jill started up the path that led into the animal park. "Hey, want to tour my new office with me?" she asked. "I'm just heading to the penguin habitat. I haven't even seen it yet."

"Definitely. You know that this whole thing is really cool, right?"

She did. Mostly. When she wasn't freaking out about the enormous pressure she was feeling.

The first thing she saw were the lemurs. She showed Evan.

"No way."

"Yep. I told you how this started as a petting zoo, right?"

Evan nodded. "Your friend Griffin joined the vet practice there, in part because of the petting zoo. It was becoming more than the one vet could handle."

"Right. The main vet got pregnant and wanted to cut back. But initially he was just taking care of otters and goats and that kind of stuff. Then Charlie came to town and decided to turn the whole thing into an animal park. Charlie not only got the lemurs but a sloth, some red pandas, and a bunch of other stuff. And Griffin." Jill smiled. "Griffin and Charlie stopped up at the motel to say hi last night. I've *never* seen Griffin happy like that. I mean, he's still gruff and stuff, but he's actually happy now. It's really great."

"There's a *sloth*?" Evan asked.

Jill laughed and continued up the path to the little hut where the sloth—Slothcrates, according to the sign—lived. She and Evan also saw the red pandas, a few peacocks, three porcupines, and four parrots.

"Up at the main barn, they also have a tortoise, several ducks, some hedgehogs, a few pigs, rabbits...a bunch of stuff," Jill told Evan. "And apparently there was talk of adding a zebra or two. Griffin had rolled his eyes about that too, but I get the impression that Charlie gets what she wants from him."

"Is Charlie on this welcoming committee?" Evan joked.

Jill felt her cheeks flush with even that little reminder of Zeke. She switched the phone's camera to show him the penguin habitat she'd finally found.

Not that it was hidden. In fact, it was right out in the middle.

Dammit.

"Ugh."

"What's wrong?" Evan asked. "That looks amazing. From where I'm sitting anyway."

"I just..." She sighed and looked at her friend again. "I knew that penguins in a small town in Louisiana would be a novelty. I know plenty of people will want to stop by and see them. The penguins are one of the most popular exhibits in Omaha, even."

"And that's bad because..."

She knew she was going to sound whiny. But this was Evan. He'd known her since they were kids. He'd definitely seen her whiny before. "These penguins are special. And not just because they're mine," she said quickly. "But this program they're a part of has a lot of stipulations."

"Okay, like what?"

"These penguins have been living a very solitary existence with A.J. as their only human contact. They're used to peace and quiet. And they *need* to have baby penguins soon. If bringing them to Autre and a whole new environment is a risk, then introducing chaos and noise, with a lot of tourists and more human interaction, could derail the entire project."

She should've thought about this more.

Though thinking about *more* than she already had seemed impossible. This had been keeping her up at night ever since she'd met the penguins a month ago.

"The project is pretty much just to keep them alive and make sure they have more penguins, right?" Evan asked.

"Yeah." Jill shrugged. "But they haven't bred in all the time A.J.'s had them, Evan. They've been kept away from any temperature fluctuations, weather threats, predators, even changes in their diets. Their environment has been *extremely* stable. But they haven't bred. They *have* to reproduce in the next year or they'll—we'll—be out of the program. Can you imagine? The foremost expert on Galápagos penguins in the United States inheriting eight of them and then getting kicked out of a program to save them because...she can't?"

"Okay, you need to calm down," Evan told her. "These penguins have belonged to you for a month. And you're just now getting moved to where you're going to settle them. Give yourself a break."

Jill took a deep breath and blew it out.

"You're going to be fine. There's no one better for this," Evan said reassuringly.

"I don't know...I mean, I *do* know that." It was a fact that she knew more about penguins than anyone else that was a part of this program. But... "These people are intimidating. They're *so* enthusiastic, for one thing," she said. "They've all already hatched new penguins. This is the only waddle that hasn't had a baby."

"I love that groups of penguins are called waddles," Evan said.

Jill had to smile. Evan knew lots of random penguin facts because of her. She appreciated her friend's interest in her passion.

"Anyway, these people have a lot of money and they are *really* into this program," Jill said.

"You should love that," Evan told her. "*You* are really into saving penguins. You should love that all of these people are too and are willing to put their money into it and, even more, take these penguins in and take care of them personally."

"I know. And I do. But they are definitely looking to me to be the expert."

"You *are* the expert."

"Yeah. With a bunch of celibate penguins."

Evan just chuckled at that.

Of course, all of that was definitely part of why she was feeling the pressure, but it was also weighing on her because a very dear friend had entrusted these birds to her, that *he'd* loved so much.

She hadn't slept well for four weeks now. In fact, last night she'd slept harder and deeper than she had since the penguins had come into her life.

She honestly was thankful to Zeke for that.

Jill looked around.

"Okay, the enclosure is right in the middle of this 'animal park', but it's pretty quiet here."

"Show me around," Evan encouraged.

She took a deep breath and focused on the structure in front of her.

The habitat itself was really beautiful. "Wow, Evan. This looks...amazing."

Of course a couple million dollars and instructions not to spare any expense probably had something to do with that.

She'd admittedly been skeptical when Griffin and Charlie had assured her that they had people who could handle this construction job, but it turned out they'd been right.

"It looks like it from my side too. Is it what you wanted?" Evan asked.

"It is. I can't tell if it's finished." She paced along the section of clear wall that looked into the enclosure.

She'd sent sketches and photographs with what the habitat should include and it looked like they'd done everything.

She switched the camera again so Evan could see.

"It's an oval shape," she told him. "About two-thirds of the perimeter is a clear wall, while the other one-third is made up of trees, rocks, and shrubbery. They made it look exactly like my sketches."

"It looks great," Evan told her.

She pointed. "It's an island of sorts. There's a moat between where I'm standing and the main land area the penguins will occupy. The moat is twenty feet across and thirty feet deep. The wall will keep the penguins inside, and other stuff out. Like humans. And wolves and bears. And alligators." Jill shuddered thinking about all of the things that could make a snack of her penguins. "So that gives them additional space to swim. The water in it and the pond on the island is temperature controlled. So is that building." She showed him the structure where the penguins could be kept in inclement weather— extreme heat, cold, or hurricanes, for instance. Yeah, she hadn't had to worry about hurricanes in Omaha. But tornadoes had been part of their emergency planning.

"That building," she said, pointing to the larger building set off behind the penguin house, "is where my office will be and the other side is storage, including the freezer where the penguins' food will be kept."

"So... is it finished?" Evan asked. "It looks complete."

"It does. It looks like they've checked every box on the list I sent. They even got the lava rocks in here."

In the distance she could hear the lemurs chattering and parrots squawking. There was the sound of a vehicle on the dirt road that ran in front of the entrance, but it was far enough off that it was hardly disturbing.

The sky overhead was bright blue, there was just a slight breeze, and the temperature was already seventy-four degrees and she could feel that it was going to get warmer.

It was going to take her some adjusting as well. Louisiana was much hotter and more humid than Kansas. Certainly the Great Plains had heat and humidity in the summer, but by this time of year the autumn air was cooling off.

"So, now that you've seen it and it's complete and they did a great job, do you feel better?" Evan asked.

She took a deep breath and thought about his question. "Yes," she answered after only a few seconds. "How the penguins adjust is still a question, but I'm so grateful that I had a place like this to relocate penguins. I'm grateful for the space, but I also really appreciate having someone like Griffin here in person. I do know more about penguins than Griffin does, but I know he'll be willing and able to get his hands dirty if needed. Or to just listen to me bitch about my penguins being little prudes."

Evan laughed. "You know I'll always listen to you bitch about your penguins not putting out."

She nodded. "I know."

Evan and Cori had been very supportive of Jill taking on this project and this crazy move and everything else that went with it. But honestly, her phone calls, emails, and video calls with Tori, Charlie, Griffin, and even the other owners—Sawyer, Maddie, Owen, and Josh—as well as Jordan, their educational director, had made Jill truly feel welcomed and like her penguins had the backing of the entire Landry clan.

Jill knew that Griffin understood the enormity of the project she was undertaking and he would take it seriously. Griffin was an animal advocate first and foremost and had done a lot of work with conservation efforts working on a tiger propagation program at the National Zoo in Washington, D.C. He was enthusiastic about this program for professional reasons first.

But he was now a part of the Landry family and the Landrys thought bringing penguins to their animal park was really damned cool.

Of course, that had added another layer to the pressure on Jill too. She knew that this was also the family business. The way they made their money. And that mattered to Griffin, her biggest professional ally here, because it was personal for him.

So yeah, bringing the penguins here was much more than just a favor to a friend.

Jill blew out a breath. "Okay, tell me this is going to be fine," she said to Evan.

"This is going to be better than fine."

So she had some conflicting pressures—the private group that needed the penguins to thrive and reproduce and the Landry family who wanted to expand their business—but surely there was a way to make this all happen.

"Right, one step at a time," she said. She looked around

again. "I kind of thought the guys who were working on the enclosure would be here this morning."

They knew she was coming to town today. Granted, she wasn't supposed to be here until this afternoon, but she'd expected at least the main contractor to be here to be sure everything was finished. He'd been great about communicating with her via text, sending her multiple questions, answering hers, and following up.

She crossed to the gate that led into the enclosure. She definitely needed to be sure the storage area was ready to go. She had big shipments of supplies coming in tomorrow, not the least of which was a truckload of fish. She supposed her office chair could wait, but it wasn't like fish could just sit on a truck for an extra day.

She pulled on the gate but it was locked. Which was good. And bad.

"Dammit." She looked at her phone. "I need to go," she told Evan. "I need to get a hold of the builder."

"I know. You've got a lot going on. But this all looks great and I know it's going to be amazing."

"Thanks, Ev. I'll talk to you soon."

"You better."

They disconnected and she pulled up the number she'd put in as "penguin builder guy" and typed out a text.

Jill: *In town early. At the habitat. Was hoping to meet you and go over things. When will you be here?*

She waited for a moment, but no little dots popped up indicating he had received her message and was replying.

She looked around. There really weren't any indications that construction was still going on. There was no caution tape anywhere, nothing draped with tarps, no piles of supplies or materials. Still, she'd like to talk to the builder. She looked down at her phone, but there was no new message from him yet.

She blew out a breath, then decided to check out more of the enclosure.

Maybe just the outside was finished and there was still more work to be done inside.

She shook the gate again, but it was tight and barely gave. She looked around, but there was clearly no other way in. But, dammit, this was *her* penguin habitat.

So she climbed over the fence.

That sounded easier than it actually ended up being. The gate was tall and the metal rods ran vertically with no horizontal beams to support a hand or foot.

She was very grateful that she made time twice a week to work out. And couldn't help but wonder how much easier this would have been if she'd worked out four or five times a week.

But she felt pretty cocky when she dropped to the pavement on the other side.

Then remembered that the moat was not only twenty feet across, but it was deep. Like penguins-could-dive-and-swim-in-it deep. And it was cold.

Dammit.

They had definitely listened to her instructions. Including the ones about the penguins preferring cooler water temps.

Still, she wanted to get over there and it looked like the only way onto the island was to go through the penguin building that sat on the edge of the island. That was also locked.

She really had no choice here.

So she prepared to jump into the water.

Then she remembered her phone.

Relieved, she pulled it out, held it over her head, and eased herself into the water instead of jumping and started doggy-paddling.

But she hadn't remembered to take her shoes off.

Dammit.

## 5

She emerged onto the sandy beach, shivering, her feet squishing in her shoes, but with a dry phone.

Which vibrated with a text as she walked across the sand and grass.

Penguin builder guy: *Running late this morning. Can meet you in an hour.*

Dammit. An *hour*? She had a lot to do today.

But what choice did she have? And she was early, after all. He hadn't been expecting her.

She toured the interior of the habitat and discovered that on her belly she could wiggle into the penguin building through the door the penguins would be using. Sure, she was a little dirty afterward, but she was thrilled too. It was all finished.

The only other thing that *had* to be completed before Thursday was the food storage facility.

Feeling pleased, though cold and squishy, Jill decided to head back to the hotel to change her clothes. But once back in her car, it occurred to her that might not be a great idea.

What if Zeke was still there? It wasn't that she didn't want to see him *at all*. In fact, she would very much like to see him again. But not right now. She didn't do morning afters. Dan was always up and out right away the next day. Or, if they stayed at his place—as she tried to do because he always had good breakfast food too—she got up and out quickly. They were both too busy for anything else. And she wasn't really the brunch type even with girlfriends or her mother.

Now that she was in Autre, her focus was even more specific. She had a waddle of penguins to take care of and she needed to have some penguin babies sooner rather than later. She also had her own habitat to worry about. She had definitely been blowing off her contractor for that. She probably should go check out her own house as well.

And hey, at least that was a place where she could get out of her shoes and socks and dry off a little bit. A place that didn't have a hot, very tempting Cajun who was *very* good with his mouth.

She pushed all thoughts of Zeke's mouth—and the parts of him that *her* mouth had really enjoyed—out of her mind and tapped her new house address into her GPS and found that she was only a mile away. Huh. She'd known that her new hometown was small but this seemed...very convenient, actually.

The tiny town size didn't bother her. She'd grown up in a small town in Kansas. From what Griffin had told her, Bliss, Kansas, and Autre, Louisiana, had a few things in common. They were small, they were full of quirky characters, and everyone knew each other's business.

Jill had to admit that she wasn't looking forward to that last aspect of small town living again. In Omaha she had not only been in a big city, but she hadn't known anyone until she'd started work. She didn't have family there and her friends were all people she got to know from the zoo. So her social circle was very small, as was the number of people who knew anything personal about her.

She turned left at the entrance to the animal park and rumbled along the dirt road for about half a mile. This was definitely the edge of town. To her right was part of the bayou with boat docks and several boats of varying sizes, including what looked to be two large fishing vessels anchored along the water. And, as she drove east, it looked as if she was coming to an area where the bayou curved behind the trees in the distance.

"You've arrived at your destination," the GPS lady told her.

"You sure?" she asked as she rolled to a stop. This was a dead-end road and there were only eight houses down here. A couple of them looked like perhaps no one was living in them. The paint was peeling, the front porches were crooked, and there were weeds growing up along the front walks.

However, three of them looked well cared for and had vehicles parked in front of them, plants in the flowerbeds, hammocks on the front porches and so on, indicating people lived there.

Then there was one house that really stood out. It looked to be nearly brand-new.

"Let this be mine," Jill said out loud as she shut the car off.

It was bigger than the others and definitely newer construction. It had a wide front porch that wrapped around three sides and was two stories with a gorgeous stone and wood combination front. The way it was positioned on the lot, it looked out over the bayou on one side and the expanse of open land with the trees in the distance on the other. Whoever lived there could watch the sunrise on one side of the house and sunset on the other side.

Jill frowned. "Do I care about sunrises and sunsets?"

She'd been living in an apartment in downtown Omaha for the past four years. It was a gorgeous place in one of the renovated buildings in the warehouse district in the Old Market area of Omaha. She hadn't sat on a porch in a very long time.

"I think I *could* care about sunrises and sunsets," she decided as she studied the gorgeous house.

She glanced at the other houses clustered at the end of the road. She also wasn't really a neighborhood barbecue type or a take-brownies-to-your-new-neighbors type, but it seemed it might be hard to avoid getting to know her neighbors in this little collection of houses at the end of this road.

"Maybe *they'll* bring *me* brownies." She really liked brownies. And she definitely wasn't a baker. It wasn't that she was opposed to making brownies or going to barbecues, of course. She had grown up in a small town and had been to plenty.

But she was a workaholic. Self-proclaimed, and proud. Unapologetic.

She took time off once in a while to go to movies, and to go home to visit her family and friends in Kansas, and to... Okay, so those were the only examples she could think of.

Her last vacation had been an exchange with a zoo in Canada where one of their veterinarians came to Omaha for a month and Jill took her place at the Calgary zoo. It was a fun way to see a new place and learn how another zoo ran their program.

"That counts as a vacation. I had to pack a suitcase and get on an airplane."

She didn't agree with Evan when he'd declared that if most of her time on her trip was spent doing something that resulted in the paycheck, it was considered work and not play. Any time she got to interact with animals, learn something new, and immerse herself in an experience, she considered that fun.

She shut off her car and got out of the car, checking the address in her emails from the contractor. She squinted at the gorgeous house with the maybe-I-do-like-sunrises front porch. Nope, the numbers on the front didn't match. Figured. She looked at the house next to it. The one with the peeling white paint, the green shutters—half of which were hanging crookedly, and the three missing front porch steps. Yep, that was hers.

"Of course it is". At least it had a front porch too. "It just doesn't have steps to *get to* the porch."

She made her way up the front walk.

"This is what you get for buying the place without photos," Jill told herself. "Location, location, location."

From the realtor's description, it had been close to the penguin's new home. That was really all she'd considered.

"That was really stupid, girl."

Price had been no object, considering she'd just come into a few million dollars overnight, but she hadn't wanted to build a new house. That was silly. She was a single woman and she didn't have time to sit around waiting for a new house to be built anyway.

She also didn't need marble countertops and twenty-foot ceilings and chandeliers and expensive furniture. She needed a place to sleep.

"And shower," she said out loud, as she looked down at her soaked clothes and shoes. She bypassed the missing steps and jumped up onto the porch from the ground.

She'd already taken off before it occurred to her to hope the porch floor was sturdy and she wouldn't go crashing through rotting wood. But it held up as she landed. She approached the front door and realized she didn't have a key to this place either. Obviously, showing up early with no appointments to see any of these building projects was becoming an issue. Still, she tried the front door. Sure enough, the knob turned, and the door swung in.

"Okay, in Autre we don't lock up houses. Or goats. But empty penguin enclosures are like Fort Knox."

But it only took her six steps inside the house to realize she had nothing to worry about. There was nothing here to steal, for one thing. And while a family of raccoons might find it a fine place to bunk down overnight, there wasn't much here that anyone would find appealing.

The house was old, and the best word that came to mind was shabby. And as far she could tell, her contractor hadn't done a damn thing.

The rooms were all empty. There was dust all over everything. The wood floor in the entryway was dirty and scarred. There was carpet in the main room off to her left that looked to be older than her grandmother. The huge front windows were dirty, two of them were cracked, and one was completely missing and was boarded up with plywood. And that wasn't new plywood as if they were in the process of replacing the window. Even the plywood was old.

She went to the wall and flipped the light switch. Nothing happened. Then again, looking around, there were no light fixtures even if the electricity did work.

"Perfect."

She was wet, dirty, cold, and homeless.

With sixteen million dollars, give or take, in the bank.

Awesome.

Yep, she was going to have to talk to the house contractor today as well. She pulled her phone out again and went into her email. She had been emailing back and forth with this guy, rather than texting.

Fine, *he'd* been emailing *her*.

She hadn't given him her phone number. It was much easier for her to keep the two projects separate. Her phone was for work almost entirely. The only people she texted were her mother, Evan, and his wife Cori. Everything else that happened with her phone was related to work.

She found the guy's email and typed out a quick message. It was similar to the one she sent about penguins.

*I got into town early, stopped over at the house. Have lots of questions. When can we meet up?*

It wasn't even a minute before she had a message back. At least *this* guy was more on the ball first thing in the morning than the penguin guy.

*Have some stuff this morning. Can meet you at the house around noon.*

She blew out a breath and realized she couldn't be frustrated. It stood to reason that he had other things already lined up for the day.

She replied, *Sounds good. See you then.*

Him: *Watch out for the front steps. There are a couple missing.*

Her: *I noticed.*

Him: *And watch yourself on the porch. There's some rotten wood and I wouldn't want you to fall through.*

Jill's eyes went wide. So, she had gotten lucky jumping up onto the porch. Great.

She took a couple of steps toward the front door and her shoe squished.

She grimaced. She really should just go back to the motel. She needed to change, and she *really* needed coffee and some breakfast.

She braced herself for more squishing and started for the front door again but stopped in the doorway. "Dammit." She didn't know where these rotten boards were, and she definitely didn't want to go crashing through the porch.

She pivoted and headed back to the house. She assumed there was a back door. "Not that you would know," she told herself. "You didn't even look at photos."

She made her way down a little hallway, noting the powder room to one side, the dining room off to her right, a room that could easily be an office—though she had that building right up next to the penguins, which was where she'd be most of the time— and stepped into her kitchen.

"Noooo. Not even a fridge?"

She really didn't care where she lived, but this house was

making her sad. It was definitely drab, but she wasn't great at envisioning things like interior decorating that wasn't already in place.

"Maybe Charlie can help." Charlie seemed stylish and put together. "I'll just give her a million dollars and tell her to go crazy." But then she shook her head. "The lawyer said you could use money to move here and take care of basic needs. That's probably like...a chair. And a fridge. And bread."

Looking around the completely bare kitchen, Jill felt overwhelmed. Not so much because she hated shopping for appliances, though she was sure that she did, she'd just never done it. She'd always lived in places that came with that stuff.

Picking out things like refrigerators and stoves seemed like such a waste of time. She just needed something to keep her food cold and to heat food up on occasion. Actually, she probably didn't need a stove and oven. She wasn't a baker or cook. Though she was under the impression that Autre, Louisiana, did not have food delivery services like she was used to.

"Ugh." She tipped her head back as she groaned.

And noticed the ceiling had nothing on it but cracked plaster and some wires sticking out from what she assumed had been a light fixture of some kind.

"Hell no. I'm not picking that stuff out too." She straightened and looked around. "I've never picked out furniture and shit! I've always had hand-me-downs and lived places that *come with this stuff!*"

She would never take light fixtures for granted again.

She focused on the crown moldings around the edge of the doorway. They were as old and dull as the rest of the house. The guy hadn't done anything with them.

Probably because she hadn't responded to his email asking what she wanted the crown moldings to look like. She'd had to Google crown moldings when he'd asked that question.

"Who the hell *cares*?" she asked the universe at large, throwing her arms wide.

Cori, her friend Evan's wife, had talked her into moving to Louisiana with nothing but her clothes. She'd insisted that Jill needed to start from scratch and that she not only didn't have enough furniture to fill a house, but that she needed new stuff if she was going to remodel the house and start a new life.

*Cori* was who Jill needed to call next.

She pulled up her friend's number on her phone and texted. *Help!*

Cori responded almost immediately. *Hey! What's wrong?*

*I know nothing about furniture.*

Cori: *Yes, I know.*

Jill: *Do you?*

Cori: *More than you do.*

Jill: *Then you do it.*

Cori: *I've been waiting for this text. Send me photos of the house and I'll help you pick stuff out.*

Jill: *I don't want help. I want you to do it.*

Cori: *\*laughing emoji\*. Fine. Photos.*

Jill held her phone up and took several shots of the kitchen, sending them to Cori.

Jill: *My kitchen at present.*

Cori: *What?! What's the contractor been doing all this time?*

Jill really wanted to blame the contractor but it was, of course, partly her fault. Not answering questions like what color she wanted the walls painted and what she wanted the flooring to look like had clearly kept him from moving ahead.

Jill: *He's waiting on me to make decisions. You know how I am about that.*

Cori: *Yes, I do.*

Jill smiled. It was nice having people in her life that understood what she was like and loved her anyway. She knew she drove her mother crazy. Actually, some of her tendency to only worry about the basics came from her mother.

Okay, *most* of that tendency came from her mother.

The rest came just from... not wanting to deal with stuff.

The fewer balls Jill had to juggle, the fewer got dropped, and the less frustrated Holly got with her. Her mother was a master ball-juggler. Jill had watched her do it her whole life.

She'd gotten pregnant right after medical school and put her career as a physician on hold to raise her children and then, when she'd tried to go back to work, she'd had to quit after only a few months because her mother had gotten sick.

Holly had been the quintessential stay-at-home mom to her four children. She attended every event and activity, had dinner on the table every night, kept an immaculate house, and the kids never had to worry about forgetting their lunch or permission slips or a pair of shoes to change into after school.

And by observing Holly, Jill had learned that it was far easier to keep track of and take care of *one* ball rather than many.

Jill knew her current habits came from the fact that her mother had always handled everything for her. When Jill had left home and been on her own, she'd needed to drastically simplify her life because she didn't have someone taking care of her.

For just a second, her thoughts went to Zeke again. But not his dirty mouth or his hot hands. Last night, he'd said that he probably wouldn't have taken the goats back to their barn if she hadn't insisted. He'd admitted it was because he knew someone else would have come along to do it and he'd said that was how things worked here for him. Other people took care of things, even if he had good intentions to help out.

That was a weird thing to have in common, but she understood that. Her mother had made Jill's life very easy growing up.

And had made her pretty pathetic at taking care of adult things now.

But how was someone supposed to learn to cook and how to get stains out of fabric and multi-task and organize if they were never taught and practiced? She could have looked things up or taken cooking classes, she knew. But she'd gotten so wrapped up in her career that she didn't have the time. Or didn't want to take the time. So Jill didn't cook, she threw things away if they got stained, and she focused on one thing at a time. Simple.

Jill: *You're hired to take care of this whole thing. Do you want the contractor's email?*

Cori: *Yes, I do. Do you want the whole house done in black and white? :-)*

Jill: *Yes.*

Black and white were her favorite colors. Yes, of course, that had to do with penguins.

Cori: *I'm not doing your entire house in black and white. But if you want a black and white bedroom I'll do that... if you let me include hot pink accents.*

Jill rolled her eyes, but grinned. Cori Carmichael Stone was a very...colorful person. She would die if all she could do was black and white. She was so good for Evan. She made sure he had fun when Evan had spent so many years trying so hard to be serious and responsible.

Jill: *Make it red, not pink and I'll say okay.*

Cori: *Deal.*

Jill: *Thank you. You know this isn't my thing.*

Cori: *\*heart emoji\*. I know. Don't worry about this. Go make some penguin babies.*

Jill: *I'm on it. The new penguin habitat, on the other hand, looks amazing.*

Cori: *Maybe the guy who built the penguin house can work on your house. LOL!*

Jill: *:-) I'll have to ask. Thank you! Talk to you soon.*

Cori: *Love you. It's all going to be okay.*

Jill felt the stinging behind her eyes. She certainly hoped everything was going to be okay. It really needed to be. Now that she was here in Autre, with this amazing penguin habitat sitting just up the road, she really had no choice. It wasn't like she could leave Louisiana if things didn't work out here. She couldn't just pack up and move eight penguins—and hopefully more than eight penguins soon—if she decided she didn't like gumbo or one thousand percent humidity.

She had to make it work here. This was where she was settling.

She headed out the back door of the kitchen, looking around and stepping carefully. There was a back porch as well. It was probably considered a mud room. They had these in Kansas too. It was a smaller room off the kitchen where people could discard muddy shoes and boots and outerwear before coming into the house. She stopped at the swinging screen door that was, of course, hanging crookedly from its hinges, and sucked in a little breath. The view back here, though... "Wow."

The back of the house looked out over the vast expanse of land that ran from this edge of town down to the bayou. It looked a little like the prairies in Kansas, but she knew from her research that as she went toward the bayou, the ground would get progressively more marshy and that the trees, vegetation, and a lot of the wildlife she would find between her back porch and the Gulf was vastly different than what she had grown up with in Kansas.

That made her heart flutter.

"This is fun. This is an adventure." She reminded herself. She was excited to be working with the penguins of course, but being here in Louisiana also meant learning about other new animals and habitats. "I wonder if Zeke would take me out on the bayou. I bet he would."

Now where had that idea come from? Why did her mind keep wandering to that guy?

Of course, it didn't take a lot of wondering to figure that one out. Zeke was hot and charming and very good with his tongue.

That was it. Simple. Just the way she liked things. She'd had an amazing night with him and it had been very straightforward. They hadn't shared back stories, they didn't share anything professionally, they didn't even know each other. Everything between them had been simple and obvious.

Except that little bit about how he didn't have to worry about much around here...

"Nope." Jill shook her head. "That was just one little thing. The rest was just sex. Really, really great sex. Simple. Easy."

She could definitely use more of that in her life.

She stepped out the back door and down the three stone steps that were definitely crumbling but were at least present as opposed to the steps in the front. She hit the ground and turned to round the house to head back to her car when she noticed him.

She froze. And gasped.

"No." But she whispered the word.

There was a fucking alligator in her backyard.

He was easily eight feet long and he was nestled in the tall grass. She wasn't even sure how she'd seen him because he wasn't moving a muscle.

"Maybe he's dead," she whispered. "And maybe you should stop even whispering."

Her mind spun, trying to remember if alligators had good hearing. What was it about adrenaline pumping through a person's veins that made them unable to remember basic facts that they should be able to come up with in a snap?

The word *snap* made her think about alligators' jaws

though. And she *did* know that they were immensely powerful and not something she wanted to get close to. At. All.

"It would be *way* too convenient if he was dead," she whispered.

*Fucking stop talking out loud to yourself!*

There, *that* was in her mind only.

And then his eyes blinked.

She didn't scream. She wasn't a screamer. But she wasn't breathing at the moment either.

She did, however, regret not reading up on what to do when you encountered an alligator in the wild.

She was a vet. She knew things *about* alligators, of course. But dammit, school had been a long time ago—she hadn't touched, or even seen, an alligator in years—and that didn't mean that *any* of that knowledge was currently retained in the brain that was chanting *you're going to be gator food on your first day? Really?*

At least that was in her mind and not out loud.

*Oh God.*

She spun and bolted for her back door, lunging inside and slamming the lightweight slab of wood behind her.

But that was evidently too much for the elderly rusted hinges because as soon the door made contact with the frame, the whole thing gave a creak, then fell. And, of course, it fell outward, essentially creating a ramp that covered the back steps that would make it very easy for a reptile to climb up into the house. With her.

She still didn't scream, but she shrieked a little now.

She ran down the hallway of the house toward the front door, ripped it open and sprang out onto the porch. She prayed the whole way across that she wouldn't step on any rotten wood.

As soon as her shoes hit the front walk, she turned and ran

to the gorgeous house with the I-could-sit-there-every-day porch next to hers.

Possibly a subconscious choice because she was also curious about getting a brief tour of the place.

But right now, what she needed was to get away from the alligator in her yard and get some help from someone who lived in a place where people regularly had alligators in their backyards.

She bounded up those front steps, all of which were completely sturdy and intact, and pounded on the front door.

She stood, breathing heavily, realizing it was during the workday and that it was possible her new neighbors wouldn't be home. But then she had heard footsteps coming closer to the door and she worked to steady her breathing and pasted on a smile.

She saw a form on the other side of the beveled glass set into the front door just before the knob turned and the door swung in.

"Hi, I'm—"

Jill's words died and her mouth dropped open as she stared at the person who had answered the door of her *neighbor's* house.

"Well, hey, cher."

"*Zeke?*"

## 6

Zeke was shocked by how glad he was to see the woman who was standing on the other side of his door.

She looked amazing.

Actually, she looked like a mess. Her hair was up in a high ponytail, but the tie had slipped and a large strand was now hanging against her right cheek and over her shoulder. She was dressed in a plain green v-neck t-shirt that was fitted to her toned body and a pair of denim shorts that hit her mid-thigh.

She was also...damp.

Her clothes weren't soaking wet, but they weren't dry. In fact, her shoes—basic white canvas sneakers—also looked wet.

She had streaks of dirt all over as well. The front of her shirt, her shorts, her arms, legs, and cheek.

Yeah, she was definitely a mess. And he felt his heart rate kick up anyway.

Still, he frowned as he pushed his screen door open. "What happened? Are you okay?"

"Alligator." She pointed in the direction of the house next door.

He glanced in that direction though didn't expect to see anything. It was probably Chuck. He was harmless.

For an alligator.

"You ran into a gator?"

She nodded.

"That happens around here once in a while." He reached out and grabbed her wrist, tugging her forward. "Come on in here."

She stopped right inside the door, right in front of him, and he became aware that he had only a towel on.

He'd just gotten out of the shower when he'd heard the banging on his front door. Everyone in Autre knew this was his house and he could only assume that someone was in big trouble pounding like that. Since he knew everyone in town and ninety-eight percent of the people who would come to his house for help were relatives, he hadn't thought much about answering the door half-naked.

Now he was thinking about it a lot.

Jill's gaze was tracking over him from his shoulders across his chest down his abdomen to the dark gray towel he had slung low on his hips.

Her eyes on him, her body so close to his, the scent of her, all combined and his body stirred.

"You came looking for me?" He couldn't even express how that made him feel. When he'd awoken alone in bed in the motel, his heart had actually sunk. He wasn't sure that it had ever happened to him before.

The women he typically went to bed with knew the expectations—that they both have as much fun as they could before the sun came up. It was kind of a Cinderella thing. He'd be Prince Charming for a night, but he was a regular working guy, who was way more likely to own a pumpkin than a fancy coach, again the next morning.

The women he barely knew would continue being women

he barely knew. The women he knew, because they'd grown up in the same town, would continue being women he ran into once in a while at the bar, a bonfire, or crawfish boil. And they might end up in the same bed again at some point. But the next day did not mean they would be having brunch together or going to the movies that weekend or to Sunday dinner at her grandma's house after church.

This time though, when he'd awakened without Jill next to him, he'd been incredibly disappointed. He'd shaken it off, of course, but now looking at her standing in his front entryway and looking at him as if she was very much in the mood for brunch and he was a giant plate of bananas Foster French toast, and hash browns—and yes, he was projecting his favorite breakfast foods here—had his body heating and his cock stirring.

He tucked his finger under Jill's chin and tipped her head back so that her eyes met his. "How did you find me?"

With her gaze diverted from his chest and abs she shook her head slightly. "I didn't. I didn't know this was your house."

"Really? What are you doing here?"

"I was next door. Then I came out and there was an alligator and I decided I should come and get someone who might know what to do about that."

"But you didn't know it would be me?"

She shook her head again. "I figure anyone who lives here would know what to do if there was suddenly an alligator in their backyard."

He felt his mouth curl at the corner. "True enough. Especially down in this part of town."

His backyard was basically all of the Landry land that ran from the edge of Autre to the bayou. His neighbors included his brother Zander, his brother Fletcher, and his cousin Mitch. They had called this end of the road Bachelor Row for the past few years since all the guys had moved into the old family homes that were clustered down here.

But now that Mitch and Fletcher were both very much not bachelors, the town was going to have to come up with something else. Plus, the house next door to Zeke was getting remodeled for the new penguin veterinarian who was coming to town. And she was a woman. So not a bachelor. So...

His eyes widened. "You said you were next door?"

She nodded. Then *her* eyes widened. "Wait, you live *here*?"

He looked down at himself, then gave her a grin. "I don't just walk in and shower at other people's houses."

Hell, he *loved* the shower he'd put in upstairs. He didn't even stick around and shower at women's houses when he spent the night.

Jill's eyes dropped from his face to his naked torso and she seemed to lose her focus again.

Laughing softly Zeke again tipped her chin up to look him in the eye. "What were you doing next door?"

"Checking out the house. But there's not much to check out. The contractor hasn't done much with it."

"Why were you checking to see what the contractor had gotten done?"

His heart was hammering harder now. But he was starting to connect some dots.

And he found the resultant line surprising, but exciting.

"It's my new house."

Holy shit.

That was...*awesome*.

Jill was the veterinarian.

He'd been corresponding with her via text and email but her texts had been about the penguins and he'd known her as Dr. Morris. Her email address had been jmorris11 so hadn't given her name away either. He hadn't put that together last night.

But now?

He was definitely putting this together now.

This meant the woman who had rocked his world last night wasn't just passing through town. In fact, she wasn't going anywhere for a very long time.

"You're the new penguin veterinarian."

She was clearly a little surprised. "You've heard of me?"

He chuckled. "Definitely. I'm related to the people who own Boys of the Bayou Gone Wild. For one thing."

She tipped her head. "Really? So you know Griffin and Charlie."

"Charlie's my cousin. Of course, I also happened to be the one who built the penguins their new habitat."

Her eyes went round. "You...what...you're kidding."

He lifted a hand to run it through his wet hair.

Her eyes followed the motion, seemingly riveted on his arm. He wasn't sure if it was the tattoo or what exactly. But he did know that Jillian was fascinated with his ink. She had traced all of it with her fingers and tongue last night more than once. And he had a lot of ink.

He dropped his hand and reached for her. "I'm also the guy who's remodeling your house." He ran his hand up and down her arm. She didn't pull away but she didn't lean into his touch either. It seemed that she was far more focused on the conversation.

"I thought that was two different guys."

"Nope. I own Landry Construction. My cousin Mitch takes lead on a lot of the animal enclosures, but I'm the one you've been texting with about the penguins. And I do most of the building and remodeling around here." He tugged her a little closer. "I've been the one emailing you questions about that house for weeks."

She winced. "Yeah. Um. Sorry about that."

"While, on the other hand, you gave me very detailed information for the penguins."

She lifted a shoulder. "I care a lot more where the penguins are living than where I will be."

"Clearly. But now that you're here, we can finish your house."

Her eyes widened again, and she stared at him. "We're going to be neighbors."

He let his grin grow slowly as he stroked his hands up and down her arm slower. "Yup."

She tipped her head back and groaned.

But it wasn't one of the hot oh-my-God-yes groans she'd been giving him last night. This was more of an oh-crap groan.

"You're clearly not as excited about that as I am," he said dryly.

Her head came up and she met his eyes. Now there was no roaming over his half naked body. She shook her head. "It just feels complicated to live next door to the guy I'm hooking up with once a month."

He was confused. "We're hooking up once a month?"

"That was what I was going to propose anyway. Friends with benefits, you know? After last night I thought that could be kind of fun."

"That would be fun. Very, *very* fun," he said. "But why only once a month? I'm up for that kind of fun way more often."

"Sure. But then it turns into more like dating or a relationship or something rather than just getting together for hot sex."

"And I take it the relationship and dating thing is something you're trying to avoid?"

"Very much so. And living next door to you means that we'll see each other occasionally and since you'll be saving me from alligators on a regular basis, we could potentially turn into *actual* friends. And that makes the hooking up even more complicated."

Having the sun up hadn't made him feel any less attracted to, slightly confused by, surprised by, and definitely amused by this woman. "But friends with benefits has *friends* right in the title."

This all sounded good to him. Having a neighbor he could get naked with whenever the urge struck, who didn't want anything else from him, sounded pretty damned great.

"I'm just really not interested in a relationship," Jill went on. "I'm not good at them. And I don't really have time for them. And I don't put the effort into them, which ends up bothering the other person after a while. Which is understandable. I'm not blaming anyone. I just really like to have everything laid out and everyone on the same page. And I like sex. It would be really perfect to be able to have amazing sex, but only when it's convenient."

Zeke gave a soft snort. Convenient hot sex. It really did sound pretty amazing.

"I don't see why we can't have that. Hell, being neighbors makes the whole thing even more *convenient*, right?" he asked.

"It couldn't be an all-night thing like last night. I don't have time for that very often."

"If you just want to walk through my door, only wearing a robe and nothing underneath to save time, and bend over the back of my sofa, I'm not gonna kick you out, cher," he told her. He was half-teasing. But only half.

She finally gave him a hint of a smile. "I can just show up on your front porch anytime I need an orgasm that I don't want to do myself?"

Something about the way she said that—whether it was the word orgasm or the mischievous little twinkle in her eye or how damned easy she was making it all sound—made heat clench in Zeke's gut. He reached up and cupped the side of her head.

He brought her in close and put his mouth against hers. "Any fucking time."

Then he kissed her.

He hadn't expected to see her again. He'd thought she was passing through. When he'd awakened alone in bed, her stuff had still been in the motel room indicating she was only out temporarily. He'd been disappointed, yes, but he'd also gotten out of the room quick. They had a hot one-night stand. That had been pretty clear. So he'd gotten out before they had to have any kind of awkward morning after. But he'd known he was going to be thinking about her for a very long time to come.

Now she was not only here on his front porch, but was staying in Autre. Even more, she was going to be living next door.

His day had gotten a lot better very quickly.

She leaned into him as he kissed her. Their tongues tangled. They both moaned and her hands started to roam over his chest and abs.

He really needed to get to work.

Except that the client who had been texting and emailing him this morning was the woman who was right now cupping his ass through his towel and pressing into him.

"Welcome to Autre," he said roughly against her mouth.

She gave a soft laugh and leaned back. "This town is not what I expected."

He grinned. "I think a lot of people say that. Maybe not for the same reason you think, but Autre surprises a lot of people."

He took her hand and started to pull her deeper into the house. "Turns out I don't have to rush off to work after all, so how about we go upstairs—"

She dug her heels in and he stopped.

"What do you mean you don't have to go to work right away? I have an entire house that needs to be remodeled."

"Your fault. If you'd answered a few emails, it would be a lot further along."

She looked slightly abashed at that. "Well, *I* have to get to work. And I have to run back up to the motel to shower again." She looked down at her dirty clothes and shoes. "I checked out the penguin habitat earlier."

He frowned. "You got dirty at the penguin habitat? What did you do? It should be all locked up."

"How about I just warn you, since we're going to be running into one another regularly, that I often end up messy, dirty, wet, and other things when I don't mean to."

"I like you messy, wet, and dirty."

She put a hand against his chest and pushed as he stepped closer. "Yeah, yeah. I also don't do the friends-with-benefits-hook-up-thing two days in a row."

"Why the hell not?"

"No time. Because it starts to build expectations. Because it makes things more complicated."

He narrowed his eyes and studied her. "I've never done friends-with-benefits. You might have to fill me in on the rules."

"I might have different rules than most."

"Well, if I'm *your* friend-with-benefits, I guess *your* rules are the ones I should know."

She studied him right back almost as if she didn't believe him. "You'll just let me take the lead here? You'll just do this however I want to?"

He leaned in and met her gaze directly. "I will do just about anything for the taste of that sweet pussy again. But now that I know you have penguins too? I'm not going anywhere. Whatever rules you've got? I'll follow them."

Her pupils dilated and he watched her catch her breath. She swallowed. Then smiled. "You're into penguins?"

"You could be bald and fat and named Roger and I'd be trying to get closer so I could hang with the penguins," he said sincerely.

She laughed. "Okay, neighbor, I'm going to go clean up at

the motel and then maybe we can meet at the penguin habitat and go over everything you've done there. Make sure everything is ready to go for when they show up in a couple days."

"Okay. But you know you can clean up at your house. I can get rid of the gator for you."

She gasped. "I forgot about that! Yes, please get rid of the gator. But what do you mean I can clean up at my house? There's nothing *at* my house."

"You didn't go upstairs?"

"No. Why?"

"Because I did redo one bedroom and bathroom. I knew whoever you were, you'd at least need that much. So essentially, you've got a motel room over there. You can't cook or do anything like that, but you have a bed and a working shower and a toilet."

She looked startled. "Wow. That's...thank you."

"Sure."

"Seriously. That's...that was really thoughtful." She wrinkled her nose. "I should have returned a few emails."

"Yes, you should have."

She looked sheepish.

"But..." This was going to sound like a come on. Especially after the conversation they'd just had. But... "There's no soap or towels or anything over there though. Do you want to borrow some of mine?"

Her gaze dropped to the towel he was wearing. And there was no way she missed the erection tenting said towel.

"Um..." She lifted her gaze to his again and wet her lips. "This is going to sound like a come on, especially after the conversation we just had," she said.

He felt surprise jolt through him.

"But," she continued. "Could I maybe just use your stuff here? That would be easier."

"Of course."

And that was the moment Zeke realized he *really* liked her.

He didn't let women use his shower.

He didn't shower at their places because he liked his shower much better. But he didn't let them shower at his place either.

Because one, shower sex was a lot more difficult and awkward than porn made it seem. Which was a bummer, because he'd installed a shower bench that he'd thought would be sexy and perfect.

And two, long hair clogged his drain.

He didn't mind snaking his drain for his *own* hair, but it was gross for anyone else's.

And yet, here he was leading Jill to the steps, and telling her, "It's the third door on the right. Towels are in the closet. Borrow whatever soap and shampoo you want. I've got a couple kinds of shampoo and body wash and some really great hair conditioner."

She lifted a brow. "You have a *couple* of kinds of body wash?"

He narrowed his eyes. "Yes."

"Why?"

He answered with the same thing he'd told his brothers when they'd asked. "Sometimes I want to smell like spring rain and sometimes I want to smell like a mountain morning "

"Oh my God."

"You only have one kind?" he asked, as if *that* was crazy.

"I have soap," she said simply.

"Just soap? What's it smell like?"

She shrugged. "Soap."

He looked at her, feeling a surge of what he could only describe as *like*. He liked her. In his family they were all boys, and most of his female cousins lived outside of Autre. Kennedy was the only Landry granddaughter who had grown up in Autre and she was...not a typical girlie-girl. But he generally knew from the girls he'd dated that things like soap and shampoo mattered to most of them.

He reached up and pulled the ponytail holder from Jillian's hair. He ran his fingers through the long tresses.

She seemed startled by that as well.

"You're low maintenance?"

She laughed out loud at that. "You have no idea."

But he wanted to have an idea. That all seemed to come out of the blue, but he wanted to have an idea what she was like, he wanted to figure out just how low or high maintenance she was, he wanted to know what kind of towels she would pick out if she was picking out her own, and he definitely wanted to be her friend-with-benefits. Though he was definitely going to press for more than once a month. Twice a month, or even three times, wasn't *that* much. Especially if they just got right to it each time.

Though the idea of *not* talking to her and teasing her and showing her the ins and outs of a good old Louisiana crawfish boil—because he somehow knew this girl had never sucked a crawfish before—made him feel like he was definitely going to be missing out.

"So yeah, go clean up, then we can go over to the penguin habitat together."

She looked down at her shoes. "My clothes are pretty dry, but I'll have to change shoes, though," she said with a sigh. "They feel gross."

"I'll get you some from Paige for now. Then later, after the penguin habitat, I'll help you move your stuff up to the house. You can definitely stay there from now on."

He now wanted to be there when she saw the bedroom and bathroom he'd remodeled. It was all he'd been able to get done in that house, and that had been driving him crazy, but he at least wanted to see her reaction to what he had done.

He always took pride in his work and he loved when people told him that it was even better than they'd envisioned.

Considering Jill had given him zero direction, he had no

idea if this was going to be better than she'd envisioned, but if she really was low maintenance and didn't care about this stuff, then it would be easy to wow her.

"Who's Paige?"

"My cousin Mitch's girlfriend. They just live three houses over. She'd be happy to loan you shoes."

Jill rolled her eyes. "I don't know about that. I have a way of ruining shoes."

"Oh?"

"I don't really think about things, like what I'm wearing, before I do things. Like this morning when I climbed into the penguin habitat and jumped into the moat."

Zeke's brows arched. "You *climbed* into the penguin habitat and *jumped* into the moat?" he repeated. "Why?"

"I wanted to get inside and see everything. And the guy with the key was running late this morning."

"Because he got *very* laid, *very* well last night and needed a little extra rest," he told her, pointing a finger at her cute little nose. "So...also your fault."

"Somehow *I* got out of bed nice and early though. Guess we know which one of us wore the other out."

"Or which of us did all the work," he returned.

She laughed.

God, he loved teasing her.

"Anyway, no worries. Paige has been here long enough that she knows what kind of footwear it takes to be on the bayou. Let me go get something from her. If you ruin it, you can replace it. You're a millionaire after all, right?"

Jill's sudden smile nearly knocked him on his ass. It was quick, bright, and full of amusement.

"Hey, that's true. I'm definitely still getting used to that."

He chuckled. "Something like that won't take long to get used to."

"I'm just not a big spender, and I have pretty much zero

taste when it comes to...everything. So, it might take me longer than most."

She was intriguing. He was often attracted to women. He made friends easily and enjoyed other people and loved nothing more than to just sit around and talk and bullshit and laugh. But there was something about Jill that actually *interested* him. Maybe that sounded shallow when it came to his other human interactions, but he just wasn't that often interested in the women he flirted with.

Well, he was interested in them as far as flirting, and having a good time, and then of course when they ended up naked, he was interested.

But most of the conversations he had that were actually fun and thought-provoking and entertaining were the ones he had with his family and friends. And most of his friends were family. He was as close to his cousins as he was to his brothers, and the entire Landry clan spent most of their social time together. He supposed that meant that he wasn't looking to women to interest or entertain him.

But Jill was already doing both. And she wasn't even trying. She only wanted to hook up with him once a month.

He was either going to throw her over his shoulder and take her upstairs and give shower sex another shot or he was going to take a big step back and insist she head up to the shower alone.

He did the latter. Which surprised him, actually.

"Go clean up. I'll get dressed and get you some shoes and then we'll go see the penguin habitat."

He was really proud of that thing too.

She took a step toward the stairs, then turned back. "Actually..."

"Yeah?"

"Do you have any food?"

That wasn't what he'd been expecting. "Food?"

She nodded. "I obviously don't have any food in my house. And I haven't had breakfast. I'm starving. I mean, we're neighbors, right? So rather than borrowing a cup of sugar, I'm wondering if you have any cereal."

"Cereal?"

"Breakfast cereal. Sugary is preferred. If it's fruit flavored of any kind, bonus points."

He shook his head. "No cereal. Sorry."

She sighed. "If you had, you would've been too good to be true."

As her gaze tracked over his naked torso again, Zeke was torn between wanting to laugh and wanting to press her up against the door and kiss the hell out of her before going down on her and making her come in his mouth.

She sure seemed horny for a girl who only wanted to hook up once a month.

And his body definitely liked her.

"I don't have any cereal, but I can feed you."

He did not mean that to sound dirty. And maybe it was only in his head.

"So you do have food?"

Yeah, it seemed that her mind was firmly on actual food rather than where his had been.

"No," he said honestly. "I don't have any food but I know where we can get some."

"You don't have *any* food? Like crackers or an apple? I'm not picky."

"I might have ketchup. And I do have beer. But I don't really eat here."

"Where do you eat?"

"My mom's or my grandma's mostly."

"You eat all of your meals at your mother's or your grandmother's house?"

"In fairness, my grandmother's place is a restaurant," he

said. "But, yeah, I eat at least most of my meals at her place. If I can't sit down to eat something, I can always pop into the kitchen to grab something. I go to my mom's at least once a week though."

Jill looked horrified. "Can you tell me where the grocery store is?"

"Yes. But I'm not going to. You're going to go get cleaned up, I'm going to get you some shoes, then I'm going to feed you, then we're going to go look at the penguin habitat."

"I could find the grocery store by myself."

"I'm sure you could."

"But I really want to see inside the main building at the enclosure."

"You didn't pick the lock or break a window?"

"I didn't even think of that," she said. "I was wet and freezing by then. But otherwise..."

He grinned. "I know." Just the amount of detail she'd given him when instructing him on how to construct the habitat said a lot about her passion for the animals and the project.

"Fine. I'll stick with you this morning. Because of the penguins."

"Understood." He paused, then said, "But once you taste my grandma's food, you're going to be thanking me for that too."

"Something you should know about me," Jill said. "If you're good to my penguins, you don't have to do much else."

# 7

Zeke got dressed quickly, trying very hard to ignore the sound of the shower running in the bathroom off his bedroom and to not wonder which body wash she was choosing. But he was grinning stupidly the entire time.

He pulled on jeans and a t-shirt and laced up his work boots. Then he headed over to grab shoes from Paige. There were a number of pairs of varying styles on the back porch and he grabbed a pair of short ankle boots that laced up since he and Jill were going to be walking around the penguin habitat.

He left a quick note that he'd borrowed the boots, though he was certain he would run into Paige and/or Mitch sometime today and could tell them then. He was also certain neither of them would care.

He headed over to Jill's house and scoured her yard, front to back and sides for any signs of stray alligators. It had probably been Chuck. The alligator made a habit of sunning himself behind the houses down here. Of course, the backyard of the abandoned house had been perfect for him and the humans since he wasn't bothering anyone there.

Until now.

Zeke was going to have to come up with something.

For one, he was going to have to teach Jill what to do and how to handle gators in her path in the future. That was definitely something that happened periodically down here this close to the bayou. For the most part the alligators were well fed from all the boat tours tossing food out so the animals would come close enough for the tourists to see them. But it was important to know to look for them in the first place.

He was sitting on the front steps of his porch when Jill came out a few minutes later. He'd put her slightly damp clothes in his dryer while he'd been at Paige and Mitch's and then tossed them back on the floor of the bathroom before she was out of the shower. They hadn't been too wet and he wasn't sure she even noticed the difference.

"Are you going to tell me where the rotten wood areas are on my porch?" she asked.

He stretched his feet. "Of course. But the strip from the steps to the door is fine. I made sure of that in case anyone was coming over to make any deliveries or anything for you."

She came to stand right in front of him. With her on the porch and him two steps down, they were a little closer in height.

"Thanks for...everything."

"You bet. And I can do whatever else you need. We can talk about your house now that you're here."

She held up a hand. "I don't—"

He captured her hand in his. "Yeah, I know you don't care."

But he wanted her to care. He wanted to talk about how to make that house amazing for her. The bones of the house were great and yes, it needed a lot of work, but that meant they could do *anything*. And she had the money. He didn't want to spend down her bank account completely, of course, but with her finances and that house, he could really stretch himself, maybe try some new, fun things.

Plus he wanted to...take care of her.

Damn, that was a weird thought.

He didn't take care of anyone.

He barely took care of himself.

But getting her shoes, helping her get cleaned up, having her come to him—even if it had been kind of accidental—about the alligator, and now taking her to eat all felt good in a way that was very different for him.

"Let's at least talk about the kitchen."

Maybe if they took it one thing at a time he could get answers from her. He could walk her through the project step by step.

The kitchen was a great place to start since she had a bedroom and bathroom.

"Okay," she agreed.

He felt a rush of relief.

"Can you get me a refrigerator that keeps my milk and yogurt cold?"

He blinked at her. "Um...of course."

"Great." She smiled brightly.

"What else?"

"That's all I really need."

He frowned. "But do you want a center island? An open concept? A pantry that—"

"I really don't care what it looks like. I'm not going to be hosting dinner parties, so I don't need anything fancy. I'm not really having any big family holiday dinners, so it's not like I need a huge oven or the double-decker convection thing my mother has. In fact, I really don't even need a full-sized refrigerator. I could get by with a dorm-sized fridge."

Zeke knew he was staring. He did homebuilding and remodels for a living. He had never had someone tell him that they didn't care about the layout of their kitchen or what their appliances looked like.

"I am *not* putting a dorm fridge into that kitchen," he told her.

"Why not?"

"Because that's ridiculous. You're a grown woman with an enormous kitchen. You will have a full-sized fridge. Actually," he said, interrupting himself. "I'm getting you an extra full-size."

"This is a matter of ego and pride for *you*?"

"Damn right."

"I don't even *need* a whole house. I could just live in an apartment."

"Well, you bought *that* house and I'm going to fucking remodel the hell out of it, so too bad."

She tipped her head, a slow smile spreading her lips. "You're hot when you get all riled up."

"You're not getting a dorm fridge even if you act all sexy," he told her.

"I'm *certain* I could convince you to put a dorm fridge in that kitchen if I had your cock in my mouth."

Heat grabbed him in the gut and he coughed. "Stop it."

"This is really important to you, isn't it?" she asked.

"Yes."

"Why?"

"Because I'm damned good at what I do. And while it's your house and I want to make you happy, I also can't stand the idea of someone not making that old house magnificent when they have the time, money, and contractor to do it."

She just studied him.

"And since you don't care anyway, why don't you just keep your sweet ass out of my way, say, 'yes, sir' when I tell you something, and be sure you pay your invoices on time?"

She smiled again. "Very hot."

"I mean it." He wasn't teasing her now. Though hearing 'yes, sir' from her in another context would be very welcome also.

"I know. I think that's why it's hot. It's not just the bossy stuff, but you're actually really into this."

"I am."

He would paint a bedroom neon orange. He would put a fireman's pole from the upstairs bedroom to the kitchen. He would turn a bathroom into a spa for a dog. He'd actually done all of those things. But because the owner had *cared*. It had mattered to them. It had been part of making the house their *home*.

But he'd be damned if he'd let some woman put a dorm fridge and nothing else in that awesome kitchen just because she didn't give a shit about anything else.

"Okay. Then you're in charge," she told him.

Thank God.

"What do you keep in your fridge?" he asked.

"Milk for my cereal and yogurt."

He paused, but she clearly wasn't kidding.

Fine. He didn't have much in his fridge either. Who was he to judge?

"Do you need an icemaker? A freezer for ice cream, frozen pizza, frozen waffles?"

She shook her head. "Nope, I'm good. I mean I assume that there will be room for ice in the freezer because they don't really make refrigerators without freezers, do they?"

He didn't think so. But he wouldn't really know. "I know a lot more about added bells and whistles rather than any kind of stripped-down version. I put a fridge in a kitchen two weeks ago that tells the weather and news of the day and keeps track of grocery lists electronically."

Her eyes widened. "See, that's another reason why buying cereal, milk, yogurt, bread, and peanut butter is the best way to live. I don't even have to keep a list."

"That's all you eat?"

"Well at night, I have this vegetable powdered drink thing.

But only because I should be eating vegetables and I don't like to buy them."

"You don't like vegetables?"

"It's more that they go bad. I forget that I have them or forget what I planned to do with them and they get rotten."

Again, he couldn't really judge. He didn't think he'd ever had a fresh vegetable in his refrigerator. But that didn't mean he didn't eat them. He ate them at his grandmother's all the time.

"Vegetable powdered drink mix?"

"It's not as bad as it sounds. Though it's not as good as it should be. Still, it's a way to get the equivalent of three vegetables for the day. And it doesn't go rotten."

She'd said bread so he asked, "And you eat sandwiches?"

He couldn't explain why, but he was fascinated by all of this.

"Of course."

"So do you like turkey or ham or roast beef or what?" He suddenly really wanted to know what kind of sandwiches this woman ate. But why? He wasn't sure he even knew what his cousin Kennedy's favorite sandwich was and he spent nearly every day of his life with her. And Jill was a little odd. And some of her oddities were kind of annoying.

*Just put a fridge in your fucking kitchen, woman.*

"Peanut butter and jelly," Jill said.

"Just peanut butter and jelly?"

"Oh jelly. I would need to put that in my fridge. Maybe I do need to make a list."

Zeke felt the corner of his mouth curling up. There was something about this woman that was just so...different.

He didn't get a lot of different in his life. His family was a bunch of crazy, quirky characters and they certainly all had their own personalities, but underlying it all was a commonality because of how they'd grown up and lived together all their lives.

The women who had come into his cousins' lives—Tori and

Juliet and Paige—had brought a breath of fresh air to the bayou. They were all from other places and had come to Autre for various reasons, but had fallen in love with the Landry boys as well as the town and the rest of the family and had stayed.

Maddie, Kennedy, and Charlie, the other girls in the family by marriage or blood, had all spent time on the bayou growing up so they'd fit right in with the Landry craziness.

Jill was turning out to be one of those breaths of fresh air. And damn if Zeke didn't want to breathe deeply.

"So you only eat peanut butter and jelly sandwiches? No other kind?" he asked.

"Peanut butter and jelly don't go bad."

Right. Back to that. So she tended to buy food that didn't have strict expiration dates.

"But milk and yogurt both go bad," he pointed out.

He wasn't sure how they'd even gotten on this topic and why he felt compelled to keep talking about it.

"They do, but I eat them every day, so they're habits and I'm much less likely to let them go bad," Jill said.

"Do you forget a lot of things?"

"A startling amount, actually."

He gave a soft laugh. He really liked her ability to be self-deprecating.

"Do you need a keeper, Jill?"

She didn't even blink. "You have no idea."

He opened his mouth to say something flirtatious about how he'd like to take care of her, but hesitated. He wasn't really a guy who took care of other people. He got taken care of. He wasn't exactly forgetful. Then again, he also never had a zucchini in his crisper drawer in the fridge. For all he knew he would forget it was there and let it go bad. He did love a good turkey sandwich, but he always ate them at his grandma's or his mom's house. How long did turkey stay good in the refrigerator? He didn't even know.

Yeah, if this woman needed someone to take care of her—or perishable food—he was probably not the guy.

Suddenly remembering the shoes, that had ironically made him feel like he was taking care of her, he held them up. "Gotcha these."

She reached for them with a smile. "These will be perfect."

"These too." He handed her some socks from his own drawer.

She took them with a questioning look. She turned the boots all directions, checking them out. "They look...pretty."

The boots were a pale pink. "They're Paige's. She does go walking around and out on the swamp boats and loves the otters, but she is not a real outdoorsy girl. And when she's with the otters, for instance, she's barefoot. I don't think those boots are really right for yoga."

"Yoga?"

"Yeah, she teaches yoga. She actually does otter yoga down at the otter enclosure twice a week."

"I'm assuming it's people doing yoga with otters around them and not making the otters actually do yoga."

"Right," he said with a chuckle. "She also does cat yoga in her studio downtown. "

"People keep telling me I should do yoga," Jill said.

"Yeah? Why is that?"

"I'm a workaholic. I don't really take time to take care of myself and I can be a little...tense about things."

"I'm sure Paige would love to have you come to class."

Jill sat down on the top step of the porch and pulled a sock and boot on and started to lace them up. "Yeah, I'm not going to do that."

"Why not?"

"I don't do very well with things that go according to a schedule."

Zeke shook his head. He wanted to keep talking to her for

hours. He also thought she was maybe a little nutty. And he definitely wanted to bend her over his couch now that he'd mentioned it.

He couldn't explain it entirely. He figured it had something to do with the fact that this woman's mouth around his cock last night had been one of the best things he'd ever felt in his life and that watching her ride him cowgirl had been like an erotic movie come to life.

He hadn't realized he was quite that easy for sex. Well, that wasn't true, he knew he was pretty easy for sex. But the idea of spending the entire day with this woman was looking like more and more fun. And in spite of having some pretty great sex in the past he couldn't remember the last time he'd wanted to spend the entire next day with the woman he'd taken to bed the night before.

"So timelines are trouble for you?" he asked. "Schedules, expiration dates, things like that just in general?"

She slid her other foot into a sock and boot. "Definitely."

"You can't just put notifications for appointments and stuff on the calendar in your phone?"

He wasn't judging. He actually ran his business according to a schedule, having start and end dates for projects, but outside of that he wasn't a huge fan of schedules and having to be certain places at certain times. He lived on the bayou and owned his own business so he didn't really have to worry about a hectic schedule.

Jill tied the boot and looked up at him. "Sure, I put things in my calendar on my phone. And then I leave my phone laying on my desk three rooms away and it doesn't really help."

They were talking about sandwiches and the fact that she didn't like schedules and timelines. Why was that so damned adorable?

She lifted a foot turning it back and forth to show off the

boots. "They are a little big. But they will totally work. Thank you."

"My pleasure."

"How did you know about putting socks on to make them fit better?"

"Growing up I borrowed boots and shoes from all of my older cousins and brothers and always needed to wear extra socks."

Both of her eyebrows went up. "There are bigger men than you down here?"

He narrowed his eyes playfully. "Not anymore. I caught up and shot past most of them. I've even got half an inch on my twin brother."

Now, her eyes widened under those arched brows. "You have a *twin*?"

His eyes narrowed further and he wasn't as playful when he said, "Not that it matters."

"Who says it doesn't matter?"

"My brother and I aren't into sharing."

He and Zander had never been with the same woman at the same time, nor could he imagine them ever doing that. They both tended to be pretty possessive. Not when it came to ball gloves and trucks and sweatshirts maybe, but definitely when it came to women.

But they *had* been out with the same woman at different times. Autre was just too small to never date a friend or brother's ex. As long as it was cool with everyone, it was fine. After all, just because you took the girl to prom when you were seventeen didn't mean she could never date another guy you hung out with. If that was the case, no one in Autre would ever date anyone else from Autre after about age fourteen.

But there was no way any other guy in Autre was touching Jill.

The thought was sudden and shocking.

But Zeke felt a powerful surge of possessiveness when thinking about Jill being with any other guy. Not just his brother, but *any* other guy.

He was going to ruin dating for her in this town. And he'd just met her. That was really a dick move on his part.

And he wasn't even sorry.

He had never cared about the sandwiches the girls he dated ate or what color their bedrooms were painted. He cared about both of those things with Jill. And now he was getting possessive. This was all very strange.

"We should get going." He pivoted and started down the walk. He heard the boots on her feet hit the pavement behind him.

"To the penguin habitat?"

"To get breakfast."

"Any chance you decided to just find me some yogurt?"

"Ellie might have yogurt."

Zeke stopped next to his truck and opened the passenger door. He waited for Jill to join him. He noted the fact that she'd been fine putting the same clothes on again after showering. Sure, it was all she'd had here, but he knew *many* women who would have insisted on changing after tromping around a penguin habitat.

No, scratch that. He actually didn't, because he didn't know too many other women who would have been tromping around in a penguin habitat in the first place.

Tori, his cousin Josh's wife. Possibly Charlie, if she got a wild hair. Bailey Wilcox, his friend Chase's girlfriend, who also happened to work for the Louisiana Department of Wildlife and Fisheries. She tromped around in worse all the time. Jordan, Fletcher's wife, would. Possibly his grandmother. Other than that, he couldn't think of many. None of the women he dated, for sure.

Jill climbed up into the passenger seat. "Who's Ellie? I thought we were going to your grandma's."

Zeke nodded. "Ellie is my grandma."

"And you call her Ellie?"

"There are a lot of grandmas and grandpas down here and several that aren't even ours by blood that seem like grandparents, so early on we all started calling them by their first names. It's unconventional down here, that's for sure. But I can't imagine calling Ellie anything else. Except maybe 'brat' once in a while or 'lovable pain in my ass'. But then again, she calls me both of those things too."

"I know what it's like to grow up in a small town with your whole family around. But if I called my grandmother anything but 'grandma' she would've gasped so loud, you would've heard it down here."

With her on the truck seat and him standing beside it, they were again at a more even height.

He took advantage and looked into her big green eyes. "You're not from Omaha then?"

"Nope, not even from Nebraska. I grew up in a little town called Bliss, Kansas."

"Bliss? Sounds like it should be a happy place."

"It is for the most part. It's a pretty typical Midwestern small town. Everybody knows your business, you've known everybody there since you've been born."

"Everybody takes care of one another and pulls together?" Zeke asked.

"Yeah. For sure."

"You miss home?"

"Sometimes. But I couldn't do my dream job there and that's always been more important than anything else. I go home to visit a few times a year."

"Dream job as a zoo veterinarian?"

"Dream job working with penguins. Veterinary school was

a good way to get credentials for that job. And Omaha was the first position that opened up that would give me direct contact with them."

"You don't like working with the bears and monkeys and giraffes?"

Jill shrugged. "Sure, they're great."

"But if it weren't for the penguins, you wouldn't have been there?"

"Nope."

She didn't seem apologetic about it, or even like she had to think about the question for more than a second.

"But when you inherited all this money and you could move the penguins anywhere, why not take them back to Kansas?"

"Griffin," she said, thinking about that question for only about three seconds. "It'll be nice to have another veterinarian around who has the level of passion for animals that I do."

"Moving back home didn't even occur to you?"

She was no longer looking him in the eye. "It really didn't. If I was back in Bliss, I would be caught up in all of the family stuff, the community stuff, my old friends. I love them all and going home to visit at the holidays or for events, like anniversaries and babies being born, is great. But living there full-time would definitely cut into my work. My family doesn't fully understand what I do or why. So they would be constantly harping on me to leave work at a decent hour and come over for dinner and to be available for picnics on the weekends or to help take my grandmother to appointments."

Her eyes flew back to Zeke's face. "It's not that I don't want to be around them or to help out. It's more that it's really hard for me to juggle everything and it's easier when I'm further away and not just around the corner for them to drop in on."

She frowned. "That sounds terrible, I know."

It did sound a little terrible. Zeke had no idea what it would be like to live far away from his family and friends. It had never occurred to him.

Being around for family picnics and to help take people to appointments along with those anniversary parties and the births of babies was what life was all about in his opinion.

He loved living in the town where he'd grown up and where all of his family had stayed. He'd loved growing up fishing and running around and swimming and raising hell with his brothers and cousins, and now that they were all older and settling down and starting businesses and doing amazing things for the community and the world, he was thrilled to have a front row seat to see it all and to be part of it. Building lemur, sloth, red panda, and now penguin enclosures for his family's new animal park was awesome. He couldn't imagine being this happy anywhere else.

"Oh my God, you're thinking it's terrible," Jill said, studying his face. "Aren't you supposed to reassure me that I'm not a bad person for not wanting to be around my family twenty-four seven?"

He gave an exaggerated wince. "I am definitely not the guy to tell you that not wanting to be around your family is a normal thing."

"Really? You love being around your family all the time?"

"Absolutely."

As if on cue his watch vibrated on his wrist and he glanced down to see a text message from his brother asking if he was going to be up at Ellie's for lunch.

"What's that?"

Zeke looked up at Jill. Then down at his watch. "This is called a watch. Since you have trouble with times and appointments, you might think about investing in one."

"It's a good thing that you're hot and have a big cock because you actually aren't that funny."

He gave a choked laugh. He was used to his brothers and

cousins saying graphic and inappropriate things out of the blue, but he couldn't say he was used to it from the women he was interested in. Except that it made him even more interested in Jill.

He leaned in close. "I'm glad my big cock made an impression."

She didn't lean back, or even blink. "Yeah, well, the way you bent me over the motel's desk chair and used that big cock on me, I think I might still have some *impressions* of the chair on my hips."

He felt like lightning had struck his head and streaked through his body.

"Damn, girl. I'm so glad you're moving in next door."

Now she did lean back. "Yep. Once a month it will be great.

"Yeah, I don't think the once a month thing is how this is going to turn out."

Her eyes were wide. "I think we need to go eat breakfast."

Okay so now she was trying to put up some barriers. Well, she could try. He wasn't going to stop her, but he also didn't think he was going to have to. She might not care what kind of sandwiches he liked, but she wanted him as badly as he wanted her.

Of course, after he took her for breakfast at Ellie's and she met the Landry clan and saw just how twenty-four-seven involved they all were, she might push even harder.

So it might just take him a while to get a refrigerator installed in her house. But he'd be happy to keep some milk and yogurt in his fridge for her to come over and borrow any time.

Grinning and feeling very optimistic—which was saying something considering Zeke had a pretty charmed life and felt optimistic ninety percent of the time—he leaned in to press a quick kiss to her lips before she could protest, then leaned back and shut the door.

He was actually whistling as he rounded the front bumper and got into the truck.

———

J ill wasn't sure why she felt trepidation as Zeke pulled his truck up in front of a plain square building that could've been anything from a storage shed, albeit a big one, to a workshop of some kind.

What it did not look like, however, was a restaurant.

There were two small windows in the front and a glass door but otherwise it was the definition of nondescript. It was a rectangular building that she had literally not even noticed when driving by on her way to her new house because it was so average.

"Do they have cereal here?" Jill eyed the building, already knowing the answer was no.

Zeke shut the truck off. "Define cereal."

"If I have to define it, the answer is no."

A bowl of cereal standing at her kitchen counter and she was done in five minutes. It'd taken more than that to drive to this place. Now they were going to have to go inside and order and wait for everything to get prepared and probably have conversations in the meantime. Everyone knew that talking while you ate made eating take longer.

Jill's inability to just sit and have a meal and conversation that lasted for more than ten minutes drove her mother insane. Her mom, like most of the town of Bliss, loved to sit around and talk. They dressed the events up with food and drink and called them barbecues and picnics and potlucks and block parties to make it *seem* like it was a meal, but truly it was just an excuse to sit around even longer and tell stories and gossip.

It had always driven Jill crazy.

It wasn't that she was opposed to eating with other people.

But her main focus was the eating and if there was some conversation on the side as well, fine, but no one needed an hour and a half to finish a hot dog and potato chips. In fact, left alone, Jill could eat a hot dog and potato chips and even have dessert done in less than ten minutes. People just needed to focus.

And no, the prepackaged Hot Cakes snack cakes that she counted as dessert weren't as good as her mother's homemade fudge brownies, but Jill was generally willing to sacrifice a little bit of homemade goodness for a saved hour in her schedule. And hey, those Hot Cakes people knew what they were doing.

"How long do you think this is going to take?" she asked as she joined Zeke at the front door to the building.

He pulled the door open and looked at her with a grin. "Longer than you're gonna want it to."

"It's that obvious?"

"That you do not want to walk in here and have breakfast with my entire family and half the town? Yes, it's that obvious. What's that about anyway? Are you antisocial, shy, or just anti-people in general?"

"I'm anti-wasted time."

"Eating breakfast is wasting time?"

"Telling my whole life story to a room full of strangers while trying to eat breakfast is a waste of time."

His grin grew. "You really are from a small town."

Then he nudged her through the doorway.

# 8

Everyone in the place looked over and when they realized there was a stranger standing in the room, they all got quiet.

Yep, she was from a small town all right. This was exactly what happened when people walked into Parker's café or Blissfully Baked—where they sold pie, not weed—in downtown Bliss.

"Morning, everyone," Zeke greeted the room.

His hand came to rest on Jill's lower back and he nudged her again, making her step forward. She took a few steps and found that he was steering her between the tables toward the back of the room even as he chatted and greeted people along the way.

None of that surprised her, of course. What *was* astonishing, however, were the people who greeted *her*. By name.

She glanced up at Zeke.

And caught him pointing at the top of her head and mouthing, "Penguin girl."

"Penguin girl?" she repeated.

He didn't look even slightly sheepish. "*Veterinarian* is harder to lip read."

She rolled her eyes. Then turned back to the room and raised her hand in a wave. And her voice. "Hi, everyone. Yes, I'm the penguin girl. My name is Jill. They will be here on Thursday. They're absolutely as cute as you think they are. But no, you can't visit them. For a while."

She added that last part without thinking. She should not have said that.

Everyone took in the information, nodded, and went back to their breakfasts.

Geez. Small towns.

Zeke pinched her side. "Just like home?"

"So much."

"What are we having this time?" the older woman behind the bar called.

She had long silver hair that was braided and fell nearly all the way down her back. She had tanned skin like that of someone who'd spent years outdoors in this hot Louisiana sun. And she had a bright smile.

"This time?" Jill asked.

"I was in here earlier. Right after I rolled out of bed." He gave her a grin. "Bragging about my amazing night."

"So you *did* brag to your friends."

"Told you I would." He gave her a hot, if slightly amused look. Then he glanced toward the bar. "Eggs Benedict and hash browns, I'm thinking," Zeke told the woman.

Jill looked up at him. "Really?"

"Cora's hash browns are amazing."

"I just told you that I wanted cereal and I didn't like spending a lot of time on meals and you ordered eggs Benedict?"

"I figure if I'm gonna convince you that taking your time with meals is worthwhile, I'd better give you some of the best food you can get," Zeke told her. He pulled out a chair at one of two long tables at the very back of the room and nudged her into it.

There were already people sitting at the tables. They looked over and smiled, but they didn't even pause their conversation as Zeke and Jill joined them.

Zeke dropped into the chair next to her and leaned back, stretching his arm out over the back of her chair and crossing one ankle over his opposite knee. He was the epitome of relaxed and laid back.

Eggs Benedict was brunch food, dammit.

How had this happened?

Last night she'd been walking back to her motel room from the convenience store with pistachios and a Diet Dr. Pepper. Now, less than twelve hours later, she'd had the best sex of her life, found out that her house contractor was the same guy who built the penguin habitat, who was also her neighbor, who was also the guy she had that hot sex with, and she was now basically at brunch.

"Rock-paper-scissors continues to be the only fair way to do this," one of the men sitting at the table with them said.

Jill instantly realized that this was Zeke's twin brother. They were clearly identical twins. Even down to the long hair. His twin had his pulled back into a bun at the back of his head. He was also obviously a cop. He was in his uniform as he lounged at the table.

Zeke leaned over. "Zander, my brother," he said softly.

Zander didn't have the same tattoos in the same places on his arms, and he didn't have a glint of gold in his earlobe, but he was incredibly good-looking, with his dark eyes, beard, and muscles. And yes, what they said about men in uniform was true. They were hot. Period.

Of course, that seemed to be a regular thing around here.

Michael, the handsome paramedic from last night was there too. Also in uniform. He gave Jill a smile and a wink.

And sitting next to him was freaking Donovan Foster.

Jill sucked in a quick breath and then realized she'd sat up straighter. She swallowed hard and sat back.

Zeke chuckled beside her. "I'm guessing you know who Foster is?"

"I, um...yeah."

She didn't watch much TV but when she did—big surprise —she tended toward nature shows, particularly ones that featured wild animals. It was no coincidence that one of her favorites had been hosted by Griffin's brother, Donovan.

She hadn't known about Donovan Foster or his show until she'd met Griffin, but once he'd spilled the beans about his TV-star brother, she'd checked him out and had been hooked.

Donovan had moved from that show to a series that was specifically produced for the internet, but she'd followed him there as well and found him charming and engaging and knowledgeable.

Griffin had mentioned on one of their recent phone calls that Donovan had been to Autre a few times and was actually hanging out now for an extended period and rehabilitating some wildlife right there in Autre. Jill couldn't deny that she'd been excited to potentially meet him and talk about their shared passion.

She'd had no idea she might be sitting at brunch with *him* though.

"I can't believe—" Zeke started.

"Shh," she said quickly. "Don't make a big deal out of it." She frowned at him. "No *mouthing* anything."

"He's done something with penguins?"

"Yeah. A couple of times."

Zeke grinned.

"I can't believe I did rock-paper-scissors even once. This is not going to be a regular thing," the man at the end of the table said.

He was even bigger than Zeke. He was wide and clearly taller. He also had longer hair, but it was loose and brushed the collar of his button-down shirt. His beard was longer and thicker and though his shirtsleeves were rolled up to his elbows, there was no evidence of any ink, at least on his forearms. He was in dress pants and wore glasses. He had a bad-boy-turned-hot-nerd thing going on.

"And that's Knox, our city manager," Zeke said in Jill's ear.

He did *not* look like a city manager.

"It's only fair," Zander insisted.

"I don't think it has to be fair. We just need to decide whose job this is going to be and that person needs to go do it. And I know it's not *mine*," Knox said.

"People can't be calling 9-1-1 for goats," Michael said. He was sitting much the way Zeke was, with his ankle crossed over his opposite knee. His left hand cradled the cup of coffee and he seemed mildly amused by the whole conversation.

"They're not my job either," the woman at the table said. "They're not exactly wildlife." She had long light brown hair that was pulled into a ponytail, though the ponytail holder was slipping down partway and her hair was hanging loose. She wore a green polo shirt that read Louisiana Department of Wildlife and Fisheries on the left side and khaki pants.

"Bailey," Zeke said to Jill.

"What about you?" Knox said to Donovan.

Donovan looked up from his plate. "What about me?"

Jill worked on looking totally casual about listening to Donovan Foster talk in person over breakfast.

"*You* could take care of the goats," Knox said.

"Definitely," Michael agreed. "You look a little like Griffin and are way more charming. The goats might like you even better than him if they get to know you."

Jill wasn't really following this conversation, but goats seemed to be a common thing around this town.

"Yeah, and you're an animal lover," Zander said, sitting forward. "We can get you a special cell phone and number. People can call straight to you. It'll be the Goat Hotline."

"It'll be like the Bat Signal," Michael said. "We'll even let you wear a cape."

"With a big goat head on the back," Zander added.

Donovan swallowed the bite he'd taken, wiped his mouth, pushed his empty plate away, and sat back in his chair. "I'll do it."

The people around the table looked surprised. Knox was the first to respond. "Awesome. I'll look into the—"

"On one condition," Donovan added.

Knox sighed. "Why is there always a condition?"

"Because grown men don't go around chasing goats down Main Street USA, unless there's a very good reason," Donovan said.

"But they do go around chasing giant salamanders?" Zander asked.

"Of course. Giant salamanders are cool. And there *was* a very good reason...I was getting paid by a television network for that," Donovan said with a grin.

"Still starstruck?" Zeke whispered to Jill. "The guy plays with salamanders."

"Shh," she hissed.

Of course she was still starstruck. Donovan Foster had rescued a baby elephant from poachers and a tiger from big game hunters. And those were just two episodes of his show. She could overlook giant slimy amphibians. Probably.

But Zeke Landry's index finger stroking up and down the outside of her arm was *very* distracting and she was now envisioning Donovan in a cape. And it wasn't doing anything for her.

"So what's this 'very good reason' you need?" Knox asked.

"There's one thing I've never done with my brand," Donovan said.

Zander and Knox rolled their eyes simultaneously.

Donovan just waited until he had their full attention again.

"Main Street USA," Donovan went on. "I've been talking to Charlie and Jordan—"

Now Zander and Knox both sighed.

Again Donovan waited.

"Okay, let's hear it," Knox said, rotating his hand in a 'come on' motion.

"As you know," Donovan said, "the ladies are big on helping the visitors to the petting zoo understand that there are interesting animals living all around them in their own backyards. That while visiting petting zoos and interesting places like the bayou is great, it's also important to understand the wildlife where they live and what they can do to protect the ecosystems right around them. Getting involved locally is a fantastic way to make advocates and activists on a larger scale down the road."

Zander was staring at him. "That wasn't even a prepared speech, was it? You talk like that all the time?"

"Well..." Donovan looked from Zander to Michael to Knox. "Yeah."

"So what do you want in exchange for being our local goat herder?" Knox asked.

"A show."

"You have a show."

"Another show."

"So do a show. The internet is free." Then Knox looked around the table. "It is free to put stuff like his show up on the internet right?"

"Jesus," Zander muttered. "What do you *want*, Donovan?"

"Money to advertise the show with online ads."

"From the city?" Knox asked. "That would take a whole

budget amendment. The Council would have to get involved. I'd have to—"

"I don't care where you get it," Donovan interrupted. "Have a car wash. Pass the hat at the next crawfish boil. Whatever."

Knox blew out a breath. "Maybe I'll just keep going to get the goats."

Finally, Zeke asked, "What the hell is going on?"

Jill tried not to be grateful he'd asked. But she kind of wanted to know now too. Dammit.

Michael looked over. "Just discussing what to do about our friendly neighborhood goat gang and Benny."

"Again? Already?" Zeke asked.

"This morning."

"Where did Benny take them this time?"

"The Methodist Church," Michael said. "Right into the sanctuary too. The door was propped open because the cleaning ladies were there."

"And four people showed up here with their bingo cards all at the same time so Ellie and Cora had to give out beer and fried pickles at nine a.m.," Zander added with a grin.

Zeke laughed. "And which of you got the call?"

They all looked at Knox. Who gave a heavy sigh as if he was *very* put upon.

"Why are they his problem?"

Jill was as startled as anyone to hear *her* voice ask the question.

They all looked at her in surprise.

Zeke recovered first. "These four—" He pointed to Knox, Zander, Bailey, and Michael. "All get the calls at different times. And they rock-paper-scissors to see who has to actually handle it. They are all *public servants*—"

The public servants all rolled their eyes.

"So *we* all think it makes sense. Zander is the sheriff, Michael is fire chief, and Bailey is with Wildlife and Fisheries.

And then Knox gets all the random calls when people don't know who else to call."

"Or when they don't want to deal with Zander," Michael said.

They all nodded their agreement. Including Zander.

"I work very hard to make it so people never really *want* to deal with me," Zander said. "That way the calls I get are actually important."

"It was Pastor Carson who called this morning," Bailey said. "So Knox couldn't swear at him."

"I never swear at citizens calling my office for help," Knox said.

"Not out loud anyway," Zander said.

Knox didn't deny that.

"I guess he knew better than to call 9-1-1 for it and figured the city manager's office would be able to handle it," Michael said.

"Sure, goat herding is right in my job description. Page three, paragraph two." Knox's tone was dry.

"But you *did* take care of it," Bailey said with a laugh. "They call you because you always take care of everything. They all know very well that eighty percent of what they call you about is not your job, but you'll get it done."

"What was I supposed to do?" Knox asked. "I can't call any of you because you'll tell me it's not your job. If I call Griffin, he'll just tell me they're not his goats. I can't call Fletcher when he's at school. He can't leave a classroom of third graders. And Jordan will just say Benny's doing her job and what a good girl she is."

"Jordan's great with alpacas, but the goats don't listen to her worth a shit anyway," Zander said.

They all nodded at that as well.

"You could call Tori or Josh or Sawyer or Maddie about the goats," Bailey said. "They *are* their goats."

"I'm not calling Tori about the goats," Knox said with a sigh. "She's got a newborn and…"

Bailey leaned in. "And what?"

The big guy shrugged. "It's Tori."

"And she's so sweet that you wouldn't want to upset her by being upset about her goats," Bailey filled in, with a knowing smile.

Knox rolled his eyes, but he didn't deny it. So, the grumpy guy had a soft side.

The rest of them laughed.

"Why not call Sawyer or Maddie or Owen?" Zander asked.

"They're always out on the bayou. What are they supposed to do? Turn around with a boat full of tourists to come back to deal with the damned goats?"

"Good point." Bailey gave Zander a look and they both grinned.

Knox was clearly put out, but he was also reasonable about the whole thing. "She *never* herds them back to the barn."

"Are these the same goats Zeke tried to kill last night?" Jill asked.

"They are," Michael confirmed.

"Were you just waiting for Benny to show up to take care of the goats?" Jill asked Zeke.

She felt his fingers grab the tips of her ponytail and give a playful tug, but he answered, "I saw something dart out in front of me and I swerved to miss it."

"But once you knew it was a goat, and that there were more of them, you were thinking Benny would come and round them up so you didn't have to actually take them back to the barn, right?" Jill asked.

"I figured she'd already herded them to the motel, actually."

"And you were just going to let her keep them there until the motel manager called Knox?"

The big man growled.

"I had a concussion," Zeke said quickly.

Jill lifted a brow. "Are you saying that the concussion influenced all of your actions last night and that you can't be held responsible for anything you did?"

He gave her a slow grin. "Oh no, things cleared up nicely after I got that *ibuprofen* from you."

She returned the grin. Then realized the entire table was watching them.

With interest.

And that Michael knew at least enough of the story—like the part where Zeke had gone back to her room with her—to make them even more interested.

"So if the goats keep getting out, why would you not just fix the gates and the pen?" Jill asked, trying to change the subject.

They all laughed.

"We've definitely tried that. There's one goat who always can figure a way out though," Bailey said.

"We don't call him Satan for nothing," Zander said.

"You call him Satan?" Jill asked. Wow, none of these people were very nice to goats.

"We *definitely* call him Satan," Knox said.

"But the girls decided that was mean, so they make everyone call him Stan," Bailey said.

Jill looked at Zeke. "The girls?"

"Tori, Maddie, and Juliet, my cousins' wives, and Kennedy, one of my cousins."

Yeah, this place was a lot like Bliss. Everyone was related to everyone else.

"Don't worry, you'll meet them all soon enough," Zeke said.

Worried wasn't exactly what she was feeling. More like exasperated. Already.

But if these people were one big happy, boisterous family, and Griffin was a part of it because of Charlie and his partner, Tori, Jill realized that avoiding all of this would take some work.

It was definitely one reason she'd liked living in a bigger city. The bigger the place, the more anonymous you could be and the more your business stayed your own. Small talk and gossip and just hanging around seemed like such a waste of time. Didn't these people know the planet was dying around them?

The climate was changing, water levels were rising, and entire animal species were edging closer and closer to extinction.

She knew from experience that it could be difficult to make people understand how penguins that lived almost entirely on an island just north of the equator had anything to do with their own lives. But that was one of the beauties of the work that zoos did.

Initially, Jill had thought she would travel the world and literally get her hands on penguins in their natural habitats. But as she'd grown up and learned more, she realized that zoos, animal parks, and preserves did a lot of important educational work as well. These relatively small groups of humans who cared about the animals directly weren't big enough to save them by themselves. Larger groups *had* to become interested.

Jill took a deep breath. She knew she sometimes let her passions and personal mission cause her to judge other human beings and how they chose to spend their time and resources. It was part of the reason she'd chosen to bring the penguins to Autre versus anywhere else.

She knew Griffin. She knew Donovan's reputation. She'd also met Griffin's friend Fiona who ran a large animal park in Florida. She knew they were all passionate about wildlife and conservation efforts. If she was going to immerse herself in this penguin project, she was going to need like-minded people around her. Who wouldn't think she was entirely crazy.

She glanced at the hot tattooed guy next to her, who had already gotten her off track and had her sitting in a rundown restaurant by the bayou waiting for a *brunch* she didn't want instead of talking about her new penguin habitat. And she realized that perhaps he wasn't someone she should spend a lot of time with.

That was too bad. He was not just hot, but funny, charming, and sweet. He'd kept her from panicking about the alligator in her yard, and he'd remodeled her bathroom and bedroom in the old house even when she hadn't returned his emails.

"Come on, let's just rock-paper-scissors this thing and get it over with," Bailey said. "If it ends up being my job today, I need to get the goats back home so I can get out and check on the alligator nuisance call from yesterday."

"You do alligator nuisance calls?" Jill asked.

"I'm the one people call if there's an alligator some place they shouldn't be."

"There was an alligator in my backyard this morning," Jill said. "Zeke took care of it, but I'd love to have your phone number for next time."

"Your backyard?" Bailey said.

"She's the one I'm remodeling Mary's house for."

Bailey's eyes went round. "So you two are neighbors now."

Jill nodded. "Evidently. Who's Mary?" she asked Zeke.

"Mary was one of my grandfather's sisters. That was her house until she passed a few years back."

"So I'm living in one of your family homes?" Jill asked. "Are you sure that's all right?"

"There are still a couple houses available for anyone else who needs one. But everybody's pretty taken care of right now. And you saw the place. It was definitely the one that needed the most work."

Jill rolled her eyes. "I'm going to need to have a talk with my realtor."

Zeke laughed. "We told Stuart that he'd get free bread

pudding for the next two months if he talked you into the house."

"You knew you had to *bribe* the realtor to sell that place?"

"We honestly did not think that he would manage it." Zander said. "Then again, we expected most people to check the house out before they bought it."

"Guess we didn't expect the new penguin veterinarian to be quite so low maintenance," Zeke agreed.

She didn't really have a response to that. After all, it was her fault she'd ended up with a house that needed renovation from basement to attic.

"Anyway, I'm happy to give you my number if you ever need anything," Bailey said. "But I have to warn you, your backyard isn't officially a place we would remove an alligator from."

"What do you mean?" Jill asked, suddenly concerned.

"Your backyard is basically part of the bayou. The alligators are protected there. That's their natural habitat."

"So you're saying that when people in other parts of town call you to remove an alligator, you technically bring it *to* my backyard," Jill said.

"Kind of," Bailey admitted. "Not actually, of course. All of that land is private Landry property, so the state wouldn't be able to relocate an animal there. However, it is protected land and while the Landry family can do most anything they want with it, there are a few rules they have to follow."

Zeke's hand moved from the back of her chair to the spot on Jill's upper back between her shoulder blades.

His big palm covered the entire space and she immediately felt the heat soaking in through her shirt. The heavy, warm touch was actually comforting. She took a deep breath and looked at him.

"Bailey can't, in her official capacity, come and remove your alligators. But I'm right next door and I'm happy to take care of anything you need."

Zander laughed and Michael gave a short cough.

Jill rolled her eyes. "I'm going to remember that, and I assume that comes with a twenty-four seven offer. So even if there's a *need* at three a.m., you're happy to answer my call."

Zeke's grin grew. "I'll give you a key. You don't even have to call."

"I'll have the Bat phone, you know," Donovan inserted. "Well, the goat phone. You can call me too."

"You're taking the phone?" Knox said. "I didn't agree to any online marketing budget for your Wildlife on Main Street show."

"Wildlife on Main Street," Donovan repeated. Then he said, "Or Going Wild on Main Street. Ties in with Gone Wild."

"*Anyway*, I didn't agree to that," Knox said.

"Yet," Donovan added.

"You sure about that yet?" Knox asked.

"There *is* a Methodist church full of goats right now that you are either going to have to take care of or put up with Zander bitching about having to take care of," Donovan said. "And those goats have definitely pooped by those pews by now."

"Puts a whole new spin on 'holy shit'," Bailey quipped. The guys groaned as she got up from her chair with a little laugh. "Okay, I seriously have to get to work. I would certainly assume that the town cop, fire chief, and city manager would also have more to do." She looked at each of the men pointedly.

"Fine. Go. Leave us with the goat shit," Zander grumped. "Seems about right that this is what my career has been reduced to."

"*You* left the force in New Orleans," Michael pointed out. "You knew what being the sheriff in this part of the world would be like."

Bailey took a couple of steps but grimaced and limped on her one foot as she rounded the edge of the table.

"I take it you saw Chase this past weekend?" Zeke asked.

"Good thing he's in medical school," Bailey said with a nod.

Jill sent Zeke a questioning look. Then regretted it. She didn't care who Chase was. Well, she *shouldn't*. He was one more person in this huge list of people that seemed to interact on a regular basis around here.

But she was curious, she had to admit.

"Chase is Bailey's fiancé. He's at medical school in D.C. They are both perfectly normal, successful, competent people. When they're apart. But whenever they're together, they are accident-prone, klutzy, and one or both of them ends up bruised, bleeding, or limping."

Jill's eyes widened and she looked at Bailey. In spite of not wanting to be interested in the stories that seemed to be swirling just under the surface with this group she was.

"Are you all right?" she asked.

Bailey nodded. "Since falling in love with Chase, I've gotten very used to staying in and taking ibuprofen."

Jill didn't press for more details, but dammit she kind of wanted to.

She was amused to watch the men, including Donovan, all make a fist, pump their arms three times, and then choose a sign for rock, paper, or scissors.

Knox and Zander both chose paper, Michael and Donovan chose scissors.

Knox and Zander groaned in unison then turned to face one another. Again, they did the fist pump and chose their sign.

This time Knox went with rock while Zander went with paper.

"Whoo-hoo!" Zander crowed. "Paper beats rock."

"I hate everything about this," Knox informed them.

He pushed to his feet and Jill watched as his big frame unfolded.

The guy was huge.

He ran a hand through his long hair, adjusted his glasses, straightened his dress shirt, and looked at them all.

"And after I get the goats back to the barn, I get to figure out where in the budget we can possibly divert funds to pave the road that leads to the petting zoo. The fish market is complaining that the increased traffic along the dirt road is kicking up too much dust in the air. Your family's petting zoo is a pain in my ass."

Zeke grinned. "And, of course, you asked them about their increased profits over the past three months from visitors to the swamp boat tours and petting zoo who stop at the market on their way out, right? And the fish we've agreed to buy from them for the otters?"

"I didn't have to ask," Knox said. "It's obvious. They put up a whole new stand. And now the whole farmer's market wants to relocate down there."

"Exactly."

Zander got to his feet as well, and shook his head. "You don't think *I'm* happy about it, do you? Do you know how many parking tickets and fender benders I've had to respond to? Things were a hell of a lot quieter when most of the visitors to the swamp boat tours came on buses from the hotels in New Orleans. Now all these people in the surrounding area want to drive down here themselves. Everyone who lives here can see the bayou on their own but not everybody has a lemur in their backyard."

"You do realize that we're going to have to talk about alligator deterrence around the animal park," Bailey said. "The more small animals you bring in, the more potential for alligators to start coming closer, looking for food."

Jill felt how wide her eyes went now. She glanced at Zeke. It wasn't that she thought Zeke could fix any and all issues with alligators stalking the small animals of a petting zoo, but for some reason her instinct was to look at him first.

"Don't worry, Kansas. We've got protections around the pens that are close to the bayou for sure."

"Alligators would definitely stalk goats." Jill frowned and looked around the group. "Especially baby goats. And you have llamas, right? Alligators could take down a small llama."

"They're alpacas, actually," Zeke told her.

"Still."

They could also hunt and eat a penguin. The habitat seemed very secure from what she'd seen this morning, but when they went back over she was going to look at it with new eyes. Being from Kansas and Nebraska, alligators were not something that she thought about on a regular basis.

"Yes, we've taken all of that into consideration," Bailey said. "I'm sorry, I didn't mean to worry you. It's just something these guys need to be aware of when we're talking about impacts the animal park is having on the town and local area."

"Absolutely," Jill agreed. "These are all important considerations. The more animals you bring in, the more scents and sounds the alligators are going to pick up and it would make sense that they would start moving in closer."

"We have measures in place," Zeke said again. "We all know how to handle gators."

Jill gave a little shudder. "So I need to be on the lookout for them in places other than just my backyard?"

"Absolutely," Zander said. "Front yard, under your porch, your car—"

"Okay, got it," Jill interrupted.

Zander grinned at her. "Don't worry. Zeke's not the only neighbor you know. I'm right on the other side."

"Really? And do you have food in your house?" She glanced at Zeke.

Zander nodded. "I do. What are you into?"

Zeke's hand moved from the middle of her upper back to the back of her neck, under her hair. Now they were skin to skin. The heat intensified. He didn't even curl his fingers into her neck, but the hold was decidedly possessive. "I've got everything she needs."

Jill looked from one twin to the other. It was clear that Zeke was giving his brother a warning.

He was warning another guy off? That was presumptuous. They were going to have a little fling at most. He couldn't be staking a claim like this publicly in front of all the other men.

Of course, she wasn't actually going to consider hooking up with his brother.

Strangely, looking back and forth between the two men who were identical twins, she found that she wasn't attracted to Zander. In a purely empirical sense, Zander was extremely good-looking and sexy just like Zeke. But she didn't feel any spark with him. Whereas Zeke's index finger dragging up and down the side of her neck had her nipples tightening and heat gathering between her legs.

"Okay," Zander said. "But if you need a cup of *sugar* or anything, you know where to find me."

He definitely put an innuendo emphasis on sugar.

Zeke gave a little growl that everyone at the table could hear.

And they all laughed at him.

Jill did like this banter. It reminded her of how she and Evan and Parker and even the quieter Noah sometimes teased.

It was the sign of true affection and friendship. Clearly Zeke didn't take Zander's flirting with her seriously, but Zander felt comfortable pushing his twin's buttons.

She also kind of liked that one of his buttons seem to be her and having another man flirting with her.

Which was stupid and dangerous and a sure way of making things unnecessarily complicated. She didn't want Zeke to be jealous. She didn't want the other men in town to think that she and Zeke were exclusive. She didn't want *Zeke* to think they were exclusive. Because she didn't want to be exclusive.

Not that she intended to date anyone else, or even sleep with anyone else. One guy was more than enough. And that was the problem. She didn't want Zeke attached to her and thinking that *he* couldn't date anyone else. She could not fulfill anyone's expectations for a relationship other than in the bedroom. It wouldn't be fair to him. And even more, it would be complicated for her to constantly be having to tell him she couldn't go out, couldn't come over, couldn't have dinner, and so on and so on.

The only relationships she could focus on at the moment were the ones between the black and white endangered birds that were going to be here in three days.

# 9

As everyone else finally said their goodbyes and headed off to work, the woman from behind the bar arrived at the table with another older woman. And an older man.

"Jill, this is my grandmother, Ellie," Zeke said.

Ellie gave them both smiles. "Here you go." She set a plate down in front of Jill first.

"And this is Cora. She's my grandmother in every way but blood," Zeke said as the shorter, plumper woman with short curly hair slid a plate in front of Zeke. "Thanks."

Cora patted Zeke's shoulder. "Hello, darling," Cora greeted Jill.

"And don't forget these." The man with them sat down two cups of coffee, two glasses of orange juice, and two glasses of water.

Jill smiled at them all even as she was inwardly gritting her teeth. She was meeting his family. She'd met his twin brother and a few of his friends. Now she was meeting not just his grandmother but his grandfather and a woman who was clearly as close to the family as his grandparents.

She understood how relationships like Zeke and Cora's

worked. Her own grandmother's best friend had been a pseudo-grandmother to Jill as well. Which was exactly how life in Bliss was more complicated than in Omaha. She didn't just have her family—which was large and extended, though nothing like the Landrys seemed to be—but she also had all the people who were important to all of the generations of her family.

Truly, her grandmother's last birthday party had been on par with the town's annual Founder's Day celebration. The whole town had turned out, and they'd had to have it at the park to accommodate the crowd. And the party had gone on all day long.

Jill hadn't gotten a lick of work done until ten o'clock that night and she'd been up until two. And extremely crabby the next day. Which her mother and grandmother had both pointed out.

"It's nice to meet you all," she said sweetly.

"Very nice to meet you. We've been excited for you to show up. So interesting to have penguins coming to town," Ellie said.

"It's wonderful that Griffin and Tori were willing and able to help me relocate them here," Jill said. "Giving them a very safe and secure and *quiet* place to breed is imperative to the success of the program."

Jill said it mostly to gauge the reaction. Did people here understand conservation and propagation programs? Did they understand that this was not going to be just another exhibit in their petting zoo?

"Tori and Griffin are wonderful," Ellie said, her affection and pride evident in even those simple words.

"Charlie already ordered the most adorable stuffed penguins for the gift shop," Cora said. "Everyone's very excited."

Right. It was just that "everyone" and "excited" were two words that were the opposite of what she was hoping for.

"You didn't bring her eggs Benedict?" Zeke asked, checking out the plates of food that had been set down in front of them.

Jill focused, taking inventory. Zeke's plate had eggs Benedict and hash browns on it. But hers looked like a bowl of oatmeal.

Oatmeal wasn't really the cold, fruity cereal she most loved, but it was an okay substitute.

"You ever had grits?" Ellie asked.

Jill looked up at her. "Heard of them, but never had them."

"It's like cream of wheat but it's made with cornmeal. Most of us down here like them savory with seasonings and cheese and hot sauce. But you can also eat them sweet. Some people will tell you that's blasphemy, but I was thinking maybe that would be something you'd like to try," Ellie said.

She looked up at her, surprised. "Did Zeke tell you I like cereal?"

Ellie looked at her grandson, then back to Jill. "No. Zeke hasn't told me anything about you at all."

Her tone definitely indicated that she thought Zeke knew some things about Jill, however.

"So what made you think I might like this?" Jill asked.

Ellie put a hand on her hip. "You know all about penguins. I know all about food. You handle those pretty black and white birds and I'll handle the feeding people around here."

Okay, well fair enough. She certainly was no great connoisseur when it came to Louisiana breakfast food.

Jill studied the bowl of grits. She had to admit that the idea of having someone else cooking for her was appealing. She'd done lots of food delivery when she was in Omaha. It saved time. While someone else was preparing her food and bringing it to her, she could work. And it was definitely better than buying her own food that would go bad or would make portions far too big for a single person to eat alone.

She hadn't had anyone cooking for her since she'd moved away from Bliss though.

Ellie shoved the sugar bowl, a bowl of butter, and a shaker of brown powder toward Jill from the other end of the table.

"Doctor them up with the butter and sugar. You can add cinnamon too. I like them that way."

Leo shuddered. "Sweet grits. That's a travesty."

Ellie shushed him. "Leave her be."

"If you like sweets in the morning, you need to try the biscuits and strawberry rhubarb jam. Or cinnamon rolls. Or her cornbread."

Jill looked at Ellie. "You make all of that?"

Ellie laughed. "No, Cora does. But he's right. Anything you want, honey."

"You must have a huge menu."

"The menu is basic," Ellie said, waving her hand. "We make a couple things each night. They work as the special. That's what most people eat. And that, of course, varies each night. But if people come and want something special and we've got the ingredients for it, we make it."

Cora nodded. "You just let me know what you like, honey."

Jill swallowed. She wasn't planning on coming back. Cold cereal at home was so much easier. But damn, she hadn't had a cinnamon roll in forever. And she really liked eggs Benedict, as a matter of fact.

"Thank you. That's so nice. I'll keep that in mind."

Ellie, Leo, and Cora hovered for just a moment, and Zeke finally said, "The penguins don't get here for a few days. She's not going to just pull one out of her pocket."

Ellie swatted him on the shoulder, but the three of them moved off and back to work.

"They're really that excited about the penguins?"

Zeke cut into his breakfast, but gave her a look that clearly said, *seriously?* "Fuck yeah. penguins are awesome. And to have them right here in Autre...who would've thought?"

Dammit, these people were so nice. And they were excited

about her penguins. She really wanted to give the penguins a quiet, peaceful place to lay their eggs and hatch a whole bunch of new babies. A bunch of loud, enthusiastic Cajuns clustering around watching would not be conducive.

What if the penguins wouldn't breed? What if they didn't lay viable eggs? What if the eggs wouldn't hatch? What if the hatchlings didn't survive?

"You're overthinking." Zeke pulled her bowl of grits closer to him, reached for the sugar, butter, and cinnamon and started adding them to her bowl.

"Hey," she protested.

"You don't know what you're doing. Let me show you how this should be."

*You don't know what you're doing.*

He wasn't talking about the penguins. She knew that. Everyone here thought she was a penguin expert. She was, of course. At least relative to anyone else here. But she was definitely feeling a little unsure.

Zeke pushed the bowl back to her and handed her a spoon. "Taste it."

She wasn't really that hungry suddenly. "I'm okay."

"Stop being a diva. Taste the grits."

She looked at him with surprise. A diva? She hadn't been called a diva before. "I'm just not hungry."

"Bullshit. You haven't eaten this morning. And you burned *a lot* of calories last night."

He gave her a grin that made her tingle in spite of the niggling thoughts of being a penguin fraud.

"Besides, once you try this you will be hungry."

Deciding that arguing with him was also a waste of time, she took the spoon from his fingers and dipped into the bowl. She took a small taste.

Huh. Not bad. She didn't mind oatmeal and cream of wheat

and this had a perfect combination of sugar and cinnamon. She looked at Zeke.

He smiled. "Right?"

"Yeah. Okay, you were right." She took another bite.

He watched her eat for a minute or so, munching on a strip of bacon. After she had taken about four bites, he pushed his plate toward her. "Okay, now try this."

He'd eaten about half. But there was plenty still left. The portions here were huge.

"You don't like grits?"

"Grits are fine. Sometimes. But they're no eggs Benedict."

"Grits are probably more my thing though," she told him. "I like simple and straightforward. Eggs Benedict is... complicated. There's lots of ingredients and it takes a lot more time."

"I hear you loud and clear, Kansas. Taste the fucking eggs Benedict."

She really did believe that he understood her analogy with breakfast food and how she preferred her life and relationships.

But she still leaned over and cut off a piece of the eggs Benedict. She took the bite, fully expecting to enjoy it.

What she hadn't expected, however, was to moan out loud.

"Oh my God," she said, after she swallowed. "That's amazing."

He lifted a hand and tugged on the end of a strand of hair. "A little extra time and a few extra ingredients are sometimes worth it."

Yeah, she didn't miss his analogy either.

She also didn't miss that it was the morning after, they barely knew one another, and he was already pressing for more.

"I'll give you that," she said. "But I don't have time for eggs Benedict in my mornings. And the grits do the job. When all is said and done, all of the food gets broken down into the same parts that your body uses for nutrition and energy. All I need are the calories to get me through the day. It doesn't really matter where they come from. So I definitely opt for simple."

"You're not wrong," he said. "But if you're only focused on what happens *after*, you're missing a lot of pleasure of the initial experience."

Yeah, yeah.

"Here you go."

They were interrupted by another woman. This one looked to be in her mid-fifties. She had brown hair the same mahogany color as Zeke's and the same brown eyes. She set a paper grocery bag on the table next to Zeke.

"Hello," she said to Jill. "I'm Elizabeth, Ezekiel's mom."

"Hello." And now she'd met his mother. Who called him by his full name. Wonderful.

"And you just happened to be coming in here and thought to bring me this...stuff?" Zeke asked, pushing the bag further under the table.

"Of course not," Elizabeth said. "Your brother texted Fletcher, who texted your dad, who texted me that you were here with the pretty new penguin veterinarian."

Jill pressed her lips together. Yep, she knew exactly how texting trees like that worked.

Zeke didn't say anything.

Elizabeth nodded and addressed Jill. "And he's not saying anything about that because he would have done the very same thing. I swear Leo and Ellie are the only people who spread more gossip than my boys."

"Knox," Zeke finally said. "Knox knows as much."

"Knox might *know* as much, but I said *spread*. He doesn't talk about what he knows the way you and Alexander do."

And Zander's full name was Alexander. Okay, then.

"Anyway, it's very nice to meet you, Jill."

"Thank you, you too, Mrs. Landry."

"Oh, Lord, there are *way* too many of those around here. Call me Elizabeth."

She really had a point about the number of Landrys. Mrs. or otherwise.

"And I used the ocean breezes dryer sheets for you," Elizabeth said to Zeke. "But if you like them, you'll have to get me some more. I'm out."

Jill looked from his mother to Zeke, then leaned to look into the paper bag Elizabeth had given him.

He pushed it further away with his foot.

"I'll see you both later," Elizabeth said with a smile. Then she turned and headed out.

Zeke blew out a breath.

"Ocean breezes dryer sheets?" Jill asked.

"She was...kidding."

Jill leaned in and propped her chin on her hand. "Was she? Or did she just hand you a grocery bag full of clean clothes that she washed, dried, and folded for you?"

"She...helps me out sometimes when I get really busy with projects. Like huge, impressive, never-before-attempted-in-Autre penguin enclosures."

"Your mom does your laundry for you," Jill summarized.

"*Sometimes.*"

"Okay."

"She *likes* doing it. She says she loves it when we let her mother us."

"Okay." Jill picked her fork back up.

"It makes her feel good."

Jill took a bite.

"And she uses those dryer sheets for other people too."

Jill swallowed and shook her head. "Zeke, I would *love* to have someone else do my laundry. I am not judging you. Go for it. Let her do it all, all the time. Hell, throw mine in with yours if you get a chance. I'll buy the next box of dryer sheets. And you can pick the scent."

He paused with his mouth open. Then shut it. Frowned. Then opened it again. "Really?"

"Of course. Having someone do my laundry for me? That's right up there with grocery delivery services."

He nodded, seeming to accept that. That was good. She *totally* meant it.

"By the way, we don't have grocery delivery services here."

She sighed. Yeah, she'd figured.

---

I t was amazing to Zeke how much he liked watching Jill eat grits. Grits were not a sexy food. They weren't even all that interesting, to be honest. They were a side dish, a base, a filler. But watching her eat the grits, when it was clearly out of her norm, and because he'd encouraged it, made him stupidly happy.

She also ate a third of his eggs Benedict and stole his last two pieces of bacon. And he happily gave them up. Which was a sure sign that he liked this girl more than most.

It was very clear Jill was holding herself back. She'd admitted as much when she'd told him she was from a small town. She knew what it was like for people to get involved in her business.

Jill was obviously a very independent person. She was used to taking care of herself. She liked things a very certain way and in the short time he'd known her she'd already made it very clear that she liked things simple and straightforward.

Zeke could get on board with that. Simple and straightforward was a great way to be. When things went as expected, it made things much less dramatic. And with a big family like his, there always seemed to be some drama, even when things were going smoothly.

Where he and Jill differed was that she clearly wasn't used to other people doing things for her. Whereas Zeke not only had a lot of people doing things for him all the time, but he absolutely loved it.

He hadn't made himself breakfast in he couldn't remember how long. And while cold cereal was fine, why would he eat that when he could drive a mile up the road and have eggs Benedict and hash browns or French toast or just about any other breakfast food made by one of the best cooks in the state of Louisiana?

Half an hour later, they pulled up by the penguin habitat next to Griffin's truck.

They found the other vet pacing in front of the habitat on the phone. It sounded as if someone was calling him about an animal that needed his attention. He was not just the veterinarian for the animals in the petting zoo but was the general vet for the local area as well. He and Tori saw cats, dogs, cows, horses, and everything in between.

"Hey, guys," Griffin greeted, disconnecting his call. "I've got to head out soon. Going to have a new colt today."

"No problem, everything here should be mostly done," Zeke said looking at Jill. "You checked the place out this morning, what do you think?"

"It really looks great. I'm thrilled that it's finished. I do want to do a little bit more with the rock formations," she said. "Did you get my email about the man-made nesting areas they're building in the Galápagos ?"

"You mean the article you attached and said, 'read this'?"

"Yes."

"I got the email."

Jill narrowed her eyes. "Did you read the article?"

"I opened the article and skimmed it. Then I emailed you back some follow-up questions."

"Which I responded to."

"Yes, and you referred me to paragraph six on page two."

Jill nodded. "Right."

"That's not really the same thing as just telling me what you wanted."

"What I wanted was what they described in paragraph six on page two."

"Well, I put the rocks in there, and figured you could tell me how you wanted them set up when you got here."

"So you waited until I got here to hold your hand through finishing the project?"

"I guess that's one way to put it."

"Why couldn't you just read the article and do what it said? The article gave you not only the instructions for it, but also the reason behind it."

"I'm the contractor, Jill. I just need you to tell me how you want things built, not all the reasons why."

"I want them built like it describes in paragraph six on page two," Jill said, clearly growing exasperated. "You're the guy who wanted me to tell you what kind of knobs to put on the drawers in my new bathroom. Clearly, you do care about details."

"I care about the details *you* care about. When you didn't email me back, even about the drawer pulls, I figured that where these rocks were set up was another tiny detail."

"But I—"

"Do I need to be here for this?" Griffin interrupted.

Jill blew out a breath. "No. We just need the rock formations configured so that they mimic what they have on the islands. The penguins need to have very safe and secure areas to build their nests. The deeper and more enclosed these little caves are, the greater the chance they will use them and will produce viable eggs that will hatch."

"There's a chance they won't lay eggs?" Zeke asked.

"We're not really sure what kind of effect the different climates, and of course the huge move across the country, and all of the changes will have on them. A.J. was not successful breeding them within captivity. I'm concerned that there's going to be some disruption because A.J. is no longer around."

"The penguins were attached to him?" Zeke asked.

"Lots of animals grieve," Jill said with a nod. "But all they will really know is that he's no longer their caregiver and that their entire environment is different. They may be disrupted just having someone new in their environment. It was part of the program that he would be the only one interacting with them so that they didn't attach to many humans. But truly, once he knew that he was sick, he probably should've brought me in so that the penguins could have gotten used to me too."

Jill felt the rising bubble of panic climbing from her stomach up into her chest and to her throat. There were so many unknowns. The penguin population was so fragile and even these eight mattered a lot to the survival of the species. It wasn't that these specific animals were fragile and vulnerable. They were healthy and demonstrated normal behaviors. Except breeding, of course. But she honestly didn't know what all of these interventions and changes would have on them.

"So then making nests and laying eggs is the most important thing?" Zeke asked.

"Yes. Absolutely. We're trying to increase the numbers of these penguins. We estimate there are fewer than six hundred breeding pairs alive today, so they are at risk for being totally lost." Jill felt the anxiety swirling through her. "We're hoping these independent captivity programs can help save them from extinction. But we have to know that they are able to thrive in these environments. We're experimenting with what those environments look like now. We have way more questions than answers. We're trying to mimic their natural environments as much as possible, of course, but captivity is different from the wild no matter what. And just as A.J. had everything set up, he got sick and now that he's passed, packing them up and moving them several states away could end up being detrimental. But we really don't know."

Zeke stepped in front of her and met her eyes directly. "Simple. Straightforward. You need these rock formations to be a certain way so the penguins will lay their eggs and make more penguins."

Jill took a shaky breath. "Yes. At this moment, the most important thing is getting those rock formations right."

Zeke gave her nod. "All I needed to know."

Jill took another breath. This one deeper, where she actually felt it expand her lungs. He'd just cut through all the B.S.

She liked that.

She felt that all of the humans around and interacting with the penguins should understand their part of the bigger picture. But he had a point. If, at this moment before the penguins got here, they needed to have the habitat constructed as close to perfectly as they could, then she needed to communicate clearly what that meant.

"You okay?" Griffin asked her.

It took her a moment to pull her eyes from Zeke's. "Um...no. I'm freaking out a little bit. There's so much pressure here. I need to keep these penguins alive. First of all. Then I need to make sure that they thrive. I have three breeding pairs and two juveniles who will hopefully breed eventually as well, and I need to get at least one of them, if not a couple of them, knocked up soon."

Griffin chuckled. "There's no reason to think that it won't work here, though, right?"

"This project with private ownership is fairly new. We don't have any reason to think it *won't* work, but we actually don't have any data to prove that it will. Will limiting their interactions with humans be better? Will having them in private, quiet spaces be better? Would they be better off if we could just have protected areas actually in the Galápagos? I mean, that seems obvious, right? But that's not the best solution in some ways."

"You can't just leave them there?" Zeke asked.

She looked at him again. He actually seemed interested and maybe a bit concerned.

Well...he asked...

"There are a number of things that threaten them. They have natural predators, of course, like sharks and giant sea lions and fur seals. Occasionally they are caught up accidentally by fishermen too. Because they are air-breathers and have to come up for air while swimming, oil spills and pollution are a huge threat. But the two biggest dangers to them right now are climate change and invasive species introduced to the islands.

"Climate change is causing more El Niño events which affects their food apply. When their food supply diminishes, they will skip nesting and won't hatch new penguins. When it's really severe, some of the adults starve.

"Additionally, cats have been introduced to the islands and they will attack and kill the penguins. The other invasive species is mosquitoes that carry avian flu. An outbreak could wipe out what's left of the penguins on the islands."

Jill paused to take a breath, but found Zeke was still listening intently. He was watching her with a mix of fascination and surprise. Possibly she was telling him facts that he found surprising. But it was also possible he was surprised that anyone could just talk non-stop about penguins like this.

Well, if he wanted to hang out with her, he was going to have to be okay with that.

"The Galápagos Islands are the only place that these penguins exist indigenously. So fighting those threats on the islands is important, but they're huge and it takes a long time to change any of that. Climate change alone is an almost over-whelming threat. So out of desperation, conservation groups have relocated some penguins to various zoos and animal parks.

"But this private group of investors decided to get together and start a new program. Having private ownership of groups of penguins cuts through lots of regulatory red tape. There is licensing and specific permissions given—these aren't black market acquisitions—and we're sharing ideas and data and working together to make the penguins successful in the program, but these people have been definitely been given special privileges to own penguins that not just everyone could get.

"Basically, the penguins become pets of individuals who have the money and knowledge to support them. Decisions can be made faster and changes implemented. Trials can be conducted. The birds get more individualized attention from the veterinarians that are caring for them. There are some advantages, certainly."

She finally stopped talking and crossed her arms, pressing her lips together.

Zeke was either going to think this was intriguing or he was going to think she was incredibly weird.

Weird would get him to leave her alone though. That would be good. She wouldn't be distracted that way.

But she wanted him to find her—the *penguins*, she meant the penguins—interesting.

The more people who found the penguins and their plight interesting, the more help they would potentially get.

Griffin looked at Zeke. "You know how you love how passionate Fiona and Tori and Charlie and everyone is about animals?"

Zeke nodded.

"Jill is the same, except that *all* of her passion is focused on penguins. So all the worry and enthusiasm and willingness to fight get directed at one particular animal—one that's endangered—and Jill gets...a little worked up."

Jill frowned at Griffin. "Worked up? About now being solely responsible for keeping eight endangered animals alive that I have been in love with my entire life? With the only real guidance being 'do whatever you think is best'? Everyone else in the program is looking to me to guide *them*. But the program is new and—"

Suddenly Zeke reached out, took her upper arm, and pulled her close.

Then he wrapped his big arms around her and gave her a bear hug.

For just a moment she was stunned. She wasn't a big hugger. She hugged people she was close to, but she lived far away from most of those people so hugging wasn't a daily occurrence. And she wasn't close to Zeke.

But he seemed perfectly at ease wrapping her up and squeezing her.

She felt a huge breath of oxygen rush into her lungs. Then it rushed out. She felt her muscles relax. And she felt her arms go up and around Zeke.

Her eyes closed and she just let him hold her.

Damn, that felt good. So she just leaned into it. A big hot guy who smelled good and felt even better, was pressing her up against his body. Who was she to fight it?

It seemed that he enjoyed it just as much because he held her until Griffin cleared his throat and asked, "And, again, do I need to be here?"

## 10

Z eke's arms loosened and Jill looked up at him. "What was that for?"

"I don't know how to give you advice about penguins. But you seemed to need a hug. And that I can do."

She wasn't much of a hugger... until now. If Zeke Landry would hug her whenever she started to get a little worked up about the penguins, not only would she get to press up against his big, hot, hard body a lot but it did actually seem to be helpful. Her heart rate had definitely slowed and the swirling tension in her stomach had loosened a bit.

She nodded. Even as she stepped back from him. "I might take you up on that."

"You know where to find me."

Jill turned to give Griffin a smile. "Thanks for greeting me this morning. But everything seems to be on track and mostly ready to go. The guys are showing up with the penguins on Thursday."

"Let's go make *sure* everything is ready," Zeke said.

"I'm going to head out and check on that horse then,"

Griffin said. "But if you need anything, you know how to get a hold of me and Charlie."

"Um, Griffin," Jill said. She wasn't sure this was the exact time to bring it up, but she wasn't sure when would be a good time. Probably the sooner the better. "Is there any issue with Charlie and the penguins?"

"What do you mean?" Griffin asked.

It had been clear last night that Charlie clearly had the gruff, semi–anti-social man wrapped around her finger.

"I just need to be sure that, Charlie, and everyone, understands what we're trying to do here with the penguins. I didn't bring them here to be an exhibition. They are here as part of a breeding program and to keep them safe. I don't want anyone thinking that they are just another attraction at the animal park. If I want to limit the number of people interacting with them, is she going to be okay with that?"

Even in the emails she had exchanged with Charlie it'd been clear that Charlie's mission and passion was growing the previous petting zoo into a larger animal attraction.

Griffin's frown deepened. "We haven't talked about it specifically. I don't know that she understands exactly what you're doing with the penguins, but she will when you explain it."

"So there is a chance that everyone is going to be confused and disappointed?" Jill asked, though it was more a statement than a question. "They all think they were adding penguins as another animal exhibit for the tourists."

"I suppose they do," Griffin said. "But I promise you that everyone will be on board with whatever you think is best."

"So people shouldn't be looking at the penguins?" Zeke asked.

"Not until we have some hatchlings," Jill said. "At least until then. If we can have some baby penguins then we'll know that keeping them here in this habitat in this climate with us as caretakers is going to work. But until then I feel like we need to control as many factors as we can. A lot of noise and traffic and human interaction could have a detrimental effect. And we just won't know until the penguins are here for a while."

Jill realized she sounded like a killjoy. People loved penguins. Penguins were incredibly cute and very interesting and not something most people ran into on a regular basis. They were a huge attraction at the Omaha zoo. She knew people would want to look at them. She was going to get to be the bad guy that brought cute, interesting penguins to town and then told everyone that they had to stay away. Great.

"If it's not good for the penguins, then we keep people away," Zeke said. "Right, Griffin?"

Jill watched the men. Griffin was a wildlife veterinarian. For as long as she'd known him, he had been a fierce protector of animals, and a huge advocate for their care.

Zeke, on the other hand, was a small town construction contractor. He said himself that he knew very little about penguins. So why did this feel like Zeke was the one being protective of the penguins and was warning *Griffin* about how he should respond to the situation?

"Of course. We will do whatever needs done to make the project successful, Jill," Griffin finally said.

"I appreciate that. I know this might put you in a weird position between me and the Landry family."

She was, of course, funding everything that was going into bringing the penguins to Louisiana. The Boys of the Bayou Gone Wild hadn't needed to come up with any money to construct the penguin habitat or plan for the care and feeding of the birds. Nor would they going forward. It really was just that they had the land and she'd wanted to be around other animal enthusiasts like Griffin, Fiona, and Tori. What they had done so far with Boys of the Bayou Gone Wild was impressive and being around like-minded people as she undertook this huge project had been comforting. But she didn't want to disappoint or upset anyone.

"The family will be fine." It was Zeke who spoke. "I'll make sure of it."

"You will?" Jill was surprised.

"Of course. I'll just explain that we're working to knock up a few penguins and we need some peace and quiet for that. My family's not great about peace and quiet, but they understand the general concept. Don't worry; I'll talk to them."

She definitely noted his use of the word "we". Again, there was that sense of protectiveness from him. She was finding that very endearing. And attractive. "I would...appreciate that."

"Sure. Everyone loves Griffin, especially Charlie, but sometimes the Landrys need to be talked to a certain way. I've got it covered."

Dammit, she was going to have to let him hang around.

Not only could he potentially be helpful, and with more than his hammer and nails, but she liked him. He'd gotten her shoes, fixed her grits, and hugged her. And if he could translate between her and his family, that would really be helpful.

"Thank you," she told him.

"But of course, we'll have to hang out," he said. "You're gonna have to teach me all about penguins so I can explain it to them."

"Hang out, huh?"

"Yeah, you have to help make me into a penguin ambassador."

Her lips twitched. "Penguin ambassador?"

"I mean, I can just tell them all to shut up and butt out, but the more I know about the penguins and why they need to be left alone, the better I can explain it."

"Aren't you the guy who just earlier said you don't need to know all the whys to things? You just need to know what I need done?"

Jill stood watching him think about that for a few seconds. Then she shook her head. This guy was unexpected. After she met him last night, she'd pegged him for a bad boy and had loved how talented he was between the sheets. And against the wall. And that desk chair...

She cleared her throat as her body heated.

Now today, he was so much more. He was funny, charming, and seemed captivated by the penguins. And maybe even by her. Which, dammit, was definitely appealing. Her professional passion had led to more than one person thinking she was a little strange. Her immediate family at the top of that list.

"So I *definitely* don't need to be here for *this*," Griffin said, looking back and forth between them. He started for his truck. "I'll let Zeke handle the Landrys at large, but I'll talk to Charlie."

"Thank you!" Jill called after him. "For everything!" she added.

She felt like a bitch for coming here and immediately shutting down all of the happy excitement over the penguins.

Griffin drove off, leaving just Jill and Zeke.

"Okay, let's get these rocks set up just right." He started for the gate to the enclosure. He pulled out the key, unlocked the gate, and then handed the key over. "It's all yours."

She felt a rush of adrenaline and she knew it was half excitement and half oh-shit-this-is-real-and-all-mine-and-I'm-in-charge-oh-shit.

She followed him inside. They went in through the penguin house to get to the island, no need to deal with wet shoes and clothes this time.

She directed him where she wanted the lava rocks that had been the one thing she had succeeded in bringing in from the Galápagos Islands, and he put them together exactly according to her specifications. Then she knelt and started digging. He joined her a moment later.

"What are we doing?"

But she noted that he started digging even before she answered the question.

"They need to be deeper."

He nodded and kept digging.

They worked together on the first one until Jillian was content. She wanted to have five nesting sites for the three breeding pairs, hoping that with some options, the penguins would each pick a site they liked.

"Do they always nest in the rocks like this?" Zeke asked.

"Usually. Sometimes they nest under bushes. Wherever they feel safe and protected and can keep the eggs cool. But the little rock caves seem to be the most popular. There's a group that travels to the islands twice a year and constructs multiple sites to supplement the natural ones so there are plenty."

"Won't they figure out they don't have any predators here?"

"Yes, maybe. Actually, food supply seems to be a better indicator of successful breeding and nesting. But they also use the rocks to keep their eggs in the shade and cool. Plus, a strange human coming in and out of the habitat and wanting to get close to observe the nests, could bother them. They'll need time to get used to..." She sighed. "Everything." There was so much going on for the penguins. And for her.

"You're willing to take this on all by yourself?"

Her eyes widened. "Definitely." In spite of the pressure and anxiety around it, Jill felt butterflies when she thought about having eggs in these nests in a few months. "This is what I've wanted to do my whole life and even if I didn't, like I said earlier, the fewer factors we have being introduced into their environment and situation, the better."

"That's a lot to take on yourself."

She shrugged. "I don't really have anything else going on." That was an understatement.

"Really? What do you do for fun?"

"Hang out with penguins."

He chuckled. "But that's your job."

"I picked it as my job because I couldn't think of anything more fun to do all day long. I don't really consider it work most days. I suppose that's why it's easy to lose track of time and let other obligations and relationships go."

"So the penguins have your heart?"

"Completely."

She knelt next to a bush and reached underneath to dig some of the dirt out. It would be a great place for a penguin pair to make a nest if they didn't like the rock formations.

Zeke crouched beside her. "So why penguins? I mean, Griffin's into all the wild animals. Tori loves all animals period. But you specifically like penguins. Do you really not like any other animals?"

Jill sat back on her heels and looked at him. There was something about Zeke that made her comfortable talking. Maybe it was just that he was asking questions. Which was kind of pathetic. Did she really not have people in her life that asked about her work?

But no, not really. Her mom and immediate family got tired of hearing about penguins so they definitely didn't ask. She'd been talking to them about penguins since she'd been eight years old.

Evan listened and thought what she did was cool, but he didn't have any particular interest that would cause him to probe further.

Griffin knew about her penguin love, of course, but again, he hadn't really probed, because he already knew a lot about the birds. Just like her co-workers and the researchers and vets she communicated with online already knew almost everything she knew about penguins.

Dan, her friend-with-benefits, had asked a few times but his eyes had glazed over about ten minutes in.

But Zeke had already heard her rant about the penguins and he was still asking for more.

"I do like all animals, of course. But I became a veterinarian specifically so I could work with penguins."

Zeke lifted a brow. "Wow, really?"

"I've loved them for as long as I can remember."

"Where did that start?"

Well, he kept asking questions. So he had to expect her to answer right? Even if the answer was strange or went on too long, that was his own fault. Besides, if he started to find her boring or strange, it would mean fewer trips back and forth between their two houses. Which could only be for the best.

"Honestly, I think it started with the books my mom read to me when I was little. She always picked books about finding your passion, and changing the world, and being who you were meant to be. The stories that she read to me and I liked the best were all about making a difference in the world and finding something that made you special and then celebrating it."

Zeke was watching her intently. He didn't seem bored. Yet.

"Then, when I was eight, my grandfather got me the book Mr. Popper's Penguins and we read it together. Have you ever read it?"

Zeke shook his head. "Nope."

"It's...whimsical," she said with a smile. "But it's...becoming my real life."

"How so?"

"It's about a man who longs to see the world and is fascinated with the exploration of the poles. He writes to an explorer he admires and the guy sends him a penguin."

Zeke laughed. "So, like the millionaire who gives you penguins in his will."

"Right. Well, that penguin gets lonely, so they get him a girlfriend from the local aquarium who is also lonely. They end up having a big family and the Poppers renovate their home to accommodate all the penguins. They are Antarctic penguins, so this involves ice and cold, of course."

Zeke grinned. "So a little different there. But I can see why you relate to having to come up with a way to house all the penguins."

"*Then*, it's so expensive to keep the birds, they decide to train them and make them into a traveling show, to make money." Jill looked down at her hands. "Eventually, though, Mr. Popper realizes that isn't good for penguins and he sends them all back to live in the wild, even though it breaks his heart."

Zeke was quiet for a long moment. Then he said, "And that's a little bit of why you're worried about your penguins being here for people to look at for money."

Her head came up. "That sounds insulting to your family, I know. I don't think they're doing any of this just for the money, Zeke."

"I know. And they're not. But sure, that's part of it. It's a business."

"I understand that."

"And this book is how you fell in love with penguins and determined to do what's right for them."

"After that, I wanted to learn all about penguins. For the next several Christmases and birthdays, my grandpa got me books about penguins, as well as stuffed penguins. Every summer, we took a trip to Omaha to the zoo and we spent half our time there with just the penguins." She could still get misty-eyed thinking about working in the same zoo she'd frequented as a child with her grandfather. "So they were special to me because of him, too. He died when I was fourteen and about that time, I read a book by Jane Goodall. Do you know who she is?"

"The lady who lived with the gorillas, right?"

"Chimpanzees," she corrected. "But yeah, that book really hit me. After that, I read everything I could find by and about

Jane. She was this force that didn't just go in and provide for the things she cared about, but made other people care about them too. I guess that, combined with all of the books about finding a way to make the world a better place and finding what you are especially good at made me realize that I wanted to do for penguins what Jane did for the chimps. That stuck with me all through high school and college. I was looking into different ways to work with penguins and realized that one of the paths was veterinary medicine. Now, I can't imagine doing anything else."

"So how did you meet A.J.?"

"He was just a nice little old man who came to the zoo every Thursday during the penguins' feeding hour. We just clicked. One project he was particularly passionate about was constructing a man-made island off of the Galápagos that could be protected from invasive species and tourism. He was working on that the entire time I knew him. But I had no idea that he actually *owned* penguins. These private investors are trying to keep that on the down low because there are groups that would probably have issue with penguins being kept in private captivity. But I'm incredibly touched and flattered by him leaving them to me."

"Why wouldn't he leave them to you? Who else would he possibly leave them to?"

"In retrospect, now knowing the whole story about when he got the penguins and when he was diagnosed, I feel like maybe he agreed to be a part of the program knowing that I would eventually take it over."

"And you're feeling the pressure," Zeke said.

"Huge pressure."

"You'll be great. You know everything you need to know, and have this great place to keep them, everything will be fine."

She studied him. Griffin had given her a mini pep talk as well, and she knew that the other investors in the group were confident in her capabilities. But there was something about Zeke believing in her that hit her differently.

Maybe it was because he didn't actually know what he was talking about. Or because he didn't know *her*. He didn't really know her credentials and even if he did, they wouldn't necessarily mean anything to him. The investors in the group knew her experience and education level. So did Griffin. And Griffin knew her history with penguins and her work ethic and her enthusiasm from being up close and around her in a work environment for a year.

Zeke didn't know any of that. He just knew what he'd seen so far. Either he was a little naïve and incredibly trusting, or he was trying to make her feel better. Either way, it was sweet. And it *was* making her feel better.

"Thank you for that."

"Anytime. Again, I don't know anything about penguins except they're cool as fuck. But I do know that beautiful women who are enthusiastic about doing good in the world are hot as hell."

She laughed softly. "You run into a lot of those?"

"Surprisingly, several here in Autre." He gave her a grin. "There's Tori, and Charlie has gotten all enthusiastic now. Jordan is really into the petting zoo, and how alpacas and other animals can help kids learn about disabilities and grief and depression and anxiety."

Jill felt her eyebrows rise. "Really?" That sounded incredibly interesting.

"Yep. And then there's Fiona. She gets excited about anything with four legs, fur, feathers, or fins. They're all beautiful women, of course, but I've definitely seen how much more gorgeous they all are when they get enthusiastic about these projects."

He tipped his head studying her face. "You're definitely no exception. Last night I was incredibly attracted to you and we had one of the hottest nights I can ever remember. But today, finding out all of the stuff you're into and all of the things you do, watching you light up when you talk about penguins, and even watching you worry about this program, has made me want you even more."

Jill's heart thumped against her chest wall and her stomach clenched. But she couldn't tell for sure if it was panic over that declaration or if it was excitement.

"You better watch yourself," she told him. "I don't want to break your heart."

"I appreciate that."

"I'm really not looking for a relationship," she felt compelled to say. "But I think we can definitely be friends."

"You know, I don't actually get the 'I hope we can still be friends' speech very often," he told her.

"Really? They don't want to be your friend after?"

"Sometimes they want more and when they can't get it, they get riled."

She gave a little snort. "Riled?"

"It makes it awkward in church when a girl I've known my whole life goes from bein' friendly to bein' snooty in one week. And my mom always knows why."

She outright laughed at that. "And what's your mom say about that?"

"Something like she says about everything I do. Last time she closed her eyes, shook her head, and said, 'Probably a madam in an Old West saloon'."

"What's that mean?" But Jill felt herself already grinning over the explanation that was coming.

"She figures she did something bad in a previous life to deserve the shenanigans of me and my brothers. Nothing too terrible. We're not *that* bad. But something sinful she's being punished for."

Jill snorted. "Your mom believes in reincarnation?"

"She's decided it's the only explanation."

Jill liked him. Dammit. She liked Dan, of course. But she liked him because he gave her exactly what she wanted. No strings attached, hot sex, no clinginess. Zeke on the other hand, was giving her a few things she was pretty sure she did not want. Like the temptation to know his family better. And the urge to spend more time with him.

And she still definitely liked him.

"Okay, then." He rubbed his hands down the thighs of his jeans and stretched to his feet. "I need to get to another project today. Do we have your rocks where you want 'em?"

She looked around the enclosure as she straightened. "Yes. They look good."

"Great."

"You have another project?" she asked.

"I actually have a house here in town to be workin' on too, but the owner won't tell me what she wants."

"Ugh. I get it. But, you'll be happy to know I've turned it over to my friend from back home. She's great. She'll answer all your questions."

"Well, hallelujah," he said. "As long as she tells me what *you* want."

"I don't care abou—"

He covered her lips with one big index finger. "Don't," he said simply.

She blew out a breath.

He moved his finger.

"Fine. Yes. She knows what I like." She had no idea if Cori actually knew her tastes. Jill didn't really have tastes. So, actually, whatever Cori picked would be Jill's taste, she supposed. "Whatever she says has my stamp of approval."

He nodded, but looked skeptical. "Fine. But your house is gonna have to wait a week or two now."

"What?"

"I started another project a town over. Helping a buddy with their new community center."

"But my house..."

"You got bumped down the list when you didn't answer my emails, Kansas," he told her with an unapologetic grin.

Well, dammit. She supposed she deserved that.

"Besides, you don't care where you live right?"

"I guess I was just hoping to catch you shirtless and sweaty with a toolbelt around your hips."

Now see, she should *not* have said that. Why had she said that? His eyes heated and he stepped in close.

"I'll bring my *toolbelt* over to your place any time you want."

Yeah, she wanted.

Crap.

"But you can use my fridge until we get you one."

She blinked at the sudden shift in topic.

"Oh. Thanks, that's really nice."

"Back door will always be unlocked."

"Okay."

"But I want to pet your penguins in exchange."

She gave a soft snort. "Is that innuendo?"

He grinned. "No. I actually want to pet the penguins. Is that possible?"

Damn, she kind of wanted him to flirt with her. But she nodded. "It is possible."

"Awesome. How about for every day you have stuff in my fridge I get twenty minutes of penguin petting?"

"I think that can be arranged."

Suddenly he stepped forward, reached up to cup the back of her head, and pulled her in and kissed her.

It was partly because she was surprised by the gesture that she didn't respond right away, and by the time she was leaning in and opening her mouth, he was already lifting his head. But he smiled down at her. "I'm glad I got to see you again. And if you find one of my socks in your motel room later—"

"I'll take it to your mom to throw in the laundry?"

He leaned in and kissed her quickly again, then let her go with a smile. "You're sassy."

Jill wasn't sure she'd ever been called sassy. Before she could come up with a response, he pivoted on the heel of his work boot and headed out of the penguin enclosure.

She watched him go. She wasn't quite sure what to think of Zeke Landry yet, but she was becoming more and more certain that she *was* going to be thinking about him.

And then, when she got home that night and found a loaf of bread, a jar of peanut butter, and a jar of strawberry jelly on her kitchen counter with a note that said, "This counts for twenty minutes of petting too. But you can decide if it's penguins I'm petting," she realized she was *definitely* going to be thinking of him.

And not smiling when thinking of him was simply impossible.

So, she decided to just avoid him.

## 11

S he was avoiding him.

By Sunday it seemed obvious.

The penguins had gotten to Autre on Thursday as planned. And no one had seen Jill since.

Apparently she was answering texts from Griffin but she'd also said she was fine, the birds were fine, and no, she didn't need anything.

Griffin, being Griffin, had been okay with that answer and had left her alone.

Zeke had too, but he'd been a lot less cool about it.

"You've been a grumpy ass for three days now," Zander told him. "And you've been bitching about her not returning your texts every time I see you. Knock it off."

"Well, it's annoying."

"Thought you weren't planning to work on her house for a couple of weeks anyway. You're still helping Jase with the Pork and Peach, right?"

"Yeah."

"So why are you texting her?"

His brother knew damned well why Zeke was texting Jill.

He liked her. He wanted her. He wanted to be sure she was okay. And he...fucking missed her.

He shoved a hand through his hair. "She's stressed about the penguins. Just checking on her."

"And how are *you* going to help with the penguins?" Zander asked. "You don't know anything about animals that could be helpful to her."

That was true. And yet, he'd had the feeling the other day at the penguin enclosure that he *had* been helpful. He'd helped calm her down. He'd made her smile. He'd helped her build penguin nesting sites at least.

When he should have been working on building things for humans.

He was kind of a mess.

"It's kind of killing you that you remodeled the bedroom on the side of her house *opposite* of your house so you can't see when her lights are on at night, isn't it?" Zander asked as he popped a shrimp in his mouth and chewed.

Yeah, it kind of was.

Zander swallowed. "That was dumb," he said without Zeke needing to answer.

"When I remodeled that bedroom, I had no idea that I'd *care* when those lights were on or off," Zeke told him with a scowl.

Zander laughed. "If it's any consolation, her bedroom *does* face my house."

"It's not," Zeke said flatly.

"And I haven't noticed her lights on. If she's sleeping there, it's late at night and she comes in, goes upstairs, and pretty much heads straight to bed."

Zeke didn't really feel consoled by that, no. Though if she was working long hours, it would explain why she hadn't called, texted, or stopped over for a booty call.

"Just stop out there," Zander said.

"Where?"

"Where the penguins are. Griffin makes it sound like that's the only place she ever is."

Zeke could believe that. "I can't."

"Why not?"

"They need peace and quiet and to get used to the new place without a lot of disruptions."

"So don't be loud or disruptive."

"That's..."

"Do that or go get laid with someone else. You're being a dick."

He wasn't going to go get laid with someone else.

That thought was swift and clear.

Dammit.

She'd ruined him for other women.

And he'd known it the first time he'd thrust inside her.

"I'm just *worried*. That's not the same thing as being a dick. You just haven't seen me do that much," Zeke said. Which was absolutely true. The last time he'd been actually *worried* about anyone had been when Leo had needed to have his gall bladder removed at age sixty-eight.

"Huh." Zander took another bite and studied Zeke. "Well, either stop worrying or go out there and make sure she's okay then."

"I'm not going to do that. I'm...giving her space."

Zander just nodded. But Zeke was certain he was thinking *what a dumbass*.

Of course, he was thinking the same thing about himself when he pulled up at the penguin habitat three hours later.

That was how long he lasted without seeing her—four days and fourteen and a half hours.

Her car was there and it was the only vehicle, so she was probably alone.

As he got out of his truck, he heard the very loud squawking-trilling sound that he assumed was the noise Galápagos penguins made.

He texted Jill. *I'm here to pet your...*

He sent that, then followed up with *penguins.*

She had, after all, had milk and yogurt in his fridge for four and a half days now. Sure, he'd been the one to put it there, but half the milk was gone and there were only two of the six yogurt cups left.

That made him feel stupidly happy.

He got a text back this time.

Jill: *Now????*

He texted back: *Yep. Come let me in.*

There was no answering text, but two minutes later, he heard the gate rattle and it swung in with a, "What are you doing here?"

He strode toward her, shocked by how happy he was to see her. "Told you. Want to pet something."

She looked...harried.

But not pissed.

He could work with that.

He held up a paper bag. "Brought you something too."

She lifted a brow. "Laundry?"

"You're hilarious. It's beignets from Cora."

Her expression brightened. "Oh."

He grinned. She ate cereal, yogurt, and PB and J because it was simpler but not because she didn't like other good food.

"But," he said, lifting them up out of her reach. "I need eyes on a penguin before you get these."

"Fine."

He relented with that. "But honestly, only if it's okay. I don't want to screw anything up. I really just came to check on you."

She gave him a little smile. "Thank you. I'm..."

God, he really wanted her to say "good".

"Really, really tired."

Dammit.

"What can I do?"

He braced himself for her to tell him to leave her alone.

"Come on in."

Oh damn, *yes*. "Really?"

"I do owe you some petting."

"I'll take any and all petting you'll give me."

He was gratified to see her eyes flicker with heat behind the fatigue and stress.

"And..."

He lifted a brow as she trailed off.

"Could you..."

"Yes," he said without needing her to finish the thought.

She swallowed. "Could I get another hug?"

He wasn't sure she could have said anything better. Not even "strip me down and fuck me".

He knew that Jill wasn't a hugger. When he'd pulled her into his arms the other day that had been clear. That she'd let him do it then, and was asking for it now? He felt like the king of the world.

Without a word, he reached out, took her arm, pulled her in, and wrapped her up.

He felt her melt into him, wrapping her arms around him, and then he felt her give a big sigh.

A sense of protectiveness shot through him and he had to consciously work not to crush her tightly against his chest.

And say something crazy like, "I've got you, girl."

Well, fuck. He'd said that out loud after all.

She took another deep breath and let it out. "Thank you."

They just stood hugging for a few minutes. Zeke soaked it up.

But eventually, she pulled back and looked up. "I needed that."

"You can have it any time. I'm right next door."

"If I showed up at two a.m. and asked you just to hug me, and that was all, that would be perfectly fine?" She clearly didn't believe that.

He wasn't sure it would be *perfectly* fine. He'd want more. He wasn't going to lie about that. But he said, "It would be fine."

She, of course, noted his rewording.

"Fair enough." She stepped back, slipping out of his arms. "Want to meet the penguins?"

"Yes. Introduce me to your waddle."

Jill looked pleasantly surprised. "You know that a group of penguins is sometimes called a waddle?"

"The site I read said it's mostly when they're moving though. I guess this would be a rookery? Unless they're in the water and they're a raft of penguins."

She smiled. "Right. You looked stuff up?"

"Had to. The crazy chick in charge of the live ones here won't let us close to 'em unless we bring her beignets. I mean, I gave her *six* orgasms the other night and I still haven't seen the live ones."

She coughed. "Damn, that's playing dirty."

"Is it working?"

"Maybe. Because you've got a point there. Those six orgasms were *very* appreciated."

Yeah, he wasn't such a good guy that hearing *that* didn't make him pretty damned proud too. "Let's go then."

She led him into the enclosure.

Zeke pulled up short as he stepped past the gate and took in the sight. He knew every inch of this place, but it was suddenly brand new to him. Because of the eight penguins....*penguins*... hopping all over the rocks and grass and sand he'd installed.

"Wow."

Jill took his hand and tugged him toward the penguin house that would let them onto the island. "Come on. You can't pet them from over here."

"I really can pet them?" he asked, following her eagerly.

"A couple of them. The others aren't really into that. Yet anyway." She led him through the building that gave the birds a temperature controlled place to hang out if the Louisiana weather got too hot or too cold for them. "Penguins aren't naturally that social with other species, including humans. But they get used to those who feed them, of course." She shot him a smile. "And they're very social with one another."

They stepped out of the building onto the island.

Jill stepped around the rocks and past a few of the penguins, heading for a flatter area. He noted there was a blanket spread out, a wide-brimmed hat, and a book and pen lying there.

"So you just hang out in here?"

She nodded. "They need to get used to me being around. Just a regular, normal, non-threatening part of their environment."

"How's it going?"

She took a seat on the blanket and he dropped down beside her.

She looked at him. "No idea."

"What?"

"I have no idea how it's going. I sit here and hang out and make notes about what they're doing. I feed them. I clean the enclosure. I talk to them. Then I'll go hours *without* talking to them. I leave the enclosure entirely and sit in my office. And...I have no idea what the right thing is."

A penguin waddled over. It cocked its head, studying Zeke.

Zeke realized he was holding his breath, hoping the little thing would come closer. If he was being completely honest, he wanted it to hop into his lap.

It didn't. But it didn't run from him either.

He blew out his breath.

Jill gave him a sweet smile. "You can touch him if you want."

"Really?"

"Reach out gently. Just a couple of fingers to start." She showed him what she meant, stroking the penguin from his head down his back.

Zeke did it, realizing he was grinning like a little kid. He didn't care. This was cool.

"He's slippery."

"Yeah, their feathers are waterproof. They're not as soft as most people think."

"They fit in down here though, smelling like fish the way they do."

She laughed. "I guess they do. You're all pretty used to that smell?"

"For sure."

The penguin waddled off and Jill and Zeke sat watching them all for a few minutes without talking.

"Okay, so you've heard *all* about my passion for penguins. What's your passion?" she asked.

He looked at her, a little surprised. But he answered easily. "Giving people homes."

"Building houses?"

"Yeah, but more than that," he said. "Taking a house and turning it into a *home*. I figure if everybody had a place they liked to go, where they could be themselves and feel totally comfortable and safe, the world would be a happier place."

She just looked at him for a several beats. Zeke let her look. It wasn't complicated.

Finally, she said, "Like what you did for the penguins."

"What *you* did for the penguins."

"Okay, what *we* did."

"Okay. But yeah. The idea is to give them a place where they have everything they need, feel totally secure, and can relax, be comfortable, and live their best life."

"That's really nice."

He narrowed his eyes. "It's why it's very important to me that people answer my emails about what kind of drawer pulls they want and what color they want their bedrooms painted."

"Oh my God, enough already."

He laughed. "Though I'm starting to figure you out, Kansas. I just need to make your house look like a penguin enclosure. Then you'd be happy, right?"

She looked around. "Well..."

He shook his head. "Be honest. There has to be *something* you care about having in your house."

"Okay...I like the shower you put in. The bedroom is gorgeous. Actually, all of it is gorgeous. You're obviously good at what you do."

"Thank you." He was. It was just a fact.

"But I guess I can be comfortable in a lot of different places. Décor doesn't matter that much. Or amenities." She drew her legs up and wrapped her arms around them. "I think I actually try not to attach too much to a place. I don't want a *home* because then it becomes too important."

Okay, *that* was not something he'd ever heard before. "Why is that?"

She met his eyes. "Because keeping up our home and making it a place that was perfect for everyone all the time wore on my mom. It was where she felt she *had* to be instead of out doing what she *wanted* to do. Home was her work rather than where she was able to relax and be comfortable."

Zeke frowned. "What do you mean?"

"My mom was a doctor. And she loved it. It was what she'd always dreamed of doing. She did her residency, but she didn't really get to work before she got pregnant with my older brother. He had a lot of health issues as a baby, so she didn't feel like she could leave him with someone else. From that point on she became a stay-at-home mom. And that's great for some people," Jill added quickly. "But it wasn't what *she* wanted. She had four kids and everyone always praised her for how well she kept everything all together, how great we all were, how clean and organized the house always was, how she managed everything. She took pride in that because it was all she had. It became important to her that our house be this perfect place where we were all safe and happy and where we liked to bring our friends and then, by the time we all graduated and moved out and she was thinking about going back to work, my grandma got sick and Mom started taking care of her."

Jill shrugged. "My mom was kind of bound down by home and family when she really wanted to be working instead. She always seemed tired and like she wanted more. She kept her license up and read journals all the time. But she never got to practice."

"So when you got the chance at your dream job, you decided to focus only on that and not let home and family and all of that distract you," Zeke said.

"Exactly."

Zeke's family was incredibly supportive. Whatever anyone wanted to try or do, everyone else was behind them. When Kennedy had wanted to go from swamp boat tour company receptionist to politician, they'd all joined her campaign. When Zander had gone to the police academy and then come home after only a year working in New Orleans, they'd all supported him. When Charlie had been fired from her big, fancy job in Paris and ended up back on the bayou and decided to expand the petting zoo, they'd said, "go for it."

That was the Landry way. Love you until you fell on your ass and then haul you up, feed you, and love you even harder.

"Okay, I hear you, Kansas," he said. And he did. A woman didn't have to have a family. And, apparently, this woman didn't have to be into home and family for him to want her more than he'd ever wanted anyone.

Maybe it was because he couldn't have her.

But he really thought it was more than that.

"I didn't mean..." She paused and bit her bottom lip. "Actually, I guess I did mean that as a warning," she said. "You're all really into family down here."

"We definitely are."

"It's nothing personal."

"I get it. And it doesn't make you weird, Jill," he felt compelled to add.

"I don't know about that." She gave him a little smile. "But it *does* make me *very* good with penguins." She looked around and her smile fell. "Supposedly."

He nudged her foot with his. "It'll be okay."

"You promise?"

"Maybe not. But I can tell you that 'oh shits' reproduce like rabbits."

"What's that mean?"

"That's what Leo always says. It means if you start thinking about all the things in a project that might make you say 'oh, shit', you'll find even more than you ever imagined."

"Ooookay," she said slowly.

"Like when I start a new building project. If I start thinking of materials not coming in on time, or one of my guys not showing up, or a ceiling beam crashing down or...there are a ton of things that *could* go wrong. I'd never start if I tried to have it all in place from the first day."

"And does Leo give any advice about how to deal with it?"

"Let it happen, say 'oh shit', and then fix it."

"You really don't put measures in place to be sure that ceiling beams don't come crashing down?" she asked.

He laughed. "Of course. But shit can still happen. And you have to just do your best to figure it out when it does."

"I've never been on my own before," she admitted. "I was the lead at the zoo with the penguins. I'm an expert. People call me all the time. But, I've never actually been the only one who would be saying 'oh shit' like I am here."

He nudged her foot again. "But you're not. We'll all say, 'oh shit' if things don't work out with these penguins."

She groaned. "I don't know if that's better now that you say that. I don't want a bunch of Cajuns disappointed in me too."

"'Oh shit' isn't 'you're shit', Kansas. It just means 'well, that didn't go according to plan, here's a beer'. Or, if it's really bad, Leo will pull out his moonshine and it'll take you two days to remember what went wrong."

She actually smiled at that and Zeke felt his heart expand. He couldn't fix things with her penguins but he could make sure she knew she had friends no matter what happened. Whether she wanted them or not.

He pushed himself to his feet. "I should probably get going. I don't want the female penguins to get attached to me and ruin *all* chances of them wanting to get it on with the males."

Jill's gaze roamed over him as he stretched to his full height. "Good thinking."

"And if you need any more hugs, just text me. You *do* have my number. Or you can just respond to one of the ten I sent you."

"It was fourteen. And okay," she said with a half smile.

He wanted to kiss her so fucking bad. Instead, he turned and made his way back to the penguin house. But before he ducked inside to leave he said, "By the way, naked hugging is also an option."

She laughed and he felt his heart swell even further.

# 12

"**E**zekiel Nathaniel Landry!"

Zeke sighed. "Do it quick," he said to Michael.

"This is going to hurt."

"I'm aware." Zeke gritted his teeth. "Do it. Now."

They had a long tablecloth wrapped around Zander's trunk to hold him still.

Michael nodded at Zander. "Okay, pull."

Zander pulled on the cloth, Michael jerked on Zeke's arm, and Zeke's shoulder popped back into place.

The pain was like a streak of lightning, arcing through him. "Motherfucker."

"Maybe I stole a dog from my neighbor's yard and relocated it seven counties away because it would never stop barking."

Zeke looked up at his mother. "Most of your scenarios have to do with you stealing things or being a sex worker. Have you ever realized that?"

His mother arched a brow. "I don't think I actually *murdered* anyone or anything. You boys aren't quite that bad. But I definitely did something that requires periodic pain and mental anguish."

Zander chuckled as he folded their grandmother's table-cloth back into a neat square. "He's dislocated his shoulder before. You know it's nothing permanent."

Elizabeth narrowed her eyes at her middle son. "All the call said was that he'd fallen off another roof."

"I wasn't on the roof," Zeke said. He rotated his sore shoulder. Dammit, that hurt. "I was on scaffolding near a tall ceiling."

"Why are you always falling off of things?"

"Because I love the TLC from Michael and getting to see your smiling face," he told her.

"Ezekiel, if you're not going to be more careful, you need to at least get a partner to work with regularly."

"I'm fine." He actually was feeling like a dumbass. He didn't fall off of things all the time. But he did climb on things that weren't entirely steady and jump off of things that he probably shouldn't from time to time.

Ignoring his mother, he looked at Charlie. "What do you mean she hasn't been in here to eat?"

Just before Michael had showed up to help relocate his shoulder, Charlie had mentioned to Zeke that she hadn't seen Jill since the penguins had showed up five days ago. Zeke had successfully kept his family from going to the penguin enclosure even though they all knew that the birds had arrived in town.

He was pretty proud of that. The Landrys weren't the best listeners, but he'd laid out a very compelling argument about why they needed to steer clear of the penguin enclosure. He also accentuated it with warnings like, "you don't want to have to pay more on your taxes this year, do you?"

He was the family's accountant. He didn't do it for anyone without the last name Landry, but he did do the books for all of his cousins and brothers and his grandma's business. From personal to business taxes, everyone trusted him to get the numbers to add up right.

That didn't mean he couldn't take off a couple of deductions though. Of course, he *wouldn't* do that, but it was a great threat. None of them had a clue about how to do their taxes, nor did they want to. He'd been doing them since he was sixteen and had taught himself how to fill out the forms.

When he'd first started, it had been a great way to make some extra spending money, but when he got older and realized how much he should have been charging them, he'd jacked their rates up right away.

"I mean she hasn't been in here to eat," Charlie said. "That doesn't mean she hasn't eaten at all, of course."

That crazy chick was surviving on peanut butter and jelly a week after being exposed to Ellie and Cora's cooking?

Okay, cereal, yogurt, peanut butter and jelly. He'd restocked the milk and yogurt yesterday.

Somehow she'd been using his refrigerator and going in and out of his back door and yet he hadn't run into her since the penguin enclosure. He was trying to give her space so he hadn't gone back there. She'd made it very clear that she didn't want to date him, so he was hoping if he respected her boundaries, when they did run into one another, she might hang around for a while.

So far, that hadn't happened.

As far as he could tell, everything in Autre was the same as it had been before Jillian Morris had showed up.

Except that he couldn't stop thinking about her.

"Here you go." His mother set something down on the table next to his elbow.

Zeke looked over. It was his sock. The one he'd left in Jill's motel room.

He looked up at his mom. "Where did you get that?"

"Ellie gave it to me. Is it yours? I figured I'd wash it with your other stuff and if it was Zander's you'd tell me."

Huh. He didn't think he'd realized how much his mother did actually do his laundry.

He glanced toward the bar. His grandmother and Cora were both moving behind the long, scarred wooden length, waiting on their lunch crowd. He looked up at Michael. "Thanks for helping."

"You want a shot for pain?"

"Naw. I'll get some stuff from Cora."

"You'll be...fine...then."

Michael probably didn't want to actually endorse the use of Cora's interventions, but he couldn't deny they were effective.

Zeke wouldn't use any of Cora's stuff until tonight. For one thing, this shoulder popped in and out routinely. This wasn't anything major. For another, Cora's stuff would knock him on his ass and he definitely shouldn't be climbing on anything when he used it. He'd learned, as had everyone in Autre, not to ask what was in the stuff Cora gave them. His grandmother's best friend had been making salves, creams, and potions for as long as he could remember. She had everything from bug repellents to natural cleaning solutions to painkillers. They all trusted her and used according to her directions and everyone was happy.

He shifted back from the table and stood. He pivoted to his mother. "I'm okay." He leaned in and kissed her on the cheek. "But thanks for worrying."

Elizabeth closed her eyes and shook her head and said, "Maybe I was a pirate."

Zeke, Zander, and Michael all laughed at that. "Your stories all tend to involve elaborate costumes too," Zander teased.

"I don't think they were considered 'costumes' back when we were dominating the open seas, pillaging and plunderin'," Elizabeth said. But her mouth was twitching.

"Right. And I'm sure there were no murderers in a pack of pirates," Michael said with a nod.

"Not the group *I* ran around with. We were in it for the gold and the rum," Elizabeth said.

Zeke laughed. "Now *that* I can believe. You still love shiny things."

"And rum," Elizabeth agreed. She reached up and patted Zeke's cheek. "I love you too. I'd like you to stay in one piece."

"As long as I've got Zander and Michael and Cora, I'm fine," Zeke told her.

Elizabeth couldn't argue with that. She'd been very grateful, out loud and often, to have so many other people helping keep track of her boys.

"And I love you too," Zeke told her.

"I know."

Zeke headed for the bar, and Ellie and Cora.

"You gonna live?" Ellie asked him as she poured beer into a mug from the tap.

"Yep. And it just proves once again that I'm tougher than cement."

Ellie snorted. "Or the times you hit it with your head when you were younger shook loose any sense of pain or fear."

"Cora, you got something for me?" he asked his grandmother's partner and best friend.

Cora smiled and reached into the front pockets of the apron she wore. She pulled out a glass jar of some kind of yellow cream and a bottle of brown powder. "Put the cream on your sore muscles. The powder goes in hot water and drink before bed."

"You're the best."

Cora gave him a sweet smile. "Wait till you see what kind of dreams you have when you use that powder before bed. Then you'll really love me."

He chuckled. Then focused on his grandmother. "You've seen Jill?"

Ellie looked over at him. "No."

"Then how'd you get my sock?"

"It was hanging on the doorknob to the back door of this place," Ellie said. "Had a note that said 'Zeke's'."

Zeke shook his head. "I don't get it. Why wouldn't she just put it on my doorknob?"

"I suppose she thinks that you need someone else taking care of your socks."

"Good Lord, she thinks I'm a dumb ass."

Ellie shrugged. "It's possible."

Ellie Landry was never going to be awarded warm-and-fuzzy-grandmother-of-the-year.

"Hey, I built her a very nice penguin enclosure."

"You can be a dumbass who can't keep his socks together and still be a great builder," Ellie said. "Lots of people are dumbasses in some areas and smart and talented in another. Have you ever met a lawyer?"

Zeke snorted. "This is what you're going to say to me instead of assuring me that I'm not a dumbass and that no one would ever think that of me?" Zeke asked, amused in spite of himself.

"Didn't you have to get her shoes the other day?"

"I borrowed some from Paige for her, yes."

"Why?" Ellie asked.

"Because she got her shoes wet."

"How?"

"Crawling into the penguin enclosure." Zeke realized how that sounded as he said it out loud.

"Right. Maybe you and Jillian have a lot in common."

"Being dumbasses?"

"Leaping before you look," Ellie said with a smile. "By the way, it's one of my favorite things about you. Sure, once in a while it ends up dislocating a joint, but some people just assume they can't make it and never even try. You, on the other hand, are never afraid to make the jump. You sometimes fall, but you get help, and then know how to cross that distance next time."

"And you think Jill and I have that in common?"

"She climbed over the gate instead of accepting she couldn't get to what she wanted."

Well, damn.

He really loved his grandmother.

And he was pretty sure he was falling for Jillian Morris as well.

"I like that spin on the dumbass angle."

Ellie smiled at him affectionately. "You're not a dumbass, Zeke. You just don't worry about much. But then why would you? You've always had a huge safety net." She looked around the room.

Zeke felt a little warmer in his chest. She was right about that. He had always had a number of people watching his back.

"Jill's not a dumbass either."

"Of course she's not. She just does dumbass things sometimes. As we all do."

Okay, he'd give Ellie that. But he couldn't resist saying, "She's passionate. And she puts the end goal in front of all the steps it's going to take to get there. Like when she wanted to get inside the enclosure. She just climbed over the fence rather than waiting for someone to get there to help her."

"But she can clean up and dry," Ellie said simply.

Exactly. All of the steps in between the starting point and the end point were details. How a person got there didn't always matter as long as they were willing to deal with the consequences of taking a different path.

"Thanks, Ellie."

"For?"

"For making dumbass moments seem perfectly normal."

She laughed. "Years of practice."

He leaned across the bar and kissed her cheek. Then he

tucked the cream and powder from Cora into his pocket and headed back to the table. Just in time, it seemed.

He got there just as Zander said, "Knox and I have good reason to go out there and look around."

"What's my reason?" Tori asked.

"You're one of the owners of Boys of the Bayou Gone Wild?" Zander asked.

"Sure, but she owns everything out there, she even bought the land from us."

Griffin looked at Zeke. "They're all yours."

"What's going on?"

"Everyone's trying to figure out a reason to head over to the penguin habitat. Their curiosity is killing them."

Zeke's eyebrows slammed together. "Nobody's going over there."

Charlie's eyes widened. "You're going to stop us?"

"If needed." Zeke put his hands on his hips. "I'm bigger and way meaner than you, Charlie."

"You think you're meaner than me?"

"You might have some scathing retorts to throw at me," Zeke told her. "But I'm mean enough to handcuff you in my shed in my workroom."

Charlie seemed to be thinking about that. And she seemed to come up with the conclusion that he was being sincere.

"I just want to be sure she has everything she needs. She doesn't need to be doing this alone. I'm perfectly qualified to help her with the penguins," Tori turned her big brown eyes on Zeke.

Tori was absolutely the sweetest of the girls. She had those big eyes, long eyelashes, and a smattering of freckles. A very wholesome girl-next-door demeanor. And it was no act. Tori was absolutely kind and sweet and generous.

However, she had learned that Josh wasn't the only Landry guy with a soft spot for sweet and kind and quirky and she wasn't above using the fact that she had all of them at least slightly wrapped around her finger to get her way.

She was also a new mom to a beautiful baby girl they were all enamored with. Eleanor Coraline Landry was the first great-grandchild, and she was named for both Ellie and Cora, who were, obviously, everyone's favorites.

And honestly, if it wasn't Jill that Zeke was protecting, he would've totally given in.

But it *was* Jill. And the fact that he was willing to turn Tori down in order to preserve Jill's peace said a lot about how much he liked the penguin veterinarian.

"Sorry, Victoria," he said using her full name. "You're going to have to wait too. I wouldn't be surprised if Jill has you and Griffin over first, but she made it very clear that the penguins need time to adjust in the peace and quiet."

"We just want to *look* at them," Zander said.

Zeke turned to his twin. "I realize that you're not big on rules. And I realize that makes you being a cop incredibly ironic, but I will physically block you from going to the penguin habitat if I have to."

Zander looked amused. "I just helped you pop your shoulder back into joint. You really think you can take me?"

"Okay," Mitch interjected, literally stepping between the two. "Nobody's taking anybody. We're all excited to go see the penguins but, clearly, Zeke and I are the only ones who have a good reason, at this moment."

Zeke frowned at him. "What's your good reason?"

"I helped build the enclosure. It makes sense that I would stop by and make sure everything was all right. See if anything needs adjusted now that the birds have been there for a few days."

Zeke narrowed his eyes. Mitch was probably the nicest of his cousins, but he still had Landry blood. That meant he would connive and manipulate to get what he wanted, if needed. "You're not going to the penguin enclosure either."

"But, Zeke—"

"Look, these penguins are endangered. They're part of a special program and they need to breed and lay some eggs. We have no idea how much all of this disruption is going to upset them. They lost their primary caregiver and have now been moved halfway across the country to a completely new environment. They need to get used to Jillian, they need to get used to the new enclosure, they need some time to adjust. If they don't and they don't have any baby penguins, the species could become *extinct*. There are only six hundred breeding pairs in the *world*. And they only lay a couple of eggs at a time and only lay eggs like three times a year!"

Everyone around the table was staring at him now.

After a moment Tori asked, "Did Jillian teach you all of that?"

"Some of it. I looked some of it up. But these birds are definitely in danger, you guys. No fucking around. If Jill thinks they need to be left alone for a few days then we're all gonna fucking leave them alone."

The mix of expressions around the table would've been comical if he was more laid back about the subject. But he wasn't. These people needed to just chill the fuck out. And they could. He knew that. They were all good people with good intentions. They just needed to understand *why* they were being asked to do what they were being asked to do.

Which, yes, he realized Jill might find humorous if she heard it considering he was the guy who just wanted to be told what to do and didn't think he needed to know all the explanations.

But dammit...now that he knew *why* the penguins mattered to her—and even more than because of their endangered status and her big heart, but the whole backstory—he realized that the whys did matter. He wasn't as laid back as he thought he was. At least not about everything.

"You feel strongly about this," Charlie finally commented.

"We should *all* feel strongly about this," he said, as he looked around the table with a serious stare. "All of us have had a negative impact on our planet, and this is our chance to do something to help right the balance." He pointed his index finger at each of them individually, then said, "So, stay the fuck away from the penguins until Jill says it's all right."

Finally, they all nodded.

"Okay, we'll stay away for now," Zander said.

"But you should know, Knox is getting phone calls from the community about when *they* can all go see the penguins," Charlie said.

"Well, Knox needs to tell the community that he doesn't know when or *if* they're going to be able to see the penguins. Maybe Boys of the Bayou Gone Wild needs to make a statement about the penguins," Zeke said. "Something to the effect that we are helping give them a *sanctuary* and *protecting* them so that we can help make a positive impact on the Galápagos penguin population, but that they may not become a regular exhibit as a part of the animal park. We can include some education about the penguins. Help everyone understand."

Charlie and Griffin shared a glance.

Finally, Charlie sighed. "Fine."

Griffin looked pleased. He met Zeke's gaze. "I've been trying to explain that if we're going to be open to bringing in threatened and vulnerable animals, whether they are endangered populations or they are just injured like the bear and wolf that Donovan is working with now, we have to be willing to keep some of them out of public view and we have to have a plan for communicating that with the community and visitors."

Donovan and Bailey had been working closely together. Bailey was often called to help rescue and remove injured wildlife and now that Donovan was right here in Autre, he was usually her first call when an animal needed some additional care before it was released.

Since he'd been here, he'd worked with a fox, an eagle, and now had a bear and a wolf. Those animals were definitely set to be re-released into the wild and had been kept separate from the animal park exhibits but they'd kept the community and interested audience updated via the website.

"Yes, we should consider the penguins a lot like the bear," Zeke said. "They need time to rehabilitate and get used to their new environment and then they need to have some baby penguins before we know if they're going to be successful here or not."

Tori gave him a smile. "We?"

Zeke realized that he used the term 'we' but yeah, he felt it. He was invested here. Did it have anything to do with Jill's silky dark hair, her gorgeous ass, and her dirty mouth? Maybe. But she'd reeled him in with the knowledge and love she had for the penguins and, frankly, their plight. Someone had to care about these animals. It might as well be all of them.

"Yeah, we. We're in a great position to do something here. We have the space, we have the enclosures, we have the knowledge collectively, and we can keep them all safe. If Boys of the Bayou Gone Wild becomes part animal park and part animal sanctuary, what's wrong with that?"

Tori nodded, then looked at Griffin, who seemed pleased. Even Charlie nodded.

"Fine," she said. "I mean, the penguins would sell a ton of tickets. But I get it. And it's still great PR for the business if we're taking care of the penguins for all the right reasons. Even if people can't actually see them."

Zeke shook his head, but smiled at his cousin. "There you go. I knew you'd come around."

Charlie regarded him as if she was trying to figure something out. "I wasn't under the impression you're giving me an option to not come around."

"You're right."

If he had to physically keep his own family members away from the penguins for the time being...or permanently, for that matter...he'd do it.

Jillian Morris had an ally and an advocate. Whether she wanted one or not.

---

$Z$ eke didn't see Jill again for three days. And when he did, it was out of his kitchen window, and clearly quite accidentally.

Of course, he also took note of the fact that she was dressed in a short tank top and panties. And nothing else. And that she was standing on the edge of her porch, holding a laundry basket, and looking around wildly as if she had no idea what to do.

He was through his house, out his front door, and down his front porch before he even thought about it.

"Are you okay?"

She whipped around to face him. "There's another alligator in my yard!"

Zeke glanced toward the side yard between her house and Zander's. Sure enough, Chuck was sunning himself on the rocks alongside Zander's driveway.

"But he's clear over there."

"He's between me and Zander's house."

"So what?" He strode across her grass and leapt from the ground to her porch.

"Well specifically, he's between my laundry and Zander's washer and dryer."

"You're going over there to use Zander's washer and dryer?"

She nodded. "He came over the other day and asked if there was anything I needed. I told him the only thing I didn't have that I needed was a washer and dryer and he offered his. He leaves his back door unlocked all the time too." She rolled her eyes.

"Ninety percent of the population of Autre leaves their back doors unlocked," Zeke informed her. "And Zander just came over? And asked if you needed anything?"

She looked up at him and seemed to fully focus on him rather than the alligator for the first time.

"He did. Brought me homemade apple butter and biscuits. Seems he heard that I like peanut butter and jelly and thought that might be a nice alternative some morning."

His fucking brother. Zeke couldn't remember specifically telling Zander that Jill liked peanut butter and jelly, but he also wasn't shocked to find out that she had come up in conversation over the last few days.

"You know he didn't make the apple butter or the biscuits, right?"

She grinned. "I didn't think that you made the bread, peanut butter, or jelly you brought me, but I still thought it was very sweet."

Fucking Zander.

"I would've brought you anything you wanted. All you had to do was ask."

"I know that, Zeke," Jill told him, moving the laundry basket to balance it on her hip now.

Which moved the one thing between his gaze and her body dressed only in that tiny tank and panties. It also pulled the tank up slightly, showing a bare strip of skin on her belly.

He didn't even pretend not to look.

"I'm just teasing you. And I'm totally on to Zander. He brought me the apple butter and biscuits so that I would let him come out to look at the penguins."

"He told you that?"

"It was obvious. The most interesting thing about me, even to tough guys who wear a badge and carry a gun, are the penguins. It's kind of always been that way."

Zeke took the opportunity to step closer and reach up to tuck a strand of hair behind her ear. "That wasn't what I was first interested in."

"And you get big brownie points for that," she told him with a little smile.

"I'm all about brownie points. So when I do what I'm about to do, I want you to think about how many brownie points I'm going to get for it."

"What are you going to do?"

Her gaze dropped to his lips and for a moment, Zeke thought about giving her the kiss she was clearly expecting. He loved that she was anticipating that and clearly wanted it. But he wanted to give her something she needed even more right now. And he wasn't really in the business of giving women things beyond kisses—and all the stuff that went with those—very often. So he went with it.

He bent, hooked an arm around her back, the other behind her knees, and scooped her up into his arms.

"Zeke!" She gasped.

"Hang onto your basket."

He turned and carried her down the rickety steps and across their joint yards to his house. She didn't wiggle or give a single word of protest.

"What are you doing?" she finally asked as he managed to open the front door while still holding onto her.

"Coming to your rescue. The way you did for me the first night when I crashed my bike in front of your motel... Oh wait, you came to the rescue of a *goat*, not me."

She laughed. "I'm never going to live that down, am I?"

He carried her to the kitchen before he swung her legs to the floor and set her down. "You're not.""

"Even now that you know I don't have the first clue how to treat a human and that my focus is always on animals? I mean, honestly, the goat is lucky I even noticed *him* since he's not a penguin."

"Nope. And you're going to feel even worse when I tell you that I just carried you across the yard so the gator wouldn't get you even after dislocating my shoulder three days ago."

She frowned. "You dislocated your shoulder?"

"Yep, happens periodically." He rotated his left arm. "I dislocated it the first time in football in high school. Now it slides in and out pretty easily. The other day I was up on some scaffolding and misjudged a step and ended up on the floor from several feet up. Shoulder popped out and my brother and Michael had to put it back in."

She wrinkled her nose. "Did it hurt?"

"Like a son of a bitch."

"You should probably be more careful with it."

He huffed out a laugh. "Not even a thank you for sacrificing to carry you in here?"

"Well, if it hurts, or would've been detrimental, I'm going to assume you wouldn't have done it."

"You're going to assume I always make the right choices?"

She shook her head. "I'm going to assume you understand there are consequences when you make decisions, good or bad. You're a grown up, after all."

That was fair enough. So, she wasn't overly worried. Hell, he'd known from the very first night that she wasn't actually the nurturing type. Unless he was black and white and had feathers, he wasn't getting too much TLC from this woman.

She looked around his kitchen. "So why am I over here? I really need to do laundry."

"So use my washer and dryer."

Her eyes widened. "You have a washer and dryer?"

"Yes, Jill, I have a washer and dryer."

"Surely you can understand why I might be surprised by that."

"Because my mother did laundry for me once?"

"Once?"

"Okay, she does it for me periodically. But yes, I have a washer and dryer and even use them occasionally." He leaned in. "Which means that you will no longer be using my brother's. Or anything else of his. You don't need to be going to my brother's house at all."

"What if I need butter? You don't even have butter in your fridge."

"Do you need butter? Because I'll fucking get a barrel of it."

"I don't need butter."

"So stop pushing me."

She tipped her head, studying him. "Are you jealous?"

"Yes, I am."

"Do we have a relationship that would make it appropriate for you to be jealous?"

"Is that how jealousy works? It only happens when it's appropriate and reasonable?"

"Okay, good point."

"But yes, I think it's reasonable in this case. We're sleeping together. He's my brother. He looks just like me, so he's obviously pretty fucking hot. It would make sense that you might be attracted to him. Except, of course, he's an asshole."

"Funny, he said the same thing about you."

"Did he? Well, you ask around. If it's between me and Zander, he's definitely more of an asshole."

"And we're sleeping together?"

"Not as regularly as I would like, but yes."

"We haven't seen each other in a few days. I thought maybe you'd lost interest."

"Definitely not. I've been thinking about you every night when I'm jerking off in bed."

Her eyes widened, but she didn't seem scandalized so much as turned on.

"You said you needed some time with your penguins. And honestly, at this point, I'm hoping to see some baby penguin chicks waddling around in that habitat really soon. And I'm hoping that when there's a couple eggs in those nests that I helped you put together, you're gonna want to have some celebratory nookie."

"Celebratory nookie? Yeah, I think I will."

"Awesome. And, for the record, anything else you want to celebrate that way, you know where to find me."

"So now I'm using your refrigerator and your washer and dryer," Jill said. "It seems maybe I should be thinking about ways to pay you back."

He leaned in. "Does that mean I can come and see the penguins again?"

She paused, then laughed. "Seriously? You'd rather come see the penguins?"

"Rather? What's my other option?"

Jill set her laundry basket on his center kitchen island.

"I think I was offering you sex in exchange for the use of your appliances."

## 13

W ell, that was new and definitely not unwelcome. "So is this a test?" Zeke asked. "Like if I take you up on that, I'm the asshole twin? Or is that a legit offer?"

"It's actually my way of saying that I really love to have sex with you and this is maybe a really good reason?"

He moved closer, bracing a hand on the counter behind her, caging her in. "You don't need a reason, Kansas. If you want sex, all you have to do is say please."

"Just please? What if sometime all I'm wanting is more homemade apple butter?"

She noted that her voice was slightly breathless as she teased him back.

"How about anytime you say please, I lead with sex and afterwards you can tell me what else you want?"

"And you're offering to get me *anything* I need *anytime*?"

He paused. "I'm going to be totally honest with you."

"I appreciate that."

"I will be able to *procure* anything you want or need. But it will very likely, technically come from someone else."

"And you see why I'm surprised that you have a washer and dryer."

He laughed. "Fair enough." He pushed back from her. "My mother doesn't do my laundry all the time."

"Hey, no judgment. If I had someone to do my laundry, I would be unapologetically in on that deal."

He believed that she wasn't judging him for that. A lot of women would probably think he was lazy or immature, or hopeless, but it seemed that Jill was just accepting the fact that once in a while his family pitched in. And that it was nice.

"Let's get your laundry started, and then maybe we can talk about the fees associated with using the machine and my water bill and laundry detergent." He grabbed her basket of clothes.

"All that stuff is surely gonna cost me," Jill said following him into the laundry room.

He really liked how open she was about wanting to have sex with him again. And how easily she teased about it. She definitely got wound up tight about the penguins, but when it came to everything else, she did seem to prefer simple and straightforward. Even talking about sex.

He set the basket on top of the dryer. Then he studied the body clad only in the tank top and panties. "You were going to wear this over to my brother's house?"

She looked over at him. "Zander isn't home right now."

"Still, what if he comes home?"

She shrugged. "I guess I would've pulled a blanket around me or something."

"You hadn't even thought of that, had you?" There was something funny about this woman who was trying to save the world by saving the penguins but who couldn't seem to think even one step ahead on any personal plans.

"This is what I have that's clean. But..."

He cocked an eyebrow. "But?"

"Honestly, I was going to throw them in too once I got over there."

Zeke knew it was irrational, but he frowned and he gave a low growl. "So you were going to sit around my brother's house completely naked?"

She lifted a shoulder. "I guess."

"I'm sure glad that Chuck was between you and Zander's place. In fact, I might build him a little house. And feed him. And make him a pet."

"Chuck?"

"The alligator that hangs out in our yards."

"You *named* him?"

He couldn't remember for sure if it had been him, Zander, or Fletcher who'd first called the reptile Chuck. "Yeah."

She gave a little shudder. "Fine. I won't go to Zander's anymore. But you definitely have to have everything I need over here then."

"Apple butter, refrigerator," Zeke said as he moved in behind her and settled his hands on her hips. "Washer, dryer, laundry detergent." He slid his hands up under the edge of her tank to the bare skin on her belly.

She shivered again but this time, he knew it was not in disgust. Or fear. That was lust.

He leaned in and put his mouth against her ear. "And a huge cock that's never been happier than when it was buried in your sweet pussy." He ran his hands up to cup her breasts. They were bare too, of course, because apparently everything else she owned was dirty. He sucked on her earlobe as he played with her nipples.

She leaned back into him with a deep sigh. "Do you have blackberry wine?"

Zeke paused. Fucking Zander.

"You drank blackberry wine with him?"

She rolled her head back and forth where it was resting on his chest. "No, he just gave me some. And it's delicious."

Okay, so he wasn't going to beat the crap out of Zander, but if he'd gotten Jill drunk and talked her into showing up at his house in the tank top and panties to do her laundry, he might have.

"I can definitely get you blackberry wine."

"This sounds like an amazing deal."

He went back to teasing her nipples. "I'm thinking for the first load, I get to eat your pussy. Second load, you're on your knees sucking blackberry wine off my cock. Third load, I bend you over and fuck you during the spin cycle."

She drew in a quick shaky breath. "Too bad I'm only doing one load."

"You've got a whole basket here, you really only doing one load?"

"I'm tempted to start separating everything if I'm going to get sex for each load." She arched her back slightly, pressing her breasts into his hands. "But I do have to get over to the penguin enclosure. I don't really have time for three loads."

He thought about saying something dirty about loads and what he could give her, but instead stripped her tank top up over her head and tossed it into the washing machine. "So everything goes in at once?"

Again, he felt like there was some great innuendo there.

Jill must've thought so too, because she grinned up at him. "I love it when it all goes at once."

He chuckled. "Let's fill it up."

She stripped her panties off as he reached for the basket. He was actually waiting for her to stop him as he turned the basket over, dumping denim, multiple cotton tees in various colors, and a bunch of white panties and bras all together into the machine. But she didn't.

He didn't bother to separate his own laundry, but he knew

most people did, and he knew that he drove his mother crazy the way he washed clothes. It was one of the reasons that she did it for him on a fairly regular basis. Probably even more often than he would want to admit to Jill, regardless of her clear acceptance.

He reached for the dials. "What settings do you like?"

"Hot and fast."

"Are we talking about laundry or the laundry fees?"

"Both."

He withdrew his hand.

"Why are you looking at me like that?"

"Because I know enough women who've yelled about how I do my laundry to know that's not actually how laundry is supposed to be done."

"Okay, but I don't want to take the time to separate laundry and do multiple loads. I get a lot of really gross stuff on my clothes so I feel like hot water is best for that, and if my clothes fade or shrink, I get more. I pretty much wear denim and t-shirts all the time."

Zeke had never paid this much attention to laundry in his life. "You weren't kidding when you said you like things simple."

"It's super easy to replace my wardrobe at any point. And it's super easy to get dressed in the morning."

"I've never met a woman like you. And I live on the bayou. The women down here aren't exactly frilly and girly, but..."

"They're more interesting?"

"That was definitely not what I was going to say. They're more complicated," he said. "Generally, anyway. You're a lot more like my grandma. She wears jeans and t-shirts every day. Her t-shirt collection is a little more eclectic. Tourists send her t-shirts from their home states when they get home after visiting Autre. But she braids her hair every morning, puts on a t-shirt and jeans, and heads to the bar where she spends the day doing the same thing she's done for fifty years with the same people she's known for fifty years." He paused. "And she loves it. It's her passion. And it probably doesn't seem like she's making the world a better place, but I think she is. That bar and that food are comforting for people around here. And it helps them all go out and do their thing—whether it's teaching little kids or taking care of animals or showing off the bayou or being a spouse or a parent—knowing they have a place to come to where they can reconnect and be cheered on and supported no matter what they're going through. She's got a part in everyone's stories and successes."

Jill was watching him with a strange expression.

"What?" he asked.

"I don't remember the last time I did laundry with a guy. I'm not sure I ever have. But I am sure I've never stood entirely naked in front of a guy and had him get sentimental about his grandmother."

Zeke huffed out a breath. "Yeah. I don't think I've ever done that before either."

"It's clear that you think your grandmother's a pretty amazing woman, so I'm going to take all of that as a compliment. If it's not, I need you to not tell me. And if it any point in the next few minutes, you start thinking about her again, I'm going to need you to stop everything and walk out of this house, and never speak of this again."

His mind and body shifted almost immediately. "Walk out of my own house?"

"Yeah. Because I don't have any dry clothes at the moment, so I can't be the one to leave."

He laughed. "Okay. What are you gonna do?"

"I'm going to have you lift me up onto this washing machine and take your first laundromat fee."

Zeke couldn't have told anyone what they had been talking about thirty seconds before she said those words.

He clasped her hips in his hands and lifted her up onto the machine.

She readily spread her knees so that he could step forward between them. He held her hips in his hands as he leaned in to kiss her. Her arms wrapped around his neck and she pressed close, opening her mouth and sighing happily.

He ran his hands up and down her back, then around to her sides again to cup her breasts, rubbing his thumbs over her nipples.

Her hands went to his hair and pulled on the tie that was holding his hair back from his face. She dropped it to the floor behind them and ran her fingers through his hair, loosening the strands.

He dipped his knees to take a nipple in his mouth, sucking gently for only a second before sucking hard and giving her a little bite the way he learned she loved that first night.

She gave a little moan and her fingers tightened in his hair. He moved one hand from her back to her thigh and lifted her leg to set her heel on the edge of the machine. The position tipped her back slightly, and she leaned, propping her elbows on the top of the console where the dials and buttons were. Zeke moved her propped leg open, spreading her thighs.

"So fucking pretty," he said, gruffly.

She took his hand and led it to her hot center. "Touch me."

Gladly. He ran the pad of his middle finger up and down her slick slit, circling her clit and loving the way her head fell back and her eyes closed. He reached for one breast, plucking at the nipple as he slid first one finger, then a second into her pussy.

Her sweet heat welcomed him, and he dragged his fingers in and out leisurely, loving the feel of her tight body clinging to him.

Her breathing sped up and a flush started to climb from her chest to her neck to her cheeks.

"Yes, Zeke. Deeper. Harder."

He picked up the pace, loving the way she felt free to direct him to what she wanted.

"More."

"Suck on me. I want your mouth too," she said.

"Where?" He'd put his mouth anywhere she wanted.

Her eyes fluttered open.

"Here." One hand slid down her stomach until she reached her clit. She circled it with her own finger as he continued to pump in and out of her.

"Fuck. Anything you want." He lowered his head and replaced her finger with his tongue. He licked, circled, then sucked.

She tangled her fingers in his hair, lifting her hips closer to his mouth.

"Yes. I'm so close."

"Come like this. I never want to do laundry without getting hard again," he told her.

The machine was rocking under her and he kept his mouth against her as he fucked her with two fingers.

It only took a few more seconds for her to clamp down around his fingers and cry out his name.

Zeke straightened immediately, pulling his fingers from her body and lifting them to his mouth. He sucked them clean as he fumbled with his fly with one hand.

She reached to help him, freeing his cock in seconds, pushing his jeans to his knees. He grasped her hips and pulled her so her ass was just hanging off the edge of the machine.

"Take your shirt off," she coaxed. "I love your ink."

He reached behind him and grabbed the cotton between his shoulders, yanking it up and over his head. He tossed it to the floor then fisted his cock,

She licked her lips as she watched. "Fuck, you're so pretty," she told him, repeating his words with a half smile on her lips.

"The stars you're about to see are gonna be pretty," he growled.

He held his cock with one hand and gripped under her ass with the other, lining them up. Then he thrust forward.

He sank deep into the tight heat that took his breath.

"Yes, Zeke!"

She was perfect. He didn't know if she was seeing stars but he sure as fuck was. Rainbow stars. Rainbow stars that sparkled and twinkled and formed the word *forever*.

He wasn't going to argue.

He pulled back, then pressed forward.

And froze.

Fuck. "*Fuck.*"

Jill frowned. "What?"

Zeke gritted his teeth. He carefully pulled out of her body. "No condom."

"Oh." Jill's eyes went wide as that sank in. "*Oh.*"

"I've got it." He met her eyes. "Okay?"

She pulled her lip between her teeth, but nodded.

He reached up and freed the lip. "Okay? I gotta hear you say it. I'll put one on and we'll keep going. Or we'll stop."

"Stopping sounds like the worst idea anyone ever had."

He gave a soft laugh as the tightness in his chest loosened slightly. "Yeah?"

"Zeke Landry, if you don't give me another orgasm on this washing machine—"

"That *will* happen."

"Okay, good. Unless *you* don't want to keep going. I mean, I'll give you a blow job or something instead. You were very generous. I'm not sure the orgasm you just gave me actually counts as *me* paying any kind of fee."

He shook his head. "You are an interesting woman."

He bent and grabbed his jeans, jerking them up and grabbing his wallet. He pulled a condom out, opened it, rolled it on, and tossed the wrapper to the floor.

"Now where were we?"

She reached for him, her hands circling his shaft and urging him forward. "I've saved your place. You were right here."

He gripped her hips as he thrust forward, sinking deep again.

Okay, the stars were still there. They maybe weren't quite as bright, but that was okay. Condom sex was good sex. And rainbow sparkly stars that spelled out forever were a lot for an accountant and a woman who preferred penguins over people.

But as he fucked the most interesting, gorgeous, unusual woman he'd ever met on top of his washing machine while it washed her plain white cotton underwear, he kind of thought that doing this forever was maybe the best idea he'd ever had.

---

Sitting at Zeke Landry's kitchen table in one of his t-shirts and no underwear after having sex on his washing machine probably should've felt stranger than it did.

It actually felt pretty nice. Or fun at least.

Jill was glad he'd caught her trying to get over to Zander's. She also kind of liked that he was jealous. Which was really stupid for a friends-with-benefits setup.

Still, his possessiveness made something warm curl in her stomach and she was pretty sure it was pleasure. But not the kind that he elicited with his tongue and fingers on her clit and nipples—though, she was a huge fan of that as well—but this was definitely a warmer, more comfortable pleasure. And there was just something about being around Zeke Landry that made her feel it from head to toe, not just in very specific anatomical locations.

She was glad for the distraction actually.

For one thing, he was right when he said that she hadn't thought through the idea of sitting around naked at Zander's house. She really hadn't. It was possible once she got over there and had her laundry going and thought about taking off what she was wearing that she would've decided against it. She also might have rifled through his front closet to find a jacket or something. But it definitely made more sense for her to sit naked underneath Zeke's shirt in the man's kitchen.

Zander was very nice and yes, extremely good-looking, and the charm had rolled off of him nearly as potently as it did off his twin brother. But she didn't feel a spark with Zander. Certainly not like she felt with Zeke. Then again, she wasn't sure she had ever felt a spark like she did with Zeke.

"Do you wanna take a shower?" he asked.

"Yeah, maybe later."

"Do you wanna take a shower *together*?"

She thought about how to answer that. Her answer was going to sound strange, she knew. "Well…"

"Well?"

"I'm actually not that big on shower sex," she admitted.

"No?"

She lifted a shoulder. "It's slippery, which can be dangerous. And tile is hard and can be cold. And then everyone has to dry off after. And if I go straight to bed, my hair gets the pillow wet."

He was staring at her.

"And then my hair is a tangled mess in the morning."

He was still staring.

"What?"

"Just…I'm not into shower sex either. And I hate wet hair on my pillows."

She wasn't sure she'd ever met a guy not into shower sex. Well, a guy who had any kind of sex on his "not into it" list.

"Then we can just stick to washing machines. And tables and couches and floors and most definitely beds."

"And walls," he said.

Her body flushed remembering their first night. "Yes, not slippery, cold, wet walls."

"Still hungry?" she asked. "Want to run next door and get my peanut butter and jelly?" Because *she* was hungry.

Zeke had said something about being on the way up to his grandmother's place for food when he'd seen her on her porch, but he didn't think taking her in there in just one of his t-shirts was a good idea. Not because anyone in his family would object, exactly, but because they'd all start begging her for glimpses of the penguins and he knew she didn't want to have to field those requests.

"Actually, I was thinking about sneaking over to a different neighbor's."

"Zander actually has food at his house?"

"He does. But don't go gettin' all soft about my brother. He's up at Ellie's just as much as I am. He might have some Pop Tarts or frozen pizza or burritos though."

"I'm fine with yogurt and cereal right here."

"No way. When you're fending for yourself, it's fine, but what kind of guy would I be to do *that* to you"—He inclined his head toward the laundry room—"and then not even feed you?"

"The kind that doesn't have any food in his house?"

"But I can *get* food in my house."

"Okay," Jill sat back in her chair and folded her arms. "Impress me."

"So do you actually eat food intended for people over the age of ten or should I stick with macaroni and cheese and hot dogs?"

She lifted an eyebrow. "I love macaroni and cheese and hot dogs. But I only eat them from the microwave."

"Of course, because it takes so long to boil water to cook the noodles, right?"

She grinned. "Actually, I meant the hot dogs. The macaroni and cheese I'm used to eating is from a place called Ruth's that delivers until eleven p.m. It's a spiral pasta with a five cheese sauce and a toasted Parmesan crust."

"I'm not even gonna *try* to top that," Zeke declared, pushing back from the table. "But Jordan is a good cook. I'll be right back."

Jill straightened as he got up from the table. "Wait, you're leaving? Who's Jordan?"

"Oh, are *you* jealous now?"

Was she? Jill thought about that for a moment. Maybe a little.

"It's not really hard for me to believe that you have women on speed dial who will cook for you at the drop of a hat."

He bent at the waist. "Thank you very much. And I do actually. If you want some real home cookin' and are willing to give me about an hour, I could get Amber over here with some fried chicken."

"Amber will cook fried chicken for the woman that you're now sleeping with?"

"I wouldn't tell her *that* before she brought chicken over."

Jill laughed and shook her head. "We're not making Amber make us fried chicken." She paused for a moment, though, and then said, "At least not today."

She loved fried chicken. Her grandmother's was the best she'd ever had, but she would bet some of the ladies down here in Louisiana could make some pretty amazing fried chicken.

"Jordan is my brother Fletcher's wife. She grew up down here and she is a hell of a cook. I don't know what she's got, but I'm guessing there's some pretty good leftovers in their fridge. I'll be right back."

Jill watched him go.

So he was able to pop into one house to get shoes for her, and now go to another to get food.

And for some reason, she had the impression that Jordan and Fletcher wouldn't mind having their refrigerator raided. Hell, it wouldn't surprise her to find out that Jordan made extra just so there were leftovers for Zeke to pilfer.

Autre was a very interesting place. It made her miss home a little bit, actually.

There were plenty of places she could show up to borrow shoes or food. Of course, all of those places would come with a million questions and definitely some judgment about why she needed to borrow shoes and why she didn't have her own food.

Around here, that didn't seem to be the case. Either they were just used to Zeke being the way he was, or they really didn't mind. Or Zeke didn't care if they were judging him.

Yeah, that was at least partly true. But she liked that about him. He was a good guy. He was clearly great at his job, judging by the penguin habitat—was which was probably not something most contractors around here had on their resumes—and her bedroom and bathroom just next door.

He'd also been very sweet when she'd told him about her passion for the penguins. And he had a sweet reason for being a builder as well. He wasn't just doing it because he didn't know anything else to do, or because he loved building, or because he was trying to make money. He actually had some heart behind it. She liked that.

He was back five minutes later with plastic containers. She had to get up and open the door for him so that he wouldn't drop any of them on his way in.

As her clothes finished washing and then tumbled in the dryer, they ate pulled pork, potato salad, green beans, and shared a pint of Coffee Toffee Caramel ice cream.

"Jordan is going to kill you for stealing the ice cream

though, right?" Jill asked, dipping her spoon in to the carton for the last bite and licking it clean.

"Yeah, I'm definitely going to have to replace this."

"You're willing to risk her wrath to feed me?"

"Jordan doesn't really do wrath. But yeah."

"I can't believe that you haven't mentioned that you haven't seen me up at your grandma's restaurant."

"I'm being good." He paused. "But you know you can go in there anytime, right? They can make anything you want."

"I know. And I explained to you that I'm not big on taking time to eat."

He nodded. And she believed that he understood. He'd actually been leaving her alone for several days and she'd been surprised by it. If she were honest, maybe also slightly disappointed.

And if she was even more honest, she truly had started to wonder if he'd lost interest. It had been a relief at the same time. For one, it always made her feel a little crappy to tell people that she didn't have time to do other things. For another, she wasn't actually sure how long she could resist Zeke Landry if he tried to get her attention and take up some of her time.

"The next time you get hungry and you want someone else to cook for you, you call up there and you tell them that Zeke said Leo would deliver anything you wanted."

Then he frowned. "No, don't ask for Leo. He will talk your ear off. And he will crow to everybody else if he gets a glimpse of those penguins. Ask for...Mitch. Mitch or Paige. I mean they'll definitely want to see the penguins too, but they can keep it on the down low, and they'd be happy to bring anything over you need."

"I get the impression everybody's pretty friendly. Wouldn't any of them be willing to bring something over? Especially if they got to see the penguins?"

"Absolutely. But the rest of them would hang out and drive

you crazy. And a couple of them would have a hard time showing up alone. They'd bring somebody with them. Mitch and Paige are pretty unassuming. You'd be able to get by with just one of them showing up and not overstaying their welcome."

Jill smiled. "Okay. Thanks for the intel."

They both sat quietly for a moment, then she asked. "What if I asked *you* to bring me food? Would you overstay your welcome?"

He looked at her for a long moment, his expression a mix of heat and amusement, and if she weren't mistaken affection. But that was weird.

"I would stay as long as you possibly would put up with me, ask a million more questions about the penguins, kiss you, and probably try to get you naked."

Her eyes widened. "Again, thank you for the intel."

He chuckled. Just as the dryer buzzed in the other room.

## 14

She'd been in Autre for six weeks.

And she'd only done her own laundry twice.

And she hadn't been to the grocery store even once.

Yet, she hadn't run out of yogurt, milk, cereal, or peanut butter.

Not only had Zeke thrown her laundry in with his—and she didn't know or really care if he'd done it or if his mother had because Jill really did like the ocean breezes dryer sheets—and kept her favorite items stocked in his house, but she had food from Ellie's for dinner every night. Which cut down on the amount of cereal and bread she went through. It also had given her an addiction to remoulade sauce she hadn't expected. And five new pounds.

Each evening the food was either on her desk at the penguin habitat...or on Zeke's kitchen table when she went over to say hi.

And kiss him.

And get him naked.

And curl up next to him for the rest of the night.

Yeah, yeah, she saw Zeke a lot more often than she'd ever seen Dan.

But Zeke was less busy than Dan had been.

Turned out, so was she.

She was still obsessed with the penguins, of course. But after making sure they were clean and fed and not pregnant, it turned out she had some free hours in her day. So, when Griffin had asked if she'd help out with a few of the other animals, she'd said sure.

Working with lemurs was cool. She also really liked the porcupines and the red pandas.

But she was annoyed with the cats. All three of them that hung out in the barn. And one of the alpacas. And Gertie the otter.

Because they were all pregnant.

The alpaca wasn't even supposed to *be* pregnant this time of year.

Jill blew out a breath.

She was trying to get *penguins* pregnant and they had no interest, but all the animals around her were getting knocked up.

Well, not *all* of them. Many of the animals wouldn't mate until spring. But that seemed the only thing saving her from being completely surrounded by baby animals of all kinds.

Except penguins, of course.

But it went even beyond cats and alpacas and otters.

And it was very, very, very ironic.

Turned out her weight gain wasn't entirely from the remoulade sauce. Or even from Ellie's amazing pecan pie.

Nope. The five pounds, and a few other symptoms, were all *Zeke* Landry's fault.

"Y ou don't have to knock, you know," Zeke told Jill as he pulled his door open. "Just come on in."

Ever since the washing machine sex—okay, the *first* washing machine sex—she'd been coming over to his place at least three nights a week. He knew a lot of it was the sex. And Cora and Ellie's cooking. But he thought maybe some of it was his company.

"Hi." Jill's gaze traveled over him but lingered first on his glasses.

He'd needed the damned things for reading since he'd been about fifteen. He was barefoot and wearing jeans and had just shrugged into a flannel to come to the door, but he hadn't buttoned up. Her gaze next got hung up on the ink across his chest and he leaned to brace a hand on the door frame as he let her look.

He drank in the sight of her in return. She was wearing loose gray athletic pants and a pale green t-shirt under a hunter green hoodie. Her hair was pulled back into a ponytail and she had no makeup on, as usual. Everything about her screamed girl next door, but that wasn't unusual. The huge lantern and the long pole with the looped cable at the end she was carrying, however, were.

"What are you doing with those?"

"In case I ran into Chuck on my way over."

"And where did you get them?"

"Zander." She held up the pole. "It's to loop around the alligator's neck, and—"

Holy shit. "I know what it's for." There was no way in hell Jill was going to be looping that thing around any alligators. "When did you get it?" She'd been coming to his house frequently.

"A few weeks ago."

"I haven't seen it before."

"I leave it out here." She leaned to set it to the side of the door.

"You've been bringing that over here with you every night?"

"Yeah."

He hadn't noticed. Of course, he was always very focused on her when she showed up.

"Zander said maybe I'd be better off just poking him with the other end of it and being really loud to try to scare him off."

"Do *not* poke an alligator with a stick, Jill." Jesus. What was Zander talking about? "Don't fucking get close enough to an alligator to poke it with a stick."

"What am I supposed to do? I have an alligator who frequents my yard."

"You avoid him. You run in the opposite direction. Or you scream really loud and I'll take care of it."

"What if you're not home?"

"You put your pretty ass back in your house and call me."

"And what if you're in another town and can't come over right away and I need to get out to the penguins?"

Zeke shoved a hand through his hair. "He's not going to attack you. I keep him well fed to avoid that very scenario."

Jill propped a hand on her hip. "You *feed* Chuck?"

"Yeah."

"Did it ever occur to you that he keeps coming over because of that?"

"I'm sure he is. But the first time he came over wasn't because I fed him and I'd rather have him eating my chicken than eating...you." He gave her a slow grin. "I'm the only one who's going to be doing that."

She frowned, instead of responding to his flirty teasing. "Yeah, about that. We need to have a talk."

Zeke didn't like the sound of that. If they had to talk about him eating her, it was either because she wanted him to do it right now—in which case she probably wouldn't be frowning—

or she was going to ask him not to do it anymore. And that wasn't really okay either.

He shifted away from the frame. "Come on in."

She ducked under his arm and stepped into the house.

"Have you eaten?" He already knew the answer to that question, but felt that it was polite to ask before he loaded up a plate of leftovers from Ellie and put them down in front of her.

Jill put a hand on her stomach. "I'm not really hungry."

That was new. She'd loved everything Ellie had sent home for her. He frowned, taking in her distressed expression. "You okay?"

She shook her head, and Zeke felt his chest tighten.

"What's wrong?"

"We should sit down."

He moved in toward his dining room table where he'd been working. "Okay. Have a seat."

She looked at the table strewn with papers. "What's all this?"

"Oh. Taxes." He pulled out a chair and dropped into it. "What's going on?"

"This is a lot of paperwork for taxes for one guy. And it's not tax season."

"Quarterly taxes."

"This is all for your quarterly taxes for your construction company?"

"No, I do everybody's taxes."

"Who's everybody?"

"Ellie and the Boys of the Bayou and now Boys of the Bayou Gone Wild. Then, besides mine for the construction company, I do Zander's and Mitch's and everybody's personal stuff during tax season."

She was looking at him, puzzled. "You do everyone's *taxes*?"

"Yeah."

"Why?"

"It's fun."

She blinked at him. "Doing taxes is a hobby?"

"Kind of. I am a CPA. And I make them pay me. But it's definitely on the side."

"Who does accounting for fun?"

"Math geeks."

She was looking at him as if meeting him for the first time. "You're a math geek. Who does accounting for fun. For his whole family on the side of his construction business."

"Yep."

"Wow."

"What are your hobbies?" he asked.

She gave him a look. "You already know the answer to that. I don't have any hobbies. It's penguins, penguins, penguins."

He sat back in his chair and again noted how her gaze traveled over his bare chest and stomach as his shirt fell further open.

"Could you button up?"

"I could. Or I could just take it off. I guess it depends why you're here."

"This is definitely a button up conversation," she told him. "Though not unrelated to the times you've unbuttoned and taken things off."

Was she dumping him? That would be weird. Everything had been going great. The sex was out of this world, they were happily living next to one another, sharing his space frequently, and having fun. They were a lot alike in many ways, actually.

He was definitely going to fight her on this. But he started buttoning up.

"Okay, spill. What's going on?"

"I'm pregnant."

Zeke's fingers froze on the fourth button. His gaze snapped to hers.

He immediately realized she wasn't kidding around.

"Oh."

Jill shifted forward on her chair, bracing her hands on her knees. She met his gaze directly. "Yeah. And it's yours. I'm not very far along, but I took the test yesterday. And..." She blew out a breath. "It was positive."

Zeke took all of that in as he finished buttoning his shirt. Then he sat for a few seconds, letting all of the thoughts and reactions swirl around in his head.

Jill was pregnant. The most fascinating, unique, beautiful woman he'd ever met was having his baby.

She was definitely not like any woman he'd ever dated before and he certainly hadn't gotten as far as to think about what their relationship might look like even a month from now, not to mention a year or more. But he liked her more than he could remember liking anyone he'd slept with in...ever.

"I have to be honest with you," she said after nearly a minute. "I'd never planned to be a mom. Like ever. I don't think I'll be very good at it."

He blew out a breath. "Okay. Well, I was definitely not planning on being a father yet. But...I guess I've always assumed I would have kids."

"So you want to have it?"

His first reaction was to say that of course he wanted to have it, but he decided he needed to actually think about her question. Not having it was an option after all.

It occurred to him that bringing a baby into his life, into *their* lives, would be a much bigger disruption to Jill's than it would be to his. He'd have a ton of help. He'd spent his entire life in Autre and already had a house and a business. Everything he was doing now was essentially what he would be doing a year, five years, ten years from now. If he had a child to take care of, it would be a huge change, but it would not significantly derail anything about his life.

Jill was in a different position. She had just moved to Autre and didn't even have a completely finished house. Of course, he could take care of that rather easily and quickly. But she was just starting a new phase of her career and he knew things weren't going exactly the way she would like them to.

"I will help you however you want me to help you," he finally said. "I have a huge support system. With you living right next door, we can easily share custody."

She blinked at him a few times without speaking.

"What?" Zeke finally asked after several seconds had ticked by.

"You mean that, don't you? Just like that? We have a baby together and keep doing...all of this." She swept her hand around. "Seeing each other here and there and just...what? Passing it back and forth?"

Zeke lifted a shoulder. "Isn't that what shared custody is? Or, you can move in here if you think that would be easier. Or, I mean, hell...if you want the baby to live here and you come and go, that's fine. Like I said, I have a ton of people who will help."

Jill stared at him. As in wide-eyed, open-mouth stared.

"You would actually take this baby and raise it and let me just visit...what? On the weekends? You'd have your family help out with babysitting and cooking and laundry and it would just be like your life is now, but with a little person living with you?"

Zeke frowned. It sounded like a good thing, but there was something about the way she said it that made it sound bad. But, with about three minutes to adjust to the news and think this through, yeah, that was all what was going through his mind.

"Yeah, I guess that's what I'm saying."

Jill pushed up from her chair and paced across his dining room, then turned back. "You realize that you and I are the last people who should be in charge of keeping another human alive, right?"

"Well..."

"Neither of us cooks. We barely shop for groceries. We barely keep our clothes clean. Neither of us keeps any kind of regular schedule. And we like that," she added, holding up a hand when he started to protest. "For me, I keep everything else in my life simple so I can focus on the one thing that I actually care about. You roll with everything because you know that you have this huge safety net behind you. You can literally jump from one piece of scaffolding to another and not worry about falling because if you do, you know you have people who will put you back together."

"I'm not understanding what the problem is. We would have that safety net with the baby too."

"But that's pathetic, Zeke. People shouldn't bring children into the world if they're not ready and able to take care of them. You and I barely take care of *ourselves* and now we're going to have a child reliant on us?"

"You keep penguins alive. You worry about them all the time. You feed them and shelter them and take care of their medical needs."

"They're penguins."

"They're endangered. If they die, that impacts the entire population worldwide."

For just a moment, she paused, seeming surprised and a bit mollified by the fact that he'd absorbed how important the penguins were, and that he was championing what she was doing. But she shook her head a moment later. "But I can leave the penguins alone. If I'm late to feed the penguins by a half hour, they're fine. I mean, they get a little pissy, but they're mostly fine. Or if one of them is sick, I take care of it, but then I go home. You can't do that with a kid. You have to be there twenty-four seven. You can't put them in a pen and leave them overnight. I'm pretty sure someone would call child protective services."

"But if a kid's sick and you can't be there, you call Grandma or Great Grandma or Aunt Somebody," Zeke said.

"Do you ever get tired of needing your family for everything?" she asked.

Zeke felt like she'd slapped him. "No. I don't."

"You are thirty years old. When are you going to start taking care of yourself? I mean, are you going to depend on your mother to do all the diapers? Are you going to call your aunt in the middle of the night when the baby has colic? Are you going to dump the kid off with your cousins when it has an ear infection?"

"First of all, I'm twenty-five. Second of all, hell yes I'm going to ask for help when I need it. Third of all—"

"You're *twenty-five*?"

He frowned. "Yes. Just turned twenty-five a few weeks ago. You really thought I was thirty?"

"Well, I didn't know that I was having an affair with someone nine years younger than me!"

His eyes widened. "You're *thirty-four*?"

"Geez, you don't have to say it like *that*."

Zeke got to his feet and faced her. "That's hot as fuck. But I don't care how old you are. The fact is, we're the same person. We both have adjusted our lives so that we can focus on what's really important to us. For you, you whittled your life down to wearing the same shirt in various colors, surviving on peanut butter and jelly and cereal, and drinking your vegetables. You gave up on remembering birthdays or anniversaries. For me, I simplified my life by letting other people help me. None of that makes either of us a bad person. And we can adjust. We can grocery shop, we can learn to cook, we can learn to do laundry."

Jill blew out a breath and tipped her head up to look at the ceiling.

Zeke just watched her for a long moment. His gut was tight

but he wasn't going to apologize for his family or for his plan to lean on them. He'd be there for any of them in this same situation and he knew they knew that. "I understand that you didn't choose this. This was an accident. But we'll make it work. You can be as involved...or not...as you want."

Jill focused on him again. "Isn't that the line the woman generally gives the guy? Tells him he can be as involved as he wants?"

"It's *our* kid. Just because you're the mother doesn't mean that you automatically have to be the one taking the reins, does it?"

"But it makes me look like a bad person, right? Lots of people will judge me for not being more involved."

"Maybe. Probably," he admitted. "But not everyone's wired the same way and it's not like you planned this and changed your mind. We did what we could to prevent it. We used condoms every time, but they're not a hundred percent. So—" He shrugged. "Here we are. We'll make the best of it."

"I still think it feels a little pathetic for us to just mess up like this and then just assume that your family will help us clean it up."

"That's what families do."

"There are other options, Zeke."

Right. Of course there were. And he needed to listen to all of that. "And if you want to talk about those, I will. But if I get a vote, I think I can be a good dad. I mean, I didn't used to know how to build a damn thing, but my family taught me and now I'm one of the best. My family's full of amazing fathers. If I was going to learn how to be a great dad and a good man, right here in Autre with the Landrys is exactly where I'd come to make that happen. Except, lucky me, I'm already here."

She seemed to be thinking all that over for a few seconds, but she also seemed touched.

"Do you think I'm a bad person? For not being more maternal or nurturing?"

He crossed the few feet that separated them to stand right in front of her.

This woman was carrying his baby. That was starting to sink in. Was she who he had imagined himself with? No. But she wasn't like any woman he'd met before, so how could he have possibly imagined that?

But she was good for him.

"You have made me into more of a caregiver than I have ever been," he told her. "My whole life I've been the one everyone else takes care of, because I'm the youngest and..." He gave her a little grin. "Because I really like it."

She gave a soft snort.

"But *you* haven't nurtured me. From the moment we met you haven't worried about me or made things easier for me or placated me. You're the first woman I've ever slept with who hasn't cooked me a single thing."

She grimaced.

"*But*," he went on. "You've not only made me happier than I've been with anyone else, you've made *me* into a caregiver. There isn't a single person in the Landry family who actually needs me. I love them, I make them laugh, I help them out, but none of them *need* me." He lifted a hand and cupped her face. "I *love* feeding you. Even if it's peanut butter and cereal, I like shopping for it. Even if I'm not the chef, I like making sure there's food is here for you. And I know you think my mom's been doing the laundry, but it's been me."

She lifted a brow.

"Okay, she did it twice."

Jill tipped her head.

"Okay, maybe four times. But the rest of the time, I did it." He grinned at her.

"What about the cleaning?" she asked.

Yeah, he knew that was a trick. She knew he hadn't cleaned the house. But the house had gotten cleaned. "That wasn't my family."

"No. Mrs. Thibodaux said she does it twice a month for you in exchange for you not charging her labor for putting on her new roof."

"That's true."

After a beat, Jill smiled. "She does a great job."

"She does. And I'll be honest, I'm *really* hoping she wants new kitchen cabinets put in or a bathroom remodel once that roof is worked off."

Jill laughed.

"Look," he went on. "I *like* taking care of you. And yeah, I don't take care of every detail myself, but it gets done and you don't have to do it. And I'm lucky you're pretty easy to take care of. But, I'm also okay with taking on something a little harder. Like a baby."

Jill's expression softened and damned if her eyes didn't get a little shiny.

But he meant it.

Even if Jill only needed him for the next nine months and then to take care of their child so that she could focus on saving the world—or at least the Galápagos penguins of the world— then he could do that. He was the one person who could step up for her right now.

That gave him a surge of satisfaction, excitement, and a sense of purpose.

He wanted this. He was sure of it.

"And I definitely do not think you're bad person, Jill. You have known who you are and what you want since you were eight years old. That's amazing. You've done everything you could to make that happen. You've made a difference in this world and you're going to keep doing that." He ran the pad of his thumb over her cheek. "Honestly? I'm pretty happy this happened because this means I have a reason to stay really close to you and watch all the amazing things you are going to do. I'm thrilled that my son or daughter is going to have a front row seat to see the way you are going to make the world a better place."

He was startled to see her eyes actually fill with tears. His thumb brushed away the first one that escaped her lower lashes.

Her hands came up to circle his wrists and she gave a little sniff.

"That was the perfect thing to say."

"Thank God. Because I was really winging that."

She gave a soft laugh. "That's how we both do most things, isn't it?"

"Yep. And most of the time it works out really well."

"Except the times when the condoms don't work."

He shook his head. "I'm thinking that maybe that was one of the best times."

She blew out a little breath. "You are unlike any guy I've ever met."

"Glad to hear it."

They just stood looking at each other for several beats.

Then she said, "You're really hot in these glasses."

"Oh, yeah?"

"And I'm thinking... I mean, you can't get me pregnant again."

Her meaning hit him and he felt a slow grin curl his lips. "That is a very good point."

"And, if I stay here, there's no chance of running into Chuck out in the yard."

Without another word, Zeke scooped her up in his arms and headed upstairs to his bedroom.

Two weeks later Jill met Zeke on her front porch when he came to pick her up to take her to Ellie's. They had taken time to let everything really sink in and talk through what they both wanted. Now they were on their way to the bar to tell the family the news.

Jill smoothed the front of her khaki pants and the lavender t-shirt and straightened her cardigan. She was dressed the way she dressed every day. She could have just as easily been going to see the penguins as she was going to see her baby's other side of the family.

Her stomach swooped at the thought. The bar was going to be full of aunts and uncles, cousins, great-aunts and uncles, grandparents, and even great-grandparents.

Zeke had warned her that he had asked everyone to gather together. He seemed to think everyone was under the impression they were getting engaged. Jill figured they were all expecting an announcement about when they could come see the penguins.

When she'd asked why they would jump to that conclusion about them, he'd said that he had never called a family meeting before. She'd said the idea of the two of them getting engaged so fast was crazy but he'd shook his head and told her she didn't know his family very well.

That was an understatement.

And that was all about to end. She did know enough about Autre and this family to know they were very similar to Bliss, Kansas, and her family, and that meant that as soon as they all knew there was a new Landry on the way, she wasn't going to get away with avoiding them any longer.

She pressed her hand over her stomach where butterflies were spinning and diving.

"Is this okay?" she asked as Zeke bounded up her front steps and stopped with only a couple of inches between them.

He looked down at her. "Is what okay?"

He seemed excited. Dammit. He'd actually been excited over the past two weeks in general. They had talked a lot, and he'd been amazingly supportive. He completely understood that this pregnancy was throwing a huge wrench in every plan she'd ever made. He'd been very reassuring about how much help he was going to be.

He'd even tried actually cooking for her one night.

It had only been grilled cheese. And he'd burned it. All three times he'd tried. And they'd ended up raiding Jordan and Fletcher's fridge again. But the attempt had been sweet.

Having Ellie and Cora cooking for their child was a really good idea, they'd decided.

"Am I okay wearing this?"

He chuckled. "To my grandma's bar? You might be over-dressed."

"But I'm meeting your entire family."

"Yeah, and most of them are just coming off a swamp boat tour. They'll be dirty and windblown," he said. "You're fine."

"So can we just walk in and make the announcement and then walk back out?"

"No, we cannot," Zeke said. "I fully intend to soak up all of the affection and praise."

"Praise?" Jill asked. "They do know how babies are made, right? And they're all doing the same thing most nights? And that an accidental pregnancy isn't exactly praiseworthy?"

Zeke shook his head. "That is not how they're going to see this. They'll see this as me having amazingly good taste in women. And then getting crazy lucky by making the best one I've ever found stick around."

"I'm just nervous."

"Why? They are definitely gonna think I'm the one who upgraded and am the most likely to screw this up. They all think you're smart and driven and passionate, and funny and charming and sweet."

"Why would any of them think that? I don't even know any of them."

"Because that's what I've told them about you."

A warmth washed over her and she felt the knot in her stomach loosen. She looked up at him. "You've been talking about me?"

"Apparently, even before I was aware of it. They all know an awful lot about you and your penguins. But over the last couple weeks, I've made a specific effort to make sure they know that I'm completely smitten."

"I suppose it would be nice for your mom and grandma at least to think that you really like the girl you knocked up."

"I *do* really like the girl I knocked up. It's not like I'm trying to convince them of this to cushion the blow or something. I want them to know I consider this a good thing."

She sighed. "You really do think this is a good thing, don't you?"

"I really do. And I promise to make it as good a thing for you as I can."

She reached out for his hand. "Zeke —"

It was then that she noticed his left hand was wrapped in white gauze.

"What happened to your hand?"

"Burned it."

"Burned it on what?"

"Um..."

She lifted both brows. "Zeke?"

He rolled his eyes. "I was making grilled cheese again."

She laughed and then pressed her lips together. "What? Why?"

"I was going to feed you before we went to the bar. I didn't know if you'd want to eat with everyone around."

God, he really was a good guy. "Grilled cheese is not working out for us."

"It's really not."

"Are you all right?"

"Probably," he said.

Probably wasn't good enough. Jill realized that she should take a look at it. She was a doctor, after all. No, not of human medicine, but she did know what to look at when it came to burns.

She hadn't seen a burn in a really long time and had never treated one on a human being, but she was willing to look at Zeke's. After all, this man had put up a fence to keep Chuck out of her yard —actually the fence extended all the way around her house *and* his so it was one big yard that she could walk across without worrying and without carrying her lasso-thingy. And he was not only willing to co-parent with her but was happy to do far more than his share. Though she kind of hoped his mom would do the baby's laundry. And that Cora would be in charge of grilled cheese.

"Let me look at it."

He shook his head. "You don't have to."

"No, really."

He reluctantly let her take his hands and unwrap the gauze. The burn looked kind of nasty. It was second-degree at least. "We should clean this. And put something on it. I can rewrap it then."

"Okay, do you have stuff to do that?"

She didn't. Of course. "No, do you have some stuff?"

"No."

"Do you even have Band-Aids at your house?"

"I don't think so."

"You realize that we're talking about having a child and neither of us even has first-aid supplies in our homes?"

"But we can get some."

Of course they could. That wasn't really the point. The point was neither of them was used to taking care of themselves and, even more importantly, other people. "What were you planning to do about this?"

"I'll let Cora and Michael look at it. Cora will have some cream for it."

Jill wasn't proud of the rush of relief that went through her, but she did acknowledge it. It was definitely not nurturing of her, but it was nice to know that there were plenty of other people who could step in when she and Zeke had no antibiotic ointment. Or food.

"Okay, let's go get you taken care of. Maybe we can take care of your burn before we tell everyone about the baby?"

"Fine, but we *are* telling them today."

Yeah, she knew that. She also knew that the announcement was going to change her life.

But hey, what was the big deal? Just because in two months time she'd gone from her normal life to being a millionaire who owned eight endangered penguins and lived in Louisiana. And was pregnant. Adding a big, rowdy Cajun family to her life was just one more detail.

They headed for Zeke's truck and he helped her up into the passenger seat. She smiled. She didn't think he was even aware of all the times he was chivalrous. She figured it was just ingrained in him. But she did like it.

As he rounded the front of the truck, she looked down at the floor. There was a pair of brown leather flats on the floormat.

Zeke slid behind the wheel and she looked over at him. "Do you need to return these to someone?"

The stab of jealousy was surprising. Not only that it occurred, but how strong it was.

They hadn't talked about being exclusive. If they had, she

probably would've told him to go ahead and date whoever he wanted. Maybe. Or would she?

In all the talk about the baby and what their lives going forward would look like, there had been no talk of other relationships, or *their* relationship in detail. They'd mostly talked as if they'd keep living next door to one another. Which sounded great to her. Though, lately it seemed she spent more nights sleeping over in his bed than her own. And somehow her box of cereal had ended up at his house. She figured it just made sense to have it near the milk.

But they hadn't *discussed* moving in together. Of course, the whole situation was only two weeks old and their conversations had not covered every single detail of the future.

"Those are Paige's. Well, they're yours now. Kind of."

Jill looked at him, processing what he'd said. "What you mean they're mine now?"

"I mean, they can be or they will be at some point or whatever." He started the truck and shifted into gear, pulling out onto the street.

"Zeke, what are you talking about?"

"You told me about how sometimes you forget to change your shoes. I figured some time I might stop by and pick you up for a date or convince you to come down to Ellie's for dinner or something, and you might need to have some different shoes. So I just figured we'd keep some in the truck. Paige said you're welcome to that pair and that brown goes with almost everything so they're probably a safe bet."

Jill stared at him, then looked down at the shoes, then back at him. "You specifically went and got shoes from Paige to keep in your truck for a future moment when I might have forgotten nice shoes and would need them?"

He glanced over, seemingly puzzled by why she was so surprised. "It's easier than running you home to change or expecting you to remember to grab shoes for after work."

"Are we going to have plans after work often?"

She waited for the feeling of panic to rush through her. Instead, she found herself thinking about how fun it would be to anticipate a date with Zeke after work.

That was weird.

He gave her a little smile. A little smile that made her very much want to kiss him.

"I sure hope so. At least we might have a parent-teacher conference or some kind of music recital or something, right?"

Her heart flipped in her chest. Oh, wow. Yeah, they would have those things. And going to them together would be...really nice. And he would be willing to just swing by and pick her up after work and would already have nice shoes in the car for her.

Jill felt her eyes stinging and her throat tighten. Damn, maybe this could work out. Maybe she could work long hours, knowing that Zeke was there for their kid—and for *her*—and that if he ran long at a job and there was a music program, there would be twenty-seven other Landrys going to that same program who could get their son or daughter there too.

"I really hope we have plans after work sometimes too," she told him.

Zeke reached over and squeezed her leg. She was glad he understood how meaningful it was that she'd said that.

But he had to return his hand to the wheel quickly because he couldn't grip the wheel with his burned left hand.

Now she really wanted to get to Ellie's so Cora could take care of him.

They pulled into the drive into the parking lot in front of Ellie's a couple minutes later and Jill immediately changed her mind.

She wasn't glad to be here at all.

The parking lot was packed. She'd never seen this many cars and trucks in front of the building.

"My God, how many people did you invite to this?"

He shut off the truck. "The whole family is here. And then a bunch of our friends from New Orleans. They brought their kids down for a swamp boat tour and the crawfish boil tonight."

"Friends from New Orleans?"

"Yeah, a bunch of people we know through Josh, Sawyer, and Owen. Josh used to work up there with them. Owen and Josh still go up and hang out with them sometimes. And those guys all have kids so they come down here quite a bit. They're thrilled with the petting zoo and that we're getting more animals all the time."

"But I thought we were just telling family today."

"They're pretty much family."

Jill sighed as he got out of the truck and came around to help her out. "Why do I feel like you all say that about a lot of people?"

He grinned down at her. "Because we do."

# 15

---

J ill was relieved that Zeke led her around to the back of the
building and in through the kitchen door. It meant she
had a little more time to gather her wits and prepare to
step out into the main part of the bar where everyone was
gathered.

She could hear the noise even from the back door. There
were a lot of people out there, and it sounded as if they were all
talking at once. Of course, the conversation was also accentuated by bursts of laughter and lots of clinking silverware and
glassware. The place also smelled amazing. Spices of all kinds
mingling in the air with the scent of beer and bourbon.

The kitchen was especially hot. There were two huge stoves
and every burner was covered, along with three ovens going all
at once. Cora stood at one of the stoves, stirring two pots simultaneously.

She looked over and immediately brightened. "Zeke!"

"Hey, Cora." He crossed to her and leaned in to kiss her
cheek.

Jill couldn't deny that she enjoyed watching Zeke with the

people he loved. It was obvious that displays of affection were quite common with this group.

"Hello, Jill. Welcome." Cora greeted her with a cheerful, sincere smile as well.

"Hi, Cora. We're hoping for a little help before we join the party." Jill gestured to Zeke's hand.

Cora stopped stirring and turned, wiping her hands on her apron. "What did you do?"

"Um..." He glanced at Jill. "I was welding. Touched the metal before it was cool."

Jill snorted at his lie. But she didn't tell on him.

Cora clucked her tongue. "You should know better."

"If I had a dollar for every time I've heard that in my life I'd be...still not quite as rich as Jill but a hell of a lot closer," Zeke quipped.

Cora bustled around him and past Jill, stepping into a tiny closet that opened off the kitchen. She flipped on a light, illuminating the room that was a pantry with shelves that extended well above Cora's ability to reach them. Cora scanned the shelves that were full of bottles and jars. She located what she was looking for and pulled a three-step stool over, climbing up and taking down a mason jar.

Coming back into the kitchen, she handed the jar to Jill. "This should take some of the pain away and also help start the healing. But he should also keep it wrapped up as well."

"Why are you giving it to her? I can take care of it."

Cora shook her head. "This cream works best when someone who loves you puts it on." She gave Zeke a smile.

Jill felt surprise zip through her. *Love?* Why would Cora say that?

Okay, Jill would go so far as to admit that she loved things *about* him. And they were things that extended beyond his big hands, his skillful tongue, his charming smile, and his huge cock. Which was saying something. She *really* loved those things.

She loved his unexpected sweetness. She loved when he tried to take care of her even when it failed. She maybe loved that even more.

That thought wouldn't leave her alone. There was something about him making her grilled cheese and knowing that it probably wouldn't work out, but being willing to try anyway on the off chance it did. That was possibly even sweeter than making her a five-course meal that was perfection.

Zeke chuckled. "Good thing we're heading up front then, lots of people out there love me."

Yeah, she also loved his confidence and his joking. Zeke didn't take things too seriously and while she was having a baby with him and that seemed about as serious as it could get, and a guy who didn't really do laundry and couldn't cook and constantly hurt himself didn't seem like the responsible adult she should be looking for, Jill thought Zeke was maybe exactly the type of guy she should be having a baby with.

She'd always thought she should go for a guy who was her opposite. Someone who would be extra careful and extra organized and could take care of all the things she would drop.

But having someone laid back, who simply put a pair of shoes in his truck for her rather than be annoyed that she'd forgotten a good pair, suddenly seemed like a much better idea. Kids forgot stuff, right? And they were picky eaters. Well, it wasn't that she was picky, but her eating habits left something to be desired, she knew. But instead of trying to change her or reprimanding her, Zeke just rolled with it.

The more she thought about it, Zeke had a lot of really great traits that would carry over wonderfully into being a dad. He wouldn't get upset about a kid coming home muddy from playing with his friends. He'd just dump the laundry in the washing machine with everything else. If the kid would only eat yogurt and peanut butter and jelly, Zeke would simply stock up on both. And if the kid made a major mistake—like ending up pregnant even when she'd used a condom—Zeke would roll with that too. He would never make her feel stupid or irresponsible or, most importantly, alone.

"Jill?"

She blinked and looked at Zeke. It seemed that he had said her name at least once before. "Yeah?"

"Should we go up front?"

She shook her head. "Let me put the cream on you first."

"But..." Then it seemed to sink in for him.

Cora just stood looking at them, smiling knowingly.

Yes, Jill was offering to put the cream on for him. That was supposedly best applied by someone who loved him. Would he get it?

He extended his hand, palm up.

Yeah, he got it. Zeke Landry was turning out to be one of the easiest people in her life. Sure, he—and the hot sex and the condoms that hadn't done their job—had complicated her life in a way no one else ever had, and yet, compared to so many things, including her current professional endeavor, he was so much easier.

He held the jar with his uninjured hand while she unscrewed the top, then looked at Cora.

"You can just apply it with your fingers," Cora told her.

"Should I wash my hands or something?"

Cora shrugged. "That stuff will kill anything that's on your skin or his."

Jill dipped her fingers into the light pink cream and then smoothed it over the burned area on Zeke's hand. He sucked in a quick breath, then let it out.

She looked up. "Okay?"

He met her gaze directly. "Very okay."

Cora handed Jill some gauze that had come from Jill had no

idea where and Jill wrapped it around his hand, securing it with tape that Cora also handed to her.

"Okay, good to go." She let go of his hand and recapped the jar.

"Yeah, we're really good to go," Zeke agreed, his voice a little husky.

They shared a little smile, and for the first time since he'd suggested them coming to tell his family the news, Jill actually did feel ready.

She had no idea what was ahead of them, for sure. However, she was quickly learning that whatever it was, Zeke would handle it. Sure, sometimes he needed some help, but he wasn't afraid to ask for it and he knew exactly where to turn to get what he needed.

Maybe Jill had just never had that. Maybe she'd just never had people she knew would be there no matter what. Maybe she'd never had people who would always know exactly what to do in any circumstance.

More, maybe her *mother* hadn't had that. Maybe her mom had been burdened by everything because she really was the only one doing it all. Jill knew that her allergy to the idea of a home life and family came from what she had witnessed with her mom. But her mom's situation wasn't hers. The people who surrounded her mom were not the same people surrounding Jill now.

Zeke held out his uninjured hand to her and she slipped her fingers in between his without hesitation. Then they walked through the door that led to the front of Ellie's bar together.

The place was loud, even by Landry family standards. Ellie's bar got nice and loud and rowdy on a regular basis. But today everything had been turned up several notches.

The gang from New Orleans was here and that always meant an even bigger good time and definitely more laughter and noise.

Zeke hesitated just on the other side of the swinging door from the kitchen. He took just a moment to absorb the room. His whole family was there. He immediately located his mom and dad and his two brothers. In addition, all of his cousins were present as well as the LeClaire family, including Naomi and Michael. Their grandfather, Armand, was sitting at the bar with Leo.

And then there was the New Orleans gang.

"Wow," Jill said.

He looked down at her. "Yeah." But he couldn't help his smile.

He squeezed her hand, trying to be reassuring. He knew this wasn't her kind of scene. She liked things quiet and actually fairly solitary. She seemed perfectly happy spending most of her time alone. It had kind of been killing him. Especially after she'd started sharing his bed more often and being in his house on a regular basis. She seriously was the best he'd ever had and he was addicted to her body, but more, he enjoyed *her*. They'd laughed over his burnt grilled cheese. They'd laughed over sneaking into Jordan and Fletcher's kitchen and stealing food after he'd burned that grilled cheese. They shared stories about their families. She'd taught him about penguins. He'd let her help him repair her back screen door. They'd laughed through a lot of all of that too.

And she was having his baby.

He honestly didn't care if she only visited the kid on the

weekends. He was looking forward to being a dad. And, cave-man-ish or not, he was loving the idea of having something that tied Jill to him.

He didn't think Jill was really going anywhere with her penguins here. It wasn't like relocating Galápagos penguins would be an easy task. But now with the baby in the picture, she would be next door for at least the next eighteen years.

He could definitely think of worse things.

He knew that his family would be expecting and asking if he'd proposed. And with any other woman, he would have by now. But this was Jill. She was special. Unique. She definitely looked at the world differently than anyone else he knew. She was also incredibly independent and upfront. He truly thought that if she believed getting married was the right step, she would've brought it up.

Because she hadn't, he was keeping that to himself. It wasn't that he thought he would never bring it up, but they were working through a lot of other things first. Hell, getting her to come to Ellie's and see his whole family had been a big step.

He flexed his left hand. But she had put cream on his hand. Cora had been partially teasing about having it applied by someone who loved you. Well, maybe ten percent kidding. Cora really did believe that not only did nature's remedies work better than anything from a pharmacy, but she also definitely believed that positive energy and emotions had a lot to do with healing.

But even if Jill had thought Cora was kidding, she'd still taken that jar of cream and treated his hand. That had to mean something.

Zeke knew Jill liked him. She definitely enjoyed spending time with him. And not just naked time. That was something. They seemed to have very little in common on the surface, but the more time they spent together, the more alike they clearly were.

They both liked things simple, neither of them got worked up about things like separating laundry, and they both would've been fine with that grilled cheese for dinner.

"Get over here and tell us your news!" Kennedy, another of his cousins, called. "I have a meeting in a little bit."

But she had a twinkle in her eyes. It was clear that she was expecting big news, and was mostly teasing him.

"Yeah, I've got to remake a pan of brownies for Fletcher's class tomorrow," Jordan said.

The pan of brownies she was replacing was the pan he and Jill had eaten out of last night.

He gave her a grin. Jordan would absolutely forgive him when she found out what kind of news he had.

"Okay, okay," he said, lifting his hands.

"What happened to your hand?" His mother was suddenly in front of them.

Zeke sighed. "It's nothing."

Elizabeth looked at Jill. "What happened?"

"He burned it."

She left out *how* he'd burned it and he wanted to kiss her.

"How bad is it?"

"It looks pretty ugly, but he doesn't seem to be in a lot of pain."

Elizabeth looked at the ceiling. "Maybe I robbed a bank or something,"

Zeke shook his head. "There you are stealing stuff again. And this is nothing. I'm fine."

"You have to learn to be more careful, Ezekiel. I worry enough with Alexander out there as a cop."

"Zander was a detective in New Orleans and basically retired down here. He goes fishing more than he does anything else. He's writing traffic tickets and dealing with kids drinking underage down by the bayou."

"Ironic that, isn't it?" his mother asked. "How many times did you all talk your way out of tickets?"

"It was training. Now he knows what to expect."

"And if you think I didn't lose years off my life while he was a detective in New Orleans, you are craz—"

"We're having a baby."

Elizabeth snapped her mouth shut and she and Zeke both turned to look at Jill.

Zeke couldn't believe that she had blurted that out.

Jill gave his mother a small smile. "Sorry. Turns out, I can't work up to it. That's what we came here to tell everyone. Zeke's going to be a dad."

Zeke squeezed her hand again, but quickly looked at his mother. Was this going to make her think she'd burned down a small village or something in a past life?

Elizabeth's face slowly brightened as the news sunk in. Her hand came up to cover her heart. "Maybe I started a huge children's charity that helped millions out of poverty."

Zeke stared at her. "Wait, what?"

Elizabeth gave him a huge, beaming smile. "I must've done something *really* good in one of my lives."

"So you're happy about this?"

"Of course I'm happy about this."

"And you think this makes up for all the bad things I've done? You think maybe you were a really good person in a past life?"

"I'm sure I've had more than one past life. A couple where I was rotten, certainly." Then she reached to pull Jill into a hug. "But I must've done something good as well," she said to him over Jill's shoulder.

Zeke shook his head. "You're crazy, you know that?"

Elizabeth winked at him. "It's what attracted me to your dad. I needed someone with a high tolerance for crazy. Growing up Landry meant he was the guy for me." Elizabeth let Jill go. Then she turned to the room, put her fingers to her mouth, and gave a shrill, loud whistle.

It shut the room up and had everyone turning to face her immediately.

"Zeke and Jill are having a baby!" she announced to the group.

Well so much for telling them the news himself.

There was a beat, while the news sunk in, then the room seemed to explode.

There were cheers, there were a few "no shits!" Leo yelled, "Way to go, boy!" and there was lots of laughing and talking.

Suddenly the crowd surrounded him and Jill. Zeke immediately wrapped an arm around her waist and pulled her up against his side under his arm.

"Okay, back off a little bit," he told his family and friends. "Give the girl some space."

He looked down at her. Jill did seem overwhelmed, but she offered him a small smile.

He kept her tucked against his side as he pushed his way through the crowd, making his way to the table. He deposited her in a chair with her back to the wall and took the chair right next to her where he could spread out and protect the space around her a bit. Everyone else filed back to their chairs, dropping into their seats.

Conversation continued for the next fifteen or twenty minutes with lots of jokes about how Zeke had welcomed the newcomer to town, how you could come to Autre and get all kinds of permanent souvenirs, and some sincere questions about how Jill was feeling, how far along she was, and if she'd told her family yet or not.

She hadn't yet, and Zeke wasn't sure what her plans were there.

After the initial wave of jokes and questions had quieted, Zeke sat back and took a deep, contented breath.

God, he loved these people. Every single one of them.

He took inventory of the room. The Landrys were gathered around their usual tables at the back of the bar. Leo and his friends were occupying the mismatched stools along the bar. The tables at the front of the restaurant were mostly filled with people from Autre, with only two seating tourists, while the tables in the middle of the room had been pulled together and were surrounded by the New Orleans crew.

Gabe and Logan Trahan were there with their wives and kids, along with two or three extra kids that belonged to other friends. Zeke recognized Caleb Moreau's son and daughter for sure.

But it wasn't Gabe or Logan who was surrounded by the ten kids from New Orleans.

Chuckling, Zeke leaned over to Naomi who was at the next table. "What's Donovan doing with the kids?"

Some were in chairs right next to him, some were standing behind him, some were on his lap. They were all watching the laptop screen in front of him, clearly enthralled by what they were seeing and what he was telling them.

Getting those kids all together and quiet at once—relatively anyway—was a damned miracle. Zeke was impressed.

Naomi was sitting back and watching Donovan with almost as much interest as Stella Trahan was giving him. Which was you-are-the-most-fascinating-person-I've-ever-met level interest.

It was clear that Naomi had a thing for the wildlife activist. Zeke wouldn't quite call it a crush. Naomi LeClaire wasn't really the type to "crush on" someone. But she clearly admired Donovan and the guy could rattle her when he flirted with her. Something Zeke had never seen another human do. Not the flirting thing. Plenty of men flirted with Naomi. But the flustered thing was definitely a Donovan-Foster-only phenomenon.

She smiled. "He's showing them some episodes of his show and telling them behind the scenes stories. Stella is particularly into the ones with him and the alligators."

Zeke chuckled. Of course she was. Stella had been five when she'd first come to Autre and taken a swamp boat tour with Sawyer. She'd been captivated with everything about the bayou ever since. But particularly the alligators. She'd maintained ever since that day that she was going to take over Boys of the Bayou when she was old enough.

None of the Landrys had contradicted the plan.

The details had changed a bit over time though. She'd gone from believing she'd marry Sawyer to proposing that she just take it over when he was "too old anymore". According to Stella, that should happen about the time Sawyer was forty-five. And yes, she knew when his birthday was and reminded him each year about his retirement plan.

She had, however, promised him that he could take a few tours out once in a while even when he was old and that he could have a chair in the front office where he could sit and tell people stories about working on the bayou while they waited for their tours.

"I think Sawyer's a little jealous, in fact," Naomi said, nodding at the eldest Landry cousin.

Zeke looked in Sawyer's direction. He was watching Donovan with the kids too. And he did look grumpy. Well, grumpier than usual. Sawyer wasn't the sunniest of the Landrys on his best day.

"Oh yeah?"

"He's pretty used to being the object of Stella's affection and admiration. But she's been sitting and talking to Donovan for nearly an hour."

"How did he just happen to pull out his laptop to show off his videos?" Zeke asked.

"I might have had something to do with that." Naomi

smiled. "Hey, he loves to talk about himself and the kids needed something to keep them occupied and not begging every two minutes to go see the otters and lemurs."

"Good thinking."

"He's really good with them," Naomi said. Her eyes were back on Donovan.

Uh huh. She was crushing. Just Naomi style. "He is," Zeke said. "He's good with most people."

"Yeah. And animals. And he can bring plants back to life."

Zeke laughed. "What?"

"Yep. Maddie said there were a bunch of plants up at the Boys of the Bayou office that had been sorely neglected and were basically dead. Donovan took one look, gathered them all up, took them home, and a week later brought back these thriving green plants."

"Come on. He went and bought new ones, right?"

"I don't think so. I think he's...Father Nature."

Zeke snorted and Naomi laughed.

"But seriously, he and Cora and Paige can go on and on about plants and herbs and natural remedies."

"No. He's into that stuff too?" Zeke asked.

"Yep. Traveling the world and being up close to different cultures, he's tried all kinds of things. He's eaten bugs too."

Zeke shook his head. "Weird."

"Hot."

"Eating bugs is hot?"

"No. Not even a little. And he's still hot. In spite of eating bugs." Naomi sighed.

Zeke chuckled. "He's so not what I would have pegged for your type."

"He *really* isn't," she agreed.

Yeah, Naomi loved to keep a low profile and hated big crowds. Even this group was a lot of people for her. Zeke knew it helped that she knew everyone here. But she'd be the first one to leave.

"You could make him love quiet time at home," Zeke told her, nudging her shoulder.

"Ha, thanks for the vote of confidence, but I'm just fine," she told him. "I know who I am and what I need. And that man"— She shook her head—"is too much."

"So when are you two going to get married?"

Zeke tuned back into the conversation on his other side just in time to hear Maddie ask Jill *the* question.

He felt Jill stiffen.

He'd been expecting the topic to come up though and he was ready. He'd been around the kids from New Orleans enough to know exactly what to do to create a diversion.

"Hey, Stella?" he called to Gabe's oldest daughter.

She looked over. "Yeah?"

"Did Sawyer tell you about the flamingos?"

Stella's eyes widened. "No!" But instead of asking Zeke for more information, she spun to face Sawyer. "We have flamingos?"

No one missed her use of the word "we".

Sawyer sat up a little straighter. "Uh, yeah. Three of them."

"Right now? Can we see them?" Grace, Stella's cousin, asked.

Sawyer looked to Gabe and Logan, the girls' dads.

They just shrugged as if to say it was up to Sawyer.

"Sure."

"But, Stell," Zeke called. "It gets even better."

She whipped around. "What?"

"Sawyer said he's gonna let *you* name them."

Her gasp was loud enough the entire room could hear it.

Stella looked back at Sawyer. "Are. You. *Serious*?"

Sawyer was clearly completely caught off guard. Because of course he hadn't decided to let Stella name the flamingos. It was possible he hadn't given the flamingos more than two minutes' thought. Zeke was certain Sawyer didn't care what they called the birds.

Until now.

Because this was the way back to Stella's number one spot.

"Of course you get to name the flamingos, Stell," Sawyer told her. "And the camels and donkeys."

"Hey!" Cooper interjected as his sister's mouth hung open in amazement. "What about the rest of us?"

"Well, it's *my* animal park," Stella told him.

"But you promised I could be the CFO," Cooper said. He looked at Sawyer. "That's Chief Financial Officer. I'm way better at math than Stella."

"You *will be* the CFO. But that's money, not animals," Stella said, planting a hand on one hip.

"If you're not nice, I won't let you buy things. Like when you want a new airboat, I'll say no."

Stella sighed as if already regretting hiring family. Zeke grinned.

"Fine," Stella told Cooper. "Do you want to name the camels? You can name *all* of them."

"Yes! How many are there?"

"Two," Sawyer said. "But there are a bunch of donkeys, and two horses, too."

"And we'll have a baby alpaca soon!" Charlie called.

"I want to take care of your flamingos when I grow up!" Grace told Stella, hopping up from her chair. "I'm going to be a vet and then we can work together *every day forever.*"

Stella, Grace, and Cooper were all the same age and were the three musketeers. Always together. Stella was definitely the leader, but Zeke wouldn't be surprised at all if the three of them really did end up living in Autre and running...well, everything.

"So, about nine more years," Zeke heard Logan, Grace's dad,

say to Sawyer. "Then they're *all* yours. All the noise, all the bossiness, all the crazy plans, all the ghost sightings."

"Grace still seeing ghosts?" Sawyer asked.

"All the time," Logan said.

Grace's connection with the "other side" had become a well-accepted fact around this group.

"They'll all blend in just fine down here," Sawyer told him. "Noise, bossiness, and big plans won't even faze us.

"What about the ghosts?"

"Who better to do the haunted swamp tours?" Maddie asked. "Those things happen late at night. We're all gonna be too old to stay up for those soon." She gave Logan a wink and they all laughed.

"I want to name a flamingo!" Jolie, Stella and Cooper's five-year-old sister said from Donovan's lap.

"*Okay,*" Stella said, clearly taking control again.

Zeke sat back. He was a freaking hero.

Sawyer was the coolest again and this had successfully derailed all conversation about him and Jill getting married.

"Okay, Cooper names the camels," Stella said. "Chloe, do you want to name the new alpaca?"

"Um, sure." The thirteen-year-old tried to seem cool about it, but it was clear she thought that was exciting.

"Grace and Jolie can each name a flamingo, and I'll name the third one," Stella decided. "Then everybody else can name the donkeys."

"A group of flamingos is called a flamboyance," Cooper told them all.

"No way," Stella said.

"Yep."

"That is a *fabulous* word," Stella decided.

Grace agreed. "We need bright and fabulous names!"

"Ms. Fluffypants!" Jolie said.

They laughed.

"Then we have to have Ms. Frillybottoms," Grace said.

"And Ms..." Stella trailed off, thinking.

"Featherbutt," Donovan suggested.

"*Yes*," Stella agreed, delightedly.

Everyone heard Griffin's groan.

And saw Donovan's sly grin.

Griffin hated most of the names for the animals at the Boys of the Bayou Gone Wild. Like the alpaca, Alpacino. Or the ducks named after the Brady Bunch. Or the goats named after the Seven Dwarves.

In part, because he hated telling people what the names were.

Zeke couldn't wait to hear Griffin introducing the flamingos to visitors now.

"Thank goodness we got that all straightened out," Stella said, slumping back onto her chair, clearly exhausted. "We definitely needed that figured out before the zebras show up. I can't handle all of this at once."

Zeke chuckled and leaned back in his chair, draping an arm across the back of Jill's chair.

"Zebras?" Sawyer asked.

Stella looked at him. "I heard we were getting zebras. Is that not true?"

"Well..." Sawyer said.

Donovan leaned over and said something quietly to Stella.

She gasped again and bounced up from her seat. "We can put *pink bricks* down leading up to the flamingo pond?" she asked.

"Pink bricks?" Sawyer asked. He looked over at Zeke.

"I'm sure we can find pink bricks," Zeke said.

"Oh," Stella breathed. "We'll call it the Posh Palace of Flamboyance." She looked at everyone proudly. "*That* will be fabulous."

"That's amazing," Donovan told her. "And I'm envisioning

pink feathered boas in the gift shop, and pink gummy shrimp at the concession stand."

Stella, Grace, and Jolie all turned wide eyes on him.

Even Chloe looked a little impressed.

"That's *brilliant*," Stella told him, setting her hand on his shoulder.

Zeke glanced at Sawyer. Who was now frowning.

Damn. Donovan was getting cool again.

"I do think we're probably getting zebras," Sawyer said.

Stella looked at him. "Probably?"

Sawyer looked at Griffin. "I mean..."

Griffin rolled his eyes.

"Sure. I think zebras are great," Sawyer said.

"Lord," Jill said quietly beside Zeke. "Do all Landry men cave so easily to sassy little girls?"

Zeke leaned in. "Yes. Especially the ones that love animals. And not just little girls."

She shook her head. Zeke chuckled.

Then raised his voice to help his cousin out one more time. "Hey, Sawyer, you were thinking we should put a big pink archway over the flamingo area to go with the pink bricks, right?" Zeke asked him. "Do you want Posh Palace of Flamboyance in glitter letters?"

Stella's eyes got wide.

Sawyer noticed and, of course, nodded. "Yes. Definitely glitter letters."

"I hope we have a boy," Jill muttered. "This is just embarrassing."

Zeke laughed, feeling pretty damned good about everything in general.

Fifteen minutes later, the noise level had dropped about twenty decibels.

The New Orleans kids had headed out to look at all the animals, especially the flamingos, camels, and donkeys. Their dads had obviously gone along and Griffin had accompanied them. Everyone knew he wanted to make sure they behaved around the animals, particularly the new additions.

Zeke knew it was no coincidence that Naomi had gotten Donovan talking about something over by the bar so he'd missed tagging along.

That was nice. Sawyer deserved to be the star to that group.

Besides, Donovan got Naomi as a fan. That was no small thing.

And Zeke thought maybe Donovan realized it.

## 16

"Here you go, honey."

Jill looked up to find Ellie at her side. She was still next to Zeke, but he was having fun talking to the group. The *whole* group. Okay, minus the kids and their dads now, but there were still *a lot* of people in here.

Jill had been mostly sitting back and letting the conversation roll around her. She had actually been surprised by, but appreciative of the way the Landrys were able to include her in a conversation by making eye contact and directing comments toward her without putting her on the spot and asking her anything specific.

Until the question about getting married came up, of course.

But Zeke had swiftly changed that subject.

With a little help from his friends.

Those kids were...a lot. And she suspected watching them was like looking back on the Landry cousins when they were those ages.

It was all just a bit overwhelming and it made her want to

crawl into Zeke's lap, wrap her arms around his neck, and rest her head on his shoulder.

Which had to be the strangest urge she'd ever had in her life.

She wasn't a cuddler any more than she was a hugger, but Zeke had a way of making her feel comforted and taken care of. And making her want more and more of it.

No, he didn't have first-aid supplies at his house and he couldn't make grilled cheese, but he made her feel sure that she would always *have* first-aid and grilled cheese if and when she ever needed them.

It was weird. And probably hormonal.

"What's this?"

But it was obvious what it was. Ellie Landry, the owner of the most popular local restaurant and a cook extraordinaire, had just set down the bowl of frosted fruity cereal. She set a tiny silver pitcher next to the bowl that Jill knew held milk.

"I thought maybe you could use some comfort food."

"I thought comfort food was stuff like pasta and grits and, around here, gumbo."

"What comforts us depends on who we are."

Jill blinked rapidly. She got fussed over by her own family, but it had been a while. She knew the teariness definitely had something to do with hormones. Still, she very much appreciated it.

"It's that obvious I needed comforting?"

Ellie pulled out the empty seat next to Jill. Jill frowned. She didn't remember there being an empty seat next to her. But before she could ponder that further Ellie was sitting and leaning in.

"You're unexpectedly pregnant. And thrown into the middle of all of this. And you've only been here for six weeks. And things aren't going so well at work. Yeah, I guess I figured maybe you needed comforting."

"How did you know things weren't going well at work?"

Ellie smiled. "Zeke talks about you a lot. Probably more than he realizes."

Jill sighed. "That's nice. Except that what he's talking about is true."

"Do you always get things right with the penguins?"

Jill thought about that for a moment. Then she nodded. "Yes. Penguins are the one thing I know for sure. I've spent my life studying them. Working with them. I've dedicated myself to them. All of my time and energy. And now, I've been entrusted with these eight and I can't seem to make anything work." She looked at Ellie. "How am I supposed to have a baby and make sure it's safe and healthy and raised properly when I can't even take care of the things that I have literally spent years figuring out?"

"Ah," Ellie said, nodding. "And that's why you need comforting."

"Yeah, I guess so. No offense to your grandson and all, but Zeke and I don't really have any business raising another human being."

Ellie chuckled. "Why is that?"

"Because we are both completely irresponsible."

"Now what makes you say that?"

"I can't get to any appointments on time. I don't remember birthdays or other important dates. He keeps falling off of things or getting hurt other ways. Neither of us should really be using a stove. If you give either of us anything other than cotton or denim we'll probably ruin it."

"The problem is that your definition of responsible is wrong."

"What do you mean? Being responsible is being able to take care of things, right?"

"Being responsible is making sure that the things that need taking care of get taken care of. And I believe it means admitting when you're *not* the best one to take care of something and calling whoever is. For instance, if something needs built or fixed, Zeke or Mitch should do it. But if your dog is sick, Tori or Griffin should take care of that. And if you need kickass shrimp creole or the best muffuletta you've ever had, you call Cora. But you want bread pudding that'll ruin you for all others, you call me."

"But shouldn't *we* be the best ones for our baby?"

Ellie scoffed. "Having a baby means you just magically know how to fix everything and heal everything and make everything?"

"I guess...not."

"I've done it five times. And those five have done it eleven more times total. And I can promise you that none of us have all the answers even now."

"But...I like having answers."

"You're going to have to get over that."

This wasn't particularly reassuring.

"If it makes you feel better," Ellie said, reading her expression. "By number five, you do know a bit more than you do with number one."

"Number *five*?" she repeated. Jill felt her stomach turn over. And she wasn't sure if it was her or the baby reacting to the idea of having *four more*.

"But I'll tell you a secret...every one of those babies will be different—thank God—so no matter how much experience you get, it won't totally prepare you. It's not like bread pudding, or building houses." Ellie shrugged. "Actually, I'm guessin' it's a lot more like taking care of penguins."

"How so?"

"For all they have in common, I'm guessin' those birds are all individuals, right? Just when you think you know what you're doin', one will surprise you."

"Or *eight* of them will surprise you."

Ellie smiled. "Exactly."

"Considering *nothing* is going according to plan with the penguins, that's not really comforting," Jill told her.

"Oh, did you think I was trying to be comforting?"

"You weren't?"

"The cereal is supposed to be comforting. I'm here to tell you that being uncomfortable is just fine. If you're not feeling discomfited about being a mom, you're not taking it seriously enough."

Jill felt how wide her eyes were. "So I *should* be worried and there's nothing that can make me feel better?"

"I don't know about should or shouldn't... you just *will* worry. So there's no sense in worrying about the worrying. What you can do about it, is ask for help. If nothin' else, havin' other people worry with you feels better than worryin' alone."

Jill thought about that. She appreciated Ellie's honesty. She wasn't saying it was all going to be all right. Which Jill wouldn't have believed.

"It's like a hurricane," Ellie said.

"Having a baby is like a hurricane?" Jill asked.

"For sure. Once it's comin', it's out of your hands to slow it down or stop it. You just have to hold on tight to something that's anchored deep, pray a lot, and get ready to clean up a lot of mess."

Jill gave a soft laugh. But...she looked at Zeke. *Hold on tight to something that's anchored deep.* Yeah. She had that.

"And cleaning up messes is easier with more hands," Ellie said. "That's all I'm sayin'."

"And there are a lot of hands around here," Jill said with a nod. "That I do understand."

"Yep. And you've got two of the best right there on that boy." Ellie's affectionate gaze settled on Zeke.

"He is pretty great," Jill agreed.

"When he has a reason to be great, he sure is."

"When he has a reason?"

"He's the baby of the family. And we've all definitely *let* him be the baby. As far as I can tell, you're the best thing to happen to him. He's been less needy in the past few weeks than ever before."

Jill felt her heart flip at that. "I didn't get pregnant so that Zeke wouldn't be the baby anymore."

"I didn't say the baby was the best thing to happen. *You*," Ellie said. "Zeke's been reading up on Galápagos penguins and the Galápagos Islands. He's been helping round up the goats when Benny corrals them, because he knows that you would be upset if one of them gets hurt. He's kept all of us away from the penguins and trust me, that is a big deal. Marcy at the grocery store told me that she's seen Zeke more times in the past six weeks than she has in the previous six years put together. Bailey told me that they've had fewer complaints about Chuck being a nuisance because Zeke has been feeding him and keeping him down by the water's edge so he stays out of your yard. Which keeps him out of other people's yards too. And all of that was before he even knew about the baby."

Jill knew she was staring. "He's been taking care of the goats and Chuck?"

"And I guarantee you that before you came to town he would've just assumed somebody else would take care of it."

"I'm not very good at letting people take care of me," Jill said. But everything in her was saying, *I want Zeke to take care of me.*

Ugh. Pathetic. If nothing else, she was *nine years older than him.* She still didn't love thinking about *that* too hard.

Ellie waved that away. "But he's doin' it anyway. Landrys aren't that great about asking for permission."

Jill thought about that. So she had been good for Zeke. And while she definitely appreciated him keeping the alligator out of her yard, Zeke didn't just *do* things for her. He calmed her down. He made her smile. He made her feel amazing instead of weird. And he actually decreased her stress levels. When he was around, she felt more confident and calm. And definitely happier.

"Do you think I'm a terrible person for never having wanted to be a mother?"

Suddenly Ellie Landry's opinion of her mattered a lot. She didn't try to explain it or figure it out. A lot of things seemed to happen suddenly in Autre with the Landry family.

Ellie scoffed. "I love pecan pie. But I don't want to eat it twenty-four seven. I love goin' to church, but I don't want to sit there twenty-four seven. Being a mom is a twenty-four seven job and it's okay to not like it every single one of those hours."

"I never planned on doing it for *any* hours though."

"Just because you *can* have a baby, doesn't mean you have to *want* to."

"I've been thinking about it a lot the last few days," Jill said. "And I don't know that it's that I don't *want* to. I just never *planned* to. And now I'm trying to adjust to this new reality. I was always given the impression by my mother that you can't do more than one thing really well. And that if there's something that you really, really want to do and you want to be the best at it, then it has been the *only* thing you do. So, a long time ago, I decided I wanted to study and work with penguins and I told myself I wasn't going to do anything else."

"And now you're figuring out there's something else you have to do?"

"Yeah, and I'm afraid I'm not going to be able to do either one well."

"Lots of people work and have kids."

"But I tend to go all in. I'm really afraid that if I have the baby and keep working, the penguins will come first."

"So what are you saying?"

"I..." Jill took a deep breath. Then swallowed. Then finally said out loud what she'd been thinking about for the past week. "I think I need to give up the penguins."

Wow. Hearing the words out loud made them feel real.

Ellie looked shocked. "You would give up the penguins for your baby?"

"Of course. It's what moms do, right?" It was what her own mom had done. "Besides it's really unfair to the penguins too. I'm not really doing a good job with them. Turns out this is all I know and...it's not working. Maybe this is the universe's sign that I'm not one who should have these penguins."

"Who should have them then?"

"There are a number of people who would take them. I've already made a couple calls."

There were three people in the Galápagos penguin project alone who were interested in adding her penguins to their collections.

"Honey, I don't want you to feel like you have to do that," Ellie said, looking concerned. "I don't know anything about penguins, but I know a lot about diapers and discipline. I can help with those while you raise those penguin babies."

Yeah, well, there were no penguin babies. But there *was* a human baby.

And she only had a few months to learn everything she needed to know about him or her.

She'd spent the past nearly ten years, learning everything she could about penguins, even more if she went way back to all the books she'd read as a kid, and, clearly, she *still* didn't know everything she needed to know.

She really did like having all the answers.

And according to Ellie—who would clearly know—she needed to get over that.

Jill looked at Zeke. *Hold on tight to something that's anchored deep.*

He was laughing and talking with his brother, but he looked over and caught her eye and gave her a wink.

At least she'd gotten that part right.

---

"Hey, it would be really great if you would stop buying my girlfriend things and doing stuff for her," Zeke told his brother, as Zeke caught Jill's eye and gave her a wink.

She'd been talking with Ellie and she looked...thoughtful.

Ellie had that effect on people.

Zander lifted his bottle of beer to his lips. "What do you mean?"

Zeke turned back to his brother. "If Jill needs anything, I'm the guy. Got it?"

Zander smirked. "Look, if my neighbor needs her drain snaked, I'm not gonna say no."

Zeke narrowed his eyes. "Jill does not need her drain snaked."

"Not at the moment anyway. I took care of that four days ago."

"You did not snake her drain."

"Well, I offered. And I made sure she knows I'm available any time she needs it."

"Stop saying it like that."

Zander smirked at him. "Like what?"

"Like you're talking about more than pulling gross, clumpy wet hair out of her actual drain." Zeke shuddered as he said it. He could handle blood, vomit, and even animal poop, but wet hair in a shower drain was disgusting.

Still, would he put up with it for Jill?

Absolutely.

"Okay," Zander said. "Then you probably don't want to talk about the *jelly* I gave her."

Zeke's frown intensified. "The *what*?"

"I totally gave her my jelly," Zander said. "A whole bunch of it. Really sticky and sweet, and—"

"Knock it off." Zeke knew Zander was just fucking with him but he still wanted to punch his brother in the mouth. Even the *thought* of another guy messing with Jill raised his blood pressure.

Zander laughed. "Relax. She came over to borrow a screwdriver for a lamp that got delivered and then we talked about Chuck a bit and she mentioned she needed grape jelly. So I traded with her. I got her strawberry, she got my grape."

"And you gave her a dog catcher's pole to use on Chuck?"

Zander chuckled. "That girl isn't going to get that close to Chuck."

"She said you told her she could at least poke him with it. Dammit, Zander, you can't have her thinking that's the way to defend herself with alligators."

Zander gave him a long look. "Jill's smarter than that. But I thought it would help her to feel a little safer if she had something in hand."

He was right, of course, about Jill being smart. Zeke blew out a breath. "Yeah. Okay. I just…"

"You want to be the thing that makes her feel safe," Zander filled in.

Yes. That was what he wanted. But it made him sound like an asshole out loud. "Yeah. But I don't want her *scared* just so I can feel like some big hero."

"I get it. And I like it. You've never gotten to be the big hero. Looks good on you."

No, he'd never gotten to be the hero before. He'd never really wanted to be. That seemed like it came with a lot of expectations and responsibility.

But a lot of things had changed since Dr. Jillian Morris had come to town.

"I just want her...to know I'm there for her. To know she can depend on me."

"She knows." Zander lifted his beer bottle to his lips again. "I asked if she needed help with the lamp and she said if she did, she knew where to find you."

Zeke felt the corner of his mouth curl. "Yeah?" It was just a lamp, but that still made him feel good.

"Yep. She even cut me off when I started to make a joke about screwing."

Zeke's grin grew and he glanced at the woman he'd accidentally gotten pregnant.

Best mistake ever.

"Just one thing you should know about your girlfriend, though," Zander said.

"What's that?"

"She's allergic to strawberries. That's why we traded jellies."

Zeke frowned. "Why didn't she tell me?"

"She thought you were being sweet and she didn't want to hurt your feelings." Zander leaned to set his beer bottle on the table. "But since she has to put up with you long term now, you should probably know that and try not to kill her."

"Shit." Zeke looked at Jill. "They can *kill her?*"

"Nah. Probably not. She said she breaks out in hives if she touches them though."

"Oh, *shit.*"

"What?"

Zeke held up his bandaged hand. "She put Cora's burn cream on me." The cream that had strawberry juice in it.

"Oh, shit," Zander agreed.

They both looked over at Jill. She was scratching the palm of one of her hands and they could see little red welts starting to show up.

"You know what," Zeke said. "Never mind what I said. Keep

helping. Any time you think we need you to step in. Jill and I both definitely need help."

Zander laughed. "You've got it, baby brother. I've always got you. And now Jill. No matter what."

---

"Here you go, darlin'," Cora said, bustling over with a jar of blueish white cream. "This will help with those hives."

Jill looked up, then down at her palms. She'd been so caught up in her thoughts about Zeke and the baby and the penguins that she'd barely registered how itchy her hands were.

"Wha—"

Suddenly Zeke was scooting his chair so he was facing Jill's and taking the jar from Cora.

Cora smiled at him. "Just rub it in right over the hives. They should clear up quick. The itching will get better within a few minutes. Reapply as needed."

"Got it."

He unscrewed the top and took one of Jill's hands, cradling it on top of the bandage over his burn. He dipped the fingers of his other hand into the cream and smoothed it over Jill's palm, rubbing in small circles until the cream soaked into her skin.

"Thanks," she said quietly.

"Always better when someone who loves you puts it on. So I'm told." His eyes met hers.

She wet her lips. Then swallowed. "Feels better already."

"And I made a note about the strawberries," he added.

"It didn't even occur to me to say anything."

"I've got you covered from here. I'll eat your share of all the strawberry shortcake and strawberry pepper jam right along with mine."

She laughed softly. "My hero."

His gaze intensified at her words and his voice was husky when he said, "Damn right."

"We're here!"

They were interrupted by a woman's voice calling from the front of the bar.

"Addison! Dana!" Ellie got to her feet, clearly delighted to see the two women who were headed for the back tables.

The women stopped and looked around.

"Darn, I think we missed them," the brunette said to her friend.

They smiled broadly at one another.

Laughing, Ellie pulled them both into a hug.

"Were you girls sittin' in your car waiting for your children to leave before comin' in here?"

The shorter woman with the lighter hair put her hand on her chest and gave a little gasp.

"What? Are you insinuatin' that we would sit outside, hidden around the corner of your bar, waiting until our gaggle of loud, rambunctious children left to go get stinky and muddy before coming in here where we could drink our liquor in peace?" She waved her hand. "Why I never," she added with a thick, clearly exaggerated, southern accent.

"I wasn't *insinuatin'* that at all," Ellie told her. "I was sayin' *exactly* that."

They all laughed.

It was clear from the way the Landrys all greeted the women that they were well known and well liked.

"That's Gabe's wife, Addison, and Logan's wife, Dana," Zeke filled in for Jill.

"That's Stella's mom?"

"Yep." He grinned. "They're awesome."

"Victoria Landry, you get over here with that pretty little girl," Dana said, motioning to Tori.

Laughing, Tori got up from her seat with Ella. She was

enfolded into a group hug as the women include lots of *oohs* and *ahhs* over the baby and asked Tori how she was doing as they led her away from the huge group of Landrys to a smaller table a few feet away.

Jill was shocked when, on her way past, Tori snagged her hand and tugged her to her feet.

"Come on. You're going to be a new mom soon. You have to talk to Dana and Addison with me."

Jill glanced at Zeke. He was smiling and gave her a little nod.

"They're great. If you want to go. I think you'll really like them," he said.

Jill didn't know how she felt about anything at the moment, honestly. So, she let Tori pull her toward the table where Dana and Addison had settled.

"I'm assuming you're gonna want hurricanes?" Ellie asked them.

Addison lifted her long dark hair off the back of her neck and blew out a breath. "Absolutely." She looked up at Jill with a smile. "Our husbands own a bar in New Orleans. They feel like they make a million hurricanes every week, so they won't make them at home. But I can't help it, I love them. So I have 'em every chance I get."

"And honestly, Ellie's are way better than Trahan's anyway," Dana said. "Don't tell Logan I said that."

"So Grace is yours?" Jill asked Dana.

"And a couple others in there too," Addison said. She looked at Dana. "God, we have a lot of kids."

"You're not kidding," Dana agreed.

"Four each, right?" Jill asked.

"Is that it?" Dana asked. "Feels like eight each." Both women laughed.

"And I still can't get enough of babies," Dana said, reaching for Ella and taking her from Tori. She propped the baby up on her shoulder, patting her back. *"Other people's* babies. Logan thinks we need to have another, but I am putting the kibosh on that."

Addison rolled her eyes. "Sure you are."

"I swear, if we're in the same room and that man sneezes, I get pregnant," Dana said. "But seriously. Four is enough."

"Four is *so many*," Jill said, without thinking.

"Trust me," Dana said. "It really is some days."

"I can't imagine four," Tori said. She looked at Jill. "We have Landry men, which means almost *too much* help sometimes, but these two started out on their own. Addison was a single mom in New York when she met Gabe, and Dana's husband..." Suddenly Tori looked a little ill. "Dammit. I'm so sorry, Dana."

Dana gave Tori a little smile. "No worries, honey." She looked at Jill. "My husband was active duty Army. He was killed in action in the Middle East."

Jill caught her breath. "I'm so sorry."

"Thank you. It was really hard. And I did do it on my own for a while. In fact, I intended to keep doing it on my own. Until Logan Trahan came along and knocked me up with that smile of his."

Addison chuckled. "We don't have to call it his 'smile'. The kids aren't around so we can use real grown-up language."

They all laughed.

"So wait," Dana said looking at Jill. "You're with a Landry boy too? Which one?"

Jill nodded and swallowed. "Zeke."

Dana's eyes widened. "I love Zeke."

Shocker. Everyone loved Zeke.

"Yep. We just found out earlier this afternoon that they pulled the Logan and Dana," Tori said. "They're having a baby."

Addison smiled. "Oh, congrats."

"Thanks." She didn't know what else to say.

"She is also the veterinarian who brought the penguins to

town," Naomi said, pulling a chair over to the table, and settling in.

"Hey, Naomi," Dana said brightly.

Addison gave her a big welcoming smile as well.

"Hey, ladies," Naomi returned.

"Penguins and a baby. That's an amazing way to start your new life in Autre," Addison said to Jill.

"Yeah. That's one word for it." Jill's tone was dry.

Addison chuckled. "Not the word you would use?"

Jill shrugged. "It's...just a lot."

"Yeah, it is a lot.

Addison's phone dinged and she pulled it out and swiped across the screen. "Clearly we need to stay here and help the new moms with advice." Addison turned her phone so Dana could see what was on the screen.

Dana groaned.

Addison then turned the phone so the rest of them could see their kids—and their husbands—in the goat pen covered in mud, holding goats, and grinning widely.

"Kids are washable," Tori said. "That's what Ellie keeps telling me anyway."

"You know the only reason that we keep letting them come down here is because you all will let them use your showers before they get back in the car," Addison said. "There was one time they came down to the petting zoo and didn't shower before leaving. My car smelled like goats for a week."

"And I did not know that a group of flamingos is called a flamboyance," Dana said, reading a text from her phone now. "And no, I do not want to know why I got that text just now."

"Do you want us to fill you in?" Tori asked.

Dana shook her head. "I'm certain it's some big wild plan that Stella and Grace came up with, and that Sawyer is enabling, and that includes glitter."

"Right on all counts," Tori told her.

Jill felt her eyes widen. "That's impressive."

Dana rolled her eyes. "Our kids are loud and wild, but there are some things that are completely predictable...big ideas, Sawyer, and glitter being three of those things."

Addison crossed her legs, clearly settling in. "We are definitely going to be here for a while. So tell us about you, Jill. You moved here with penguins. We actually heard all about that in the petting zoo's newsletter. You met and fell for Zeke. None of us are surprised about that. So now what?"

Wow. That really pretty much summed it all up. It sounded a lot simpler than it felt. "I..." She looked at the four women she was sitting with and was suddenly struck by the urge to be completely candid. "I can't do anything that doesn't have to do with penguins. I can't multitask at all. I can't cook. Like, I can't even boil an egg without boiling the pan dry. I've never changed a diaper or babysat, in spite of the fact that I have two younger siblings. And I'm pretty much freaking out about everything about having this baby."

None of the women at the table looked particularly shocked by the fact that she was freaked out.

"Why no diapers if you had younger siblings?" Addison finally asked.

"My mom. She was a perfectionist. So she did everything herself."

"I was a little bit like that," Addison said. "When Stella was a baby, it was really hard for me to let anyone else in. Actually, even up to the time I met Gabe."

Jill swallowed. There was something about these women and how they were so open and honest about the fact that their children were handfuls and that they weren't out there doting on every moment with them at the petting zoo.

"My mom was a doctor," Jill told them. "Well, she went to medical school. But she got pregnant right after she graduated and my oldest brother had some medical issues when he was a baby. She was too worried to let anyone else stay with him, so she quit and stayed home and proceeded to have three more kids in the next five years.

Dana's eyes rounded. "Wow, that's close together."

"I think that when she had to give up her dream job, she decided that if she couldn't be the world's best doctor, then she'd be the world's best mom and threw herself into that entirely. She did it all herself. And did it wonderfully. One thousand percent."

"So that means that you didn't learn to do diapers, or cook, or..." Addison said, clearly letting Jill fill in the blank.

"Anything. I decided to be a penguin expert when I was just a kid. She fully encouraged me to throw myself into my career, I think in part because she didn't have that. But even when I was young, she encouraged me to have an all-encompassing interest. We never did things like bake cookies together. I never even had chores. Looking back, she was always pushing all of us to get out of the house. We used to joke that it was the only way she could keep it clean, but I really think it was because, while she was so determined to have the perfect house and kids, she resented it and wanted us to have interests in anything *but* homemaking."

She looked around the table for reaction to that.

None of the women really gave her one though. They seemed to be just taking the information in. None of them were judging her. No one seemed shocked or appalled.

"It seemed like I had it really easy growing up. While my friends had to help out around the house and watch their younger siblings, all I had to do was...whatever I wanted. It wasn't until I left home that I realized she really hadn't helped me out. I didn't know how to do anything to take care of a home."

Everyone sat quietly for a moment.

Then Addison said, "You *have* to come to our support group."

"Support group?" Jill asked.

"Yeah, that's actually how we got to know each other." Dana looked at Addison. "Gabe and I knew each other first. We were both in a single parent support group. Some of us were raising family members, some of us were single parents because of divorce or because we had lost a spouse. But we all came together to support one another. Then, as we started getting married, we all kept getting together. So some of us are still single parents, some of us are married parents, but the truth is, as a parent, you always need support."

"Yeah, one of the games you have to definitely watch us play is Mine Is Bigger Than Yours," Addison told her. "We have a big whiteboard, and we all write down the biggest thing we screwed up with our kids since the last meeting. Then, as a group, we rate them from best to worst. And whoever has the worst fuck up gets the traveling trophy."

"Seriously?" Jill asked.

Addison nodded. "Seriously. We all mess up, all the time, and it's okay to admit it. And hey, almost everyone walks out knowing that at least *one* person messed up even bigger than they did."

"And the one who messed up the most for that week gets to take home the big gold cup filled with chocolate," Dana said.

"Okay, the chocolate is an important detail," Tori said.

They all laughed again.

"And then, you can watch us play, I Love Them, But..." Dana told her. "When your kid gets older you can participate too, but I think just watching us play will give you a lot of peace of mind."

Jill found herself leaning in and resting her elbows on the table. "How do you play that one?"

"We take slips of paper and all write down the asshole

things our *kids* did during the prior two weeks. We fold them up and toss them into a hat. Then we take turns randomly pulling them out and reading them to the group. You drink every time you had something similar happen and felt the same way. It's kind of like Never Have I Ever...but with the ways your kids are trying to drive you insane."

"And we end up *wasted*," Addison said. "Because we've all had all the same stuff happen at some point. Which is the purpose of the game. It's a safe place to talk about the fact that you love your kids, but they also make you nuts. Then a couple of the husbands come and pick us up and take us all home. And we all leave reassured that our kids are normal-ish and, even better, so are we."

"And who is watching the kids during this time?" Tori asked, clearly fascinated.

"The dads. Of course, now there's so many kids, they actually get together and watch them as a group," Addison said. "It's the same thing we do when they have their book club night."

"Your husbands have a book club?" Jill asked.

"Yep. And it's an erotic romance book club."

"No way," Jill said.

"Seriously," Tori said. "Josh even goes."

"They actually read romances?" Jill asked.

"Judging by some of the new ideas Logan has brought home, I can attest to the fact that yes, they really do read erotic romances," Dana said with her hand up as if making a pledge.

All the women laughed. Again. Jill couldn't remember the last time she'd sat with a group of women her age and enjoyed it this much.

And not talked about penguins the entire time.

"Also," Addison added, looking at Jill. "We'll teach you how to boil an egg."

Jill shook her head. "Honestly, I don't want to boil eggs."

Addison shrugged. "Fair enough. But, be warned, we also

do school snacks together. If someone has to decorate like four dozen cookies, we all pitch in. Or we brainstorm birthday party ideas or hell, sometimes we fold laundry. All of these never-ending tasks that are simply easier when you have extra hands."

That was so much like what Ellie had said about extra hands for clean-up, Jill was suddenly choked up. She wouldn't have the first idea how to decorate four dozen cookies. She'd hire it done, clearly. But someday she was going to have to throw a little boy or little girl a birthday party. She was so screwed.

Except...

She looked at the two women who had literally walked into her life twenty minutes ago. Then at the two women who had been here for six weeks, but who she'd been avoiding because... that was just what she did. And suddenly, she wasn't feeling quite so in over her head.

They'd done that in twenty minutes.

Imagine how great she would feel after a couple of these moms' nights with them.

"That sounds really good," Jill finally said. She looked at Tori. "We'll both go, right? To the support group?"

Tori nodded enthusiastically. "Absolutely. I can't wait."

Addison's phone dinged with another text and she groaned softly. But she opened the message. Then sat up a little straighter. "Oh, they're going over to the alpacas with Shay. Jordan's meeting them down there." She looked up. "Caleb and Lexi are friends from the group. Their little girl, Shay, has a brain injury from a car accident. Lexi has been talking with Jordan about the new program she'd put together and Lexi's been so excited to see how Shay reacts when they try some of the activities with the alpacas. I promised to record it since Lexi's working in the ER tonight."

"Of course, you should go," Jill said.

Dana and Addison stood. Dana handed Ella back to Tori and they gave the new mom and Naomi hugs. Then they both smiled at Jill.

"It is really nice to meet you, Jill," Dana said.

"You too," Jill said honestly.

"And Zeke will have to come to erotic romance book club," Addison said with a sly smile.

Jill felt her cheeks heat as her first thought was, *Zeke doesn't need an erotic romance book club for ideas.*

Addison noticed her blush and gave her a wink.

## 17

Addison and Dana left, and Tori got up as Ella started fussing. "This support group stuff will be fun," she said.

"I think so too. Thanks for introducing me to them."

Tori squeezed her shoulder. "Of course."

Jill focused on Ella. The baby was squirming and fussing against Tori's neck, but Jill had a sudden sense of contentment herself.

"And maybe, if you're willing, I could get some babysitting practice in with Ella sometime."

Tori's face lit up. "That would be amazing. We have tons of babysitters, of course, but our kids are going to be so close in age and are going to grow up together. I'd love for you to be close to Ella."

Jill felt her throat tighten and she had to swallow hard before she said, "Yeah. That's true."

Oh, God. Their kids were to be close in age and were going to grow up together. Ella was going to be her child's closest cousin. Reality slammed into Jill as Tori gave her a bright smile and then headed for Josh.

"Hey."

Jill took a deep breath and turned to look at Naomi, the only person remaining at the table with her. Naomi was so quiet and unassuming. She just sat back and watched the people around her, taking everything in, not needing to interject or ask a million questions.

"Hey."

"Want to take a walk?"

Jill *so* wanted to take a walk. How did Naomi know that?

"I would love that."

Naomi scooted her chair back and stood.

Jill glanced over at Zeke. "I'm going to take a walk with Naomi," she called.

Somehow she knew he'd be pleased that she'd enjoyed her talk with Dana and Addison and Tori and he'd be really happy she was spending time with Naomi.

He looked surprised, but said, "Okay, but don't you be havin' any plantano frito without me."

Naomi laughed. "Fried plantains," she explained to Jill. "A Haitian dish my grandmother makes. Zeke loves them." She looked at Zeke. "If we get any, we'll bring you some." She dropped her voice so only Jill could hear her. "We're not going to my grandma's."

"Fair enough." Zeke gave Jill a long look and she knew he was asking if she was okay.

She gave a little nod.

He gave her a satisfied smile in return.

And all of that was the strangest wordless exchange she'd ever had with another human being.

And it made her chest feel warm.

Jill followed Naomi out of Ellie's. They took a right at the front path, which would lead them away from the swamp boat tour company offices and the petting zoo.

They walked for several yards without speaking.

It was nice to find someone here who knew how to just enjoy a quiet moment.

That lasted for about twenty more steps.

"I know you're worried about—"

"I know you're friends with Zeke —"

They spoke over one another.

They stopped walking and turned to look at one another with mutual smiles.

"I am friends with Zeke," Naomi said. "He's a great guy."

"He is. I didn't want to give you the impression back there that I'm unhappy about being with him or about the baby. I'm not. I'm...actually really happy to be with Zeke. And I'm adjusting to the baby news."

"I'm glad to hear that. But I didn't want to take this walk to talk about Zeke or the baby," Naomi said.

"Oh." Jill frowned. "Then what did you want to talk to me about?"

"Well." Naomi shook her head. "I can't believe I'm doing this."

"Doing what?"

"Sticking my nose in where it doesn't belong."

"Now I'm *really* curious." She hadn't been around Naomi LeClaire much, but Jill got the impression the other woman was thoughtful and considerate. If she had something to say, Jill wanted to hear it.

Naomi took a breath. "I wanted to tell you a story about a polar bear."

Jill faced her more fully. That wasn't even close to what she'd been expecting the other woman to say. "A polar bear?" Jill repeated.

"Yes." Naomi tucked her hands into her pockets. "There was this polar bear, Hugo, on my show. He and his trainer, Greg, worked together for about two years. Then Greg's wife, Tracy, got cancer. Greg, obviously, was very stressed and sad. And as

Tracy's illness progressed and Greg's depression got worse and worse, we noticed that Hugo got depressed too. It was like he was feeding off of Greg's emotions. When Tracy had a good day and Greg was in a better mood, Hugo would have a good day. When Greg was especially sad, Hugo would have a terrible day."

Naomi paused. Jill didn't say a word.

"When Tracy passed away and Greg was in mourning, Hugo wouldn't do anything for us for almost two weeks. And even after that it took a really long time for him to get back to normal. It was crazy and I don't know if I would've believed that if I hadn't seen it myself, but it seemed that Hugo was feeling what Greg was feeling." Naomi met Jill's gaze directly as she spoke. "That was the most remarkable instance, but I saw animals and humans bond in really amazing ways over the years."

Jill knew she was staring, and she sincerely was trying to focus on what she knew Naomi was *really* trying to tell her. But she was distracted.

"Jill?"

"Yeah?"

"Did you hear me?"

"Every word," Jill said with a nod. "Like...the words 'your show'."

Naomi sighed, but smiled. "I figured you'd notice that."

"What did you mean by that?"

Naomi studied her for a moment. Then nodded. "The TV show I was on."

"You were on a *TV show*?"

"From the ages of eight to fourteen. It was called Zoey At the Zoo."

Jill gasped so hard she thought she'd probably sucked in a mosquito or two. "Oh my God. You were Zoey."

"Yes."

"You're Naomi *Williams*?"

Naomi lifted a shoulder. "A stage name."

Now that Jill thought about it, she vaguely recalled knowing that Naomi Williams had been originally from Louisiana. "I've seen some of the show. I'm..." She cleared her throat. "...a little older than you. But the show was huge. I definitely knew of it."

"Yeah. It was huge," Naomi agreed.

"I just...I'm stunned."

"It's the best kept secret in Autre," Naomi said. "I was born here. My family is from here. For generations, really. When I got cast on the show, Mom and I moved to California, but everyone else stayed here. When the show ended, I was fourteen. I retired and we came back here. But Autre keeps the secret. If anyone ever comes through and asks if I live here now, they lie."

"Wow, that's kind of amazing."

Naomi smiled. "It's very amazing. I live a very quiet life now, completely out of the spotlight. I have no interest in anyone knowing who I am and no interest in returning to that life at all."

"Thank you for trusting me," Jill said, realizing what Naomi had revealed to her.

"I'm not worried," Naomi said. "I've been listening to Zeke talk about you for weeks. I know you're one of us."

That hit Jill right in the chest and she had to work to pull in her next breath.

She knew the Landrys had accepted her into their circle. She knew she was automatically included because of Zeke. And the baby. But she hadn't really let it in.

That was...pretty awesome.

"But just because I'm not interested in a public life, I still have a lot of love for wild animals and all the people who work with them," Naomi went on, spreading her arms wide. "And the fact that they're building this animal park right in my backyard, is kind of crazy and ironic. I feel like I should be a part of it. Somehow." She let her arms drop. "Charlie and Jordan are two of my best friends and they keep insisting that I don't need to do anything I'm uncomfortable with, but there are so many talented, wonderful people here and if I can help at all, I really want to." She gave Jill a small, sincere smile. "I'm sorry you're struggling with the penguins. It made me think of Hugo so, after listening to you talk about your mom and everything, I finally decided to share."

"You think maybe there's something like that going on with the penguins?"

"Zeke told us about A.J. About how he was the only one taking care of the penguins and how he was sick most of the time. How you didn't meet them until he passed. And how they've only been with you since then and that you've been..."

"Uptight. Worried. Stressed. Anxious."

Naomi gave a soft laugh. "Yeah."

Jill thought about that. She believed what Naomi had told her about the bear. Animals could be very sensitive, and she'd also seen some amazing bonds between humans and animals as well as some instances of across-species bonding that were surprising and hard to explain. "You think the penguins are grieving A.J.? And picking up on my tension?"

"You're the expert," Naomi said. "I just thought I'd mention it." She paused. "Actually, I *wasn't* going to mention it. But then you were talking about your mom and the baby and I realized that maybe you could use another perspective."

"Why do you think this has to do with my mom?"

"Zeke talks about how one of the things you have in common is that you both like things simple and don't mind other people helping out and doing things for you. You said your mom actually kept you from learning *how* to take care of yourself with even the basic stuff like cooking and laundry."

Jill nodded.

"But I'm guessing you don't consider things simple with the penguins. I'll bet you know what each of those penguins weighs down to the ounce and I'll bet you monitor their vitamin intake daily, and I'm sure that you've noted details about every single one of their behaviors down to which part of the enclosure they each prefer."

Jill shifted her weight from one foot to the other. That was all scarily accurate.

Naomi noticed. "I was around animals and their caretakers every day for six years. I know a TV show and an endangered penguin project are different in a lot of ways, but I also know how people who love the animals they're caring for act."

"It's all stuff I've always done for the penguins at the zoo. But now, these are *mine*. I'm the only one taking care of them. And they were entrusted to me by a friend as his dying wish. And...yeah, I've definitely been uptight about it."

"Because you're a perfectionist like your mom."

Jill straightened in surprise. "No. I'm definitely not. It took me twenty minutes to find my phone this morning. And it was in my pocket the entire time. I got downstairs and was about to walk out the door but I couldn't remember if I'd taken *my* vitamin this morning." She grimaced. "So I took two. And that is obviously not something I should do often. Though I should probably look up what extra prenatal vitamins will do to me."

"Why were you so distracted?" Naomi asked.

Jill opened her mouth to reply, realized what her answer was, realized Naomi already knew what her answer was, and snapped her mouth shut.

"You were thinking about the penguins," Naomi filled in.

Jill sighed.

"You're not a perfectionist in *everything* the way you think your mom was, but you are about the thing that matters the most to you. And after talking to Addison and Dana, I hope you see that there's a very real possibility that your mom *wasn't* perfect in every way behind the scenes. I'm sure Stella and Cooper and Grace and Chloe and the others think Addison and Dana are though."

Jill let that sink in. And tried to think of who her mom might have hung out with and talked about mom stuff with. She couldn't come up with anyone. And that suddenly made Jill sad. She didn't even have a child yet and she was already looking forward to time with other moms.

"Can I say something else?" Naomi asked.

"Please. This has all been really helpful."

Naomi looked relieved. "Thank God you think so. Okay, look, I don't know your mom. It sounds like she really did try to do it all on her own. But I'm wondering if, even though you want to be perfect for the penguins, you might consider forming a little support group for penguin caretakers. Like the group you'll have with the moms."

"Wow, that would be nice," Jill said. "I'm usually the one that people come to when they have questions and, until now, I've always had answers. But I'd love to have a group I could talk to." She shrugged. "But all the other programs are going well."

"I was thinking it might be helpful to talk to someone who was dealing with the *exact* issue you are," Naomi said. "As in *these* penguins. Here."

"But no one else *is* dealing with these penguins."

"Maybe they should." Naomi reached out and squeezed Jill's arm. "I'm saying that, you don't mind when people cook for you and help with your laundry and you're open to help with the baby. Why not let someone help you with the penguins? Don't take it all on yourself. Get a penguin buddy. And, even if he...or she," she added quickly, "... can't actually make the penguins procreate, at least you'll have someone to talk to about it."

Jill let that sink in. It would be nice to bounce some ideas off of someone. Or maybe just complain to.

"And maybe you'll relax a little and the penguins will pick up on that too and that will help," Naomi went on.

"Yeah. Maybe."

"Really? You'll consider letting someone help?" Naomi seemed surprised.

"Sure. Can we have wine? Like Addison and Dana do with their group?"

"Well, *you* can't. At least for a few more months."

"Dammit." Jill's hand went to her stomach. "That's right." She really wasn't used to being pregnant. She hadn't had a bit of morning sickness and she felt pretty normal overall. "Seriously. I definitely need people taking care of me. I almost *forgot* I was pregnant."

"You're fine. No one's going to let you drink any alcohol, Jill."

"Thank God." She really did appreciate knowing she had people looking out for her. "Did you work with penguins on Zoey At the Zoo?" Jill asked.

"No. That was one thing we didn't have," Naomi said.

"That's fine. If you can just come out and spend some time in the enclosure with them so they get used to you, then we can—"

"Oh, not me," Naomi broke in, holding her hand up. "I'm sorry. That's not what I meant. I was talking about Donovan."

Jill was surprised. "Donovan said he wanted to work with the penguins?"

"Not in so many words. But...I'm sure he does. They're animals, after all. I can't *imagine* that he would say no."

She had a point. "I can't believe I could be working with Donovan Foster," Jill said, shaking her head. "No offense," she said quickly. "Zoey At the Zoo was a much bigger show than his, but his was more my speed."

"No offense taken. I've seen every episode of his show," Naomi said. She held her hand up again. "But do *not* confirm that for him."

"So is this plan about the penguins a way for you to get him to stick around a little longer without *confirming* for him that you want him to?"

Naomi waved that away. "Donovan Foster is not what I'm looking for."

"Uh huh."

"But," Naomi said, giving Jill an I'm-done-with-that-subject look. "I think *he's* looking for *something*. Something that's more...meaningful. Something with more purpose. He and Griffin have a complicated relationship and they're starting to get closer. And Donovan's moved around so much, that he's never really put down roots. I just..." She shrugged. "I don't know what he wants for sure, but if it's roots and relationships, then Autre is a pretty amazing place to be. I think maybe giving it a little more time wouldn't hurt him."

That was for sure. Roots and relationships were unavoidable here, it seemed.

"Do you think Donovan would play Mine's Bigger Than Yours with me?" Jill asked.

Naomi actually gave a soft snort. "I'm sure of it."

Jill laughed. "I mean regarding things we've screwed up with animals we've taken care of."

Naomi nodded. "Yeah. That too."

Jill smiled as they turned and headed back for Ellie's.

Strangely, she was actually looking forward to comparing things she'd screwed up with someone else.

"Those two penguins are never going to have chicks, Jill. You have to accept it."

Jill looked at Donovan. "You're right. I can't believe I didn't see it before."

It had been a week since Naomi had convinced Jill to ask Donovan to help out with the penguins.

As if by magic, the day after Donovan stopped by the enclosure and spent time with the birds, one pair of penguins had actually built a nest. Jill had cried real tears of joy.

Five days later, they'd realized the penguins that were taking turns sitting on the eggs in the nest were both females. The eggs were infertile and weren't going to hatch.

Donovan turned to face her, leaning against the rocks. "Yep. We have lesbian penguins."

Yep.

Which didn't bother her. Except that it was going to make it very difficult to have babies.

Jill looked at the two penguins who were standing next to the pond, tapping each other's beaks affectionately.

Same sex couples were actually common among penguins and she wasn't sure why that hadn't occurred to her before as one of the reasons for a lack of baby penguins.

"So, we need to figure something out here," she told Donovan. "Those two ladies pairing up means that two of our males are left without options."

"You need to get more penguins," Fiona said from beside Donovan.

She was in town checking on the camels, donkeys, and horses she'd brought last week. Because of her connections in the world with people who cared for exotic animals, Jill had asked if she'd stop over at the penguin enclosure. Asking for help and input was already getting easier.

It hadn't yielded any results yet. But the asking was easier.

Yes, more penguins was an option.

"Or we send the males to another program where they have more females." Jill glanced at her eight. She didn't want to do that, but it was hardly fair to keep them here if there was only one interested adult female for three males. Penguins mated for life. Once Greta chose a mate, the other two would be out of luck.

"Come on. At least think about adding more penguins," Donovan urged. "Penguins live in much bigger groups than this in the wild. Maybe they just don't have enough friends. Besides, you have four more penguin names to use."

She looked at him quickly. "You know what their names are from?"

"Come on. Of course I've read Mr. Popper's Penguins."

Jill grinned. She really liked Donovan Foster.

"You know, the small group could be a part of their general depression and why the straight pair hasn't mated yet," Fiona said. "He's right that having a larger rookery could make a difference."

"Naomi thinks they might be depressed too," Jill mused, watching the two juvenile penguins dive into the pond. They wouldn't be mature enough to mate for another year.

"Does she?" Donovan straightened slightly. "What else did Naomi say?"

That she'd been a world-famous actress at one time. But Jill didn't know who knew that secret and she wasn't about to betray her new friend's confidence. "That my stress might be rubbing off on the penguins and that I need a friend to help me brainstorm and to complain to when things don't go well," she said honestly.

He grinned. "Well, you've got one and a half."

"Am I the half?" Fiona asked.

"Yep."

"Because I'm short?"

"Because you're not here all the time," Donovan said, looping an arm around her shoulder.

Fiona only came up to his chest.

"And because you're short," he added.

She stuck her tongue out at him, but said, "I'll admit, if these birds need some positivity and enthusiasm, he's the guy."

That was for sure. If anyone could be the balance to Jill's anxiety, it would be Donovan.

"I think having you spend more time with them would be great, if you're willing. And I'm up for any ideas you have."

"You mean besides getting more penguins or shipping the two males off to someone else?"

"Both of those things are on the table," she admitted. "I have to at least consider sending those two somewhere they'll be better off."

"Fine. But could we start with two more females first? Just two more. That's not a huge commitment but we could see if we can make things better before we give up."

"How about we get the one straight pair we have to have some chicks?" Jill said. "Let's do that and then talk about what's next."

"Okay," Donovan agreed. "Fair enough." He looked at the penguins. "We could read to them. Or show them movies or something."

"Movies?" Jill asked. "Seriously?"

"Like porn? To get their libidos going?" Fiona asked.

Donovan laughed. "I was thinking films with ocean sounds like they'd hear in nature. Or hell, even cartoons. More for enrichment and stimulation. But hey, I'm open-minded."

Jill shook her head. This was what her career had come down to. Planning raunchy movie nights to try to get a bunch of penguins laid.

"Sure, let's just project porn up on the side of the penguin enclosure here in sweet little Autre, Louisiana," Fiona said. "That definitely won't bother anyone."

Donovan chuckled. "Sweet little Autre, Louisiana? You haven't been here long enough. Or hanging out with enough of the locals." Then he leaned in. "Or are you thinking about a *specific* local who that would bother *a lot*?"

"Definitely. That man is an uptight, prudish rule-follower." Fiona fanned her face. "And *oh* do I want to rile him up."

"Who?" Jill asked, looking back and forth from Donovan to Fiona.

Donovan chuckled. "Knox."

"The city manager?"

"Yep."

She looked at Fiona. "Wow. You seem like total opposites."

"We are. Total."

"You think Charlie would want to sell tickets to our porno movie night?" Donovan asked. "We could have the kids' movie night down with the baby goats and adult movie night up here with the penguins." He grinned.

"I just hope Charlie will call it Porn with the Penguins," Fiona said. "And not Penguin Porn, because that sounds like a whole different thing."

They all laughed.

Donovan started toward the parking area. "Okay, serious idea that we can implement right now."

"I'm listening," Jill told him, falling into step beside him with Fiona on her other side.

"Penguin Parade," Donovan said.

"A penguin *parade*?" Jill repeated. "What do you mean?"

"We take them on a walk around the animal park. Let them see something new. Interact with some other animals. Stimulate them."

Jill was already shaking her head though. "I don't know. Part of the program is to keep their environment controlled."

"Well, babe...," Donovan said.

And yes, she made a note of the fact that *Donovan Foster* had called her "babe".

"This controlled environment thing isn't workin'."

Jill blew out a breath. He was right. Obviously.

"And you think taking them on a *walk* will help?"

"Shake things up. It's an enrichment activity that lots of other places have used."

"What if that makes things worse?" But she frowned even as she said it.

"Can you have fewer chicks than zero?"

Jill ran a hand through her hair. "Yeah, okay."

"I mean, you have kept them pretty solitary and quiet and undisturbed," Fiona said, nodding as she considered Donovan's suggestion. "And it sounds like A.J. did the same. Maybe they're bored. Maybe they need a little excitement."

Jill looked back at her eight feathered charges. She had to admit that her first instinct was to say no to taking the penguins out of their safe haven and potentially rattling them. But at this point she was willing to try anything.

"Okay, I'm game. What do you think this looks like?"

"I'd say two or three of us walking with them right down this path, keeping them together and out of trouble," Donovan said. "We'll walk them down to see Slothcrates and Larry, Curly, and Mo. And the red pandas. They can look but won't get up real close."

"Yeah, we'll shut the rest of the petting zoo down to visitors during that time," Fiona said. "It'll only be an hour or so. We'll do it during the week, mid-afternoon, while the kids are still in school since we get busier after that."

"Okay, let's give it a try. Again, it's not like they could get *less* interested in being parents," Jill said.

And she was going to quit thinking about how ironic it was

that, while she had been trying to get three penguins pregnant, she'd managed to get herself knocked up instead.

"Speak of the big, hot, I-want-to-do-all-kinds-of-naughty-things-to-him devil," Fiona said, as they passed Slothcrates's enclosure.

Jill glanced at Fiona. "What?"

"Knox is here." Fiona lifted a hand and waved.

Jill looked toward the parking area. Sure enough, Knox was leaning against the side of Fiona's huge, grape-purple truck.

"I'm still surprised by you being into him," Jill said. "You seem so different."

"We are. But two matches side by side are just two matches. Gasoline poured on more gasoline...nothing happens. But you put a match to gasoline? *That's* how you get heat."

Jill's eyes widened. "A lot more than just 'heat'."

Fiona grinned. "Right?" She picked up her pace down the walkway.

Jill followed. She wanted to see this suddenly.

"Hey, Fritz," Fiona said to Knox as she drew close.

"Nope," he told her, pushing away from her truck and stretching to his full height.

He was a very big guy. He was an inch taller than Zeke and definitely wider through the shoulders.

"His first initial is 'F' but he won't tell anyone what it stands for," Fiona told Jill. She tucked her hands in her back pockets and peered up at Knox. "But I'm going to get it out of him someday."

Knox rolled his eyes. "I'm here about the donkeys."

Fiona smiled. "You met them?"

"Yes. All five of them," Knox said.

"Aren't they sweet?"

"Not the word I was looking for. I also noticed both camels."

"And the two horses, I presume."

"Why are you annoyed about those?" Jill asked. "Donkeys

and camels and horses should get along fine with the alpacas and—"

"I'm not annoyed," Knox said.

Fiona looked surprised. "Oh. Damn."

He *almost* smiled. "Donkeys, camels, and horses don't even need any special licensing in Louisiana."

"We've done *all* the paperwork for everything else," Fiona said. "Every animal I've brought to Autre is obtained legally and fully licensed. And they're doing great here. They're happy and well cared for and—"

"Causing an increase in traffic which is causing more congestion and tearing up the roads not to mention the increased number of *people* who are generating more litter and, even when they do manage to get stuff in the trashcans, they're filling them up a lot faster," Knox said.

"We've put up signage and enlisted the help of the church youth group to do garbage clean-up once a week and all the waste from the animal park is recycled or composted."

"We?" Knox asked her, instead of commenting on her solutions.

Fiona frowned. Then nodded. "Yeah. We."

"Your park is in Florida."

"My *other* park is in Florida."

He looked at her for a long moment. "I see."

Fiona lifted her chin. "Good."

Jill looked back and forth between them. Wow. She wasn't so sure they needed a match or gasoline. There were sparks all over. Even while they were talking about traffic and composting.

"If you're not annoyed by the new animals and you're not here about paperwork, why *are* you here?" Fiona asked.

"Tell me about the new animals."

"What about them?"

"Why are they here?"

"Why not?"

"Fi," Knox said.

Fiona's eyes widened at the use of the short form of her name. "What?" Her voice was softer.

"Tell me about the animals and why you brought them here."

"Fine. We...rescued them."

"You and Colin?"

"Yeah."

"Who's Colin?" Jill asked.

"Her boyfriend."

"My friend."

They spoke at the same time. And Jill noted that their description of Colin was different. In an important way.

"And business partner," Fiona added.

Knox didn't say anything to that. But he was watching Fiona intently.

"Anyway, yes, Colin and I rescued them. We got a call about a farm where the animals were being neglected and abused. The cops went in, but they took us along to actually take care of the animals."

"You do that a lot," Knox said. It wasn't a question.

But Fiona narrowed her eyes. "You looked into me."

"Of course, I did. Long before there were camels here."

She pulled in a breath, but finally said, "Yeah. We do it a lot."

"You don't run an animal park. You run an animal sanctuary."

"It's both. We have a few cool animals that people come to see and learn about. Like our giraffes. Those ticket sales help us support the ones that need a sanctuary instead."

"And you brought these animals here instead of keeping them yourself?"

"We can't keep them all. Unfortunately, there is always a

need to recruit new places that will take in rescued animals. And we actually rescued these here in Louisiana." Fiona put her hands on her hips. "Some of the people I work with in Florida let some people in Louisiana know that I had a connection to a place that could be a new sanctuary."

"Fortunate that they'd already built a barn and big pen for the zebra Zeke wants so much."

Fiona smiled. "It was really serendipitous that he'd already built the pen and barn, wasn't it?"

Knox studied her. Finally he asked, "Do the Landrys know you're turning their animal park into a sanctuary?"

She smiled. "Yeah. I mean, I did also bring them flamingos and they're just for fun. But"—her voice softened—"these people were on the path already. I just nudged them a little."

"Why them?"

"They've got the space and the resources. And the hearts."

Knox nodded. "I agree."

"You just think it's good because the sanctuary animals won't be on display so they won't cause increased traffic and trash."

He didn't deny it. Instead, he pulled the driver's side of her truck open. "Can we....talk?"

Jill and Fiona both arched brows.

"Talk?" Fiona repeated.

"Yeah. I'd like to talk."

"About?"

"About the animals you've rescued."

"The donkeys and camels?"

He gestured toward her truck. "All of 'em."

"*All* of them? All the animals we've rescued? It's been a lot."

"Good thing you like to talk."

"I like to do a lot of things. Especially with big, hot, growly men."

"Is eating ice cream one of those things?"

She paused, clearly surprised. Then grinned. "It is."

"Then get in the truck."

Fiona looked at Jill. "I guess I'm going out for ice cream."

Yeah, Jill wasn't so sure that was what she was going out for.

She watched Knox help Fiona up behind the wheel, then round the huge purple vehicle and climb up on the passenger side.

As they drove off, she thought back to eating ice cream with Zeke.

And she suddenly wanted more.

And she wanted more of whatever was going on between Knox and Fiona too.

———

Jill knocked on Zeke's door two hours later.

"You really have to stop knocking, cher," he told her when he answered.

"I have something to ask you," Jill told him.

Zeke had something to ask her too. Actually, a number of somethings. Did she want to spend the night with him, how was she feeling, was she allergic to anything besides strawberries, was the strawberry allergy genetic and would their baby have it, did she like the name Magnolia, had she really liked the crawfish or had she just been faking it for Ellie's sake, and about a million other things.

Instead, he tucked his hands into his back pockets and just waited.

"I'm going back to Kansas. I'm leaving tomorrow. I want to tell my friends and family about the baby."

He looked at her with surprise. "That's great."

It really was. If she was going to tell the people in her life about the baby, then she must've fully come to terms with moving forward. Maybe she was going to ask him to go with

311

her. He mentally went over his projects for the next few days and decided that he could definitely rearrange and go along.

"So I wanted to ask if you would take care of the penguins for me."

Okay, he definitely had not been expecting that.

"Really? Are you sure? Why not Griffin or Tori or Donovan?"

"I will definitely let them all know and maybe have them check in, but the penguins really just need someone to show up and feed them and talk to them and hang out. Donovan will definitely be spending time up there. But they all have other stuff going on. Not that you don't," she said quickly. "I know you do. And this is kind of a lot. You don't have to spend all day there, like I do."

"It's not too much to ask. This is what we do. We help each other out."

"It would mean a lot to me. I guess..." She took a deep breath. "I know that everyone else understands that the penguins are important and I know they would take good care of them, but there's something about you that's different. I feel like you..."

He stepped forward. "I'll take better care of them because I'll be doing it for you. Not just because I like you and respect you and admire what you're doing and want to support you like they all would, but because I'm in love with you."

Her eyes went wide and she sucked in a little breath.

He lifted a hand and cupped her cheek. "Are you really shocked?"

She wet her lips, but didn't say anything.

"It's why you asked me. Maybe you hadn't put it in those words in your head, but you understand that I feel differently about you than they all do. We're not just neighbors and we're not just friends with benefits, and we're not just two people who accidentally got pregnant together. I will take better care of these penguins than anyone else but you. Because for me it's about more than the penguins. It's about you."

She was pressing her lips together now. But she finally said, "Yeah, I guess that's it."

"I'm glad you realize that."

"I'm glad you feel that way."

"Because that means your penguins are in good hands?"

"That..." She smiled up at him. "And because it makes how I feel about you make more sense. I love you too, Zeke."

He was amazed by the surge of pleasure and desire that went through him hearing her say that.

He knew that Donovan and Fiona were helping her with the penguins more than he could. He knew that his grandmother had given her advice that had somehow calmed her down about the pregnancy in a way that he couldn't. He knew that Dana and Addison had invited her into their mom group. Even his brother had given her jelly she could eat when he'd given her jelly that would've caused an allergic reaction.

But none of that mattered. It was okay for those other people to help her with things he couldn't. Because no one would love her the way he did, and it was because of him that she had those people in her life.

He knew that Jill had spent the last few years in Omaha living a fairly solitary life. He knew she'd done it by choice. But he loved that she was now not only living but *appreciating* a life where she had people who would help her out and who she could depend on.

She could have her penguins, her amazing career saving the planet, along with people who would have her back, who would be there when she needed them, and a guy who would love her, exactly the way she needed to be loved.

"You know, I'm going to let you make this call, but if you ever want to be like the penguins and mate for life, I'm right next door."

She smiled up at him. "I've been thinking about that. I think that could be a really great idea."

"Yeah?"

"I like your shower better than mine. And I mean, you do have a refrigerator and washer and dryer."

He laughed. "That's true."

"But I was thinking we could keep my house too, and you could finish it, and we could use it for when people come to visit. I mean, I have friends and family who would love to come to Autre and do the swamp boat tours and see the animal park.

"And it seems like there's an awful lot of people here who come from somewhere else originally, and just happened to land in Autre for little bit and then fell in love. Tori and Paige both have family back in Iowa, Juliet's family is in Virginia, Bailey is from Minnesota. It wouldn't be so bad to keep the house as a family house."

Zeke's heart squeezed hard. "A family house."

"All those people will come down here to visit and after about ten minutes with the Landrys will be considered family, right?"

"Absolutely right."

Jill smiled. "So I'm going to head to Kansas and tell everybody the news and then invite them down to meet everyone."

"You know, you're making me really glad I knocked you up."

She smiled, her heart swelling. "You were already glad about that. I saw how emotional you got watching all those kids at Ellie's and I see you when you watch Josh with Ella."

He nodded. "I was thinking about our kid growing up with Tori and Josh's. And I know my other cousins are going to start having kids. I know Jordan and Fletcher are already trying."

Jill's eyes widened. "Jordan and Fletcher want to have a baby?"

"Yep. Jordan's always wanted to be a mom. They'll probably have six."

"Oh my gosh, do they want ours? I mean, that keeps the baby in the family, and—"

"That's not funny," Zeke said. "It's not a casserole dish that you just pass around to family members."

Jill laughed and stepped forward, wrapping her arms around his waist, and giving him a hug. "I don't know about that. Your grandma and I had a long talk and it sounds like the kids in the family did get passed around to different relatives all the time. A weekend here, an overnight there. Don't think that I'm not going to take everybody up on wanting to borrow ours whenever they want."

Zeke wrapped his arms around her and squeezed her. "Okay, fair enough. At least that way the kid will have a chance to eat something other than peanut butter and jelly or grilled cheese."

## 18

Jill pulled up across the street from Blissfully Baked, the pie shop in her hometown of Bliss, Kansas.

It wasn't an established business from her childhood. The shop had been started just a few years before by a man named Rudy Carmichael. Rudy had been, unbeknownst to everyone in the community, a billionaire from New York, who had been driving past Bliss when his Cadillac, Elvira, had broken down. His little bit of time in the town had convinced him to turn over a new leaf. He'd moved to Bliss, opened the pie shop, and lived the remaining months he had left before he died of cancer.

His will had stipulated that his triplet daughters had to move to Bliss and run the pie shop for a year in order to inherit their billions. So, Cori, Ava, and Brynn Carmichael had blown into town like a tornado of sass and class, and had quickly stolen the hearts of three of Bliss's most eligible bachelors—Jill's best childhood friend Evan, and his buddies Parker and Noah.

The three couples were now easily the six most influential and beloved people in town. And the pie shop was booming.

As she got out of her rental car, Jill couldn't help but smile. She'd borrowed Zeke's idea about telling everyone the news at once and had asked her mom and dad to meet her here where she could make the big announcement to them and to Evan and Cori at the same time.

Sure, her group was *a lot* smaller than Zeke's, but that was good. The pie shop was a lot smaller than Ellie's bar.

The bell above the door tinkled merrily as she stepped inside.

The pie shop also smelled like sugar, cinnamon, chocolate, and coffee rather than cayenne and beer. And the people gathered were all talking quietly at the various tables dotted throughout the bakery rather than lounging at one big family table and yelling things like, "No fucking way!"

It was such a stark contrast to walking into Ellie's that Jill paused for just a moment on the other side of the threshold.

But as soon as Evan noticed her, he came straight toward her with a huge smile.

"Jill!"

Her name caused everyone in the room to turn and several to rise from their seats.

Evan hugged her first, then passed Jill to her mother.

"I'm so happy to see you! This is all so mysterious, though," Holly Morris declared.

"I'm so happy to be here. I've missed you," Jill told her, avoiding the subject of the mystery. For now.

She was passed person to person, hugged and exclaimed over appropriately, until she ended up in front of the bakery case facing Cori Carmichael Stone.

"Welcome home! You didn't give me much time, but we were still able to put together a party."

It was the first time Jill had a second to look around the bakery closely. Cori was well known for her party planning and being able to turn even the most mundane events into something fun and special.

Jill now noticed the black-and-white theme that included everything from the plates, to the paper cups they were using, to the mini cakes she had set out across the top of the bakery case.

The pie shop still did mostly pie. Their specialties were cherry, apple, and sometimes peach. Just the way that their father had done it. But they had expanded to cakes, cookies, and even macarons.

The cakes were black and white but they were shaped strangely. Until Jill peered closer.

They were shaped like penguin parts.

"What is this?"

"Watch," Cori said with a grin. "Ruby, come here, baby."

Jill turned to see a little girl with bright blond curls come running.

If Cori hadn't called her Ruby, Jill wouldn't have known which of the three-year-old blondes this was. Each Carmichael triplet had given birth to a daughter, all within two weeks of one another. They were cousins, but the little girls could have easily passed for triplets themselves.

Ruby was Cori and Evan's daughter.

"Show Jill what we do with the cakes," Cori told her daughter.

"Make pengens," Ruby said. She took two mini cakes that looked like flippers and slid them next to a cake shaped like a penguin body.

"Oh my gosh," Jill laughed. "You made penguin puzzle cakes."

"I was trying to be creative. Honestly, I was making penguins and a flipper fell off. While I was using frosting to glue it back on, it occurred to me that we could just have all the pieces and parts be separate and people could put them together themselves."

"Because heaven forbid we just have a square cake with a picture of a penguin on it," Evan said dryly. But he was smiling as he slipped his arm around his wife's waist.

"Oh, you love when I get creative," Cori told him, giving him a not-at-all-subtle look.

"That I do."

Ruby's cousins, Cara and Michaela, joined Ruby at the table near the window and started putting their penguin cakes together as well.

Ava and Parker and Brynn and Noah joined their daughters while Cori and Evan stayed with Jill.

"So what's this big news? I was shocked that you wanted to bring everybody in here," Cori said.

"Sometimes there are things that happen that you need to make a big deal out of," Jill said, thinking fondly of the Landrys.

She was getting used to that way of thinking. There was never a dull day in Autre.

A few months ago if someone had told her she'd be living in a town where chaos could erupt at any moment, she would have told them that sounded like a nightmare, but now, she was seeing it for what it was. The Landrys lived life loud, boldly, and fully. And, to their credit, when someone didn't want to share in the loud boldness, they didn't push. They let everyone be who they were and do things the way they needed to.

However, they did insist everyone live life fully.

Jill didn't know if she would ever really feel like she was doing the mom thing right. She didn't know if she would ever completely love it or would want to do it more than once. But she did know that her child would have a very full family experience. Her child would be fully loved, fully protected, and fully supported. And that was what really mattered. It might not all come from Jill—in fact, it *wouldn't* all come from Jill—but that was okay.

"So how are things going? I can't believe you're back visiting already," Evan said as he and Cori and Jill took chairs at the table where Jill's mom and dad were sitting. "You just got to Louisiana with the penguins. And I know you've been stressed about how things are going with them. I'm surprised you would leave them already."

"Yeah, you haven't even finished decorating the house," Cori said. "All that gorgeous furniture and decor I ordered for you is just sitting in that front room on a stripped down, unfinished wood floor beside unpainted walls."

She had unwrapped one chair and a lamp, but then she'd started spending her off time at Zeke's and...she'd basically forgotten about the chair and lamp. And everything else.

Jill nodded. "Yeah, things haven't been going exactly according to plan. But I have a lot of help there. In fact, do you guys want a little tour of where the penguins and I are spending our time now?"

Her mother perked up. "A tour?"

"Yes. I mean, you should definitely come to Louisiana for a visit. The family there, the Landrys, own a swamp boat tour company and this petting zoo that's turning into an animal park. There's also a restaurant and bar that serves home-cooked authentic Cajun food. It's quite the tourist experience. But today they're taking the penguins on a little parade around the animal park. They're introducing them to the other animals. We thought it would be a good enrichment activity to give them some additional stimulation. They are live streaming it as it happens. I thought maybe you guys would enjoy watching it with me."

It had been Donovan and Charlie's idea, of course, to do the parade today. Jill suspected it had something to do with her not being there, as a matter of fact.

She knew that Donovan thought she was being overly cautious with the penguins. He wouldn't have done the parade if she had absolutely shut it down, of course. She had agreed to this. But she didn't think it was a coincidence that today was the day he decided the penguins should go for the walk.

Charlie had texted her that it was going to happen and Naomi had agreed to live stream it. Of course, that wasn't just for Jill's benefit. They could've simply done that by video call or recorded it for her.

The livestream would go up online to reach out to the people following the park. Charlie felt it was a great way to give the community and their patrons a glimpse of the penguins since they were not being allowed to visit them in person.

"I'd love to see them," her mother said.

"Absolutely. It'll be cool to see some of the people you're spending time with now," Evan said.

Jill gave him a look. She had told him and Cori about Zeke. Well, that she was hooking up with the hot guy who lived next door. Who also happened to be her contractor.

Jill pulled her laptop out of her bag and set it in the middle of the table. She logged in and pulled up the channel where the livestream would be happening.

They'd already started. She knew Naomi was behind the camera. Jordan was in front of it and was already introducing what everyone was going to be seeing.

Jordan already did a number of talks for the park, educating people about the various animals and talking about the special needs that many of them had.

"There they are!" She pointed at the screen. "That's Magellan," she said, indicating the penguin in the lead. He was waddling along the path looking side to side. He seemed curious and she couldn't help but smile.

"They are going to take them to meet the lemurs and the sloth. I think they're going to also take them by the flamingos. I don't know if they'll go over to the otters and alpacas today or not. But we also have some red pandas that have recently joined the park and there are porcupines and hedgehogs, and a bunch of goats and other barnyard animals for them to watch and interact with."

They watched for little while, listening to Jordan's explanations of what was going on. Jill supplemented Jordan's narrative with the penguin names and who each of the humans were.

It was strange how hard her heart thumped when Zeke came on screen.

He looked amazing.

He was dressed in jeans and work boots, as always, but he was also wearing sunglasses and a Boys of the Bayou Gone Wild t-shirt. The black cotton clung to his chest and shoulders, and made the ink on his tanned arms stand out. His hair was pulled back into a ponytail and the sun glinted off the gold hoop in his ear.

He looked sexy and happy and suddenly she couldn't wait to get back to Autre.

He was herding two penguins in front of him. They, of course, seemed to want to go in two different directions. Because the camera kept panning from Jordan to the penguins and because the penguins were scattered in different directions, it was difficult to see them all at once. At the moment she could only see five. The most she'd seen on screen at one time was seven. But she knew that Donovan, Zeke, Griffin, and Zander were all helping with the penguin herding. Jordan was also there and she knew that not only was Naomi behind the camera, but Charlie would be keeping a close watch over the entire proceeding.

"This is amazing," her mother said. "It looks like a lot of fun. It seems much more laid back and casual than things were at the zoo."

"Oh, it's definitely that."

"Do you like that?" her mother asked.

"Because I want two beaks!"

"No! You have to share!"

"I don't want *any* flippers!"

They all pivoted to look to where the little girls were sitting as cake flippers went flying.

Cori shook her head. "Ruby, you have to share the beaks." She dropped her voice to a mutter for the adults only. "The effing things those girls find to fight about is insane."

Jill grinned. "They're insane or they're driving *you* insane?"

"Honestly? I'd be insane if I wasn't doing this with Ava and Brynn. And the guys. I realize it's hilarious and ridiculous that it takes six adults to raise three little girls but, I can't imagine doing it any other way."

Jill felt the urge to say, "Aw." But caught herself just before saying it out loud. Evan and Cori would think she'd lost it. "Aw" was definitely not a Jill word.

At least it hadn't been before. But she also wanted to tell them about the games I Love Them, But... and Mine's Bigger Than Yours. Cori and Evan had a built-in support group here and Jill knew they'd love it.

She smiled, thinking about her support group waiting back home.

Yes, home.

In Louisiana.

One of the girls suddenly shrieked loudly and grabbed another's penguin cake. That one—Jill thought it was Cara— shrieked even louder and then yelled, "You're *yucky!*"

"Oh my *gosh!*" Evan exclaimed. "Cori, did you see what that *penguin* just did?"

Cori gave Jill a look. "Sometimes you just have to be even louder than they are." Then she pivoted on her chair. "Wow, yes! These penguins are *so cool!*" Cori pulled her phone from her pocket and typed in the web address of the live stream. She took it over to her daughter and nieces. "Look, you guys! Penguins!" The little girls all leaned in to look.

"I like that one!" One of the girls pointed at the screen. As if she hadn't just been screaming about cake.

"No, *I* like that one!" the cake-grabber yelled.

"Well, *I* certainly don't like all the *very loud talking*," Parker informed them all. Loudly.

One of the little girls sighed heavily at that. Jill pressed her lips together. In that moment, it was clear that was Ava's daughter, Michaela.

"Oh, my goodness," Holly said. "I can barely hear myself think."

Which was funny. Three months ago, Jill would have thought this was all incredibly, annoyingly loud as well. Now it seemed...well, still loud. But tolerable.

Hanging out with the Landrys was training her for motherhood in many ways.

"I think we should all get *even louder*," Noah announced, scooping one of the girls up, making her gasp and giggle as he propped her on one shoulder, then grabbed another, putting her up on his other shoulder. "But we should go *outside* to be loud. Let's go be loud *penguins* outside. We'll have our own parade." Which was also funny. Noah was easily the quietest of these three guys.

"Yes!" all three girls said at once.

Loudly.

The girls and their dads exited the building with Brynn tagging along with the Autre penguin parade still on Cori's phone.

Cori turned her attention on a customer who'd just come in and Ava headed to answer the bakery's phone.

"Do you like it?" Holly asked again.

Jill focused on her mom.

"Do I like what?"

"The animal park."

"Oh. Yes. I actually like it a lot. It's nice to have free rein. And to be able to do whatever I want."

Her dad, who'd been very quiet up to this point, looked at her thoughtfully. "Is that really true?"

"Of course. You know that I didn't always agree with the zoo director and the Board of Directors in Omaha."

"But it's a lot to do all alone."

It was.

Her gaze flickered back to the laptop screen.

But she wasn't alone.

"I have something to tell you both," Jill said. She took a deep breath. "I'm going to have a baby."

Her parents both jerked back slightly and stared. They said nothing for several long seconds.

Her mother seemed to recover first. "I see."

Jill noted her look of disappointment. "I know you think this is going to derail everything."

"Of course it will." Holly shook her head. "But there's nothing to do about it now. Will you be turning the penguins over to someone else? Will you be coming back here?"

"No." Jill shook her head. "I'm staying in Louisiana. With the penguins. And with the baby's father."

Her mother frowned. Disapprovingly.

Jill knew what she was thinking. Now that Jill was pregnant and wouldn't be able to focus everything on her career, she was going to have to focus fully on being a mom.

"That was fast," her father said.

"I know." It had all happened very fast. "But I'm in love with him. And he loves me too. We are definitely going to raise the baby together." Jill reached for the laptop and turned it to face her parents more fully. She pointed at Zeke. "That's him. Zeke. Ezekiel Landry. He owns his own construction business and he's an accountant. And obviously, he helps me whenever I need anything."

She smiled, watching him. He was talking to a man she didn't recognize. He actually looked a little upset at the moment. She frowned. What was going on? No one else was supposed to be in the park right now, but it was possible someone had wandered in. In Autre, people would generally assume putting up a "We're Closed" sign would suffice in keeping people out.

Maybe the guy had come in uninvited and gotten a little close to the penguins. It would be like Zeke to be protective. Possibly overly so. But that also made her smile.

"So you're going to keep working with the penguins?" her mother asked.

Jill felt the knot that had been in her stomach for a week, tighten. "Yes. But not in the same way." She swallowed. "I'm going to keep them in the animal park, but I'm pulling them out of the endangered penguins program. They're just going to be penguins. No propagation program. No research. Just a group of penguins living a happy, protected life."

The penguins were happy. So they wouldn't have chicks. So what? They were safe and healthy. They shouldn't be shipped off to another program, uprooted again, separated from their waddle. Maybe Jill had been stressing them out, but she was their human, the one they knew. And without the pressure of the program hanging over her, she could relax and then so could they.

Sure, she was potentially going to have to give a few million dollars back to A.J.'s estate but she hadn't discussed all of this with his attorney yet. If that was the case then, she'd have to find a way to fundraise a lot of cash.

Holly actually looked sad and reached for her hand. "I'm so sorry. I...I really wanted you to have everything you wanted, Jill."

Her mom's words hit her. "That's the thing. I do have what I want. I have work that matters. Just because it's not a formal program doesn't mean those animals don't matter. And I have a baby on the way. And I'm in love. And I have friends and family." She smiled at her mom. "The only thing I don't have is a nice, simple, perfectly laid out plan."

"You seem okay with that," Holly said, studying her face.

"Yeah, I am."

"Jill," her father said.

She blew out a breath. "Yeah, Dad?"

Her father pointed at the computer screen. "I think Zeke wants to talk to you."

Confused, Jill leaned in to look at the computer screen. Zeke's face filled the entire thing. Clearly he had taken the camera from Naomi.

"Jill, answer your phone. We need to talk."

She swallowed. What was he talking about? She glanced around for her phone. It was in her bag. She dug for it, pulling it from the outside pocket.

"This guy is here telling me that these are his penguins," Zeke said. "You need to call me."

Oh. Crap.

The guy he'd been talking to in the background was one of the investors Jill had called about the penguins? What was he doing there? The guy must've gotten on a plane immediately and flown to Autre.

She quickly pressed the button to wake her phone. There were three missed calls from Charlie, three missed calls from Naomi, and seven calls from Zeke. There was also a missed call from Donovan, one from Griffin or at least Griffin's phone, and three other numbers that had to be Autre numbers.

She looked at her parents. "And I'm definitely not going to be doing this alone. Probably anything alone. At all. Maybe ever again."

Her mom looked from the phone to her face to the computer and back to Jill. "He seems really upset."

"I'm sure he is."

"He thinks this means you're leaving him?"

"No, he thinks I'm getting rid of the penguins."

"He's attached to them?"

"He was attached to them even before he really knew them. Just because they were important to me. But now that he's been around them, yeah, I think he really cares about them. These people are..." Jill shook her head, laughing softly. "I have never met anyone who just embraces a new idea, a new person, a new situation with open arms and minds and hearts like these people. It's almost like they are constantly ready for an adventure."

"That's appealing to you? The woman who buys the same shirt in every color and eats the same food over and over, because she doesn't want to try anything new?"

Jill looked at her mom with surprise. "I don't do it because I don't want to try something new. It's because I don't want to have to worry about all the little details that I thought were silly. But I realize that even cereal and sandwiches can actually both be special." Ellie giving her a bowl of cereal in the middle of a restaurant that was famous for the food, the ingredients Zeke had gotten for her sandwiches, Zander trading her jellies...those had mattered.

"I think that I wasn't ready to worry about other details because I was so focused on the penguins all this time because I knew what I was doing there." She looked from her mother to her father. "It *is* a lot of work when you're doing something all by yourself. When it matters so much to get it right, but you don't have anyone to help you. And yes, I probably had people in Omaha who would've cared and would've supported me if I'd let them in. But I didn't. I kept myself in this little bubble where I was the only one who could do it right."

She understood her mother. If her mom had taken being a mom as seriously as Jill had taken her passion for the penguins, it would've been hard to let someone else in, to trust that they would do a good job. So, even as overwhelming as it got at times, her mom took it all on herself.

"But now that I have all of these people there helping me and supporting me and wanting to be a part of it all, I realize that I can definitely care about more than one thing. Passionately. With my whole heart. There is room in my life and my heart for multiple things."

"What made you let *them* in with the penguins when you didn't let anyone in Omaha in?" her mom asked softly.

Jill smiled. "That's the thing. I didn't *let* them in. They just barged in. They don't really care if you don't want them to love you. They do it anyway."

Her mom reached out and covered her hand. "I hope this is everything you dream it will be. And I hope that my...ideas about motherhood"—She took a breath and blew it out—"don't mean that you won't ask me for help if you need it. I probably won't do everything the way you would want me to, but I'm very willing to pitch in."

Jill squeezed her mom's hand in return. "I know. I'll call you. A lot. And I'll be back to visit. Heck, I'm kind of hoping that once the baby is older, he or she can spend part of the summer with you guys."

Her mom shook her head. "You know, maybe I should've done more of that kind of stuff. I would have been a *better* mom if I wasn't doing it all a thousand percent all the time."

"For the record, you did a great job. I mean, we might've gotten our wires crossed in my understanding of what being a working mom was, but I know you always loved me."

"Very much. And, what I hear from my friends is that being a grandparent is wonderful because it's your second chance to get things right."

"And you can send them home when you're tired." Jill's father added.

Jill's phone had been on silent, which was why she'd missed nineteen calls from Autre. Now that she was holding it, however, she noticed when it started ringing again. And that it was Zeke's number.

She lifted the phone to her ear. "I'm not giving the penguins away."

"You're damn right you're not. I told the guy to get the hell out of here. I hope I didn't ruin whatever this relationship is with this group you've got going, but dammit, Jill."

"I did call him about it, but I changed my mind. And it doesn't matter if you ruined the relationship. I'm done with that program. The penguins are just our penguins."

"Good. Now get your sweet ass back down here, and let's raise some kids and penguins together."

"*Some* kids?"

"I figure the first three or four are practice. By number five, we'll know what we're doing."

"We are *not* having five."

"Okay, I guess, like the fried chicken, I could probably recruit some other women to pitch in."

"You're not as funny and charming as you think you are."

He laughed. "Then it's a good thing I have a washer and dryer."

Her eyes were watery, but she nodded. "I'm going to spend one more day here with my family and friends and then I'll be home."

There was a beat of silence on the phone. Then he said, "You called Autre home."

She sniffed. "I know. And I meant it."

"Good. Now tell me that you love me." His voice was rough.

"I love you, Zeke. Very, very much."

"I love you too."

"I'm so glad." She smiled.

"And so, all of that considered, I feel like now is probably the best time to tell you that...we lost Ferdinand."

Jill froze. "You...what?"

"We lost Ferdinand. He wandered off. Went exploring. Just like the real Ferdinand, right?"

He gave a little chuckle but Jill knew that even he didn't believe she was going to let him off the hook that easily.

# 19

"What do you mean by *lost*?"

"I mean, while I was chewing that guy's ass, Ferdinand wandered off. Apparently, I was making a bit of a scene. And so everyone else was paying more attention to me and making sure I didn't punch the guy and didn't notice the penguin waddling off."

Jill wasn't sure what exactly she was feeling. She was aware that she should be feeling panic. But strangely, she wasn't.

"Obviously, you're all going to go look for him."

"They already are. And I'll join them in a minute. But I wanted to tell you about it as soon as possible."

"And when I was in another state and couldn't kill you?"

"That too."

"Okay. Well...keep me informed."

Jill realized that she was possibly just in shock.

But she didn't feel in shock. She supposed that somewhere in the back of her mind she'd realized that losing a penguin was a risk. But sitting right beside that thought was the realization that the people there in Autre were probably more panicked than she was. And that they would do everything they could to find Ferdinand and make sure he was safe.

"No tips on where to look?" Zeke asked.

Jill laughed at that. "You know the area far better than I do."

"But you know penguins."

"I know penguins in captivity and what they're like on the Galápagos Islands. I would say it's unusual for anyone to really know about penguins on the Louisiana bayou."

Zeke blew out a breath. "Fair enough. So you're not breaking up with me?"

"Would that do me any good?"

"Are you asking if I would just leave you alone and be fine with the mother of my child never speaking to me again? The answer to that would be no."

"I figured. So it's probably better that I just forgive you for this, since I know you didn't mean for it to happen, and give you a chance to fix it."

"That's very reasonable."

"Thank you. Hey, Zeke?"

"Yeah?"

"Go find our penguin."

She knew he noticed the "our".

"Yes, ma'am." His voice was a little huskier. "And, maybe hurry home?"

"I'll be there soon."

They disconnected and Jill sat back in her chair with a sigh.

"You're a lot calmer than I would've expected." Her mother eyed her curiously.

"I figure there's not much I can really do. The best people are down there. They know how to get around the bayou, and when they find him, if he's hurt, Donovan and Griffin are there." She lifted a shoulder. "Ferdinand is in good hands. I don't need to be there." She thought about that with a little frown. "You know, that's kind of a nice feeling." It felt strange, but good, to be able to turn it over to other people and trust that it was going to be okay.

"Still," Holly said. "When you needed your appendix out, I couldn't perform the surgery, but I still wanted to be there in the waiting room. And I definitely wanted to be there when you opened your eyes."

Jill looked at her, studying her mother's face. Her mom had been a good mom. She may have given Jill some strange ideas about motherhood, but it wasn't entirely her mom's fault. Jill had taken from it what she wanted.

Jill had very much enjoyed being able to focus just on being a penguin expert. It had definitely been easier. A lot like doing her laundry all in one load and cereal for dinner. It was possible that she had just not let herself think about doing anything else because the way she was doing things was easy.

"I love that you're here and I love the good news you shared," Holly said. "But I know you want to be there when they find Ferdinand."

"I'm sure I won't be able to get a flight right away, anyway," Jill said. "I'll call and see when I can move my flight to, but it's not a rush."

But she did feel her heart pounding. She needed Ferdinand to be okay.

"Why don't you just use our plane?" The question came from Ava Carmichael.

Jill looked over. It seemed that the rest of the pie shop had been listening in.

"Your plane?"

"Yeah, we have a private plane. We're happy to fly you back to Louisiana."

"You have a *private plane*?" Jill asked. Her eyes flickered to Evan, who had come back in at some point.

He chuckled. "Don't let the blue jeans fool you. They're still billionaires."

Two hours later Jill landed on the small landing strip outside of Autre. Apparently, Bennett Baxter, Kennedy Landry-Baxter's husband, also had a private plane and he landed it here often.

She called Zeke via video. He answered after only two rings.

"Hey, Kansas."

"Hey, I just landed, can you come get me?"

"I'm so glad you're back."

She took her suitcase from the pilot and thanked him. Then she said to Zeke, "Yeah, come get me."

"That's going to be just a bit of a problem."

Jill stopped walking. Then sighed. "Why, what's going on?"

"I'm just a little...tied up. I'll send Michael."

"Have you found Ferdinand?"

"We did actually."

Relief flooded through her.

"Is he okay?"

"We think so. A bit freaked out, but not hurt."

"You *think* so?"

"Yeah."

She narrowed her eyes. "Zeke, let me see Ferdinand."

Zeke grimaced. Then he switched his camera and she saw Ferdinand on the screen. In a net. And he was hanging in midair.

"Zeke, why is my penguin hanging in a net, from a tree?"

"It was Donovan's idea to keep him up away from the alligators."

Jill felt her heart thunk hard against her ribs. "*Alligators?*"

"Yeah, they had him cornered."

"They? How many?"

"Just three."

Jill gasped. "Three? There were *three* alligators stalking my penguin?"

"Honestly, that's good. There could've been a lot more."

"But he's safe?"

"I mean, we still need to get him down now."

Jill realized there was something strange about the perspective of what Zeke was showing her.

If Ferdinand was in a tree, why was Zeke seemingly on the same level rather than looking up...

"Zeke, are you up in the tree too?"

"Well, someone had to come up here to get him down."

Of course he'd been the one to climb up.

"And why haven't you gotten him down?"

"I'm waiting for Donovan to get a handle on the second alligator. He got away from him. So now he's loose and stalking both of us. And he's pissed."

Jill closed her eyes and took a deep breath. "So my penguin *and* my fiancé are both hanging from a tree being stalked by an alligator? Is that right?"

"Yeah, but...wait, did you just call me your fiancé?"

She nodded. "It makes the most sense, doesn't it? Of course, I'm starting to think that with you and this family, making sense is not the primary criteria for anything."

Zeke gave her a big grin in spite of hanging from a tree with alligators underneath him. "Yes, I will marry you, Jill."

"Then how about you get down from that tree *safely* with my penguin so that we can celebrate that."

"As soon as they get this alligator under control."

"How long will that take?"

"Naomi is live streaming it so Donovan's taking his sweet time and making it dramatic."

"Are you telling me that Donovan is *showboating* for the camera while my *penguin* is hanging from a *tree*?"

Zeke turned the phone so she could see Donovan.

Her eyes widened. Donovan was *not* showing off. He was trying to get behind a very large alligator while the thing hissed and thrashed. His head was in the loop of cable at the end of the long pole Zander was holding.

"Uh, Zeke. Is that *my* alligator pole?"

"Do *not* try this at home," he told her firmly.

Hell. No.

Suddenly Donovan lunged forward onto the alligator's back, immediately leaning onto the top of the gator's snout to keep its mouth shut.

Jill shrieked.

"A gator's chomping power is immense but a man can overcome their strength to open," Zeke said quickly. "Now that he's holding the thing's mouth shut, we're good."

"Holy crap," Jill muttered. She was riveted to the scene.

Donovan wrapped the gator's mouth so it couldn't open, then he and Zander carried the thing to Zander's truck.

"He's going to relocate it down the way," Zeke said. "That will give us time to get down."

"I can't believe I missed seeing all of that in person by just minutes!" Jill exclaimed.

Zeke grinned into his camera. "You know you're getting touched by the crazy, right?"

"It was kind of inevitable, wasn't it?"

"Indeed it was."

---

An hour later the alligators had been moved to another location and released, Zeke and Ferdinand were both down from the tree, and they had an amazing video for the Boys of the Bayou Gone Wild website.

Charlie was ecstatic. The more of this kind of stuff to go along with the Gone Wild name, that had initially been tongue-in-cheek, the more visitors they were going to have, tickets they were going to sell, and donations they were going to get.

Ferdinand was a little ruffled, a pun Donovan made at least three times, but only had a couple of scrapes for Jill to treat. He was back in the enclosure with the rest of the penguins and Zeke and Jill headed home to...do laundry.

They did actually throw Zeke's dirty clothes into the washing machine, but they also made very good use of the top of the machine and the spin cycle.

Afterward they sat at his kitchen table with grilled cheese sandwiches. They were slightly overdone but definitely short of being burnt.

Zeke watched her as Jill took the first few bites. Then he said, "You're not sending those male penguins away."

Jill paused with her sandwich in front of her mouth. She frowned. "What?"

"After I kicked that guy out of the park and hung up with you, Donovan told me that you were thinking about sending the male penguins away so they could find mates somewhere else. You're not doing that. And you're not pulling out of the program."

Jill swallowed and set her sandwich down. "I'm not?"

"No. Dammit. You are not giving up on those birds because of the baby. You *can* have it all, cher." He reached out and covered her hand. "I'll make sure you do."

God, she really did love him. "I *am* pulling out of the program, Zeke."

"Jill—"

"And I'm starting my own program."

He paused. "What?"

"I'm keeping the penguins. And I'm getting some more. I just want the penguins to be...whatever they're going to be. If they want to mate, great. If they don't, great. If we have baby penguins, great. If we don't, great. I just want them to be safe and healthy and a part of Boys of the Bayou Gone Wild. I don't need a big, private, national program. I just need you all. And so do they."

He was staring at her. But his love for her was so obvious Jill felt like it was wrapping around her. Like a hug.

"There is another member of the private program who is feeling in over his head. He called while I was at the airport on my way home and asked if I would take *his* penguins. He's got ten. And I said yes. He's going to give me money to keep his penguins and I think I can make a very convincing pitch to A.J.'s attorney about letting me keep the money to support ours." She squeezed his hand. "I do have the best penguin habitat of any of them after all."

"That's..."

"Perfect," she filled in. "It'll be perfect. However it all ends up."

"Yeah." His voice was gruff. "And there's a chance Columbus and Magellan will find mates then, right?"

"There's a chance. And if not, then—" She shrugged. "We'll still have lots of penguins for everyone to look at."

"You're going to let everyone see the penguins now?"

"Yep. Everyone. The town. The tourists. If nothing else, we can let our penguins be educators and ambassadors for endangered species everywhere."

He shook his head. "Damn, girl. I'm so glad I knocked you up."

She laughed. "Me too, *cher*."

He gave her a huge grin at her use of the endearment. "So..."

She lifted an eyebrow. "So what?"

"You're really not mad?"

"About you losing my penguin and risking his life and your own?"

"Uh...yeah."

"How can I be mad? I know if you'll all do what you did for

my penguin then you'll definitely do it for my kid. And I suspect that you've probably been stuck in a tree before and it will happen again. Whether or not there's penguin or kid involved."

"Fair enough. And damn right I would do that for a kid. Ours or any other."

"And here's where you could reassure me that you will do whatever you can to keep our kid from being stuck in a tree in the first place. Particularly one surrounded by alligators."

"Well, baby doll, we're gonna be raising a bayou boy. There *will* be gators in his life."

"Or a bayou girl."

Zeke nodded. "Yeah, and they tend to be even more trouble than the boys."

"Even the ones who become adopted bayou girls?"

He leaned in, cupped the back of her head, and pulled her in for a kiss. "Oh yeah. In my experience, they're the ones who flip your world *totally* upside down."

# EPILOGUE

*Four months later...*

Zeke's phone vibrated in his pocket and he shifted the pouch in his arms to his left side to reach for it.

It was Jill. And it was a video call.

"Dammit."

That wasn't, of course, how he generally felt about a call from his fiancée, but he didn't want her to know that he was running around outside as a hurricane was approaching.

He looked around. Ellie's was the only place he could duck into to take the call. It was where he'd been headed in the first place so he started for the door. But once he answered the call inside, where nearly half the town was gathered, it was going to be hard to hide that something was up.

Of course, the sheets of torrential rain and nearly forty-mile-per-hour wind outside were pretty tough to ignore too.

He yanked the door open, slid the hood of his rain jacket off his head, and swiped the screen to connect the call.

He smiled at the love of his life. "Hey, cher. How was your meeting?"

Was he trying to distract her from the rivulets of water running down his face and the noise of the crowd behind him bringing supplies and people in from all over town?

He ran his hand over his face and cradled the pouch he held closer to his chest. Yes, he definitely was.

But he also absolutely wanted to know about how her meeting in Denver had gone. He was so grateful her doctor had cleared her to fly on the private plane to Colorado even though she was past the sixth month of her pregnancy. She was coasting through the pregnancy. She hadn't had a bit of morning sickness or even a backache so far. Her doctor didn't feel there was any reason to worry about the travel. And, as he'd told Jill at her checkup two days ago, they had fabulous OBs in Denver if she did need anything.

So, she was several states away as Hurricane Clare shifted course and edged up into Louisiana a bit rather than just blowing by to Alabama the way she'd been expected to. Which was the one bright spot in this whole thing. Having Jill and the baby far from this chaos was awesome in his opinion.

Jill's face brightened. "Oh, it went so well. Not only are we going to add ten more penguins but one of the pairs has already had chicks twice. And Ken has established a very healthy trust that goes along with the birds. It's going to be amazing."

Ken was another of the private investors who'd joined the penguin protection program but had realized that he'd rather Jill take his portion over as well. He'd heard from William, the first to ask Jill to add his penguins to her collection, how well Jill's expanded rookery was doing and he'd called two weeks ago.

"I'm not surprised," Zeke said. "You're absolutely the person who should be taking care of *all* of the penguins."

Zeke's heart swelled with love and pride. Jill was not only glowing because of her pregnancy, which had been one of the easiest Ellie said she'd ever seen. She was also absolutely over the moon with her growing waddle of penguins. Ever since they'd added the ten penguins from Phoenix, the original eight had perked up and been happier and healthier than ever.

There had actually been a very successful pairing between Greta and Ferdinand. Of course, Donovan insisted that Greta had been impressed by Ferdinand's big adventure and bravery when faced with three alligators and that's what had sealed the deal.

And sure enough, Columbus and Magellan had both found girlfriends. The first four penguin chicks born in Autre had hatched a month ago and there were three more on the way.

"Well, thank you," Jill said. "And thank you for the shoes."

He grinned. "You needed them then?"

She rolled her eyes. "Of course I did. And you put them in the perfect place."

He'd tucked her dress shoes into the leather bag she packed with all of her files, including information and stats on the penguins currently on-site in Autre, plus her plans for the future of her program and how it differed from the program A.J. had been a part of. He'd figured if she got to the meeting and had forgotten her shoes, that was the perfect place to put a back-up pair.

Then Jill peered closer at her screen. "Are you at Ellie's? Why are there so many people there? Are you all having a party?"

"Um, yeah. Kind of."

"So hurricane parties are a thing in Autre, huh?"

They were. For sure. He'd been to several *really* fun ones.

And he was busted. "Uh...so you know."

"That Hurricane Clare is estimated to hit about two hundred miles east of Autre and that you guys should be taking precautions and preparing? Yes. I do have a weather app and the internet," she said. "Plus my pilot told me we won't be taking off tonight because we won't be able to land in Autre."

"I thought you weren't comin' home until Thursday." Which was two days from now.

"We got everything ironed out quickly and I thought I'd surprise you." She lifted a forkful of something to her mouth and took a bite. She chewed, swallowed, then asked, "So is this going to be a thing? Chaos is going to erupt every time I leave town?"

She was taking this in stride. Zeke was amazed. And proud. She'd definitely learned to roll with things. An absolute necessity when living with the Landrys.

"In fairness, I think there's plenty of chaos when you're here in Autre too," Zeke said with a grin. "I mean, things got pretty crazy two nights ago."

"Well, sure," Jill said, laughing. "But we'd just told everyone that we were having twins. We expected *that* to result in a lot of emotion."

Twins. He still couldn't believe it. He and Jill had, of course, known for weeks but they'd told the whole family the other night. And yeah, it had gotten crazy. Good crazy. Happy crazy. Loving crazy.

"So, not hurricane chaos, but yeah, there's always going to be *some* crazy down here," Zeke said. "I'm glad you're learning to roll with it."

Jill sat back and put her hand on her big belly. "And thankfully these babies are your kids. They are completely laid back. I sleep well, I can eat whatever I want and don't get sick or heartburn or anything. We are all three absolutely fine." Jill lifted another forkful of food to her lips.

Zeke grinned. He'd worried at first that adding a pregnancy on to everything else Jill had going on would ratchet up her stress levels, but it really did seem that she'd become more relaxed as the pregnancy had progressed. "Where are you?" he asked.

Jill swallowed and wiped her mouth. "I'm still at Ken's place. He and his wife offered me a room for the night when he heard about the storm. I mean, his house does have *twelve* bedrooms and nine baths, so it's not like I'm putting anyone out." She grinned. "I am now eating some of the most delicious five cheese and spinach ravioli I've ever tasted in my life with home-made French baguettes and a spinach, beet, and goat cheese salad that's to die for."

Zeke laughed out loud. Jill's appetite had increased dramatically and her palate had absolutely expanded beyond yogurt and peanut butter.

"Beets though? Yuck," he said.

"They're really not so bad. Plus they're making me feel less guilty about the chocolate silk pie I'm going to have for dessert."

They didn't know if they were having girls or boys or one of each yet, but he was putting his money on at least one boy. Jill was eating like a Landry boy at least, that was for sure.

"So you're fine," he said.

"I'm totally fine. But I am worried about all of you."

Zeke felt relief wash over him. They had weathered hurricanes and tropical storms numerous times. It was always a bit of a cause for concern, of course. They had to be prepared and none of them took the storms lightly. But they were out of the path of the most serious part of the storm and they had plenty of supplies and people to take care of whatever happened.

Now, though, they had a number of animals that they also had to protect and care for in the midst of the storm. But having Jill safe and sound miles and miles from the storm was making it easier for him to concentrate on the work that needed to be done.

"Been through this before, cher," he assured her.

"Before you had penguins, though."

"I know. I just came from there. They're all inside and that penguin house is made of concrete and steel. They've got fresh water and we have generators hooked up to the freezers so the fish will stay frozen even if the power goes out. I'll be over to check on them again as soon as the worst blows over. As for people, we're all gonna huddle together right here. Again, plenty of water and food and generators."

"What about the other animals?" Jill asked.

"They're all in shelters with food and water. Even if we can't get shipments in for a few days, we're fine on supplies. We went around and took down all the signage and posts and chairs and tables and anything else that might get blown around and cause damage, so the park is pretty bare. We secured all the windows and doors. And now we just have to wait it out."

Jill nodded, seemingly reassured. "What about the eggs?"

"Well." That was the one thing that they'd really had to improvise on. He held the little pouch that he'd been carrying up to the screen. "I've got the eggs."

Jill stared. "You're carrying the penguin eggs around with you?"

"The penguins are kind of riled up. They were walking around the penguin house making a bunch of noise. They can probably sense the storm and they were very offended that we made them go inside and they don't really want to be cooped up in there. I tried to reassemble one of the nests inside, but they didn't even go look at it. I tried putting the eggs in a blanket, but they completely ignored that too. I asked Donovan what to do and he said we should put them in a pouch and keep them with one of us, so that they were safe and tended and stay warm." He shrugged. "He said I might have to be the surrogate now. Like when the kids have to carry around a bag of flour and pretend it's a baby in health class? I might just have to keep them with me all the time."

"And you'd be willing to do that?" she asked.

"Of course."

"You don't have to. We can take turns."

"We'll figure it out." He didn't mind, actually. But it would definitely make it difficult to put up drywall and to climb up on roofs for a while.

"Is that a...lunch bag?" Jill asked.

He nodded. "It's one of those insulated lunch bags. I use it to take food with me to job sites. I lined it with an old t-shirt. It's really soft and keeps them nestled in there so they don't get jostled around."

Jill slowly shook her head back and forth. "I really love you, Zeke."

He grinned. "I really love you too." He paused. "This might not work, right?"

She lifted a shoulder. "It might not. But," she added, "it's the best we can do. We'll deal with whatever turns out."

Zeke felt his heart swell again. She'd come a long way from the all-about-the-penguins perfectionist he'd first flipped over. She was getting a lot better at understanding that what they were doing was perfect simply because they were doing it out of love.

"Can I talk to Donovan?" Jill asked.

The last few months, Donovan had become her right-hand man taking care of the penguins. Zeke appreciated the hell out of the guy. He had a way of balancing Jill. Zeke was able to calm her down when she got worked up and worried, but Donovan had a way of helping her be more creative and think outside the box.

"He isn't here right this minute."

Jill frowned. "Shouldn't he be? It sounds like the storm is getting bad."

"He probably should be," Zeke admitted. "But he is out doing a rescue."

"He's *what*?"

But the question didn't come from Jill. Zeke pivoted. Then swore under his breath. Naomi had been walking behind him and overheard what he'd said about Donovan.

She came over. "Where's Donovan?"

"He's out doing a rescue. But he should be back soon. He's been gone for a while." Zeke grimaced. He probably shouldn't have said that last part.

"Where? What kind of rescue?" Naomi asked.

"Route twenty-four. Three bear cubs, I think."

"So he's out in the middle of a hurricane, trying to rescue baby bears?" Naomi asked.

"I think he got two of the three already. He's trying to find the third now."

Naomi lifted a brow.

Zeke relented and nodded. "Yeah. Basically. Except that this is not a hurricane, Naomi." He said that for her sake, and for Jill's.

"Semantics. This is a really bad storm. With tons of wind and rain. And the guy's from Kansas, Zeke. What does he know about hurricanes or tropical storms?"

"Hasn't he traveled the world? He's never been in a hurricane before?"

"Do you really think his TV producers would've put him out there in a *hurricane*? As far as I know he was always in these gorgeous places in perfect weather where everything always works out." Naomi scowled. "And who's with him?" She looked around the room, as if doing an inventory of the people present.

"No..." Zeke realized too late that he should not say that Donovan had gone out alone.

Naomi planted her hands on her hips. "He's out there alone? In this storm? Trying to rescue baby bears?"

Zeke sighed. "Come on, Naomi, you know him. Of course he is."

She shook her head. "I can't believe you people let him do some of this stuff. Where's Griffin? How could he let his brother go out in this?"

"We all have our hands full here. Griffin is working on getting the other animals secure."

"Where's Michael?" Naomi asked of *her* brother, again looking around.

"Michael is the fire chief and a paramedic. He's doing what Zander's doing, as he should. They're keeping *people* safe and secure," Zeke said. Zander, Michael, Knox, and other members of the community were going door-to-door, making sure residents were transported to safer places where they could shelter or at least had supplies for the night and were ready to hunker down.

"Naomi," Zeke said, gentle but firm. "You need to relax. Donovan is a professional. As soon as he grabs that third cub he'll be coming back up here."

"Except that he'll stay out there until he gets that cub. Because that bear's life is more important to him than his own," Naomi said.

She started for the door. Zeke frowned.

"You know she's going after him, right?" Jill said from the phone.

Zeke looked down at her. "You're not going to tell me to stop her?"

"Actually, somebody *should* probably go after Donovan," Jill said. "If he's never been in a hurricane before he might not realize how fast this could get bad. And she's right, he's going to stay out there looking for the animal. Unless someone convinces him otherwise. Naomi is smart. She can handle this. And him."

"Naomi's pretty light. I could easily grab her," Zeke mused.

"You have three penguin eggs that you need to not crack," Jill reminded him. "And I don't think you can stop Naomi. She seems determined to make sure Donovan is okay if no one else will."

"Yeah, what's that about?" Zeke asked.

"What that's about," Jill said with a soft smile, full of emotion, "is that we don't get to choose who we fall in love with."

He gave her a heartfelt nod. "Thank God for that."

———

"What in God's name do you think you're doing?"

Donovan wasn't really surprised to hear Naomi LeClaire's voice as he was dying. She was perfect angel material. Beautiful. Serene. Elegant. Calming and soothing.

And absolutely capable of making a man want to atone for all his past sins just to see her smile.

At the moment, however, she was definitely not smiling. In fact, she looked kind of pissed.

She stopped right next to him, staring down, her hands planted on her hips. "Get off the ground, Donovan," she said.

Or rather she yelled. But that was because of the torrential downpour of rain battering the pavement—and them—and the howling wind. Probably.

"Have I drowned? Did something hit me in the head?" he asked.

"It better have, because if I drove out here to find you lying in the middle of the road in a hurricane on purpose, *I'm* going to hit you in the head," she informed him.

He blew out a breath and sat up. "I'm doing it on purpose." He held up a hand. "For a very good reason," he added quickly.

"Yeah, bear cubs," she said. "I heard. "You need to get your ass in the truck and get back to town."

He had never heard Naomi yell. Or say *ass*. Or look mad.

This was...interesting.

He frowned up at her, having to squint because of the rain. This wasn't a *hurricane*.

Yet.

"What are *you* doing out here? You should be back in town at Ellie's with everyone else, where it's safe."

Crazy woman.

She gave him an oh-you-did-not-just-say-that look. "Get in the truck, Donovan."

"There's one more cub."

"So you're lying next to a dead bear trying to get the cub to come to you?"

That was exactly what he was doing. He noted, and loved, that Naomi was not squeamish about the bear carcass right behind him. "Yep."

"You're nuts, you know that?"

"I've heard that a time or two." Or twelve. Or twenty.

Naomi crouched next to him. Her long black hair was in braids and the braids were gathered back and tied at the back of her head. The rain ran off her hair and her face, down her bare arms. The pale yellow tank top she wore was plastered to her body and her denim jeans were soaked, as were the black boots she wore. Yet she still managed to look completely polished and put together.

He'd never met a woman like her. He had no doubt that she really did think he was crazy. Yet here she was, in the middle of a not-quite-a-hurricane-but-definitely-not-just-a-rainstorm, trying to talk sense into him. And the strangest thing was, it was probably going to work.

Not too many people in his life had been successful in making him think twice about the things he did. But Naomi LeClaire had a way of making him take an extra second to ask *is this a terrible idea?* before he jumped into something. He'd only known her for ten months but he now had flares and duct tape in the glove box of his truck, bungee cords and a shovel in the back, and ibuprofen and hand sanitizer in the pockets of the utility vest he often wore when he was out working. And she hadn't lectured him or *told* him to get any of it. The items had simply shown up in his truck and pockets at one point or another.

But he'd known they were from her.

And now she was yelling at him.

He should probably listen.

Of course, he hadn't done that prior to coming out here in the storm and live-trapping two of the three black bear cubs. Nor had he done it before tromping around in the underbrush on either side of the road where he assumed the third cub was. Nor had he done it before deciding to lie down next to the bear's dead mother's body, hoping the bear would come back seeking safety or nourishment. But now that Naomi was here, he was definitely thinking that perhaps he shouldn't be out here in the storm alone.

"Just a few more minutes. These cubs have been on their own a couple days. He's gonna know to find shelter and food, but he's young. He's gonna come back to his mom. It's bad enough that he's out here alone. But with the storm, we may never find him again."

"But—"

"Go look in the back of my truck," he said.

She glanced at his truck, then back to him. Then blew out a breath and headed over to his big black Ford Raptor. The truck bed had a cover on it and she folded it back. Inside was a live trap with two black bear cubs that were about four months old.

She came back a couple minutes later. "Fine. Have you seen him at least?"

Donovan grinned. In addition to being gorgeous and a calming force and someone who took care of everyone around her—including him, for some reason—Naomi was also an animal lover.

She was damned near perfect as far as he could tell.

"Yeah, caught a glimpse. He ran off that way." Donovan pointed to the west as he got to his feet.

"What happened to the mom?"

"Hit by a vehicle, it seems."

"These poor babies."

"I know."

She met his gaze. "It's really not safe out here for you either. At least you got two of the cubs. I know it's heartbreaking to think about leaving him behind, but come on. Your safety is important too."

Donovan couldn't look away from her. A part of him recognized that of course she would say something like that. Most human beings would be pleading for another person to keep themselves safe in a storm like this. But honestly, Donovan wasn't used to people worrying about his safety. Griffin, sure, but Donovan had worked his ass off to keep things from Griffin that would make his brother worry.

He hadn't made tight friendships in college on purpose, and when he'd been shooting his original TV show and then more recently, his YouTube series, the risks he took and the dangerous situations he'd found himself in worked for ratings. It was incredibly rare for someone to tell him to be careful. This was nice.

And it didn't hurt that she was incredibly beautiful. If you had to be fussed over, being fussed over by a gorgeous woman was definitely the way to go.

Still, there was an orphaned bear cub out here.

He looked around. "Fuck."

He felt her hand on his shoulder. "I know. But you need to be safe too. And if something happens to you, who's going to take care of the other two bears?"

Well, his brother, Griffin. Or Tori. Or Jill. Or one of several wildlife veterinarians at the Audubon Zoo in New Orleans.

But instead of saying any of that, he nodded. "Okay."

Because if something happened to him, then Naomi would have to get those two bear cubs back to town for care from another veterinarian. And suddenly he realized that she was out here risking herself in the storm because of him. If anything happened to her, he would hate himself.

"Hey, what are you doing out here by *yourself*?"

"I'm not by myself. I'm with you."

"You didn't have to come."

"Someone did," she said firmly. "And with everything going on in town, everybody else is crazy busy."

She was definitely the type to just step up and do what needed done.

Damn. Suddenly, he needed to get *her* back to town. "Okay, let's go."

Once he got the cubs settled, maybe he could put Naomi in charge of watching over them and he could sneak out and come back down here.

"Donovan, there!" Naomi suddenly pointed off to the right.

He glanced over and, sure enough, saw flash a of black fur moving between the trees.

He took off without a word, jumping down the embankment and sliding about two feet before getting his boots under him. The bear cub was frightened, but also disoriented without his mom to lead him and definitely vulnerable to coyotes, bobcats, and other bears. It hadn't gotten far from its mother's body and Donovan knew it had been coming back to check in.

The poor little guy. Lost, lonely, and confused, and probably starving. As hard as he would work to rehabilitate the cub, at the moment, the animal's condition would work in Donovan's favor. The bear would be weak and that would make it much easier to sweep him up and get him into the truck with his brother and sister.

Donovan dodged around a tree and ducked under branch just as the bear came around a bush. It stopped, sliding on the wet leaves, and dove under another bush, scampering up the hill. Swearing, Donovan slipped and then charged in that direction.

But he pulled up short as he came over the crest of the roadside ditch.

Naomi was holding the cub and talking to him softly, her shoulders hunched as if trying to keep the rain off of him.

Donovan felt a strange warmth in his chest. This woman was definitely an angel.

He strode toward them without a word and opened the back of the truck, helping her get the cub into the crate with his brother and sister. They huddled together at the back, giving him sad looks with their brown eyes. They were scared and weak, but they were safe now. He'd make sure of it.

He turned back to Naomi, not sure what to say but opening his mouth anyway.

She was already heading for her truck.

Right. Because they were in the middle of a major storm.

"You want to ride back with me?" he called over the wind and rain.

She paused with her hand on her door and shook her head. "I have to get the truck back."

Yeah, that made sense. It was silly to leave it out here. But he had the urge to insist she stay with him.

It was his fault she was out here. He had no right to insist she do anything his way.

Dammit.

"Be safe," he said.

He wasn't sure the last time he'd told someone that. He took plenty of chances and didn't need to be babysat. People calculated their own risks and rewards.

But suddenly, looking at Naomi, he felt protective. Coming out here after him was the first time he'd seen her do something that wasn't completely safe and rational.

She was always composed and cool and seemingly unruffled. He'd seen her help her brother splint his finger with a popsicle stick and duct tape without even grimacing. She'd pulled both of those things out of her purse, by the way.

He'd seen her take a third cookie away from her nephew and replace it with a fork and simply point at a bowl of sweet potatoes. She hadn't needed to say a word. Andre had sighed, but he hadn't given even a peep of an argument.

He'd seen her get up from the table, disappear into Ellie's kitchen and then reappear with a glass of milk, cross the room to a table of tourists, and hand the glass to a guy who'd bitten into a pepper way hotter than he was able to handle.

She just noticed things. Then fixed them. Made things better. Took care of things. And people.

Maybe she wasn't an angel. She was more like a goddess.

Especially standing there in the rain, looking gorgeous and more competent than any single person he'd ever met, and like she didn't need anyone or anything.

"Oh, if I get blown off the road and into the Gulf, I will absolutely appear to Gracie Trahan so she can give you a message from me," Naomi called to him.

He laughed. And made a definite mental note. He'd learned that the sweet little blond girl he'd met a few days ago, who'd helped named the flamingos, saw ghosts. And he believed it.

He also believed this goddess would come back and give him a piece of her mind if he caused her untimely demise.

"Let's *definitely* not have that happen," he called back. "Grace doesn't need to learn all those bad words at such a young age."

Naomi shot him a grin and then climbed up into her truck. Donovan felt like he'd been punched in the gut. Damn, it was really too bad he was firmly in the friend zone with this woman.

They made their way back to Autre. He'd only been about five miles out of town, but those five miles in the wind and rain felt like fifty. When they finally pulled up next to the rehabilitation center that Boys of the Bayou Gone Wild had constructed, Donovan realized that he'd been tense during the entire drive in a way he hadn't been going out to the bear rescue. And he knew it had everything to do with Naomi being in the other truck.

He quickly went around back to unload the bears and Naomi met him at the tailgate.

"You didn't have to come over here with me."

"You've got three bears and two hands. Figured you might need some help." She took the other end of the crate.

When they got to the door, he yanked it open and she ducked inside as he struggled against the wind to shut the door behind them.

Finally it thudded shut, blocking out the storm.

The building was very basic, but Donovan loved it. It had everything he needed and it was the first time he'd felt like he really had a solid home base. He'd hadn't been in one place with his wildlife rescue and rehabilitation work for this long... ever. He'd started traveling the country right out of college and had never stayed in one place more than a month or two. He'd been in Autre for nearly a year now.

The Landry boys had put the building up and it was incredibly sturdy, with a concrete floor, steel and wood walls, and a high ceiling. There were windows up high but most of the light came from electric lights positioned throughout the building.

There were pens and kennels of all sizes to house the various animals that he brought in for rehabilitation. Each one had a door that opened to an outside pen as well. Of course, tonight, all of those doors were not only closed but had been secured with additional plywood.

There were also some interior play and exercise rooms and he had an examination room and an office in the building as well.

He headed for the examination room first.

He was dripping all over the floor, as was Naomi. As soon as he set the crate of bears down, he tossed her a towel from one of the cupboards.

"I've got extra clothes here," he said as he wiped his face and then ran the towel over his hair. "Never know when I'm going to get dirty or bloody or both."

She smiled. "I'm sure that's true."

"Want a t-shirt? Maybe some shorts that have a drawstring would work? We do have a washer and dryer. We have to launder blankets and towels and rags all the time. We can throw our stuff in to dry."

"Yeah, that'd be great," she agreed.

He headed for the locker room they'd put in. Jason Young, country music's biggest new star and a local boy, had made a huge donation to the park and the company had used some of it for this rehab facility. One of the things on Donovan's wish list had been a shower. Again, working with injured and sick wildlife came with a lot of unexpected...dirt. And other things. Being able to wash off and change clothes was handy. He spent a lot of nights up here as well. It made him feel better to be close to the animals that needed more regular monitoring. So in addition to the shower, his office had a sofa, a coffeepot, and a microwave. He even had a rollaway bed he could pull out if he needed more than a nap on the couch. The place actually seemed homey. And it gave him a place to go when he felt weird about crashing at his brother's place with Griffin and his girlfriend, Charlie. The two lovebirds deserved their own space. They didn't need Donovan in their way all the time.

He grabbed a t-shirt and jeans for himself and a t-shirt and athletic shorts for Naomi. They were going to be huge on her, but at least it was better than her own soaked clothes.

He changed before going back out, then pointed her in the direction of the locker room.

Sure enough, when she came back out, she was swimming in his shirt.

And then she said, "The shorts didn't really work. Even with the drawstring."

Donovan's eyes dropped to her long legs. Her long, *bare* legs. "Wha—" He cleared his throat. "What do you mean?"

He knew exactly what she meant.

"But the shirt's really long, so I'm good just like this."

Like this. Meaning without shorts. Or, obviously, her jeans. Or anything else.

He was *not* going to ask if she was wearing panties.

He was *not*.

"How can I help?" she asked, moving in next to him as he examined the second cub for any abrasions, cuts, or other injuries.

She smelled amazing. How could she smell amazing? They'd been outside in a rainstorm. She'd been holding a bear. A muddy baby bear.

"Uh. Um..."

She looked up at him.

Her brown eyes, a warm chestnut color, were so gorgeous. He wanted to cup her face and just stare at her. He wanted to run his hands over her cheeks and down her neck and over her shoulders. Then he wanted to bring her up against him. He wanted to cup her gorgeous ass and press her close.

His gaze dropped to her mouth. He definitely wanted to taste her lips. He'd seen them berry colored, a pinkish color, and crimson red. And yeah, he was now realizing how obsessed he was with her lips. He'd been cataloging her lipstick shades. Apparently. But today she wasn't wearing any lipstick or gloss. And God, he wanted to kiss her.

"Donovan?"

Did she sound breathless? Surely not.

"Yeah," he finally managed. "Yeah. We, um, need to get them fed."

He moved around the table to the cabinets, pulling out the ingredients to mix up the food—similar to baby cereal—they'd try first. If that didn't work, they might have to bottle feed the cubs.

Two of the cubs took the cereal right away. The third, the one Naomi had caught, was less inclined.

"We'll have to give him a bottle."

"Can I do it?" she asked eagerly.

Donovan laughed. "Sure. Let's get them settled in the pen."

Donovan prepped the bottle and they moved the cubs to one of the pens in the main portion of the building. Naomi propped up against the wall and Donovan gave her a blanket, the bear, and the bottle. The cub gratefully started nursing.

She looked up at him. "Well, this is good, right?"

It was very good, because the blanket was covering her legs and the flash of white panties he'd seen when she'd gotten down on the floor.

"Yep. For now. He needs the calories. But we don't want him getting dependent on us."

She nodded and looked down at the animal. "You think they've been on their own for two days?"

"Probably about that."

"Poor babies."

He watched them for a moment. She looked so beautiful like this. She should look bedraggled, shouldn't she? Just having been out in a rainstorm? Her hair still wet? Wearing his clothes while hers dried? But no. She looked soft and happy, if slightly amazed to be holding a baby bear. And...she wasn't wearing a bra. The shirt was big on her and fell off one shoulder, but now with the bear on her lap, it pulled more tightly against her breasts and her nipples were obviously hard and there was nothing between them and the soft cotton.

Donovan cleared his throat. "I'll be back with more supplies."

He took his time, but nothing was going to actually work to get the image of the sexiest and most amazing woman he knew, holding a baby bear, out of his mind. So he returned with more blankets and bedding as well as a few toys five minutes later.

They were babies. They'd need things to explore and to play with as they gained strength and learned to climb and forage on their own.

They scampered to the far corner as he rolled the first car tire into the enclosure. It would provide something for them to explore and climb on.

Naomi got to her feet and Donovan didn't look away fast enough to avoid the flash of panties he got.

Or maybe he didn't really try that hard.

Naomi joined him as he made a few trips from the supply room, adding two more car tires for climbing, a plastic barrel with the bottom cut off for the cubs to explore, and a large plastic igloo they could turn into a den. He'd add some logs and branches as well when he could get back outside.

"So, now we need a plan here," Naomi told him, surveying the pen. "There's a big storm brewing and you need a plan for not just the bears, but all the other animals that you're housing here. And for *yourself*."

"I've only got a beaver and a wolf. And they're doing fine right now. Plenty of supplies. I checked in and they're restless, I'm sure sensing the storm, but they're safe."

"Okay, good. So now that these guys are settled, you can come up to Ellie's."

"I'll stay here till the storm blows over. So I'm on site for anything."

Naomi sighed. "Of course."

"I stay here a lot," he told her. "Part of the job is to be on site for any needs."

"I know."

"The rollaway bed I have here is actually pretty comfortable."

"Did you actually sleep on the ground and camp out as much as they made it seem on your show?" she asked.

"Maybe not quite as much as they made it seem," he admitted. "But I've definitely slept in lots of tents and on cots and in rundown cabins and in my truck many, many times."

"Fine," she said, handing him the empty bottle.

"Fine? That I stay out here?"

"You probably should. Unlike the other animals, your animals are hurt. You probably should be here in case something crazy happens and you can't get back to them or if they get spooked and hurt themselves or something."

"How bad is the storm supposed to be?"

"You're from the Midwest, right? I assume you've been through tornadoes?"

"Several."

"So kind of like that. But bigger. And with lots more water."

He sighed. Tornadoes could make a hell of a mess.

"The eye of the storm is supposedly going to hit quite a bit east of here. But we could have a lot of water. And these damn storms can shift. So nothing's for sure until it's sure."

"Okay, then let's get you back up to your family."

He turned and stepped out of the pen, holding it open for her. She stepped out and he closed it behind her, turning the latch.

She shook her head. "My family is fine. There's lots of them and they're all together. Plus they're with the Landrys up at Ellie's. They don't need me. And Michael is out doing his fire chief and paramedic thing. If anyone needs anything medical, he's the one they're gonna need, not me."

"But you've got duct tape and super glue in your purse," he teased.

She gave him a half smile. "And Cora's got all of her potions and creams in the back room."

True enough. He leaned in. Yep, she definitely smelled amazing. "Are you offering to stay out here with me?"

Why would she do that?

"Donovan, the storm is no joke. But *you* are the greatest risk to *your* health and safety."

He gave a soft laugh. That wasn't entirely inaccurate. He was an adrenaline junkie. Unapologetic. He lived life hard and fully. He might die young, but he wasn't gonna die with any regrets.

"You're afraid I'm going to go back out there in this storm?"

"God only knows what idea you might get in your head," she said with a nod.

"Well, I do have food and water out here. And blankets and all of that. Phone. Internet. As long as they don't go out. But I've only got the one rollaway and the sofa."

Naomi lifted her chin. "You don't think I can handle a rollaway?"

"Naomi LeClaire, I think you can handle just about anything."

She seemed pleased by that response.

Suddenly, a loud boom sounded overhead and the lights flickered and went off.

"Well...dammit," Donovan said.

He pulled his phone from his pocket, swiping his thumb

over the screen and lighting the immediate area with a soft glow.

"Guess that rules out watching any Netflix while we wait it out."

"Guess so," Naomi agreed.

"So, maybe—"

Naomi suddenly stepped close, took a hold of his shirt in both hands, and pulled him in. "I'm really glad you didn't die out there rescuing those bears," she said softly against his lips.

Then she kissed him.

❦

*Thank you so much for reading Flipping Love You! I hope you loved Zeke and Jill's story!*

There is so much more to come from Boys of the Bayou Gone Wild and the Landry family!

**Donovan and Naomi are up next in Sealed With A Kiss!**

*You might also find it fun to know that Jillian first appears in **Diamonds and Dirt Roads**, book one in the Billionaires in Blue Jeans series! You can get to know her friends Evan and Cori and her hometown of Bliss, Kansas in the **Billionaires in Blue Jeans series**, available now!*

**Sealed With A Kiss**

***What's a girl to do when her celebrity crush needs her to be his fake girlfriend?***
***Keep her damned feelings to herself, of course.***

Child TV star turned adult wallflower Naomi LeClaire has vowed never to return to the spotlight.

But when she's stuck in a storm with Donovan Foster, the hot, charming, wild-life rescuing internet sensation, and she finally gives in and kisses him...and a few articles of clothing end up on the floor...suddenly her simple, quiet life is tossed upside down.

Especially after the paparazzi catches a heat-of-the-moment kiss. Now everyone assumes she's his girlfriend and, when she realizes that's the best way to keep Donovan out of trouble, Naomi agrees to play along. Even though it puts her center stage with her private life in very public view. Again.

They're a whirlwind of opposites-attract chemistry the fans love, but they'll surely blow over faster than a Gulf Coast hurricane. As long as they can keep straight what's real and what's just a once-in-a-lifetime fantasy.

**Find out more at
ErinNicholas.com**

♋
**And join in on all the FAN FUN!**

Join my **email list!**
http://bit.ly/ErinNicholasEmails

And be the first to hear about my news, sales, freebies, behind-the-scenes, and more!

Or for even more fun, join my **Super Fan page** on Facebook and chat with me and other super fans every day! Just search Facebook for Erin Nicholas Super Fans!

# IF YOU LOVE AUTRE AND THE LANDRYS...

If you love the Boys of the Bayou Gone Wild, you can't miss the Boys of the Bayou series! *All available now!*

My Best Friend's Mardi Gras Wedding (Josh & Tori)

Sweet Home Louisiana (Owen & Maddie)

Beauty and the Bayou (Sawyer & Juliet)

Crazy Rich Cajuns (Bennett & Kennedy)

Must Love Alligators (Chase & Bailey)

Four Weddings and a Swamp Boat Tour (Mitch & Paige)

---

And be sure to check out the connected series, Boys of the Big Easy!

Easy Going (prequel novella)-Gabe & Addison

Going Down Easy- Gabe & Addison

Taking It Easy - Logan & Dana

Eggnog Makes Her Easy - Matt & Lindsey

Nice and Easy - Caleb & Lexi

Getting Off Easy - James & Harper

---

If you're looking for more sexy, small town rom com fun, check out the

## The Hot Cakes Series

*One small Iowa town.*

*Two rival baking companies.*

*A three-generation old family feud.*

*And six guys who are going to be heating up a lot more than the kitchen.*

Sugar Rush (prequel)

Sugarcoated

Forking Around

Making Whoopie

Semi-Sweet On You

Oh, Fudge

Gimme S'more

---

And much more—

including my printable booklist— at

**ErinNicholas.com**

# ABOUT THE AUTHOR

Erin Nicholas is the New York Times and USA Today bestselling author of over forty sexy contemporary romances. Her stories have been described as toe-curling, enchanting, steamy and fun. She loves to write about reluctant heroes, imperfect heroines and happily ever afters. She lives in the Midwest with her husband who only wants to read the sex scenes in her books, her kids who will never read the sex scenes in her books, and family and friends who say they're shocked by the sex scenes in her books (yeah, right!).

Find her and all her books at
www.ErinNicholas.com

And find her on Facebook, Goodreads, BookBub, and Instagram!